Praise for Rebecca Kertz and her novels

"*A Wife for Jacob* is sweet and reminds readers that love is a gift."
—*RT Book Reviews*

"The caring nature of the Amish community...is well demonstrated."
—*RT Book Reviews* on *Noah's Sweetheart*

"*Jedidiah's Bride* reminds readers to count their blessings despite life's hurdles."
—*RT Book Reviews*

Praise for Marta Perry and her novels

"[A] well-written story..."
—*RT Book Reviews* on *Buried Sins*

"While love is a powerful entity in this story, danger is never too far behind. Top Pick!"
—*RT Book Reviews* on *Season of Secrets*

"*A Christmas to Die For*...is an exceptionally written story in which danger and romance blend nicely."
—*RT Book Reviews*

Rebecca Kertz was first introduced to the Amish when her husband took a job with an Amish construction crew. She enjoyed watching the Amish foreman's children at play and swapping recipes with his wife. Rebecca resides in Delaware with her husband and dog. She has a strong faith in God and feels blessed to have family nearby. Besides writing, she enjoys reading, doing crafts and visiting Lancaster County.

Marta Perry realized she wanted to be a writer at age eight, when she read her first Nancy Drew novel. A lifetime spent in rural Pennsylvania and her own Pennsylvania Dutch roots led Marta to the books she writes now about the Amish. When she's not writing, Marta is active in the life of her church and enjoys traveling and spending time with her three children and six beautiful grandchildren. Visit her online at martaperry.com.

REBECCA KERTZ

A Wife for Jacob

&

MARTA PERRY

Buried Sins

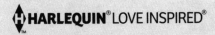

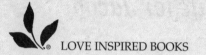

LOVE INSPIRED BOOKS

Recycling programs for this product may not exist in your area.

ISBN-13: 978-0-373-83891-2

A Wife for Jacob and Buried Sins

Copyright © 2016 by Harlequin Books S.A.

The publisher acknowledges the copyright holders of the individual works as follows:

A Wife for Jacob
Copyright © 2015 by Rebecca Kertz

Buried Sins
Copyright © 2007 by Martha Johnson

www.Harlequin.com

Printed in U.S.A.

CONTENTS

A WIFE FOR JACOB

Rebecca Kertz

For my dearest husband,
whom I love with all of my heart…
I feel blessed that I met and married you.

Beloved, let us love one another,
for love is of God; and everyone who loves
is born of God and knows God.
—*1 John* 4:7

Chapter One

Lancaster County, Pennsylvania

The windows were open, allowing the warm breeze of early autumn to flow throughout the two-story farmhouse. Anna Zook sat in the family gathering room, folding laundry from a basket of line-dried clothes. She pulled out her youngest brother Peter's light blue shirt, held it up for inspection and then laid it across the back of the sofa.

It was quiet. Her mother, Peter and her sister Barbara had taken her grandparents up north to see her *grossmudder's* sister, Evie, in New Wilmington, an Amish community north of Pittsburgh. Her older brother Josiah had left early this morning to visit the Amos Kings, most particularly his new sweetheart, Nancy. *Dat* was making some repairs to the *grosseldre's* house while her grandparents were away.

As she reached into the basket for another garment, Annie glanced at Millie, sleeping on the floor not far from her feet. Every day she thanked the Lord that *Dat* allowed her to keep her dog inside the house instead of out in the barn where the other animals were kept. In her community, most pets were excluded from homes, but Millie was special, at least to Annie. And her father was kind to understand what Millie meant to her.

She spread an apron on the cushion beside her, smoothing out the wrinkles before laying it on top of Peter's shirt. Millie lifted her head and eyed Annie briefly before closing her eyes and lying back down. Annie smiled tenderly at the animal. Millie was a black-and-white mongrel—"mutt" Peter called her—with soulful brown eyes and a mouth that looked as if she were smiling whenever she sat up, panting for a treat. She loved Millie; the dog gave her unconditional affection, following her wherever she went. It had been Millie who had helped her get over the heartache and loss of Jedidiah Lapp. When he'd talked of being friends, she'd known he was telling her that he was no longer interested in her as his sweetheart.

I'll not be hurt again, she thought. Only by marrying for practical reasons would she keep her heart safe. *I'll wed a church elder or a widower with children, someone who will appreciate me and be happy to have me as his bride.* Then after the wedding, she would learn to become fond of her husband. No handsome young man would hurt her again.

As she folded pants, socks and undergarments, Annie frowned. Lately, her mother had been hinting that she wasn't getting any younger. "You should find someone to marry and soon," *Mam* had said.

How could she find someone to marry? Didn't they have to show an interest in her first? She tried to think of all the older men who were free to marry. Preacher Levi Stoltzfus. Amos King's brother Ike, newly back in his home community from Indiana, where he'd lived with his wife before she'd passed on.

Annie loved it in Happiness. Whomever she married must stay here. Charlotte King had married Abram Peachy, their deacon, and she was happy raising Abram's five children. *If I can find someone as nice as Abram, I'll be content.* First respect, then love will follow, a safe kind of love that brings only peace rather than heartbreak.

She picked up a stack of socks and set them carefully in the laundry basket. Next to the socks, she placed the folded undergarments. Suddenly, Millie rose up on all fours and began to bark fiercely.

"Millie!" she scolded, startled by her dog's behavior. "Stop that this minute!" What was bothering her?

But the dog continued to bark as she scurried toward the window, rose up on her hind legs, propped her front paws on the windowsill and then barked and whined as she peered outside.

"Girl, what do you see?" Annie frowned as she approached, looking over the dog's head to search the yard for the cause of the animal's agitation. And she saw the ladder against the *grosseldre's* house leaning crookedly against the gutter. Suddenly apprehensive, Annie searched for her father and then saw him, lying on the ground not far from the base of the ladder.

"Dat!" She rushed out of the house and ran to him. Millie slipped out behind her, but Annie cared only to get to her father to see if he was all right. Millie hovered nearby, wanting to get close enough to sniff *Dat*, and Annie had to scold the young dog to stay away.

"Dat," Annie breathed as she knelt near his head.

He groaned. "Annie—" He tried to rise and cried out with pain.

"Nay," she said. "Don't move. We don't know how badly you're hurt."

Her father lay with his eyes closed, looking paler than she'd ever seen him. "I'll go for help. Stay where you are." She leaned closer. "*Dat*, can you hear me?"

"Ja," came his soft whisper, then he grimaced.

Annie stood, and raced barefoot through the grass and down the dirt drive as fast as she could, her heart thudding, her fear rising with each step. It wasn't safe to try to move him herself. She had to get help.

"We had a *gut* morning," Jacob Lapp said as he steered the family's horse-driven market wagon from Bird-in-Hand toward home. "*Dat* will be pleased that we picked up the lumber."

"*Ja*, and *Mam* will be happy we bought everything on her list and so quickly," his younger brother Isaac said.

Jacob flashed him a glance. "You helping *Dat* with the repairs at Abram's?"

"*Ja*, 'tis why he wanted the lumber this morning. The shed on the deacon's property has become unsafe. Abram is afraid that one of the children will get hurt."

Jacob silently agreed. A building that wasn't sturdy was an accident waiting to happen. "They'll have plenty of time to fix the shed today," he said conversationally. "It's a *gut* day to be working outside." His brothers were handy with tools, expert in construction. Jacob could handle a hammer as well as any of them, but he didn't want to work in that occupation for a living.

He sighed. He wanted what his older brothers had: a wife, a home and work that would provide for his family. His older brothers had found their life paths. Noah was an expert cabinetmaker with a thriving business. Jedidiah, his eldest brother, owned a small farm and supplemented his income with construction work when it suited him.

But me? I help Dat with the farmwork, but I don't want to be a farmer, nor do I want to work in construction. And I don't have Noah's talent for making furniture. He had no idea what his special God-given gifts were, and until he discovered he had any, he'd not be thinking of marrying. He wouldn't wed until he could provide for a family.

As he drove down the main road, past Whittier's Store, and continued on, Jacob pushed those thoughts aside and enjoyed the scenery. The only sounds were the horse's hooves hitting pavement and the occasional rev of an engine as a car approached and then passed.

Suddenly, he saw a young Amish woman running barefoot down the road. She stopped and waved at them frantically as they drove past. *"Schtupp!"*

Jacob pulled the buggy to the side of the road. Once he'd reined the horse to a halt, he sprang from the vehicle and hurried back to see what was wrong. He recognized the young woman immediately. "Annie!" She was Annie Zook, a friend from childhood and his brother Jed's former sweetheart.

Annie hesitated. "Jacob?"

"Ja." He studied her with concern. "Annie, is something wrong? Can we help?"

She glanced from him to Isaac as if she wondered if they could help. *"Dat's* hurt!" she exclaimed. "He fell off the roof of my *grosseldre's* house!"

Jacob hid his alarm. "Is he conscious?"

"Ja," she cried, "but he's in pain!"

"I'll stay with you," he told her, "while Isaac goes for help." Isaac climbed out of the vehicle and approached. Jacob addressed his younger brother, "I'll drive to the

Zooks', then you take the wagon. Find a phone and call 911." Isaac nodded, his expression turning anxious before he got back into the vehicle. Jacob helped Annie into the buggy, then he climbed in and took up the leathers. *"Yah!"* he cried, spurring the horse on.

The horse's hooves pounded against the macadam road. Jacob drove down the dirt lane to the Zooks' farmhouse, hopped out and helped Annie to alight. He turned to his brother. "Hurry, Isaac!" he urged. "Try the Martins or Whittier's Store."

"I will." Isaac slid over and grabbed the reins. "Don't worry, Annie. I'll get help." Then, he set the mare to a fast pace as he steered the animal back to the main road and toward the nearest available phone.

"Where is your *vadder*?" Jacob asked.

"Over here," she said. He accompanied her past the main house to where her father had fallen.

Jacob felt his heart beat faster as he saw the ladder, which looked like it would topple over. He noted the danger to Joe, who lay on the ground a few feet away. "Hold on, Joe!" He rushed to move the piece of equipment a safe distance from the *dawdi haus* before he returned quickly to hunker down near the injured man's head. "Joe?" he said softly. His fear rose when the man didn't immediately respond.

"Dat!" Annie sobbed, clearly terrified. *"Dat*, open your eyes—say something! *Please!"* She touched her father's cheek. *"Dat*, Jacob Lapp is here. Isaac has gone for help."

Joe's eyelashes fluttered and then opened. "Annie?"

Annie crouched next to Jacob. *"Ja, Dat!* Jacob and me. What hurts?"

"My leg," he gasped.

Joe tried to rise, then cried out and reached toward his left leg. Jacob immediately stopped him. "*Nay.* Don't move. You could injure yourself more."

Joe leaned back and closed his eyes. "Burns," he whispered. "Feels like fire."

"Hold on." Jacob's gaze met Annie's. "An ambulance will be here soon," he assured her.

Her blue eyes glistening with tears, she nodded. "I didn't know what to do."

"You did the right thing, leaving him be to get help." Jacob felt a little catch as he studied her. He'd never seen her looking so vulnerable. He rose to his feet and offered her his hand. She appeared reluctant to take it and rose without help.

It seemed like forever, but it must have been only ten minutes till they heard the ambulance siren. Jacob managed a smile. "Help has come."

"Thanks be to God," she prayed. He could see that she was trying to pull herself together.

The ambulance drove closer, rumbling over the dirt lane toward the house. "It was just you and Horseshoe Joe home?" Jacob asked softly, using the nickname that Annie's father went by in the community.

"*Ja. Grossmudder* and *Grossdaddi* wanted to visit family in New Wilmington. *Mam*, Barbara and Peter went with them."

"And Josiah?"

Watching as the ambulance pulled into the yard and stopped, Annie hugged herself with her arms. "At the Kings. He left to see Nancy early this morning."

"When Isaac comes, I'll send him to tell your brother." Jacob noted her shiver and studied her with a frown. "Are you cold?"

"Nay," she whispered. "I'm fine."

He could see that she wasn't, but he kept silent. Jacob glanced downward and saw blood along the side of her left foot. "You're hurt!" he exclaimed, upset for not noticing before.

"'Tis nothing," she assured him.

The ambulance had stopped, and three men climbed out of the vehicle. Jacob approached to explain the situation to them and then took the men to Joe before he returned to Annie. "You should have someone look at your foot."

"Nay—"

"Let me see it," he said firmly. She seemed taken aback by his brusqueness, but she obeyed and raised her left foot. He hissed at what he saw. "Now the other one." The right foot looked as bad as the left. The bottoms of both her feet were scratched and bleeding; the soles looked angry and sore. "What did you do to yourself?" he said gently. Running barefoot, she must have stepped on broken glass.

"Dat fell. I couldn't worry about shoes!" she cried, almost angrily.

Jacob nodded. "I know. I would have done the same thing. But now that your father is getting help, you must take care of yourself. Your *dat* is going to need you. You don't want to get an infection and be ill, do *you*?"

His words seemed to calm her. She sniffed as she met his gaze. *"Nay."*

"I'll run inside and get something for you to wear on your feet." He turned to leave. "I'll just speak with these men first to see if they can take a quick look—"

"Jacob!" Annie's call stopped him in his strides.

He spun back. *"Ja?"*

"Don't bother the men. They're helping *Dat*. I can wait. You'll find black socks in the laundry basket in my *grosseldre's* kitchen. I did their laundry but haven't put it away yet." She gestured toward her grandparents' cottage. "And my *grossmudder's* old sneakers are by the back door. We wear the same size shoe. I can wear those."

Jacob studied her, noting the anxiety playing on her lovely features, the look of fear in her glistening blue eyes. Tendrils of blond hair had escaped from beneath her white prayer *kapp*. She wore a full-length black apron over a lavender dress. Jacob noticed the way her bottom lip quivered, as if she was ready to break down and cry. But she didn't. She remained strong.

"I'll get you the socks," he said softly. Inside the *dawdi haus*, he found the pair of socks right where she told him they would be. He grabbed them and the navy sneakers, brought them outside and handed them to her. "Your *dat's* in *gut* hands, Annie. These men know what they're doing." She nodded. "They'll get him to the hospital. You'll need to go there, as well."

"Ja," she said, glancing toward where the men bent over her father. She held on to the socks he'd given her but made no effort to put them on.

"Do you need help?" he asked quietly.

"Nay. I can do it." But she didn't move. She watched the men working on her father.

"Annie," he said. "Do *you* need help?" Without waiting for her answer, Jacob gently took the socks from her and hunkered down near her feet. "Hold on to my shoulder."

He tried not to think about the fact that he was holding Annie's bare foot as he carefully pulled on the first sock and then the second one. Within seconds, he felt satisfied that her injured feet would be protected. He rose and, without meeting her glance as she bent to put on the shoes, turned to watch the ambulance workers.

As two men lifted Joe onto a stretcher, the driver approached them. "Are you relatives?" he asked.

"*I* am," Annie said as she straightened. "I'm his daughter."

"We've secured his neck in a brace, and we've done what we could for him. It looks like he may have fractured his leg. We'll be taking him to General Hospital. They'll do X-rays and check for other injuries." The dark-haired man wore a white shirt and pants and a white jacket embroidered with the red insignia of the ambulance company. "Do you want to ride with us?" he asked Annie.

She hesitated. *"Ja."*

"That's fine," Jacob said. "We'll make sure Josiah gets to the hospital."

A car rumbled down the dirt drive and stopped near the main farmhouse. As Jacob approached the vehicle, the door on the driver's side opened and Bob Whittier stepped out. "Isaac called from the store," he said. "Rick Martin was there. Your brother told us what happened." He paused, studied the scene. "Do you need a lift to the hospital?"

Jacob shot Annie a quick glance. "Annie's going in the ambulance with Joe. I'll take the ride." The kind *Englisher* nodded and Jacob returned to Annie's side. "I'm going to follow behind the ambulance with Bob."

Annie didn't seem pleased. "You don't have to come."

"Ja, I do. You shouldn't be alone." He paused. "I'll stay until your brother gets there." He watched as the EMTs carefully shifted Joe onto a stretcher. "Looks like they're getting ready to move him."

"I need to get my purse," she said.

"Where's Isaac?" Jacob asked Bob as Annie hurried toward the farmhouse.

"Rick is taking him to the Kings to tell Josiah what happened. As soon as he can, Rick will bring them to the hospital."

Annie returned with purse in hand, and Jacob stood beside her and Bob as the EMTs placed Joe carefully into the back of the vehicle. He heard Annie's sharp little inhalation, and he felt the strongest desire to comfort her, tell her that Joe would be all right and she had no reason to worry, except that he didn't know the extent of her father's injuries. He settled a hand on her shoulder and felt her jerk as if startled. He drew his fingers away.

One of the ambulance workers approached. "We're ready to go."

"I'm coming," she said.

Jacob couldn't help himself from reaching for her hand, just for a moment, to give it a reassuring squeeze. She broke away and hurried toward the ambulance. The memory of her shocked look stayed with him as he climbed into the front seat of Bob's car and buckled his seat belt. They were nearly at the hospital when he heard the light toot of a car horn behind them. He glanced back to see Rick's car. He was glad that the *Englisher* was able to bring Josiah so quickly.

He could tell Bob to turn around and take him back. Annie didn't want him at the hospital. But she would just have to tolerate his presence. He wasn't about to go home without learning if Joe was all right. It was the correct thing to do.

"Your father needs surgery. He has a displaced fracture of the tibia and fibula in his left leg, the two bones that make up the shin. He hit his head when he fell, but I don't think that injury is severe. Looks like the leg suffered the worst of it. We'll do a CT scan to be certain. He'll need surgery to repair the damage."

Annie nodded. "Will he be all right?" Her fear rose with each revelation the doctor made.

"There are no guarantees, but his prognosis looks good. We're running tests to make sure an underlying condition didn't cause his fall, but from what your father told me, I don't believe that's the case."

"When can we see him?" Josiah asked.

Annie glanced at her brother, who was frowning. He looked impatient, agitated.

In direct contrast, Dr. Moss looked confident and competent in her white lab coat. "You can see him for a few minutes before we take him up to surgery," she said. A nurse approached with a clipboard. "Excuse me." Dr. Moss studied the chart and nodded. She spoke privately with the young woman before she returned her attention to Josiah and Annie. "I'll need one of you to sign a consent form."

While her brother waited for the form, Annie flashed Jacob a glance. She was keenly aware of his presence. When their gazes caught, she looked away. Why had he come? He said that he'd stay only until her brother arrived, but Josiah had arrived the same time as Jacob. She wanted him to leave. But how could she make him go after the way he'd helped with *Dat*? He cared about her father and she had to respect his feelings. She recalled the image of young twelve-year-old Jacob hanging on to her father's every word as her *dat* taught him about blacksmithing.

Disturbed by the memory, she tried to focus on Josiah, now bent over a clipboard with pen in hand. But she remained acutely aware of the man behind her. She glanced at him out of the corner of her eye. She was relieved to see him deep in conversation with his brother Isaac, Bob Whittier and Rick Martin.

Tall, with dark hair like his eldest brother Jacob wore a royal blue shirt with suspenders holding up his *triblend* denim pants. He held his black-banded straw hat in his hands. She dared to examine his face. His features were a beautiful combination of his *mam* and *dat*—Katie and Samuel Lapp. Annie scowled and Jacob turned, caught her gaze. She gasped, looked away. How embarrassing to be caught staring. To her dismay, she sensed his approach.

"Are you all right?" Jacob asked softly.

She shook her head. "I will be once I know my father is all right."

"He spoke to us," he said. "That's a *gut* sign." He offered her an encouraging smile. "I'm praying for his quick recovery."

Tears sprang to Annie's eyes. "I appreciate that." It was a kind thing for him to say, but then Jacob had been kind to her from the first moment he'd jumped out of his buggy and offered his help. And she'd been anything but kind to him.

A nurse appeared from behind them. "You may see your father now but only for a few minutes. We'll be taking him up to surgery shortly. Only immediate family may see him."

"Thank you," Annie said. She turned to Jacob. "I'll let you know how he is as soon as I can. I don't want to keep you."

Jacob smiled. Amusement flashed in his golden eyes. "You're not keeping me from anything. I'll wait for you."

"I won't be long," she said as she turned away.

"Annie," Josiah interrupted, "we have to go now, or we'll miss our chance to see *Dat*."

She hurried to join her brother, and they headed into the emergency room for a brief visit with their father.

Jacob waited with Annie and Josiah while Horseshoe Joe was in surgery. He could tell that Annie was anxious. Josiah was quiet and didn't have much to say. Within the hour, Nancy King arrived, greeted them and then sat next to Josiah. Annie's brother's expression brightened; he was obviously glad to see her.

Jacob glanced at the couple, then averted his gaze. Nancy had been *his* sweetheart, if only for a short time. They had parted ways after she'd gone with her grandparents to visit relatives in North Carolina. On her return, something was changed between them. It was almost as if they'd never spent time together. And then Nancy had begun walking out with Josiah.

He'd felt hurt at the time, but later when he'd thought about it, he realized that he hadn't been too upset by the breakup. God had helped him understand that Nancy King wasn't the woman he was intended to marry. If he'd loved Nancy as much as Noah loved Rachel or Jed loved Sarah, he might have tried to win Nancy's affection again. But he hadn't; he'd simply accepted that their relationship was over.

Thinking about marriage, Jacob knew that he had nothing to offer a wife. If Nancy hadn't gone away, he might have married her, but he didn't know how he would have provided for her, or for any woman he courted with the intention of marrying. He was getting older now and had to think about his future.

"Jacob?" Annie interrupted his thoughts. "Dr. Moss warned us that this would be a long surgery. It will be another hour, at least, until *Dat* is in recovery."

"I'll wait," he said. She hadn't always been a prickly thing. Her breakup with his eldest brother Jedidiah must have changed her.

Annie stood, and he followed suit.

"Restless?" he asked her.

She nodded. "It's going to be a long while yet."

"Let's go downstairs for coffee," he said, expecting her to refuse. She surprised him when she agreed.

"Josiah, we are going down to the cafeteria for coffee," Annie said. "Would you like to come?"

"*Nay.* I'll stay," her brother said, and Nancy edged closer to him. His expression softened. "If we hear anything," he told his sister, "we'll let you know." He had taken off his hat and he held it between his knees, twirling the brim.

Jacob saw that Josiah was more upset than he'd originally let on. "This is an awful thing, but the Lord will help your *vadder*."

Josiah stared at him a second and then gave a nod. "*Ja.* When you are done," he asked, "would you bring up coffee for us?"

"*Ja*," Jacob said with a slight smile. "We won't be long." He knew Annie would want to return as soon as they'd entered the cafeteria. She wouldn't be able to help it; he could tell she was terrified that something awful would happen to her father during surgery.

He followed her into the elevator, pushed the button and stood silently, studying her as he waited for them to reach the bottom floor. She didn't look at him once during the entire ride. It didn't bode well for their having coffee together. He would just have to somehow put her at ease.

Chapter Two

Jacob studied Annie across the table as she sipped from her cup of coffee, set the mug down and stared into its contents. The hospital cafeteria was quiet. The long institutional-type tables were empty except for Annie and him and two female nurses and a male hospital worker, who occupied another table on the other side of the room. It was too late for breakfast and too early for lunch. "How's the coffee?" he asked softly.

She lifted her gaze from the steaming mug. *"Gut."* He could see the sheen from the rising moisture on her forehead. She looked at him a moment, her blue eyes shimmering with unshed tears, then glanced away. He could see how the events of the morning had taken a toll on her. "Jacob, I appreciate your help with *Dat*," she said, almost reluctantly.

"I didn't do much—"

"I don't know what I would have done if you hadn't stopped to help," she admitted.

"I wouldn't have left you," he assured her. "I knew something was wrong the minute I saw you." He frowned. "How are your feet?"

She blushed as she shifted briefly to glance beneath the table at her grandmother's navy sneakers, worn over her grandfather's black socks. "They are fine. They barely hurt."

"Must have been broken glass alongside the road."

"I was so scared, I just ran," she admitted. "I didn't take time to look down." Her blond hair was a beautiful shade of gold beneath her white head covering. After the blush of embarrassment left her, she looked pale, too pale.

"May I get you something to eat?" he asked. She looked lovely and vulnerable; he wished he could do more for her.

Annie shook her head. "I'm not hungry."

"We've been here for over two hours and the only thing you've had is that coffee. Once your *vadder* is out of surgery, you may not have another opportunity to eat. How about a sandwich?" When she declined, he said, "A cookie? A piece of cake?"

She didn't answer. He heard her sniff. "Annie." Jacob hated to see her troubled, but he understood. *"Annie."*

She looked up, started to rise. "We should get back."

He stood. "I'll get the coffee for Josiah and Nancy. You can go ahead if you'd like."

She shook her head. *"Nay* I'll wait for you," she said, surprising him. "You may need help with the coffee."

Jacob paid for the drinks for Josiah and Nancy, and on impulse, he purchased two large chocolate-chip cookies. He tucked them under the coffee fixings in the center of the cardboard cup holder. He was back with Annie in less than a minute. There'd been no one in line at the register. "I grabbed sugar and cream for the coffee," he told her. She inclined her head.

He silently rode with her on the elevator up to the surgical floor. The doors opened and Jacob waited for Annie to precede him. To his surprise, she suddenly stopped and turned to him. "What are we going to do, Jacob? How will we make do, when *Dat* can't work?"

Jacob considered the woman before him, noting the concern in her expression. "I can help out in the shop, and our community will be there for you, too."

She shook her head. "You don't have enough experience. You could do more harm than good."

"I'm not a boy, Annie. I can do the job." There was a charged moment as awareness of her sprung up inside him. Jacob shook it off. "If I don't do it, who will?"

"I don't know." She seemed to think about it. "I'll have to ask *Dat*."

She had grabbed his hat from the table, where he'd set it down when he'd gone for the coffee for her brother and Nancy. Now she fingered the brim nervously.

"We are friends, aren't we, Annie?" he asked. "I remember seeing you in the open shop doorway when we were *kinner*, watching me with your *dat*."

She hesitated, then smiled slightly. "I was sure you would burn yourself with the hot metal, but you never did."

"Not that you ever saw." He remembered her as a young girl, the first girl he'd ever liked.

Her expression turned serious. "Jacob, it's nice of you to offer your help, but we can't accept it."

"But if Joe agrees?" he said softly.

"Then I guess the decision will be made." She continued down the hall toward the surgical waiting room.

Jacob fell into step beside her. He studied her bent head, admiring the beauty of her profile. She looked pale and tense, and he didn't seem to be able to help. He saw Josiah leave the waiting room up ahead and approach.

"How's *Dat*?" Annie asked.

"No word yet from the doctor." Josiah nodded his thanks as Jacob handed him a cup of coffee. He declined sugar and cream and grabbed the other cup for Nancy.

Inside the waiting room, Jacob set down the cardboard cup holder, accepted his hat back from Annie and then took a seat near her. They waited in silence. He retrieved and handed her the wrapped cookies. "For when you're hungry."

Annie's eyes locked with his. She opened her mouth to say something but then nodded silently instead. Jacob found that he couldn't look away.

"Are those cookies?" Josiah asked, capturing Annie's attention.

"*Ja*, Jacob bought them." Annie handed him one, and Josiah beamed.

"*Gut* thinking, Jacob," Josiah said before he unwrapped the treat and broke it in half. He handed a piece to Nancy and then took a bite of his own.

Jacob smiled. He was pleased to see Josiah enjoying it, even more pleased to note that Annie had kept one for herself.

It wasn't long before there was a light commotion right outside the waiting room. Soon, others within their Amish community arrived, having received word of Joe's accident. As the newcomers entered the room, he got up and moved away to give Josiah and Annie the time to be comforted by their friends. Among the new arrivals were his parents—Katie and Samuel Lapp—Josie and William Mast and Mae and Amos King. Annie and Josiah rose, and their friends immediately surrounded them.

William Mast took off his hat, held it against his chest. "How's Joe?" he asked Jacob.

Jacob acknowledged the older man. "He's still in surgery."

"Any idea how long?" the older bearded man asked. When Jacob explained it could be another half hour or more, William left to stand near his wife, Josie, who was comforting Annie.

Josie moved aside, and Jacob's mother stepped in to give Annie a hug. She spoke briefly to her and Josiah before she moved back to allow others to talk with the Zook siblings.

His *mam* turned and saw him standing outside the group. She approached. "How bad?"

"Bad enough." Jacob was conscious of Annie across the room. He glanced over briefly to see how she was faring, before he turned back to his mother.

"Isaac stopped by the house to tell us," *Mam* told him. "You never know what can happen." She touched his arm. "What was he doing on the roof?"

"Trying to repair a leak."

"Why didn't he ask for help? Joe knows your *dat* or one of you boys would have done the work."

"Perhaps he wanted to do it himself." Jacob held out his coffee toward her. "Would you like a sip?" After his mother declined, he drank from the cup, grimaced, then walked toward a trash can and dropped the remainder inside. "Good choice," he told her with a grin.

"Jed would have come, but he's working construction today and there was no way to reach him." *Mam* glanced briefly toward the Zook siblings. "Sarah stayed at the house with Hannah. And Noah—"

Jacob nodded. He knew exactly why Noah hadn't

come. He was worried about leaving his wife, Rachel, who had lost their baby a month before her due date. Even now, months later, while she appeared strong to the outside world, Noah continually fretted about her.

The double doors leading to the surgical area swung open and Dr. Moss, dressed in green medical scrubs, stepped out and approached Annie and Josiah.

Jacob worried about Annie as she moved to stand next to her brother so Dr. Moss could inform them of the outcome of her father's surgery. Nancy King stood on Josiah's other side. He saw Josiah reach out to clasp hands with both women. Dr. Moss spoke at length, but from where he was, Jacob couldn't hear. He stepped closer.

"The surgery went well," the doctor said. "Your father is in recovery now. You'll be able to go back and see him for a few minutes, but don't be alarmed if he doesn't respond. It will take him a while to come out of the anesthesia…"

Jacob saw Mae King slip an arm around Annie, watched as Annie leaned into the older woman for a moment's comfort before she straightened. Her eyes narrowed as she looked about. Her glance slid over him without pausing before it moved on.

They'll take care of her, he thought as he studied the group who were doing their best to be there for Joe's children. Annie didn't need him now. It was time for him to leave, to see what needed to be done at the Zook farm while Annie and Josiah stayed close to their father.

"I'm going to head back," he told his parents as his father joined them.

His mother studied him, gave him a slight smile. "We'll stay for a while."

"You have a ride?" his father asked.

"Bob Whittier." Jacob glanced at the clock, noted the time. "He should be here soon."

Samuel nodded. "Are you going home?"

"Nay," Jacob said. "I thought I'd go to the Zooks' farm first."

Rick Martin pulled into the Zook barnyard late that afternoon to drop off Annie and Josiah. He promised to return the next morning to take them back to the hospital. After Rick had left, Josiah sighed and ran a hand along the back of his neck. "I'll check on the animals."

Annie watched him walk away. "Are you hungry?" she called. "I can fix us something."

He stopped and turned. *"Ja,"* he admitted. "Anything will do."

As her brother walked to the barn, Annie headed toward the farmhouse. She froze in her tracks. *Millie*, she thought with alarm. Where was Millie? In all the commotion, she'd forgotten to put her dog back into the house before leaving for the hospital.

"Josiah!" she called. "Please watch for Millie. She got out of the house earlier."

Josiah scowled but agreed. "She'll come back eventually."

Annie opened the screen door and the inside door swung open. It didn't surprise her that she hadn't locked it after she'd grabbed her purse. Her one thought had been to get to her father.

She entered the house and wandered into the gathering room. Annie stiffened at what she saw. All of the laundry was stacked, neatly folded, inside the laundry basket. She experienced a chill. Someone had been here. *But a burglar wouldn't fold laundry*, she thought.

She heard a short bark and was startled when Millie scurried into the room, wagging her tail happily. Annie bent down to rub her beloved pet's fur. "How did you get in here?"

"Annie," a deep voice said.

She gasped and spun toward the man who'd entered from the direction of the kitchen. *"Jacob?"* She rose to her feet, stared at him. "What are you doing here?"

"Sorry." His golden eyes studied her with concern. "I didn't mean to frighten you. I stopped by to look for Millie and found her. I suddenly remembered her running about before we left."

"You shouldn't have come." She peered up at him with caution. "You folded the laundry." Why would he fold laundry? The men in her Amish community didn't fold laundry! It was an unheard of thing for any man to help with women's work. "Why?"

He shrugged. "You didn't get the chance, so I thought I'd finish it for you." He flashed a brief glance at the clothes before refocusing on her.

Her spine tingled. "I could have done it."

His lips curved with amusement. "I don't doubt it."

Millie licked her leg, demanding her attention. "You found Millie."

"I found her chasing a cat through the fields." He traced the edge of his suspenders with his fingers. "The door was open, so I brought her in."

Watching, Annie wondered why her heart suddenly began to beat faster. "I forgot to lock the door."

"Not to worry. No one disturbed the house." Jacob was suddenly there beside her.

Overwhelmed by his nearness, she stepped back. "No one but you," she accused.

She heard him sigh. "You look like you're about to collapse," he said quietly. "Come. You've had a terrible day. Sit and I'll make you some hot tea."

She sat down. "I can make my own tea."

"*Ja*, I'm sure you can." He narrowed his eyes at her from above. "But I'd like to make you a cup. Is that a problem?"

Feeling foolish, Annie shook her head. Reaction to *Dat's* accident took over and suddenly cold she started to shake. She looked at him, but she couldn't seem to focus. She felt warmth override the chill and realized that Jacob had grabbed the quilt from her father's favorite chair and gently placed it around her shoulders. With mixed feelings, she watched him leave the room. He wasn't gone long.

"Here you go." Jacob held her hot tea. The sofa cushion dipped beneath her as he sat beside her. He extended the cup, and when she didn't immediately respond, gently placed it within her hands, his strong fingers cradling hers until she became overly conscious of his touch.

She realized what he was doing, and she jerked back. "I've got it," she said, relieved that he'd let go and that she hadn't spilled any. He stood, and Annie felt the heat from the mug. She raised the rim to her lips.

"Careful!" he warned. "It's hot." He seemed upset as his golden eyes regarded her apologetically. "I shouldn't have let it boil."

"It's fine, Jacob," she said irritably. "If the water isn't hot, it's not a *gut* cup of tea." Annie took a tentative drink. The steaming brew was sweet. She felt revived after several slow, tiny sips. She looked up at him. *"Danki,"* she said when she felt more like herself again.

Jacob gave her a slow smile that did odd things to her

insides. She fought back those feelings. He studied her a long moment until he was apparently satisfied with what he saw. "Did you see your *vadder*?" His voice was soft as he moved the laundry basket from the sofa to the floor and sat down.

Taken aback by her reaction to him, Annie fought to stay calm. "*Ja*, we saw him. Once he was in his hospital room. When he finally woke up, he told us he was tired and wanted us to go home." She drew a deep breath. "Jacob, I'm fine, You don't have to stay—"

He nodded. "Where's Josiah?"

"In the barn."

"I took care of the animals earlier," he said.

The front door slammed. "Annie," Josiah called out, "the animals have been fed and watered—"

Annie met his gaze as her brother entered the room and stopped abruptly. "Jacob took care of them."

Jacob rose to his feet. He and Josiah stared at one another a long moment, and Annie remembered suddenly that Nancy King, the girl Jacob had fancied and lost, was currently her brother's sweetheart.

"I appreciate what you did for *Dat*." Josiah extended his hand.

She watched the interaction between the two men and then saw Jacob smile. They shook hands and stepped back.

"I should go," Jacob said. Annie watched him grab his hat off a wall hook. "You both need your rest." He hesitated. "I made sandwiches. I put them in the refrigerator."

Annie blinked, shocked. "You made yourself at home."

He raised an eyebrow at her tone. "*Nay*. I simply fixed a meal for friends in need." He jammed his hat on his head. He gave a nod to her brother. "Josiah."

"Jacob." Josiah inclined his head.

As Jacob headed outside, Annie felt as if she'd been too mean-spirited toward him, and it didn't set well with her. It wasn't the way of her community or the Lord—and it wasn't like her to behave this way, either.

Annie followed him, stopping to stand in the open doorway as he descended the porch steps. "*Gut* day to *you*, Jacob Lapp," she called out to him.

He paused and turned. "Rest well, Annie Zook," he replied and then he walked away, without glancing back.

Annie felt awful as she watched him leave. Contrary to her behavior, she had appreciated having Jacob nearby. His quiet strength and presence had soothed her during the crisis with her *dat*. She reminded herself that he was her childhood friend, and she shouldn't worry about spending time with him. He wasn't Jed, and he wasn't in the position to break her heart.

Chapter Three

"Aren't you done with that family?"

Jacob buttoned his light blue shirt without glancing toward his twin brother. "Which family?"

"The Zooks." The mattress springs squeaked as Eli sat and kicked against the bed's wooden frame.

"What are *you* trying to tell me?" He knew what Eli was hinting at, but he wanted to hear him say it.

"I'm reminding you that while Horseshoe Joe was *gut* to you, you can't say the same for his daughter."

Jacob sighed as he pulled one suspender over his shoulder before drawing up the other one. "So, I once liked Annie, and she liked Jed. I got over her years ago."

"So you say." Eli rose from his bed, bent to pick up a shoe, which he pointed at Jacob. "Mark my words. She still pines for him, Jake. Even though he's married to Sarah now."

Jacob grabbed the black shoe, and with a teasing look Eli retrieved the other one from the floor for him. "And I shouldn't help Horseshoe Joe because Annie likes Jed?" He snatched the second shoe from Eli's hand and set both back onto the floor. He pulled on his socks.

"Nay," Eli said. "I just want you to be mindful of the past. I know *ya* like the back of my own hand, like you know me." He grinned, and his blue eyes crinkled at the corners. "We are twins after all." He plucked a straw hat off the wall peg.

"We are?" Jacob replied with feigned surprise. He grinned as he snatched his hat from his twin's hands and tossed it on the bed. "I'm not a boy, Eli. Neither are you. And I'm not pining for Annie." Although he was very glad he'd been able to help in her time of need. "Do you ever think about marrying someday?"

"Ja, I think about it." Eli ran a hand through his golden-blond hair. "But until I find the right one to wed, I'll not be thinking too much of it." He grinned, displaying even white teeth.

Jacob laughed. He loved his brother, not necessarily more than the rest but differently, with the love born of brothers who'd entered this earth on the same day. *A relationship which started in* Mam's *womb,* he thought. The connection between them was strong. They'd been raised from the cradle together, although no one looking at them would believe them twins. Eli's hair was as fair as his was dark. Day and night, someone had once said of them. They might be different in looks, but that was all. They were close, often sharing each other's thoughts, sometimes finishing each other's sentences.

Eli, more than anyone, had understood how he'd felt when Annie Zook had finally won Jed's attention. They'd been sixteen years old, and although it had been years since he'd stopped hanging about Zook's Blacksmithy, hoping for a glimpse of Annie, his loss hadn't been any less painful. He was over Annie, and she certainly didn't care for him. So why was she so wary of him? Simply because Jed was his brother?

"You don't have to worry about me." Jacob slipped on his shoes, then propped a foot onto a wooden chest to tie his shoelaces. "Annie made it clear that she only tolerates me because I stopped to help Joe. Once the ambulance arrived, she wanted me to leave." He lowered his right leg and raised his left.

"But you stayed anyway," Eli pointed out.

"Ja." Jacob finished up and straightened. "I went to the hospital *and* the *haus*." When he'd returned home the day of Horseshoe Joe's accident, he had confided in Eli how he'd gone to the Zooks' to check on the house and Millie, and dared to stay to help out. Annie hadn't liked it, although she'd seemed grateful that he'd found her dog. "Why should I care what she thinks? I was concerned about Joe. And I was worried about her dog."

Eli laughed. "You were worried about the dog." His brother regarded him with sympathy, as if Jacob were fooling himself to think that his time at Annie's had anything to do with an animal. "And now you're going to talk with Horseshoe Joe, to see if he'll let you take over his work in his shop until he is well. From what I've heard, his recovery could take twelve weeks or more." Eli paused. "That's a long time.

"Ja, I know, but I'll be available if *Dat* needs me." He retrieved his hat from the bed, then preceded Eli out of their room and down the stairs to the first floor. "If I have to, I'll work part-time in the shop and the rest at the farm."

"As long as Horseshoe Joe agrees," Eli said from behind him.

"As long as Joe agrees to what?" Isaac asked as he came out from the back of the house.

"Jacob is going to offer to work in the blacksmith shop while Joe recovers," Eli told their younger brother.

Isaac shrugged as he continued past them. "I'm sure Joe will appreciate it," he threw back over his shoulder, before he started up the stairs.

"Jake, I hope you know what you're doing." Eli followed his brother into the yard. "Helping Joe will put you in frequent company with Annie.

"It will," Jacob said. "And her sister Barbara. Shall I worry about her, too?"

Eli chuckled. "Maybe you should."

"Jacob!" *Dat* exited the house and approached. "Heading over to the Zooks'?" Jacob nodded. "I'd like to go with you."

"I'll bring around the buggy." Jacob flashed a cheeky glance at his twin brother before he headed toward the family's gray buggy, parked near the barn. As he climbed into the vehicle and grabbed up the leathers, he thought of what his brother had said, and he knew that Eli was right. He had liked Annie Zook as a boy, and she had liked—still liked—his brother Jed. But he was no longer a boy. He was a man who could control his emotions. Besides, without any means to offer a wife, he'd not be thinking of courting or marrying anytime in the near future.

"When are you going to think about marrying?"

Annie looked up from the piecrust she'd been rolling on a floured board on the kitchen worktable. "*Mam*, who said I don't think about it?"

Her mother went to a cabinet and withdrew a tin of

cinnamon. "I don't mean about marrying Jedidiah Lapp. That one is taken. It's time you looked elsewhere."

"I know that." She set down the wooden rolling pin and then wiped her hands on a tea towel. "It's not as if I can marry the next man who walks through that door," Annie said patiently as she carefully lifted the edge of the crust and set it into the pie pan. With skill born of experience, she molded the dough against the sides and then turned under the excess along the rim before she pressed the edges into place with a dinner fork.

Mam set the cinnamon tin within her reach and then began to cut up a stick of butter. "Annie," she said softly. "I know Jed hurt you, and I understand that you've decided it would be better for you to marry someone older—"

"*Much* older," Annie said with a smile for her mother. "A man who will care for me and accept me as I am. It's a *gut* plan."

"Maybe," *Mam* said, nodding. "I don't know that you should limit your choices. You're not getting any younger."

"*Mam!*" Annie began to core and cut up fresh cooking apples.

"'Tis true." *Mam* started to help her, grabbing an apple and slicing it in half. "The thing is, Annie, your *vadder's* accident is going to hurt us financially. I have faith that his hospital bills will be paid, but with him unable to work in the shop…"

Annie recalled Jacob Lapp's offer to help, then she promptly forced it from her mind. Jacob had apparently taken her at her word that he couldn't fill in for *Dat*, and that was fine. "What does *Dat's* accident have to do with me marrying?"

Mam had cut up two apples, and she reached for a third. "We'd like to see you settled with a husband, someone who can provide for you."

She felt the blood drain from her face. "You and *Dat* want me to wed so that you don't have to provide for me?"

"Nay," Mam said, "that's not what I'm saying at all. Your *dat* and I love you. But we—*I*—worry that you've not considered your future. You're a caring young woman. You'll make some man a fine wife."

"I'll not approach a man and ask him to marry me," Annie said, horrified at the idea.

"Nay." Mam dumped the apples into a large bowl, which she pushed toward Annie. "I'm simply saying that if a man shows interest in you, you consider him seriously."

Annie sprinkled sugar and cinnamon over the apples and stirred them through. "I will," she said, "if one shows interest." She didn't have much to worry about. No man since Jed Lapp had taken notice of her yet.

Mam smiled. *"Gut.* I like having you here—it's not that."

She felt herself relax. "I know you want only what's best for me."

"Ja," Mam said. "I want what's best for all of my children."

The thud of footsteps resounded on the front wooden porch—the new covered porch with the wheelchair ramp, built by the church community men to help with her father's recovery.

"Miriam?" Samuel Lapp's voice called out as he approached the screen door.

Annie smiled as her mother left the kitchen to greet Samuel. She liked Jedidiah Lapp's *dat.* He was a kind, caring man, who loved his family and was always available for whenever anyone within their church community needed him. As she continued to work on the apple pie, she heard murmuring voices. Samuel must have come to visit with her father. She carefully spooned the apples onto the crust, aware of when her mother entered the kitchen. "*Mam*, would you pass me the container of brown sugar? I left it on the counter."

The container of brown sugar was set before her. She looked up to smile her thanks and then promptly froze at the sight of Jacob Lapp, standing on the other side of the table, watching her with his laughing, golden eyes.

"What are you doing here?" she snapped. His dark hair looked neatly combed despite the fact that he had obviously just removed his hat upon entering the house. His jaw was clean shaven, like all of the other unmarried young men within their village of Happiness. She lifted her gaze from the smooth skin of his chin and cheeks to a nose that was well formed and masculine, up to those twinkling tawny eyes of his. It felt like dancing butterflies flitted across her nape as some unknown emotion passed over her. Disturbed, she quickly looked away.

"Your *mudder* sent me for the pitcher of iced tea. *Dat* and I have come for a visit with your *vadder*."

Her heart raced as she narrowed her eyes at him. "The tea is over there," she instructed, "in the refrigerator." She gestured toward a back room. Aware of her flour-and-cinnamon-dusted hands, she quickly went back to work, fixing the crumb topping that would form the upper "crust" of the apple pie. She was aware that Jacob hadn't moved. She could feel him studying her and pretended she didn't notice until her mother returned from the family gathering room, where her father spent the better part of his days recuperating.

"Did you find the iced tea, Jacob?" *Mam* asked.

"Annie just told me where to find it," he said.

"I'll get it," her mother offered as Jacob moved closer to the worktable.

He leaned forward, nearly invading her space. She stepped back and glared at him. He simply smiled at her. "That looks *gut*," he said. "I always enjoy being in the kitchen on *Mam's* baking day."

Annie paused, looked up. "Making an apple pie?" she taunted.

A slow smile curved his handsome lips. "I don't cook, but I've helped a time or two." Her mother returned from the back room and handed him the iced tea. He held on to the glass pitcher and said, "Nothing like a slice of hot apple pie, fresh from the oven on baking day."

"Except maybe a piece of warm apple pie with a scoop of homemade ice cream." *Mam* went to the pantry and took out a tray of cookies. "Pie won't be done for a while, how about these instead?"

"These are great." Jacob grinned, and Annie told herself that she wasn't affected by his smile or his good looks.

"Annie made them," *Mam* said, and Annie wanted to cry out with frustration.

"You helped." She measured out the brown sugar, dumped it in a small bowl and added the butter her mother had cut up earlier.

Jacob grabbed a chocolate-chip cookie from the plate and took a bite. "Delicious."

Annie shot him a glance and felt her heart flutter at his look. "It's just a cookie," she said, her tone sharp.

There is no need to be hostile, she reminded herself. She drew a calming breath and managed to smile. "I'm glad you like it."

Why was he here? Why did he seek her out? Had Jed said something to him about her? She didn't want to know, for she feared the truth might hurt her.

"I'll take these into the other room." Jacob sniffed, as if detecting a scent. "I can smell them. Lemon?" He took another whiff and nodded. "And this one here smells like almond extract." He held up the plate with one hand. "I'd sure like to try that pie."

Annie saw Jacob smile at her mother, felt the bright light of it and looked away. She was relieved when he left the room with the refreshments, for she didn't want to notice anything about him—or to remember the attractive, teasing twinkle in his eyes while he ate one of her cookies.

"Jacob!" Horseshoe Joe sat in his chair with his leg cast propped up on a padded stool that Jacob's brother Noah had made for him.

"We were just talking about you," Samuel said.

Jacob raised his eyebrows as he approached with iced tea and cookies and set them down. "What about?"

"Joe wants to ask you something," his father said.

He glanced back and forth between the two older men. *"Ja?"* He was pleased to note that Joe looked much better since his return home nearly two weeks before. The color had returned to the older man's cheeks. But Joe couldn't get around well yet.

Joe tried to adjust his leg, and Jacob's *dat* helped him shift it to a more comfortable position. "You must know that I still have weeks of recovery before me." Jacob nodded. "I go back to the doctor next Tuesday." The older man suddenly seemed uncertain. "I was wondering, Jake…"

Concerned, Jacob placed a hand on his shoulder. "What is it, Joe?"

"Would *ya* consider taking over for me until I'm well?" Joe asked quickly. Seated next to him in a wooden chair, Jacob's father was nodding.

Jacob stepped back. "You want me to take over your work in the shop?" He thought of Annie. Maybe he shouldn't accept the job. He didn't want to antagonize the woman further, if he could help it. But how could he deny Joe his assistance, especially since the thought of returning to the art of blacksmithing tempted him?

Joe nodded. "If you would. I know you're busy, but you would be a big help, if you could. If not, I'll understand." He reached up to rub his bearded chin. "I'll pay you for your work."

"*Nay*, if I do this, you'll not be paying me." Jacob picked up the cookies, placed them within Joe's reach and then chose to sit across the room. He suffered a moment of doubt but couldn't ignore the expectant look on Horseshoe Joe's face. He sighed inwardly. Annie wouldn't like it, but he had to help out Joe. "I'll be more than happy to help *you*, Joe." While the idea of working in the shop thrilled him, it also gave him a little chill. "It's been years since I helped—bothered—you with my interest in blacksmithing. I was only a boy."

"At twelve, you were hardly a boy. You have a talent for the job, son. I had faith in you then, and I have faith that you can do the work now." He grinned. "And I'll be nearby if *ya* happen to need me."

"Josiah doesn't want to step in?"

Joe shook his head. "He never learned about forging metal, never wanted to. You are the only one who took an interest in my work and my business. You and my girls, Annie and Barbara, who liked to watch when they were younger."

"And I liked to be in the thick of everything," Jacob agreed.

"*Ja*, you did." Joe exchanged glances with Jacob's father.

"Will *you* do it, Jake?" his father asked.

"Heat and bend metal, watch it glow?" Jacob grinned. "*Ja*, I'll do it."

"Do what?" Annie asked as she entered the room with clear glasses. She set them down, picked up the pitcher and began to pour out the tea.

"Jacob's agreed to fill in for me at the shop," Joe said.

"That's nice of him," Annie said after a lengthy pause. When she shot him an angry glance, Jacob raised an eyebrow at her.

He noted a bit of flour dust on her cheek and in her hair. She wore a patchwork apron over a spring-green dress. A few strands of her blond hair had escaped from the edge of her prayer *kapp*, where she must have wiped cinnamon from her forehead with the back of her hand. The cinnamon was still there—barely. He could detect the scent rather than see any of the spice's warm brown color.

As she worked to fill each glass, he watched emotion play across her features. It moved so fast no one else might have noticed, but he did. She wasn't happy that he'd be coming to the farm daily. She hadn't known about her father's plan. Jacob felt a smile start, but he stifled it until she briefly looked his way, and then he released it.

"That will be a great help to *Dat*," she said, turning away, and his amusement grew.

"*Ja*, I'll be around to help every day—" he glanced toward Joe "—or whenever *ya* need me to come."

"Can you start tomorrow?" Joe asked.

Jacob looked to his father. "Can you make do without me on the farm?"

His *dat* nodded. "I've plenty of help." He turned toward his friend. "Tomorrow will be fine, Joe."

"Then I'll be here then." Jacob watched Joe reach for a cookie. Recalling his enjoyment of his first one, he reached for another. Annie Zook was a fine baker. He flashed Annie an admiring glance as she turned to stare at him, before she looked away. He continued to study her. For some reason, she always found fault with him. He didn't know what bothered her about him, but he was sure he'd find out eventually. For now, he had to concentrate on doing a good job at Zook's Blacksmithy. "I'll not let you down, Joe," he said.

Horseshoe Joe swallowed before answering. "Never thought *ya* would." He grinned as he brought the cookie to his lips. "I know you'll do me proud," he said before taking another bite.

"If not," *Dat* said, "he'll have to answer to me." His teasing tone made Jacob smile.

"It's not you I worry about, *Dat*."

"*Nay*, it's your *mudder*." And the three men laughed together at his father's remark, while Annie scurried out of the room.

Chapter Four

Jacob stood in the center of Zook's Blacksmithy and examined the shop. He felt a little nervous pull in his gut. Could he do this and do it well? His attention focused on the tools hanging on the wall: metal tongs, cross-peen hammers and other various tools for shaping metal, before it moved to the steel anvil not far from the brick forge.

You must be careful you don't burn yourself, Jacob, Joe had warned him time and again when he was a boy. *Hold these tongs just so—* The man had shown him how to use the tool. *These will get hot, as well.* He had gestured toward his leather apron. *This garment protects my clothes from sparks and heat.*

One particular day after Jacob, as a young boy, had been coming to the shop for weeks, Joe had pulled out a slightly smaller version of his leather apron and handed it to him. Jacob had accepted the garment with wide eyes, pleased that Joe trusted him enough to let him try his hand at blacksmithing.

The memory of Joe's patient voice calmed him. Suddenly, everything within the shop seemed familiar again.

He just had to remember all the things that Joe had taught him, and he'd do fine.

"Jacob."

Startled, Jacob spun, surprised to see Joe in his wheelchair. Annie stood behind him in the open doorway, looking beautiful in a light blue dress, black apron and with a white prayer *kapp* on her golden-blond hair. She appeared concerned for her father. In direct contrast, Horseshoe Joe looked pale beneath his white-streaked brown beard. He had left his hat in the house, and his tousled graying hair made him look much older than his forty-some years. "Joe, *ya* shouldn't be here. You should be resting and recovering."

Joe nodded. "I just wanted to check in on your first day here. Is there anything you need? Anything you want to know?"

The memory of Joe's teachings gave Jacob the confidence to smile. "I remember everything you taught me. I'll be fine."

"I never doubted that," Joe replied. "You make sure you stop a time or two and come to the house for something to eat."

"If I get hungry, I will," Jacob said. He smiled at Annie. She glanced quickly away and he turned his attention back to Horseshoe Joe. "Do you have a list of any back orders?" he asked.

"Ja," Joe said. "Annie, push me closer." He gestured toward the other side of the shop.

"Dat..."

"I'm not going to work, daughter. I'm hardly in a position to do anything but sit—and even that's getting painful." Annie pushed her father's wheelchair farther into the room. "This is fine, Annie." Joe gestured toward a wall shelf. "Jacob? See that notebook? Inside, you'll find a list of special orders. Not horseshoes but cabinet hinges, tools for specific use and other requests."

Jacob pulled the book from its nesting place on the shelf. He flipped through pages, seeing Joe's notes. "This will be helpful."

Joe looked tired. "There will be the usual orders for horseshoes. Abram Peachy has been patiently waiting for me to shoe one of his mares. If you can take care of that soon, I'd appreciate it." Jacob saw a hint of tears in the older man's eyes. "*Danki*, Jacob."

"I'm grateful you had the patience to teach me about blacksmithing when I was younger," Jacob replied.

"I enjoyed having you in the shop, interested in my work." Joe smiled.

Jacob grinned. His good humor dimmed as he met Annie's gaze briefly before returning his attention to her father. "Go home and rest. Things will be fine here."

Joe's smile was weak. "I think I'll do that."

"It was *gut* of you to visit me on my first day," Jacob said. He gave Annie a nod, and she acknowledged it politely. He knew that she would take good care of her father.

As she pushed Joe from the shop, Jacob sighed. *Annie.* He had a lot to do and he didn't need his thoughts muddled with Annie Zook and whether or not she approved of him. A blacksmith's job took concentration, skill and patience, and he planned to ensure that Zook's Blacksmithy continued to run smoothly in Horseshoe Joe's absence.

Annie pushed her father up the wheelchair ramp and into the house. "You'll be resting now, *Dat*?"

Her father sighed. "*Ja.* I'm feeling weak."

"'Tis to be expected. You've done too much today." She eyed him with concern. "Is your shin hurting?"

He nodded. "I'll just sit in my chair and put up my leg."

"Do *ya* need a pain pill?"

"*Nay.* I'll be fine. Would you get me a cup of tea?"

Annie smiled. "I'll bring you some of your favorite cookies, too." She helped him move to his favorite chair. With Annie's help, he set both of his legs onto the stool Noah Lapp had made for him and closed his eyes.

Annie picked up a quilt, spread it carefully over his legs and tucked it in near his waist. "I'll be right back, *Dat.*"

He acknowledged her with a small sound that told her he might be ready to sleep. Still, she left the room and entered the kitchen to put on a pot of tea. As she placed the kettle on the stove, she thought of Jacob. It was strange to see him in the shop again. Watching him take stock of Zook's Blacksmithy, she became overly conscious that he was no longer a boy but an attractive man.

I'm older and wiser; I won't make the same mistake twice. She wouldn't fall for another Lapp brother.

When the water was hot, she poured it into a teapot and added two bags. She'd enjoy a cup, too. Her mother and sister were not home; they were next door at her *grosseldre's* house.

When the tea had steeped, she poured out two cups. After filling a plate with treats, she went back to the gathering room and her father. Her *dat* opened his eyes when she entered the room.

"*Gut,*" he said. "Those cookies look delicious." He smiled when Annie placed his tea just the way he liked it on the table beside him.

"I put more than one kind on the plate," she said as she offered him a napkin and extended the dish.

"They're all my favorite," he said with a weak grin. There was a tired look about his eyes, but there was enjoyment, too. Annie was happy to see it. "Annie." Her father captured her hand as she turned to leave. "Take the boy something to eat later."

Annie frowned. "Boy?"

"Jacob," *Dat* said as he took a bite.

"Jacob's not a boy, *Dat*." She held out the plate for him.

"Man, then," her father corrected as he selected another cookie.

She opened her mouth to say more but promptly thought better of it. "I'll make him something to eat."

"How about that leftover chicken potpie of yours?"

"*Mam* made it." She rubbed her nape with her left hand. "I'll bring him a bowlful and something to drink."

"*Nay*, Annie. Invite him to eat lunch with us," her *dat* said. "He's doing me a favor by pitching in."

"Are *ya* sure he'll do a *gut* enough job for you?" she asked. She was upset that Jacob hadn't waited for her to talk with her father about the idea.

"He'll do a fine job." *Dat* took a sip of his tea. "I taught him well."

"But he was only eleven or twelve then," she said. "That was a long time ago."

"He's a natural. He hasn't forgotten what to do." Her father smiled. "Shouldn't your *mudder* be back by now?"

Annie shook her head. "She and Barbara are cleaning for *Grossmudder*."

"And you had *vadder* duty," *Dat* said sadly.

She settled her hand on his shoulder. "*Dat*, 'tis my pleasure to be here for you."

Her father regarded her with affection. "I know."

Annie saw her *dat's* eyes brighten as he caught sight of her dog, Millie, curled up in her bed. He'd grown attached to the dog since his accident.

"Millie," she called softly. The dog picked up her head. "Go sit by *Dat*." As if she understood, little Millie rose from her bed and went to lie next to the base of Joe's chair. "Watch him for me, girl."

"Bring Jacob some water when you ask him to lunch. Working in the shop makes a man thirsty," Joe said as he closed his eyes.

Annie stiffened. *"Ja, Dat,"* she said dutifully. In the kitchen, she filled a large plastic jug with water. She then grabbed a cup and a plate of cookies before she reluctantly headed out to the barn.

Jacob pulled out the tools he needed to make the horseshoes for Abram Peachy's mare and stoked up the fire in the forge. He could use the propane torch but not today. He wanted to do it the way he'd first been taught. The leather apron Joe had bought for him still hung in the shop, as if it were only a day rather than years since he'd visited last. Jacob fingered the material. It was too small for him, and so he put on Joe's. Next, he pulled on gloves to protect his hands.

The shop was warm, the heat from the fire a bit overwhelming as he set metal into flame until it glowed an orange red. Next, he hammered it into the shape of a horseshoe on the steel anvil. The sound of his cross-peen hammer against the glowing metal filled the room, rewarding him with a sense of familiar satisfaction. He hammered, checked the metal, fired it up again and hammered some more, then he suddenly became aware of someone's presence. He didn't have to look toward the doorway to know who had entered the shop. "Annie," he said without looking up. "Do you need something?"

"Nay," she called back, to be heard over the ring of iron against steel as he continued his work. "I've brought you a drink."

Jacob stopped pounding, set down his tools and glanced her way. "Water," he said with a grateful smile.

She carried the refreshments to the worktable on the opposite side of the room. *"Dat* said you'd be thirsty."

"Ja," he said, watching her closely. "I could use a drink." She poured him a glass of water and offered it to him. He nodded his thanks and took a sip. "Just what I needed."

"I brought cookies, too." She placed the plate on the workbench within his reach. "For whenever you're hungry," she added. *"Dat* said you're to join us for lunch."

"You don't have to feed me," he said carefully.

"We've got plenty. So, you'll come? *Dat* will be pleased if you do."

"And you?" he dared to ask. "Will *you* mind?"

She blushed. "I'm asking you, aren't I?" Her expression became unreadable. "We're grateful that you're handling *Dat's* work."

"First see how I do before you're too grateful."

"Dat has confidence in your abilities, so I do, too." She touched a hand to her prayer *kapp.* "You will come?"

He noted the vibrant gold in her blond hair. *"Ja,* I'll be there. I wouldn't want to disappoint Joe." He locked gazes with her.

She looked away. "I'd better finish my chores—"

He glanced down at the cooling metal. He would have

to fire it up again before he could continue the job. "And I better get back to work."

She hesitated. "If there is anything you need before then, come to the *haus* and let us know."

He nodded and turned his attention back to the forge, conscious of the exact moment when Annie left the shop.

Annie was stirring the pan of chicken potpie when she heard her brother's voice coming from the front of the house.

"Jacob!" Peter cried. "Come eat!"

Although she listened carefully, Annie couldn't hear his reply, but she recognized Jacob's deep male voice.

"Bread done?" *Mam* entered the room from the other side.

"Ja," Annie said. "Fresh from the oven and ready to be sliced. I took the butter out of the refrigerator."

"I'll open a jar of chow-chow," her mother said, referring to garden vegetables canned in a sweet-and-sour mix.

"I made a pitcher of iced tea this morning," Annie told her. "And lemonade." She filled a pitcher for those who preferred water.

Peter entered, followed closely by her father in his wheelchair. *"Dat,* I would have brought you something to eat." Her voice trailed off when she saw who stood behind the chair.

"Hallo," Jacob said as he pushed Joe's chair farther into the room. "It smells wonderful in here."

Mam turned from the kitchen counter with the dish of chow-chow. "I'm glad you could join us, Jacob."

"I'm happy you asked." He flashed Annie a look that made the heat rise in her face.

Annie scrambled to move furniture to accommodate her father's wheelchair at the table. Then she turned to the stove, where she ladled their meal into a large ceramic bowl. "I hope you like chicken potpie."

"*Ja*, 'tis one of my favorites." Jacob smiled as he took the seat where instructed, next to her father. "Did *ya* make it?"

Annie shook her head. "*Nay, Mam* did."

"You helped with the pie squares," her *mam* said.

Annie had, in fact, rolled out the dough thinly, and she'd cut it into one-inch squares. Unlike the pie-crusted potpies made by the English, the Amish recipe for chicken potpie did not have a two-part flaky crust surrounding the cooked chicken and vegetables, nor was it baked in the oven. The women in their Amish community cooked the chicken in a stockpot until the meat was tender and the water became broth. Then they added vegetables and seasoning. Once the time was right, they stirred in pie squares, similar to the dough the English used in their chicken-and-dumpling recipes. Annie had learned the recipe from her mother at a young age, and over the years, she'd become skilled at making the thick, tasty dish.

The wonderful scent of chicken and the lingering aroma of baked bread permeated the kitchen, smelling delicious. Annie set the bowl on the table and went back for the bread. She placed the basket next to the main course.

The meal was simple, but there was plenty to eat. Annie put a hefty amount on each plate while her mother passed around the chow-chow bowl.

"Bread?" Annie extended the basket toward Jacob. "There's butter and strawberry jam."

Jacob smiled as he took a thick, crusty slice but he declined the toppings, apparently preferring to eat his bread plain.

"Where's Josiah?" her mother asked with a frown.

"He's coming. He's out in the fields," Annie told her. She heard the front door open and footsteps as someone entered the house.

Joe smiled. "There he is now."

Annie saw her brother walk into the kitchen and note Jacob's presence.

"How goes it in the shop?" Josiah asked pleasantly as he took a seat next to Annie, who sat across from Jacob.

"Just getting used to it again," Jacob said, "but it's beginning to feel like home."

Her brother looked relieved, and her father appeared pleased. "Let me know if you need anything," Josiah said. He addressed his father. "It's nearly harvest time, *Dat.*"

Dat nodded. "Find out when the others are bringing in their crops. See if anyone can help out here one day."

Jacob spoke up, "Next week." He tore his bread in half. "We're all planning to come here on Tuesday."

"We'll need to cook and bake for the workers," her mother addressed Annie.

Annie nodded. "All the men are planning to help each other with the harvest?" she asked Jacob.

"Ja." Jacob forked up some noodles. "Everyone decided it would be quicker that way."

Annie silently agreed. Without help, it might take an Amish farmer and his sons several days to bring in their crops and properly store them. She had a feeling the community men had decided to pitch in at each farm because of her father, so that *Dat* would feel better about accepting help. "We should cook for the week."

Her mother picked up the breadbasket and passed it to her eldest son. Josiah took a piece and handed it to Peter. "I'll make dried-corn casserole," *Mam* said, "and macaroni salad to start."

The topic of conversation became centered on the harvest and how each family would have help each day, depending on the size of their land and their crops, and the offerings that the women of the house would bring to share at the community food table.

Annie decided to talk with Josie Mast, their neighbor, who together with her husband, William, knew most of what was happening within the Happiness community. Josie and William were always ready to lend a hand.

Annie remained conscious of Jacob at their kitchen table, enjoying his food and the conversation with her family. Across from him, she was able to study him unobtrusively. He looked solid and strong in his burgundy broadcloth shirt and *triblend* denim pants. He had removed his leather apron, as was appropriate, before coming to the house. He must have washed up outside, for there was no sign of soot or dirt on his face or hands. He'd undoubtedly left his hat in the shop, for his dark hair looked clean and shiny in the sun filtering in through the kitchen window.

He raised an eyebrow. Embarrassed to be caught examining him, she blushed and looked away. "Did everyone have enough to eat?" she asked as she rose. "There is plenty more on the stove."

When everyone claimed that they'd eaten enough of their meal, Annie left to retrieve dessert from the back room.

"Fresh apple pie," she said as she reentered the room, "with homemade ice cream."

While her family exclaimed their delight, it was Jacob's slow, appreciative smile that set her heart to racing. "I've been eager to taste your apple pie," he said.

After preparing several servings, Annie watched Jacob enjoy his portion and experienced a rush of satisfaction. All too soon, he was done eating, and he rose.

"Back to work," he said. "The meal was wonderful, topped off by a delicious dessert."

He didn't meet Annie's eyes as he thanked her parents for having him at their table. Then he left, and Annie noticed that the house seemed different with him gone. She didn't want to think about it too closely as she worked to put away food and clean up. As she was washing dishes, she thought about Jacob Lapp again and smiled.

"Annie," her mother said, "Preacher Levi will be coming for supper tomorrow night. What shall we make?"

Annie thought about it. The preacher was a frequent dinner guest. "Fried chicken?"

Mam nodded approvingly. "And make something special for dessert."

"Ja, Mam." Maybe a cobbler, she thought. She could use a jar of the peaches she'd canned this summer. She mentioned it to her mother.

"*Gut* idea, Annie. And let's make some sweet-and-vinegar green beans to go along with the chicken."

Her thoughts returned to Jacob. The meal with him had been pleasant. In the midst of her family, she'd been able to relax and truly appreciate his company. He'd been polite, teasing at times, occasionally catching her glance with a look that made her feel warm inside. She recalled Jacob the boy and couldn't help comparing him to the attractive man he'd become. She felt an infusion of heat. He was like a brother to her, she reminded herself.

Or was he?

Chapter Five

The sun shone warm and bright in a clear azure sky, and there was barely a breeze on harvest day at her family's farm. Annie stood outside next to her brother Josiah, watching as gray buggies drove down the lane toward the house and parked in a row in the barnyard. Other families came in horse-drawn wagons, some of which pulled farm equipment behind them. It was Monday instead of Tuesday, the day Annie and her family had expected the help. On Sunday, the community had decided to harvest their farm first after learning about her *dat's* appointment with the doctor on Tuesday. When they were done with their farm, the workers would move from one neighbor's farm property to the next, until everyone's crops were harvested.

Annie, her sister Barbara and her mother had spent hours cooking and baking to prepare for this week. Today the food would be served on tables set in the yard between their house and the *dawdi haus*—their *grosseldre's* cottage. Josiah and Peter with William Mast and Abram Peachy had set up tables of plywood on wooden sawhorses. Eli Shrock, Amos and Mae King's son-in-law, had brought the church's bench wagon earlier. Amos had come with Eli, and the two men, with Peter's help, had unloaded benches for everyone to sit on while they ate.

Annie set the tables with the linens that *Mam* used for such occasions. As the men and their families got out of their vehicles and approached, she felt satisfied that the day would go well. Josiah left her side to speak with Noah Lapp and his brother Eli, who had ridden in with his older brother and sister-in-law.

"Annie!" Rachel Lapp approached with a smile. She carried a large platter covered with plastic wrap.

"Cupcakes," Annie said with a grin. "The workers are going to love these."

Rachel glanced toward the food table, where Annie and her *mam* had put out breakfast for the crew. "You've been busy."

Annie gestured toward Rachel's cake dish. "So have you."

"Annie!" *Dat* sat on the porch in his wheelchair.

"Coming, *Dat*," she called back. She gave Rachel a half smile. "This is hard for him."

Rachel nodded. "Maybe if you push him closer so that he can watch the workers?"

"That's a great idea." Annie glanced toward her father. "I'll talk with you later." Rachel's husband, Noah, came up behind his wife. "Noah," she greeted him with a nod before she excused herself to help her father.

"*Dat?* You all right?" she asked as she climbed the porch steps.

"*Ja.*" Her father watched as families exited their vehicles, and the workers moved toward the field. "I should be out there helping."

She crouched before him, looked up. "*Dat*, you can't

work, and everyone understands that. You need to stay here, and rest."

"Annie. Joe."

Annie turned and was startled to find Jacob Lapp on the stairs behind her. She rose quickly to her feet. "Jacob." She felt suddenly breathless. He looked ready for a full day's work in his royal blue shirt, navy coat and black suspenders and navy *triblend* denim pants. Her study of him fell to his black work boots before lifting up to his golden eyes.

"I thought Joe might like to watch us," Jacob said.

"I'd like that, Jake." Her father looked pleased. "Can't see anything from here."

Annie felt concerned, despite the fact that she thought the move a good idea. "What if you get tired?"

Her father smiled. "Then I'll have one of the boys bring me back."

"Not to worry, Annie," Jacob assured her. "I'll see that he rests if he needs it."

Annie didn't answer as she watched while Jacob pushed her father's chair down the ramp. She sighed. Until today, she hadn't seen or spoken with Jacob since he'd eaten lunch with them on his first day of work in her *dat's* blacksmith shop. According to her father, Jacob came to the shop each day, completed his work, then spoke briefly with her father before heading home. He'd been coming for days, but he hadn't bothered to stop into the house and say hello.

Why should he seek her out? He was helping her father, not her. It wasn't Jacob's fault that she couldn't stop thinking about him. Was it?

Annie sighed. There had to be an older man in the community who would make her a fine husband. Maybe if she prayed to the Lord He would show her her future husband. *Please, Lord, help and guide me. Help me to know Thy will.*

Mam came out of the house behind her. "Where's your *vadder*?"

Annie gestured toward the yard. "Jacob's taking *Dat* down for a better view." Once the workers continued to the other side of the farm, her father would no longer be able to watch them. *Maybe by then, Dat will be ready for a nap.*

Unbidden came a mental image of Jacob Lapp's smile. Annie pushed him from her mind as she went back into the house, where the women were preparing to set out more food.

"Will you be all right here?" Jacob asked Joe as he rolled the older man into a shady spot in the yard, with a good view.

"This is fine, Jacob." Joe stared as the workers walked into the field with their farm tools.

"Horseshoe Joe!" William Mast called. "How *ya* feeling?"

"Not too bad," Joe replied. "Doing as well as can be expected."

"You take care of yourself, and don't *ya* be worrying about anything. Your boy Josiah knows what he's doing, planning which areas to be covered by whom."

"I'm going to get to work, Joe," Jacob said. "I'll check back later to see how you are."

"I'd appreciate that." Joe seemed settled as he waved and answered his neighbors' and friends' inquiries about his recovery.

Jacob felt satisfied that Joe would be fine as he left to

join his brothers Isaac and Eli. Minutes later, he grabbed his corn hook and climbed onto a wagon drawn by a team of Belgian horses. They headed toward the field area they'd been assigned. Isaac drove the team while Jacob and Eli hand-husked corn. With each swipe of the hook, Jacob snagged a stalk, then cut off an ear, husked it quickly by hand and then he threw the cob into the back of the wagon. Jacob worked quickly, moving down the row, with Eli working beside him, to cut the crop from the stalks that Jacob missed. At the end of the row Isaac turned the wagon, and Jacob and Eli shifted to work the next row, cutting, husking and tossing the husked corn behind them.

In another area, workers shocked corn by using a horse-drawn binder that cut down the stalks to the ground. Men followed behind, gathering and then standing them on end, with their tops leaning together in tepee-like fashion. Still other community men worked with a corn picker that was pulled by horses. Cornstalks were pulled into the chain-driven machine, which mechanically removed the ears from the shoots and husks. The ears were tossed through a passageway into a wagon pulled behind the picker. Only a few knew how to work the equipment, which could jam and be dangerous, especially its chains, which gathered the crop.

Jacob preferred husking the corn by hand. It might seem time-consuming, but each ear that was tossed into the back was ready to be dried before it was stored. He had shocked corn, as well, and he felt satisfaction in seeing the tents of stalks, in rows along the fields.

"We should get this acreage done before the midday meal," Eli commented as he bent to the work.

"*Ja*, but there is still the hay to bring in." Jacob inspected the corn he'd just shocked and, satisfied, threw it in with the others before he reached for another. "Although we'll have plenty of help."

"*Ja*. It won't take long, not with everyone pitching in." Eli hand-husked from another stalk and tossed the clean ears in the back of the wagon.

They worked for a time, then decided to break for lunch. Jacob accompanied his twin brother back to the house and the food waiting there. Isaac stayed with the team and waited for them to return with food for him.

"How are things with Annie?" Eli asked.

"I barely see her," Jacob replied, taking off his hat and wiping his brow with his shirtsleeve.

"Is staying away your doing or hers?"

Jacob shrugged. "I've been busy. Why would I seek her out?"

"Because you like her," Eli said with quiet understanding.

"I'm keeping my distance and getting the job done. That's all I need to do until I'm finished at the smithy."

"That could be a long time, Jake." Eli gestured toward Annie, who was arranging baked goods on the dessert table.

"I'll manage," he said. Somehow he would work hard, keep his distance from Joe's daughter and, in so doing, protect his heart. Not a chance that he'd be disappointed again by Anna Marie Zook.

"If you say so, Jake," his brother said, but he sounded unconvinced.

Annie stood by the dessert table, ready to slice a piece of cake or pie for a worker when she saw Jedidiah Lapp chatting with his wife, Sarah. She watched them a moment—she couldn't help herself. She'd been heartbroken when Jed had broken up with her years before, and she'd hurt from the loss when last year he'd courted and married Sarah Mast, William Mast's cousin from Delaware.

Watching the affection between them, the way he placed a hand on her arm, the soft smiles they exchanged, Annie felt pain. Seeing the two of them together was a reminder of what she didn't have. She wasn't jealous. She understood now that Sarah and Jed's marriage was God ordained.

Annie wanted a husband—and a family. As *Mam* had pointed out, she wasn't getting any younger. But how could she marry when no one showed an interest in her? She blinked back tears. She'd work hard to be a wife whom a husband would appreciate. She wanted children, to hold a baby in her arms, a child to nurture and love.

She sniffed, looked down and straightened the plates. The drinks were on one end—pitchers and jugs of iced tea and lemonade, and there were bottles of birch beer and cola.

"May I have some lemonade?" a deep, familiar voice said.

Annie felt a jolt and looked up. "Jacob." His expression was serious as he eyed her. She glanced down and noticed the fine dusting of corn residue on his dark jacket. "Lemonade?" she echoed self-consciously.

"*Ja.* Lemonade," he said with amusement.

She nodded and quickly reached for the pitcher. She kept her eyes on the task as she poured his drink into a plastic cup, only chancing a glance at him when she handed it to him.

"How is the work going?" she asked conversationally.

"We are nearly finished with the corn. We'll be cutting hay next." He lifted the cup to his lips and took a swallow.

Warmth pooled in her stomach as she watched the movement of his throat. "How's *Dat*?" she asked. She had seen him chatting with her father earlier.

With a small smile, Jacob glanced toward her *dat*. "He says he's not tired. He claims he's enjoying the view too much." His smile dissipated. "He'll be exhausted later."

Annie agreed. "I'll check on him in a while." She hesitated. "Are you hungry? I can fix you a plate—"

His striking golden eyes met hers for several heartbeats. "*Nay*, I'll fix one myself." He finished his drink and held out his cup to her. "May I?"

Heart pumping hard, she hurried to refill it. With a crooked smile and a nod of thanks, Jacob accepted the refreshment and left. The warm flutter in her stomach became a painful burning as she watched him walk away, stopping briefly to chat with Noah and Rachel, his brother and sister-in-law, at another table.

She thought about their conversation. He seemed different, but then she hadn't seen much of him since that first day. She had stayed away from the shop. She didn't want to interrupt him when he was hard at work. Her sister Barbara had been the one to offer him meals lately, and Barbara had informed them that he'd accepted a snack, but that he'd been bringing a packed lunch from home.

Annie followed his progress as he headed toward the food table, grabbed a plate and talked with Josie Mast, who stood behind the table and served up his supper.

"Annie." Rachel smiled at her as she approached. "You look thoughtful."

Annie nodded. "Rachel, have you ever felt like you've

done something wrong and don't know how to make it right?"

"*Ja*, years ago when I was hospitalized after Abraham Beiler's courting buggy slipped off an icy road, and I was thrown into a ditch."

Annie had heard about the accident not long after Rachel, the new schoolteacher, had arrived in Happiness. "Why did you feel as if you'd done something wrong?"

"After the accident, Abraham never came to visit me in the hospital—not once, even though we were sweethearts. I wondered what I had done to ruin his affection for me. And I mistakenly felt as if I was being punished."

Annie felt sympathy for what Rachel had suffered. "That must have been awful."

Rachel nodded. "But then God brought me Noah. Things happen to us that we can't control," she continued. "I believe that the Lord has a plan for us. He watches over us and gives us strength when we most need it. I know now that Abraham and I were not meant to be together. It is Noah who God chose for me, and I am grateful to the Lord for giving him to me."

"*Ja*, you and Noah are meant to be," Annie said with a smile. "As Sarah and Jed are."

Rachel grinned. "As there is someone God has chosen for you. You just don't know who yet."

Annie glanced toward the food table, where several men were having plates of meat, vegetables and sides dished up for them. "I pray the Lord finds me someone soon," she confessed softly. She felt Rachel's sympathetic touch on her arm.

"I believe it will happen." Rachel looked back to see the line of workers. "I'd better help out Josie."

"You're a kind person, Rachel." Annie smiled at the young woman with genuine warmth.

"So are you, Annie. You're a *gut* daughter and sister, and you're always willing to help anyone."

As she watched Rachel join Josie on the other side of the room, Annie thought of her behavior toward Jacob. She caught sight of him with his brother Eli. The contrast of Jacob's dark hair and Eli's light locks struck her, making her think of their differences and similarities as they disappeared into the barn. They came out a few minutes later, Eli carrying tools, Jacob leading Nosey, one of her father's workhorses.

As if he sensed her regard, Jacob glanced in her direction. She started to lift a hand to wave, but the somber look in his expression stopped her.

The workers completed the fall harvest at their farm. Annie watched as her fellow church members packed up their belongings and left with their families. William Mast waved as he drove his shock wagon with its team of mules away from the fields, past the house.

His wife, Josie, exited behind her. "We finished wrapping the leftovers."

"I'll help carry them out to your buggy," Annie offered.

"*Nay*, you'll be keeping them."

"But everyone will be at your farm next." She straightened her head covering.

Josie smiled. "*Ja*, and everyone has been cooking and baking to prepare for tomorrow, as well."

Annie nodded. It was true. She, *Mam* and Barbara had made several cakes and pies for the week's harvesting, as well as potato salad, dried-corn casserole and sweet-and-vinegar green beans.

"We appreciate the help," Annie said softly. She fondly regarded her father, who still sat in his wheelchair in the yard. All day he had refused to come inside to rest.

"How is he feeling?" Josie asked, her voice quiet.

Annie frowned. "He believes he is mending too slowly. He thinks he should be walking again."

"He is rushing his recovery. It bothers him to see others do his work."

"*Ja.* I wish I could help him. *Mam* has loving patience, but it has been difficult. *Dat* is a *gut* man, but this has been hard for him."

Josie's touch on her arm comforted her. "Things will get better."

Annie agreed. With God's help, everything was possible.

"We'll be heading home. *Ellen!*" Josie called into the house for her daughter.

Within seconds, Josie and William's twelve-year-old daughter, Ellen, exited the residence. "*Mam*, Miriam insisted we take this cake for *Dat.*"

Annie smiled. "It's William's favorite."

Josie hesitated and then grinned. "If Miriam insists." She called for her two sons, who had been playing ball with Abram Peachy's boys. "Will! Elam! Time to go!"

Annie watched with a smile as the Mast boys climbed into their family buggy, followed by their mother and sister. She waved as they left and followed the buggy's progress as it headed along the long dirt drive toward the main road.

Soon, other families followed suit, gathering their children before going home. It had been a wonderful day,

Annie realized. She enjoyed her church community, the way everyone was there to help when someone needed it.

Annie entered the kitchen to find her mother and Katie Lapp seated at the table, sharing a pot of tea. Millie lay curled up in the corner.

"Annie," Katie said with a smile, "will you join us?"

"Ja." Annie pulled out a chair. "Where is Barbara?" Her sister had been out of sight for most of the day.

Mam poured her a cup of tea. "She's upstairs gathering the boys' clothes for washing."

Annie rose to her feet. "I'll help her."

Her mother placed a hand on her arm. *"Nay*, Annie. Sit. There is no hurry to do the wash. This is Barbara's doing."

Annie felt concern. *"Mam*, what's bothering her? She's been quiet and doesn't talk with me like she used to." Barbara had seemed distant ever since her return last week from their great-aunt's house in New Wilmington. Her sister and she had always been close, but something had changed. Annie knew she'd been spending a lot of time with her father. Did Barbara feel slighted?

"Your sister spent time with a boy in New Wilmington," *Mam* said.

Annie widened her eyes. "She didn't tell me. She used to tell me everything." She reached for the sugar bowl, moved it closer to her cup.

"She got her feelings hurt. David chose another girl to be his sweetheart, someone from his local church community."

"I didn't know. Why didn't she tell me?" Annie repeated as she stirred a spoonful of sugar into her tea.

"Embarrassed maybe," Katie suggested. "You're her

older sister. She may have thought you'd think her foolish."

"She didn't know the boy long," *Mam* said.

"But long enough to lose her heart and have it broken," Annie said with a new realization of why Barbara had been acting strangely. She would have to talk with her sister in private. Tell her that she understood how Barbara felt.

Barbara entered the room as she rearranged the garments she carried over one arm. "*Mam*, I found Peter's clothes on the bedroom floor. He's in the shower—" She looked up and stopped when she saw *Mam*, Katie Lapp and Annie seated at the table.

"Want a cup of tea?" Annie invited with a smile.

"The clothes—" Her sister appeared anxious.

"Put them in the washer, Barbara," *Mam* said. "We can take care of them later."

Barbara crossed toward the back room, where the propane freezer and washing machine were kept. Annie heard the clink of the lid lifted, and the thump seconds later after her sister had dropped it closed.

Annie smiled encouragingly at her sister as Barbara reentered the kitchen. She pulled out a chair for her and then rose to take another teacup from the cabinet. "Anyone want a cookie?" she asked.

"Not me," *Mam* said.

"I'll have one," Katie replied, and Barbara agreed that she'd have one, too.

"Where's *Dat*?" Barbara asked as she accepted the tea that Annie poured for her.

"He's still out in the yard." Annie stood. "I should check on him."

"No need," a deep voice said, making Annie jerk.

She turned to see Jacob Lapp behind her father's wheelchair. Heart thumping hard, she focused on her father. *"Dat."* Unable to help herself, she felt drawn to the younger man. "Jacob. I didn't hear you come in."

"Joe." Her mother rose and hurried to his side. "You must be tired."

"I'm fine, Miriam." Her father smiled and Annie was pleased to see him happy. "Jacob has asked me to help out in the shop next week."

Annie frowned. "Are you sure that's a *gut* idea?"

"I told him only for an hour." Jacob held her glance briefly before he looked away. Annie felt a sniggle of disappointment.

Mam examined *Dat's* face and nodded. "That would be *gut*." Annie saw her smile gratefully at Jacob.

Josiah entered the kitchen. "I've brought in the mail." He flipped through the envelopes and then frowned as he drew out one in particular. He handed it to *Dat*. "From the hospital."

Annie watched her father as he opened the envelope. He turned pale as he read the bill. She saw how he fought to compose himself as he refolded the paper and stuffed it back in.

"Joe," Katie said as she stood with her teacup in hand, "whatever it is, you know our church community will pay the expense."

"This is too much, even for our community," *Dat* said wearily.

"Then we'll hold fund-raisers. As many as it will take to pay your bill." Katie took her cup to the sink and washed it.

Samuel, Jacob's father and Jacob's twin brother, Eli,

entered the kitchen. "What's wrong?" his *dat* asked as if sensing the tension in the room.

"Joe received his hospital bill in today's mail," Katie said as she returned to her seat, and Annie saw her flash a concerned glance toward *Mam*.

Samuel placed a hand on his friend's shoulder. "Don't *ya* worry, Joe. We'll find a way. The burden isn't yours alone."

Joe nodded but remained silent. Annie saw the look on her father's face; any happiness he'd had at joining Jacob in the shop next week had disappeared under the weight of debt.

"Don't worry, Joe. We're all here for you," Jacob said, and Annie looked at him with gratitude. When he favored her with a warm smile, she felt her stomach flip-flop.

Annie looked away, her heart racing as the Lapps got ready to leave a few minutes later. They would gather at the Masts the next day and then move on to Abram Peachy's place after bringing in the harvest there.

It would be a busy week, but she would be seeing Jacob every day. She felt a wash of pleasure that turned to fear as she recognized a subtle shift in her feelings toward him.

Jacob stood by the buggy, grabbed hold to lift himself in. But then he paused to glance in her direction, and she experienced the startling impact of his golden regard. Heart hammering hard, she raised a hand to wave. She inhaled sharply when he grinned, touched the edge of his hat brim as he acknowledged her with a dip of his head.

"Tomorrow," he mouthed.

Her spine tingled as she moved her lips, "Tomorrow."

Chapter Six

Annie's *Dat* was sleeping late; yesterday's church service and this past week's busy harvest had tired him. *Mam* thought he would easily stay abed until nine o'clock, a late hour for someone who usually got up at five in the morning before his accident. *Mam* and Barbara were busy at *Grossmudder's* house, leaving Annie at home in the kitchen, baking fresh cinnamon rolls. Peter had gone to the Masts to help William paint the rear side of his barn. Josiah, having finished his morning chores, had gone to visit his sweetheart, Nancy King.

Annie felt a sense of purpose. She hurriedly filled a thermos with coffee and placed two warm cinnamon rolls on a plate. With peace offerings in hand, she headed out to the shop to talk with Jacob, a funny feeling in the pit of her stomach as she approached. She heard the ring of steel against steel as she neared the shop door. Annie paused at the threshold to observe Jacob work.

With royal blue shirtsleeves rolled up to reveal his forearms and a leather blacksmith's apron tied about his neck and his waist, Jacob held the piece of metal within the tongs, examining it from every direction. Annie didn't think he noticed her as he fired up a propane blow-torch, held it against the piece of iron, before turning off the torch and then transferring the glowing metal back onto the anvil. He raised his hammer and banged the iron into shape. Suddenly, as if he sensed her presence, he looked up and without a smile set down the metal, tongs and hammer. He stepped away from the anvil and gave a polite nod.

"Annie." He had taken off his hat and hung it on a wall peg, and his dark hair looked a bit mussed as if he'd run his fingers through it.

She offered him a tentative smile, raised the thermos and plate. "I brought you coffee and cinnamon rolls." She held her breath, expecting him to refuse her offering.

A gleam entered his golden eyes. "Homemade?"

She gave him a genuine smile. "Is there any other kind?" She approached and handed him the plate. "May I pour your coffee?"

Watching her carefully, he inclined his head. "I didn't expect this."

"I know I haven't been in to talk with you," she began as she unscrewed the cap and filled his cup. She kept her eyes on the steam wafting from the hot brew as she extended it toward him.

"You came to talk?" he asked as he accepted the drink. "About what?" He appeared interested as he sipped the coffee.

Annie looked away in a sudden rush of uncertainty. Then she forced herself to look straight into his eyes. "I owe you an apology," she began confidently. "You were nothing but kind to me after *Dat* had his accident, and I was rude and ungrateful—" She felt the heat rise in her cheeks but met his glance head-on. "I'm sorry. I am very grateful for what you did for *Dat*. We all are. The Lord can't be happy with me."

He didn't laugh, didn't smile. He considered her as if he were searching the depths of her soul, and she shifted uneasily. "No apology needed," he finally said. He drank from his cup again.

"*Ja*, there is," she said. She wanted them to be friends like they were when they were children.

Jacob picked up a frosted cinnamon roll and viewed it from every angle. "This would be a *gut* apology if I needed one," he said before he took a bite. She watched him chew and swallow with great enjoyment. "Fortunately, I don't need one."

Annie watched him with confusion. She was surprised that he had brushed off her rudeness. She felt the tension within her ease, wondered why she was relieved and why making friends with Jacob should matter to her so much.

He took another drink. "How did you know how I like my coffee?"

She felt the focus of his golden eyes on her. "I saw you make it for yourself one day."

He looked surprised but pleased. "Do you want a cinnamon roll?"

She shook her head. "*Nay*, I brought them for you."

"I'm happy to share," he said with a smile, and Annie felt her heart beat rapidly. He extended the bun but she shook her head. "Will your *vadder* be coming in today?"

"*Ja*," she said. "He slept late this morning. He will be over later. It was nice of you to ask him to come. But it won't be easy having him here when you're trying to get work done."

"Has he been underfoot in the house?" Jacob jumped up to sit on the top of the worktable.

His easy movements drew Annie's attention to his muscled arms and long legs. "*Nay. Dat* has no wish to interfere with our housework. But the shop—that is his place. He is bound to give advice—some of it unwanted."

"That's where you're wrong, Annie. I learned a lot from your *vadder*. I spent hours taking his advice. It will be a pleasure to have him here."

"And he will love being here again. His heart has always been with forging metal, more so than with farm-work."

Jacob nodded. "He has your brothers to handle the farm for him. It is a *gut* arrangement."

Silence reigned for several seconds, and Annie began to feel self-conscious.

"You know Jed and Sarah are happy together," he said suddenly, the non sequitur startling her.

"*Ja.*" She blinked, felt her face burn. "Their marriage is God ordained."

"You believe that?" He eyed her skeptically over his cinnamon roll.

"*Ja*, I do." She examined him without embarrassment. "Why do you doubt it?"

"You were Jed's sweetheart."

"For a short time," she said, feeling a little pang at the memory, "but it wasn't meant to be."

Jacob sipped from his coffee and set the cup down on the table beside him. "Last Monday, during the harvest, I saw you watching him. It brought you tears."

Annie reached up to finger the string on her prayer *kapp*. "I know I shouldn't, but I was wishing I had someone, too, that I could be as happy as Jed and Sarah, and Noah and Rachel." She bit her lip. "I hope to marry…" she trailed off. She had no business telling him about her plan to marry an older church member, to have a happy marriage like Charlotte had with Abram Peachy.

"You hope to marry whom?" he prompted softly.

Embarrassed, she looked down at her shoes. "I've decided it would be best for me to marry someone older within our church district. Someone like Abram Peachy."

"Abram is married to Charlotte."

She gave him a look. "I know. I merely want to have a family like Charlotte does." *To have someone accept me for who I am, to look at me with quiet love and contentment.*

"And you believe that you will find happiness by wedding an older man?" His voice was soft.

Annie nodded. She would care for her husband, enjoy a safe kind of peaceful affection. She would know that with him, she'd never have to worry about a broken heart. And as time went on, her fondness for him would grow into a deep, abiding love. She was silent as her mind raced with images of her future.

"Annie." Jacob's deep voice drew her from her thoughts. "Is something wrong?"

She shook her head, feeling foolish. "*Nay.* I am fine." She felt suddenly uncomfortable for all she'd revealed to him. "I should go back to the *haus*. I have work to do." She gave him a slight smile. "*Dat* will be out after breakfast." She turned to leave.

"Annie—"

She stopped and spun around.

"Your *dat*, he is all right?"

She was pleased by his concern. Her discomfort eased. "He is worried about his medical expenses."

"We will raise the money." Jacob set down the plate and pushed off the worktable.

"I know, but it worries him still. He feels that he made a grave error in trying to fix the roof."

"We all make mistakes. He was doing a *gut* thing— that is never a mistake."

"*Danki*, Jacob," she said. He raised an eyebrow in question. "For helping *Dat*," she added. She turned to leave.

"Annie," he called. She paused and faced him. "I sincerely doubt the Lord is angry or upset with you."

She blushed. She didn't know what to say. So she remained silent as she hurried to escape his intense regard and startling words.

The women of the community met on Wednesday to plan a fund-raiser dinner for Horseshoe Joe. Annie, her sister Barbara, and *Mam* sat in Katie Lapp's gathering room, listening to the others talk.

"We can do a breakfast or supper," Alta Hershberger said. Alta was Annie's aunt, whose late husband had been *Mam's* brother. The woman was kind but a bit of a busybody. She had two daughters, Mary and Sally, and it was Alta's deepest wish to see each of her girls settled with a husband and family.

"Supper would be best, I think." Mae King jotted down some notes on a small pad. "Fried chicken? What else?"

"The English love chicken and dumplings. We could make that." Josie Mast sat in the chair next to Annie's. She raised her cup of tea to her lips, took a sip.

"We should keep it simple, but we do need to consider who will come and what the English like to eat," Katie said as she entered the room with two plates of cookies.

"Rachel made these," she murmured as she extended the plate to Annie and her mother.

Annie and Rachel exchanged looks across the room. Rachel winked and gifted her with a smile.

"Do you think dinner is the best way to go? We can serve breakfast with muffins and pancakes, waffles, eggs and toast." It was Charlotte Peachy who spoke up.

"It would be easier, I suppose," *Mam* said.

"I think we should do a supper first, then later do a breakfast," Nancy King said as she rose to grab a small plate on which she put three of Rachel's homemade cookies.

There were fifteen women in the room. They had a brief discussion on the merits of hosting a supper versus a breakfast. Annie watched the women with a small smile. Nancy King caught her eye, and her lips curved up in shared amusement.

The women's conversation stopped abruptly when Samuel and his twin sons entered the room. The silence seemed deafening to Annie.

Samuel looked at his wife. "A meeting?"

Katie nodded. "To discuss the fund-raiser for Horseshoe Joe."

Samuel appeared pleased. "A supper?"

Annie was conscious of Jacob and Eli, standing behind their father. To her dismay, Annie found her interest taken up mostly with the dark-haired twin with the stunning golden eyes. "Supper or breakfast—we're trying to decide."

"Why not do a supper first?" Samuel suggested. "Hold it on a Friday evening? The English enjoy eating out on Friday nights."

Jacob stepped forward, and Annie got a good view of

his handsome face. He towered over his father by five inches. Eli was as tall as Jacob, but there the similarity in their appearances ended. "Jacob. Eli," Annie dared to speak up. "What do you think we should do—a supper or a breakfast?" She felt a flush of warmth as Jacob studied her as he mulled it over. When he didn't answer immediately, she turned quickly to focus on his fraternal twin, but Eli was busy discussing the merits of whether or not to host a supper with her sister Barbara.

After much discussion, the community women decided to hold a chicken supper the following week on a Friday night. Samuel and his sons left, and Annie was able to relax and plan the dishes her family would contribute.

Soon, *Mam* and Barbara were ready to leave. Annie stood and finished a conversation with Rachel and her sister-in-law Sarah. "We'll bring the desserts," Sarah said and Rachel agreed. "Sarah loves to bake, and she's good at it."

Annie nodded. "So are you," she said. She smiled at Sarah. "I've had a piece of your chocolate cream pie," she admitted. She no longer felt awkward in Sarah's company. She had told Jacob the truth; she had come to accept Jed and Sarah's marriage. Seeing them together no longer upset her.

As she left the house, Annie saw Abram Peachy helping his wife into their family buggy. "They are happy together—Charlotte and Abram."

"Ja," Rachel said from beside her. "I've never seen Charlotte happier, and she loves the children. Little Ruthie took to her from the start. It's hard to believe how much Ruthie has grown. She's nearly six."

"There she is with her brother Nate," Annie observed.

They stood silently for a moment, then Noah came out of the barn with Jacob.

"Time for home." Rachel smiled at her husband as he approached.

Annie saw the way Noah looked at Rachel and the warmth in his wife's expression as she regarded him with affection. They were fortunate to have found each other.

She watched as families departed, enjoying the view, feeling a bit wistful that she had no husband or children to share her life. Suddenly, she realized that she was no longer alone. Jacob stood behind and within a few feet of her. She glanced over her shoulder, then turned to face him. "Jacob."

"Annie." His lips curved upward. "Why are you standing out here all alone?

Because I have no one to call my own, she thought. "I'm enjoying the view."

He shook his head as if he were disappointed. "Come into the *haus*. Your *mudder* and sister are still inside."

Silently, she followed him in. "*Mam*, are we staying for a while?" Annie asked, conscious of Jacob next to her.

"*Nay*, 'tis time to leave." *Mam* stood. "We have much to do for this fund-raiser. Katie, *danki* for everything."

Jacob's mother nodded. "'Tis my pleasure, Miriam. I will talk with you later to finalize the fund-raiser menu."

Her mother glanced in Jacob's direction as she, Annie and Jacob exited the house. "Jacob. It's *gut* to see you again as always. How are things going in the shop?"

"*Gut*. Horseshoe Joe is an excellent teacher. I feel as if I'd never left."

"Has he been behaving?" *Mam* paused on the front porch.

"*Ja*. It's *gut* to have his company," Jacob said. "I feel

like a young boy again, learning how to tackle various jobs."

"What kind of jobs?" Annie wanted to know. She was curious and in no hurry to leave.

"There is a certain skill in reworking an old horseshoe to extend its use," he said as he peered out into the yard, before refocusing his attention on Annie. "He's been teaching me how to create more traction on the bottom of an older worn horseshoe." He smiled. "For your *vadder*, it's an easy thing. I've become accustomed to the work now, though."

Jacob seemed to enjoy his surroundings. It was clear that he loved his family. Earlier, his eyes had been soft as he'd looked about the gathering room, apparently studying all the ladies who had come to meet in his parents' house. For a long minute, Annie hadn't been able to take her eyes off him. As was the custom, he had hung up his hat when he'd come inside. He had retrieved his hat and held it by the brim. His dark hair was shiny and looked newly combed. He wore a maroon shirt and navy *triblend* denim pants, held up by dark suspenders. His shirtsleeves were rolled up slightly, revealing strong, muscled forearms.

"We'd better get home," *Mam* said as she continued down the steps. "Peter is waiting for us. He has chores to do, and I know he's eager to get started. He won't leave your *vadder* alone."

"Take care, Jacob," Annie said softly as she followed her mother.

"I'll be at the shop tomorrow," he said. "Maybe I will see you then."

Pleased by his parting words, Annie joined her mother and sister near the buggy. She climbed into the front seat and picked up the leathers. *Mam* sat up front on the other side, while Barbara took a seat in the back.

As if unable to help herself, Annie glanced toward the Lapps' front porch. There Jacob stood, watching her. With a funny feeling in her chest, she waved and felt glad when he lifted a hand in response. Although she somehow managed to carry on an easy conversation with her sister and mother during the buggy ride home, she couldn't get him out of her mind.

A week later, Jacob stood in the doorway of Abram Peachy's barn, wondering how they were going to set up the tables for the dinner fund-raiser. He heard the rumble of an engine and stepped outside as a large flatbed truck was backing up to the barn. His father directed the vehicle into position, until with a call of "ho!" he instructed the truck to halt.

Jacob was surprised by what the truck carried: long banquet tables and plastic chairs.

When the vehicle came to a complete halt, the passenger door opened and his brother Jed hopped out. He came to where they stood at the back of the truck. "Matt is on the volunteer fire department. The men wanted to help, so they offered us the use of these—no charge."

Samuel looked pleased. "That is kind of them."

The driver shut off the engine and climbed out of the vehicle. Matt was Jed's construction-job foreman.

"What do you think?" he asked with a grin.

"We can certainly use these. Thanks," Jacob said to the *Englisher*. He reached onto the truck and pulled off two chairs, which he leaned against the barn. Other available workers followed suit, hauling out the furniture and setting them with the rest.

As he worked to prepare the area inside the large fairly new space that was Abram's barn and church-gathering place, Jacob thought of the women who would be arriving soon to ready the tables. He imagined Annie carefully spreading linens over every available banquet surface and then arranging each place setting with care. That was something he'd noticed about her whenever he visited the Zook farmhouse. Whether it was serving cookies and iced tea or cake and coffee, she took care in whatever she did, making a plate of goodies look nice or remembering what he liked in his coffee.

Annie. The way she was always in his thoughts, he was in dangerous territory. He mustn't make the same mistake twice. He had loved her once, only to get his heart trounced. He couldn't afford to fall for Annie a second time.

A buggy pulled into the barnyard and Annie stepped out. Jacob drew a sharp breath. *Dear Lord, keep me strong. Keep me safe from loving Annie.*

He watched her approach and felt a hard jolt. It was too late. He had fallen in love with Annie, and he didn't know how he was going to get over her a second time.

Chapter Seven

Annie climbed out of her family's buggy and then reached in for the box of tablecloths, plates, eating utensils and napkins. She turned toward the barn. "It looks like they're just setting up the tables now," she said to her sister.

"*Ja*. There is Josiah," Barbara said. "Look! They have long tables and folding chairs!"

Annie nodded, but her attention wasn't on the furniture being unloaded from the back of the truck. It was on the men doing the work—her brother Josiah, Amos King, Samuel Lapp and his sons—and Levi Stoltzfus who had come to help out. She looked from one man to the other, settling briefly on Jacob before quickly moving on. Levi glanced over and waved. Annie grinned and waved back. She was happy to see him. She always felt comfortable in his company.

"Girls, hold up," *Mam* said. "What are we going to do about these pies and cakes?"

Annie turned carefully, her arms full. "Why not leave them where they are until we can get one of the food tables set up? Unless you want to ask Charlotte if we can store them in her pantry."

Mam nodded. "If we leave them here, the boys are liable to find and eat them."

Annie agreed. Cradling the box of items, she approached the barn. "Noah," she greeted. "Amos. Samuel." Her heart skipped a beat as she and Jacob locked gazes. "*Hallo*, Jacob."

"That box looks heavy," Jacob said as he reached out to take it from her.

"Danki." She followed him inside the barn and checked the placement of furniture.

She saw Jacob study the room. "Where would *ya* like me to put this?"

Annie gestured toward a table along the wall. "There would be fine." He set the box down and she managed a smile for him when he faced her. "The room looks *gut*. We'll be able to handle a lot of paying guests. Who gave us the use of all this?"

"The fire department. Jed's construction foreman, Matt Rhoades, is a member."

"Gut, gut," she said. "The English will be more comfortable on chairs than on our benches."

"Ja," he agreed and she could sense him studying her as she inspected the room.

His scrutiny made her feel suddenly uncomfortable. "I should get to work. I have a lot to prepare."

He nodded. "I have things to do, as well."

"I appreciate the help," she offered as he started to walk away.

He stopped, glanced back. "'Twas my pleasure, Annie," he said silkily.

Heart thumping hard, Annie watched him walk away.

She had to focus on the task at hand. She drew in a steadying breath as she reached into the box for the tablecloths. Instead of plastic, the churchwomen had decided to use linens instead. She envisioned how the room would look when the tables were covered and place settings done and felt pleased.

"Annie, where are the plates and napkins?" Barbara asked. Annie hadn't missed her sister's approach. She gestured toward the box.

Barbara flashed a grin as she headed toward it. Their relationship was back to normal after a sisterly discussion last week. They shared a bedroom, and one evening, after they'd gone upstairs to bed, Annie had broached the subject of David Byler, the boy Barbara had fallen for during her visit to their great-aunt Evie's in northern Pennsylvania. At first, Barbara had been upset, almost defensive, until Annie had offered sympathy while talking of her own heartbreak over Jedidiah Lapp.

"I feel foolish, Annie," Barbara had whispered into the dark silence of their bedroom. They not only shared a room but a bed large enough for two.

"Why?" Annie had asked. "Because you fell in love? There is nothing wrong with loving someone." They had lain side by side in their white cotton nightgowns, their hair free from their head coverings, unpinned and flowing well down their backs—Annie's golden blond and Barbara's rich dark brown. When she was younger, Annie had shared a room with Joan, their eldest sister. Joan had lain next to her each night and shared private, whispered conversations, usually about the boy Joan liked and later married, while other times they had discussed Annie's feelings for Jedidiah Lapp. Barbara and she, closer in age than Joan and her, shared a friendship beyond being sisters. Barbara's distance from her after she'd returned from her trip with their *grosseldres* had hurt. Once she'd learned the truth of Barbara's painful experience, she was able to offer her sister kindness and understanding—and the assurance that Barbara had neither been foolish nor rash.

As she and Barbara worked together to set up the tables for tonight's dinner fund-raiser, Annie felt good. She had missed their quiet conversations. Now they gave each other frequent smiles as they discussed how to arrange each place setting.

Annie stood back to admire their handiwork. "We need five more tablecloths."

"Katie Lapp mentioned bringing more, in case we need them," Barbara said.

"So did Mae King."

Several women entered the room, among them their mother, Miriam, with Katie and Mae. Each woman carried a metal rack with an aluminum chafing dish and a can of gelled cooking fuel.

"The room looks *gut*," *Mam* stated as she approached.

"We need more tablecloths," Barbara said.

"The extras are in the buggy," Katie said. "Noah told me about the tables and chairs."

Mae King set down the chafing dish. "I hope we have a *gut* turnout."

"I think we will," Katie said. "We've had over a week to get the word out. The boys put posters in all the local stores and in the shops at the Rockvale Outlet Mall and Tanger Outlets. Bob Whittier told everyone who came into his store."

"I hope so." Annie wanted this fund-raiser to be a success for her father's sake. *Dat's* worry over his medical bills was taking a toll on his recovery.

"After we're done setting up, we'll head home," *Mam* said. "Later, we'll come back with the food, an hour and a half before dinner starts."

Alta Hershberger entered the barn. "Miriam, the place looks nice."

Mam smiled. "It should do the job."

"Where do you want these?" Annie's aunt seemed genuinely happy to help out.

Mae gestured toward a table. The women discussed the arrangements. Except for the dessert portion of the meal afterward, they would be serving their guests. Several side items would be set out family style while the younger women, including Annie, Barbara, Nancy King and young Ellen Mast, would be on hand to make sure that no one left hungry.

The women finished dinner preparations and departed. Annie, Barbara and their mother discussed the fund-raiser as they drove home in their buggy.

"We have plenty of seats for our guests," Barbara said.

"*Ja*, now we should pray that we see a *gut* profit."

"'Tis a fair price, *Mam*," Annie said. She directed the mare onto their dirt driveway. "Rick Martin's bringing his family, and he told his friends. The dinner fund-raiser will be successful."

"I pray that it will be so," *Mam* said somberly.

Annie reached out to clasp *Mam's* hand. "I have faith, *Mam*. You must, too." She drove skillfully down the drive and into the barnyard. Josiah and Peter had returned home earlier in their market wagon. She lifted a hand to smile and wave at Josiah in the yard. "The Lord will guide us in our time of need," she told her mother. "He has been *gut* to us. *Dat's* injuries could have been worse."

The silence in the buggy, as the vehicle came to a complete stop, felt heavy. Annie thought of what might have happened if her father had injured himself more severely. What if he'd broken his neck or cracked his skull?

"We have a lot to be thankful for." *Mam* smiled at her as she climbed out. "Come, we have much to do yet."

The fund-raiser was a success. Jacob stood near the door and watched as the diners enjoyed the dinner prepared by the women of the Happiness Amish community. Earlier, he had gone home to wash and change his clothes. He looked for where he might be able to help. He observed the young women—including Annie—attending to their dinner guests.

There were bowls of sides on the tables: potato salad, green beans, coleslaw, dried-corn casserole, sweet-and-sour chow-chow and fresh home-baked bread. The women went from guest to guest to inquire about their choice of meat—fried chicken, roasted chicken or roast beef—and whether or not they preferred other sides.

So far the people who'd come were pleasant. The first to arrive had been the Zooks' neighbors, Rick Martin and his wife and children—a teenage son and daughter. Store-owner Bob Whittier, with his brood, came soon afterward, followed closely by his other relatives and friends.

The first seating was filled to capacity. As their guests left after dessert, others came in to take their place.

He wondered how many meals had been served so far. *Two hundred? Three hundred? More?* His mother looked pleased. He prayed that the amount raised would be enough to pay Joe's medical expenses.

"Jacob!"

"Rachel." With a smile, he approached his sister-in-law. "Need help?"

"*Ja*, there is more bread in Charlotte's kitchen. Would you mind getting five loaves?" She moved the breadbasket toward the front of the table.

Jacob nodded. "Do *ya* need anything else?"

"*Nay.*" She glanced about the room. "Have you seen Noah?"

"He is outside with Arlin, helping him set up a table to sell his woodcrafts. Our uncle wants to help with Joe's expenses. He's suffered medical bills with our cousin Meg and appreciated the help he got from his community."

"That's kind of him." Rachel spied her husband and waved at him. She flashed Jacob a smile. "Keep Noah away from the dessert table. Tell him there is chocolate cake at home for him. I don't want him sampling the fund-raiser treats."

Jacob laughed. "I'll tell him and be right back with the bread."

Rachel smiled her thanks. Grinning, Jacob turned and stopped short. Annie Zook stood directly behind him with baskets of rolls, biscuits and muffins.

"Annie." She looked lovely in a light blue dress that matched her eyes, over which she wore a black apron. Silky tendrils of her golden hair peeked out from beneath her white prayer *kapp* and caught the light. Her smile reached her bright blue eyes. Her pink lips and pretty nose were exquisitely formed. *A glorious vision from God.*

Startled by his thoughts, he said, "I have to get bread."

Then he excused himself and left. He stopped once briefly to speak with Noah before he headed toward Charlotte Peachy's kitchen.

Except when he helped carry items to the food table, Jacob seemed to avoid her, she noticed. When it came time for him to eat dinner, he chose to sit in his sister-in-law's area, a fact that bothered her greatly. She thought they were friends. At times, he talked and teased her, but on other occasions, he would eye her with a strange look that was disconcerting.

She watched from a distance as he smiled and laughed, at ease while talking with Rachel. Eli Lapp entered the room and approached his twin. Eli saw her and grinned. Her heart lightened as she waved at him.

"Annie!" *Mam* called her from the kitchen doorway, just a few feet away. "We're almost done," she said. "Did you eat?" Annie shook her head. "Well, get something, daughter. You've been working hard. You need to eat, and not only from the dessert table."

"Ja, Mam," she said without argument.

Toward the end of the evening, Charlotte Peachy approached. "We've done well." She beamed. "Almost four thousand dollars!"

Arlin Hostetler, Katie Lapp's brother, entered the barn behind Charlotte. "And I sold over eight hundred dollars worth of merchandise," he said with a grin. He turned the money over to Charlotte.

"Nearly five thousand dollars in all," Charlotte corrected.

Annie blinked back tears. *"Danki.* You don't know how much this means to us."

"I think I do," Arlin said.

Annie sniffled and wiped her eyes. "What would we do without all of you?"

Mam approached. "How much did we make?" she asked, and Charlotte told her. "Thanks be to God!" Her eyes filled with tears.

"Let's clean up," Charlotte said. "I'll give this cash to Abram to lock up until tomorrow."

Annie, her mother and all who had helped to set up or serve pitched in to clean up afterward. When they were done, after the women promised to gather and discuss a future Saturday breakfast fund-raiser, families left for home.

"We did well at the fund-raiser today." Annie felt pleased that the breakfast had been such a success.

"Ja," her *mam* said, "the money will be a good payment toward the hospital bills."

Annie murmured her agreement. Perhaps now her father would feel less stressed about the state of their finances, she thought with relief.

Saturday morning Annie started her chores. She did the wash and hung it on the clothesline with Barbara's help. The day was sunny but a bit cooler than it had been yesterday.

"There's a nice breeze," Annie said.

"Ja, the clothes will dry in no time." Barbara reached into the wicker basket and withdrew one of Peter's shirts. She fastened the bottom hem on the line with wooden clothespins. "Have you decided what to make for supper?" she asked casually.

"Ja, meat loaf, mashed potatoes and peas." Annie picked up a wet pillowcase and shook the wrinkles from

it before pinning it into place. "I'm thinking cherry cobbler for dessert."

Barbara was quiet for a few moments as she continued to hang the damp garments. "Do *ya* think that's *gut* enough?" she asked.

"For Levi?" Annie frowned. "Barbara, the preacher has been coming to our house for dinner once a week for months. He always likes what we fix. Why should tonight be any different?"

Barbara secured a lavender dress to the clothesline and then faced her sister. "I just thought we could do something special for him."

"Any particular reason?" Annie asked.

"Nay," she murmured. "I just thought, since he is a preacher…"

"Levi would be the first to tell you that he is no different than the rest of us." Annie sighed. "Stop worrying, Barbara."

Later, as she worked to fix the cherry cobbler, Annie grew thoughtful. *Is Barbara right?* She stirred the cherries until they were coated with sugar. Should she be fixing something special for the preacher? She frowned as she dumped the fruit into a large baking pan. *Nay, he always likes what I fix.*

Next, she worked to prepare the crumb topping made with cinnamon, sugar and dry oatmeal, which she sprinkled over the cherries and dotted with dabs of butter.

She'd have to watch Levi this evening to see if he was enjoying the food or just being polite. Annie picked up the cobbler pan and put it in the refrigerator.

Preacher Levi Stoltzfus was an honest man. He wouldn't come to supper every week if he didn't enjoy the food, she realized. She smiled. Just as she had told

Barbara, there was no cause to worry that Levi wouldn't enjoy the meal. Levi Stoltzfus was a kind older man, who would make someone a good husband. He came to dinner often because he'd lost his wife in childbirth two years ago.

She went still. Were Barbara and *Mam* trying to play matchmaker? Was that why Barbara was worried about whether or not Levi enjoyed tonight's meal?

Annie laughed softly, scolding herself for her silly concern. *Mam* hadn't said a word about Levi, and the preacher was a frequent visitor so his visit was nothing out of the ordinary.

Nay, she thought. Barbara was just being Barbara, worrying about something for no reason.

Preacher Levi would make me a fine husband... He'd be kind to me, treat me fairly and I would never have to worry about him breaking my heart.

Unbidden came thoughts of Jacob Lapp with his twinkling golden eyes and warm smile, and Preacher Levi was temporarily forgotten.

Chapter Eight

Annie was at the stove, stirring potatoes, when she heard her sister's voice in the front room.

"Preacher Levi!"

"*Hallo*, Barbara. 'Tis nice to see *ya* again," he replied pleasantly. Seconds later, they were in the doorway.

"Levi," her sister said with warmth. "Are you hungry? We're having meat loaf for dinner."

"It smells wonderful." He entered the room behind Barbara.

Annie turned. "*Hallo*, Levi," she said with a smile. "Dinner is nearly ready. We'll be having mashed potatoes, buttered baby peas and fresh yeast rolls with the meat loaf." She grabbed the pot from the stove, set it on a hot mat on the countertop and reached for the butter. "What would you like to drink?"

"I'll get it," Barbara piped up. "Iced or hot tea? Lemonade? Coffee?"

"Iced tea would be fine." He flashed Annie an amused glance as Barbara hurried to retrieve the pitcher from the refrigerator in the back room. She raced back into the kitchen where she withdrew two glasses from a cabinet. She filled one to the brim with tea and handed it to Levi.

Mam entered the kitchen. "*Hallo*, Levi."

"Miriam." He smiled. "I appreciate the standing dinner invitation."

"'Tis always a pleasure to have you, isn't it, girls?"

Annie agreed while Barbara nodded.

"Where's Joe?" Levi asked.

"In the gathering room," Annie said. "Would *ya* mind telling him that it's time to eat?"

"I'd be happy to." As the minister left to visit with their father, Barbara turned toward her and exclaimed, "Why did you ask him to tell *Dat*? He shouldn't have to do anything. He's our guest."

Annie sighed. "Barbara, Levi wanted to see *Dat*—couldn't *ya* tell? And he is more like family than a guest." After stirring the potatoes, she drained the liquid from the pot into the sink and grabbed the masher.

Barbara looked taken aback. "But he's the preacher!"

"And you and I are Joe and Miriam's daughters. Does that make us any less in the Lord's eyes?" She worked the potatoes into a fine mash, added butter, milk and seasonings. "Barbara, would you please put the peas on the table? And maybe some jam as well as butter."

Soon supper was served and Annie called everyone to come and eat.

"Your *vadder* and Levi will be right in," *Mam* said. "I'm going to get your *grosseldre*."

"What's for dinner?" Peter asked as he passed his mother and entered the room. Annie gestured toward the table. "Meat loaf!" he cried, sounding pleased.

Josiah came in behind him and reached down to snag a piece of bread. "Looks *gut*."

"Josiah!" Barbara scolded. "Save some for supper."

Josiah gave her a look. "This *is* supper time, sister."

"Smells wonderful," Levi said as he pushed *Dat* into the room and into position at the table.

Soon *Mam* had returned with Annie's grandparents, and everyone was seated and ready to eat. The meat loaf was passed around, followed by the vegetables and bread.

"Levi." *Mam* handed him the dish of peas. "How long has it been since Rebecca passed on?"

Annie heard her sister gasp from beside her.

"Two years," Levi murmured.

"It must get lonely in that big house of yours." *Mam* smiled as she spooned mashed potatoes onto her plate.

"*Ja*, it can be," the preacher admitted.

Annie frowned. Levi had lost his wife in childbirth along with their baby. The preacher had no family left in Happiness. His parents had passed away ten years ago, leaving Levi and his five siblings. His two sisters had married and moved with their husbands to Indiana, while his eldest brother had died three years after their mother and father. Not long afterward, Levi's two living brothers had left Happiness and followed his sisters to Indiana.

Levi hadn't minded when his family moved away, for he had met and happily married Rebecca Troyer. Rebecca and Levi had wanted children, and at first it seemed that it wasn't meant to be. After five years of marriage, Rebecca and Levi had rejoiced that they were finally to have a child. Only it had all gone wrong, and Rebecca, who had suffered a difficult pregnancy, had endured a childbirth that had taken her life and their baby's.

Much to Annie's relief, her father changed the subject and asked Levi about the preacher's corn harvest.

Levi smiled. "*Ja*, it has been a *gut* year. The weather

was fine for us. Now we have to think of next year. I was thinking of trying to plant some…"

The conversation turned to farming and from farming to this visiting Sunday.

"You will come tomorrow, won't you, Levi?" Barbara asked.

"With all the fine food you provide? *Ja*, I'll come." Levi had finished his plate and taken seconds. *Mam* rose to remove his dish when he was done.

"Annie made chocolate cake and cherry cobbler," *Mam* said as she carried the dessert to the table.

Levi smiled at Annie. "They both sound wonderful, but I'd like a piece of cherry cobbler."

"Annie is a *gut* cook, Levi. She will make some man a wonderful wife." *Mam* continued to extol Annie's talents, causing Annie's face to redden.

"Mam—"

"'Tis true, Annie," *Mam* said.

"*Ja*, you do cook well," Levi told her gently.

"She will make a fine wife, *ja*?" *Mam* asked.

Annie could feel the intensity of Levi's regard. *"Ja."* He appeared thoughtful, and she wished she could be anywhere but here at this moment.

"Miriam," *Dat* said, "you are embarrassing the girl, and you are forgetting your youngest daughter. Barbara is a fine cook, as well."

Annie was suddenly grateful that the attention had shifted to her sister, who didn't seem the least embarrassed by it. She frowned. *What is* Mam *doing?* She gasped. *Trying to make a match!* She closed her eyes. This wasn't the way to find a husband!

The preacher was a nice man, it was true, and he was attractive with his golden-blond hair and blue eyes. And she did feel comfortable around him, but something inside her rebelled at her mother's interference in matters of her heart.

Later that night, in her room, the memory of that moment mortified her. Levi Stoltzfus? Annie shook her head. She couldn't think of this now. She couldn't. Was her mother so determined to get her out of the house that she would push her toward Levi when the man wasn't ready to court or marry again?

"Annie?" Barbara's voice came out of the dark.

"Ja?" She stared up at the ceiling, not seeing anything but the images inside her head.

"Do you like him?"

"Who?" Annie rolled to face her.

"Preacher Levi."

"Ja, he is a nice man." He was more than a nice man, she thought, but she didn't want to be pushed into a relationship by her mother or her sister.

"Mam seems to think he should be for you."

Annie sighed. "That was obvious at dinner."

"What are you doing to do?"

She thought long and hard before answering. Levi would make her a fine husband, but he would have to be the one to show interest in her. "What can I do? 'Tis God's will that will decide."

Monday morning, Jacob was hanging up his hat in the shop when he heard a sound behind him.

"Jacob."

He spun, startled to see her. "Annie! You're here early."

"I couldn't sleep."

Jacob became concerned. Annie looked exhausted; there were dark circles beneath her eyes and a look of anxiety in her expression. His worry for her grew. "What's wrong? Is it Joe?"

She shook her head. "*Nay, Dat* is doing well. He goes back to the doctor this week."

"What's wrong, then?"

She blinked up at him, then looked away. "You'll think it's silly—"

"Something is worrying you, and I doubt it's silly."

She wandered about the room, running her fingers over the items on the worktable: a metal fire poker…different sizes of tongs and cross-peen hammers.

"Annie—"

"I think my *mudder* is trying to make me a match," she rushed to say.

"A match?" He stared at her. *With whom?* "You think she's trying to find you a sweetheart?"

"Sweetheart, *nay*." She stopped fidgeting to face him. "A husband."

"Your *mudder* wants to marry you off?" Jacob thought of other families within the community. It was possible. Not everyone was like his *mam* and *dat*, who had married for love and were happy to see their children discover the same happiness on their own.

"Preacher Levi comes to the house every week for supper," she began.

Jacob nodded. The preacher came to their house often, as well.

"The last time Levi ate with us, *Mam* suddenly mentioned his late wife and how long it had been since Rebecca had passed on—"

"Surely it was just an expression of concern for our preacher," he suggested as he reached for his leather apron. He slipped it over his head and tied it in the back at his waist.

Annie shook her head. "After reminding Levi how lonely he must be in his big house, *Mam* praised my cooking." She looked horrified, and he fought not to smile. "And then she told him what a wonderful wife I'd make." She blinked back tears. "It was humiliating."

"You said that you'd wanted to marry an older man." He gathered his tools and placed them within reach. "Levi is older. What's wrong with him?"

"There is nothing wrong with him," she said. "He's a kind man. Once he is over his late wife, I believe he will make someone a *wonderful* husband."

Jacob felt his heart skip a beat as she spoke. Levi Stoltzfus sounded like the perfect husband for her. "Then I would consider what you want and take your time to decide," he said.

"I could do that. It's not as if they will force me to marry him." Annie smiled and looked relieved. "That is sound advice. *Danki*, Jacob."

He nodded as he watched her closely.

Annie glanced about the shop. "I don't see any food in here. Would you like coffee and a cinnamon bun?"

"Ja." He grinned. "You are a fine cook, Annie Zook," he teased. "You'll make some man a wonderful wife one day."

She flashed him a look that told him she didn't mind his teasing. "I'll bring your coffee and roll." She suddenly looked mischievous. "Or I'll send Barbara out with hard-boiled eggs and castor oil." She laughed as she left, and the sound of her laughter was like music to his heart.

Jacob felt a burning in his stomach. He didn't like the idea of Annie marrying Levi; he didn't like the idea of her marrying anyone but him. But if he had to pick an older husband for her, then Preacher Levi would be his choice.

He sighed. He seemed destined for heartbreak. He'd thought he could work in the shop and keep his emotions under control, but he'd lost that battle. He loved Annie. He wanted her for his wife. If being friends with her was his only choice, he'd take it. Friendship was better than having no relationship with her at all. But would he feel the same after she married someone else? Could he endure watching her with another man, holding his children? He wanted Annie to be happy and if her happiness meant her marriage to Levi Stoltzfus, then he would pray to the Lord to help him accept it.

Preacher Levi Stoltzfus wasn't the only man that *Mam* invited to take supper with the family. The following Wednesday, Joseph Byler arrived, much to Annie's surprise. Joseph was a young man who tended to be overeager in everything he did. He was the son of Edna and the late John Byler. He was single, eighteen, and while he was attractive, he irritated Annie.

Joseph's presence, along with *Mam's* questions and comments regarding Annie's cooking skills, made Annie realize that Joseph was only the second in what could potentially be a long parade of prospective husbands invited by her mother.

Annie confronted *Mam* after Joseph went home. "What are *ya* doing?"

Her mother shrugged. "You promised to consider any man who showed an interest in you."

"But *Joseph Byler*? I can't possibly spend time with him. He is…*annoying*."

Mam stared at her. "Annie!" she scolded.

Annie stood at the sink, drying the last of the supper dishes. "Would you want his attention?"

"He's a nice young man."

"*Ja*, too young. I want an *older* husband. I'll not accept him if he asks to court me. It wouldn't be fair to give him hope."

Her mother sighed, apparently accepting defeat. "I agree he can be overwhelming."

"Trying, you mean." Annie wrinkled her nose.

Mam gave her a look. "You need to think seriously about your future. If not Joseph, you must consider someone else." She paused. "What about Levi?"

"I'm not sure he's over his late wife."

"But you like him."

Annie nodded. "*Ja.* He is a kind man."

"There are other available men within our church community. All hope isn't gone yet," her mother assured her.

Annie raised her eyebrows. "I never thought it was." She frowned. "*Ya* think I'm so awful that no man would ask to court me on his own?"

"*Nay*, daughter. But you can't live in the past. You're getting older, and I'd like to see you settled with a husband and children."

"Miriam!" Joe called from the other room.

"Coming!" *Mam* touched her cheek. "Things will work out for the best, Annie. They always do." And she left Annie wiping the countertop, wondering what she would do if she didn't find a man with whom she could be content.

Levi Stoltzfus was definitely a better choice than Joseph Byler.

Please, Lord, give me the courage to accept Thy will and be happy.

* * *

The church community put on another fund-raiser for Horseshoe Joe, this one a breakfast. Jacob stood along one wall, looking for the best way to lend a hand. Today, the breakfast was to be held in the firehouse. Jed's boss, the firefighter who had arranged the use of tables and chairs for the dinner, had come to the bishop and offered the use of the large hall. Seeing the merit in the size of the room and the location, Bishop John accepted the offer. With the breakfast announced on the sign outside, Jacob knew the fund-raiser would be a success.

This morning the tables were lined with rolls of paper. It was 7:00 a.m., and soon people would arrive to eat.

Jacob saw his two sister-in-laws and Annie setting up. The cans of cooking fuel beneath the stainless-steel chafing dishes were lit and ready to go. His *mam*, Mae King and Miriam Zook were cooking scrambled eggs, pancakes, sausage, bacon and ham. Jacob made his way to the kitchen. The scents coming from the room were wonderful. They made his mouth water.

"Need any help?" he asked.

"Jacob! I'm glad you're here." His mother gestured toward a large metal pan on the worktable. "Would you take the sausage to the food table?"

"Ja, Mam." He lifted a metal lid to inspect the contents. He hadn't eaten yet this morning, and the delicious aroma wafting up from the breakfast sausage patties made his stomach rumble.

"When you're done with that, there'll be a dish of pancakes ready," Mae King asked.

"I'll be back soon." Jacob picked up the chafing dish and carried it out to the dining area. He passed Annie as he made his way out.

"Jacob," she said. "What do you have there?"

"Sausage." He enjoyed taking stock of her.

Her cheeks were flushed from rushing about, preparing for the event. "Rachel will tell you where to put it."

Jacob inclined his head. At the food table, he set the full serving dish into a rack, as instructed, and as he headed back to the kitchen, he experienced an awareness of Annie across the room.

Annie watched Jacob chat briefly with Rachel before he set down the breakfast meat and left. With lingering mixed feelings, she scrutinized the food table. Everything was as it should be. She went to the kitchen and picked up the scrambled egg pan. She hurried toward the dining room and stumbled against Joseph Byler. "Joseph, you startled me!" she gasped, stepping back.

"Let me carry that for you," he said.

Annie kept a firm grip on the dish. "It's not heavy. I can manage."

"I insist." Joseph observed her with gleaming eyes as he started a tug-of-war with her over the metal pan.

Annie inhaled sharply and released it. "Take it to Rachel, please." She hurried back to the kitchen, eager to be away from the young man. "Are the pancakes ready?" she asked Mae as she entered the room.

"Ja." Mae wiped her hands on her cooking apron. "Dish is almost to the brim."

"I'll take these out to keep warm," Annie stated as she picked up the pan of pancakes. She hesitated then sighed. "Here comes Joseph Byler."

"He is a nice young man," *Mam* insisted.

"I'm not interested."

Joseph made a beeline in her direction as soon as he

saw her. Annie managed a weak smile. "Next to the sausage," she instructed as she handed him the pan.

"I'll take care of it." He looked serious before he turned and left.

Annie watched him walk away, then sighing, she went to the drink table where she checked the large container of iced tea. She set out plastic cups and placed a hot mat where she would put out a thermal coffee decanter later. Another would be used for hot water for tea or hot chocolate. She eyed the area to decide what needed to be brought out now and what should wait until later.

As she turned, she saw Joseph Byler heading her way. She closed her eyes briefly and prayed. *Dear Lord, please grant me wisdom, patience and understanding so that I may deal kindly with Joseph Byler.* When she opened her eyes, Jacob Lapp was in her line of vision. She sent him a pleading look as she glanced pointedly toward Joseph. Jacob grinned and followed the young man as he approached.

"Annie, how else may I help?" Joseph asked.

"You can give Isaac and Eli a hand as they set up the last of the chairs." Jacob gestured toward the other side of the room. "I'll stay and help Annie."

Joseph opened his mouth as if to object, but then he nodded politely and left.

"May I carry something?" Jacob teased, his golden eyes twinkling.

Annie made a face at him and then laughed. "Would you like to?" she asked seriously.

"*Ja*, but I don't want to seem overeager like Joseph." Jacob glanced in the other man's direction.

"You're *not* Joseph," she said and felt her face heat.

"I can use the help." She felt an odd sensation along her spine as he took her measure.

"What do *ya* want me to do?" he asked.

"We have several more food dishes in the kitchen. You can help me carry them out to the dining room." She examined the buffet tables. "More breakfast meat," she decided. "And fried eggs, if they're ready."

"Lead the way, Annie, and I will be happy to carry them for you."

Annie felt a tingling at her nape, overly aware of his strong presence behind her, as she preceded him into the kitchen.

"Back so soon?" Mae King asked.

"Came for the fried eggs," he said. He picked up the large metal dish.

"*Mam*, are there more muffins and sweet rolls?" Annie asked.

"*Ja*, in the backroom."

Katie wiped her hands on her cooking apron as she moved from the stove. "After you take those out, Jacob, would you help Annie by carrying the jams and jellies for the breadbaskets?"

"*Ja, Mam.* Anything else?"

"You can make sure the girl eats breakfast before we open the doors to our guests," Mae said.

Annie felt the warmth of Jacob's regard. "I will," he promised, and Annie looked into his twinkling golden eyes and blushed before she quickly headed into the other room for the breadbaskets.

"I don't see Joseph," Jacob said a short time afterward as they reentered the large dining area together. "Would *ya* like me to find him for you?"

Halting, Annie shot him a look. "Not funny." He

shrugged and then chuckled. She responded to his good humor and joined in the laughter. "Come, Jacob, we need to put these on the other buffet table."

"May I sneak a muffin?" he said as he set down the jam and jelly tray next to the two large baskets that Annie had carried in. "I haven't eaten breakfast."

"You're not sneaking if you ask permission," she teased.

"*Gut* point." He snatched a chocolate-chip muffin and glanced about slyly, then took a small bite. He looked so comical that Annie grinned.

"Well?" she said. "Is it worth getting in trouble over?"

He feigned a frown. She couldn't miss the amusement in his golden eyes. "Am I in trouble?"

She smirked. "You *are* trouble." And as they shared laughter, Annie found great enjoyment in his company. As she turned to head back to the kitchen, she caught sight of her sister standing several feet away, staring at them. She met Barbara's glance and, to her dismay, watched as her sibling made an about-face and rushed toward the kitchen.

"Ach, nay," Annie murmured.

"What's wrong?" Jacob asked, moving to her side.

"I'm afraid you'll be in the hot seat next. My sister saw us laughing, and now she's run to tell my *mudder.*" She paused, gave him a worried look. "Be careful or you'll find yourself invited to dinner."

"Not a chance." Jacob glanced toward the kitchen doorway. "Your *mam* doesn't consider me as a potential husband for you. I have no job and no prospects." He smiled slightly. "See? So there's no need to worry. Just remind her that I'm too young for you."

Annie tilted her head at him. "Too young?" she murmured.

"*Ja*, I'm not your type at all, an older member of our church community." He grinned. "Coming?" He gestured toward the kitchen, and she inclined her head.

Annie followed slowly as Jacob went on ahead. *He's right*, she thought. That was exactly what *Mam* would think—that he was a young man without means. And Jacob was everything she wanted to avoid in a man. She closed her eyes, felt a rush of pain. Why did she suddenly feel so sad?

Chapter Nine

Annie was in the yard, feeding chickens, when Jacob exited the shop and approached. "*Gut* morning!" she greeted with a smile.

"*Gut* morning. You are out early." He reached her side, dipped his fingers into her bucket and scattered a handful of feed.

She was conscious of him beside her, looking handsome in his maroon shirt and *triblend*-denim trousers. "*Mam's* gone into town with *Dat*. He has a doctor's appointment. Barbara and Josiah left for the Amos Kings' earlier this morning." She smiled. "Me? I've got a full day's chores." She threw another fistful. "You?"

"Ike King is bringing in his gelding. When I'm done in the shop, I'll head to Noah's." He captured her glance, causing warmth to rise up from her nape. "Jed is out with a construction crew, and Noah needs help with deliveries."

Annie broke eye contact with him until she could regain her balance. "What time will Ike be here?" She knew that Noah Lapp's furniture shop did well. Noah was an excellent cabinetmaker and the demand for his work had increased since he'd opened his business.

"Any minute now. I've come to watch for him."

"Do you have time for coffee?" she asked.

"*Nay*, but I appreciate the offer."

A buggy on the dirt drive drew Annie's attention. Beside her, Jacob called out a greeting and waved to Ike, who drove the vehicle.

Ike parked his buggy close to the shop entrance. He smiled as he climbed out. "Mornin'!" he greeted. "Fine day today." He was a man in his late thirties with a beard along his jawline. All Amish men grew beards after they married. Only Ike was a widower.

"Great weather to be out and about," Jacob agreed as he walked toward the horse and rubbed the gelding's nose. "I don't imagine we'll see many days like this before the cold rushes in."

The older man nodded. Studying him, Annie knew that Ike had left Indiana and returned home to Lancaster County after his young wife's death. Ike resembled his older brother Amos about the eyes and in the shape of his chin, but Amos's beard had streaks of gray while Ike's was reddish brown.

"Where do you want him?" Ike asked Jacob, referring to the animal.

"Inside." Jacob worked to help Ike unhitch the horse and then he instructed the other man to follow him into the blacksmith shop. "See you later, Annie."

"*Ja*, Jacob." She smiled at Ike, who didn't immediately follow. "Are you waiting? You can come in for coffee or tea."

"That is kind of *ya*, Annie, but Amos is coming to

fetch me. I'll be back later when Jacob has finished shoeing young Abraham here."

"*Gut* day to *ya* then, Ike. I must get back to work. I'll see you on Sunday." Annie watched him as he joined Jacob, and the two men stood outside the shop, talking for a time.

"Annie!" Levi Stoltzfus approached from the direction of her grandparents' house, drawing her attention. The handsome preacher wore a spring-green shirt, black suspenders and black pants.

"Levi!" Annie grinned as he drew near. "I didn't expect to see you today."

"I thought I'd stop and visit with your *grosseldre* this morning." He appeared pleased as he reached her side.

"I'm sure they appreciated the company." Annie regarded him with warmth. "*Mam* sees the changes in them as they age, and since *Grossmudder's* last illness and hospital stay, she worries about them."

The preacher nodded. "*Ja.* They seem to be getting around well now, though." He took off his black-banded straw hat and held it in his hands.

"*Ja*, thank the Lord." Annie scattered the last of the chicken feed, then chatted with Levi about the weather, the farm and the upcoming winter.

"I should be getting back," Levi finally said. "I've got chores to do."

"As do I." A warm breeze stirred the air, and Annie closed her eyes, enjoying the sensation. She heard a sharp inhalation of breath, and she quickly opened her eyes to catch an odd look on Levi's face.

"Annie, before I go…" He suddenly looked uncomfortable. "I was wondering—"

Annie regarded him with concern. "Is something wrong, Levi?"

"Nay." His expression cleared. "I... Would you consider going for a buggy ride?"

She felt her breath hitch. "You want me to go for a ride with you?"

He nodded, looking very much like a young schoolboy. "I'll understand if you—"

"I'd like that," she said hurriedly, and the idea of spending time with Levi seemed a sudden answer to her prayers. Jacob had told her to consider what she wanted. She wanted an older husband like Levi. Didn't she?

"Friday evening, then?" he said. "Or do *ya* have plans?"

Annie smiled as she shook his head. *"Nay.* Friday would be fine."

Levi looked relieved and genuinely happy. Annie felt a moment's doubt but pushed it away.

"We can talk about it tomorrow night," he said.

"So, you still plan to come to dinner?" she teased.

"I wouldn't miss your cooking, Annie," he said seriously.

"Roast beef?" Annie noted his expression and felt only slightly uneasy. The feeling passed as she reminded herself that this was Levi Stoltzfus, a man who had been coming to dinner every week for months.

"Ja. Sounds delicious." He put on his hat. "I will see *ya* tomorrow, Annie."

She had always felt at ease in Levi's presence. Why should that change just because he wanted to take her for a buggy ride? Because he realized that he liked her? She smiled and waved as he walked away. Annie turned toward the barn and saw Jacob Lapp standing near the shop entrance. Jacob gave her a look that made her feel uncomfortable before he and Ike disappeared into the shop.

Heart thumping hard, she hurried to store the feed, then shooed the chickens into a fenced area and secured the gate. With thoughts of Jacob and Levi swirling in her mind, Annie headed toward her grandparents' house. She had work to do.

As she approached, she spied her grandmother in the yard, watching a robin.

"It won't be long before they'll be gone for the winter," she said of the bird. "*Grossmudder*, did you and *Grossdaddi* have breakfast?"

"*Nay*, I wasn't hungry earlier."

"You had a visitor," Annie said. "Preacher Levi."

Grossmudder nodded. "*Ja*, he is a *gut* boy, that Levi." She fixed Annie with a look. "A fine preacher. He would be perfect for you."

Annie laughed, although her heart wasn't in it. She couldn't forget the strange look Jacob had given her. Why should he disapprove?

Her sister was back when Annie returned home. "You weren't gone long."

"*Nay*," Barbara said. "I'd planned to do the laundry, but I see you already put in a load." She tightened the strings of her white apron, making sure the cape was neatly tucked inside.

"Is Josiah back?"

"*Ja*, he is in the barn seeing to the horses."

"Would *ya* help hang the sheets to dry? I put them on before I went over to *Grossmudder's*."

"*Ja*, I'll be glad to help. 'Tis too nice a day to be indoors."

"I'll meet *ya* outside," Annie said. She gathered the clothes from the propane washing machine and set them in the laundry basket. Then she headed outside and saw Barbara hanging the clothespin bag on the line within easy reach. Annie set down the clothes.

Barbara reached in to grab a sheet while Annie hurried to catch hold of the other end. With a snap of the wet fabric between them, they pinned the fabric on the line and then reached down for another.

"How are the Kings?" Annie asked conversationally.

"They are well. While I was there, Amos's brother Ike came to visit."

Annie secured a pillowcase. "Ike was here, too. Jacob made shoes for one of his horses this morning."

"Ike is a nice man," Barbara commented.

Annie reached up to swat away a bug. "*Ja*, he is pleasant."

"He is a widower," Barbara said casually.

"*Ja*, I heard." Annie fastened a bath towel to the clothes rope.

Barbara pulled a white prayer *kapp* from the basket, pegged it to the line by its strings. "He would make a *gut* husband."

"*Ja.*" Annie smiled. "Are *ya* interested?"

"Me?" Barbara looked stunned. "*Nay*, I'm thinking of you."

Annie stared at her. "Why would *ya* think that Ike and I should be man and wife?"

"*Ya* want an older man, don't *ya*?"

Annie frowned. "How do you know that?" Had Jacob said something to Barbara? She felt a burning in her stomach.

"*Mam* told me," Barbara said. "It is a *gut* plan, Annie."

Annie was aghast. "You didn't say anything to Ike, did you?"

"*Nay.* I would not do that."

Relieved, Annie continued to hang clothes. "Thanks be to God," she murmured beneath her breath. To her sister, she said, "You don't need to be looking for a husband for me. It will happen in the Lord's time." She hesitated, then confided, "Levi has asked me to go for a buggy ride with him."

"I see." Barbara hung up a blue dress. "Then you like him."

"He is a *gut* man." Annie wondered if she was trying to convince herself.

"'Tis true." Barbara handed her one end of a sheet, and the sisters worked together to secure it on the line.

As they hung the laundry, Annie noticed that her sister had become suddenly quiet. "Barbara, is everything all right?"

Barbara looked at her and nodded. *"Ja."* Her smile didn't reach her eyes. "Come. We have a lot to do yet."

Later, as she prepared supper in the kitchen with her mother and sister, Annie wondered about her sister's sudden change in behavior. Why? Because of Levi's invitation to go for a buggy ride? Barbara had made a big fuss over Levi the last time he'd come to dinner. Was Barbara sweet on Levi? If so, what should she do about her outing with the preacher? She couldn't back out now. Could she?

Annie was thoughtful as she took the ham, green beans and potatoes out of the oven. She'd think of something. She didn't want to hurt her sister.

"Annie," a masculine voice said.

"Reuben!" She smiled. "Come in and sit. Where's your sister?"

Reuben hesitated. "She didn't come."

"How is Rebekkah?" Barbara asked as she entered the room. She didn't seem surprised to discover him there.

"She is *fine*. She is with our *grossmudder* this evening."

"Is she all right—your *grossmudder*? The rest of the family?" Annie asked. "It's been a while since we've seen all of you."

He nodded. "It's been months, and *ja*, they are all doing well."

"You are just in time." Annie pulled the tray of yeast rolls out of the oven and turned with a smile. "I hope you brought your appetite." She set the tray on pot holders on the countertop.

"Reuben." *Dat* entered the kitchen on crutches. Annie automatically pulled out a chair for him, and he maneuvered himself to the table and sat down. Peter, Josiah and the *grosseldre* came to the table.

"I heard about your accident, Joe." Reuben eyed her *dat* with concern. "It looks like you're getting around."

"*Ja*, although my progress is slower than I'd like it to be."

"Things will improve, and soon it will be just a story to tell your grandchildren." Reuben accepted his plate from Barbara, who had added meat, potatoes and succotash. "My *vadder* does well after his injury."

Annie saw her *dat* nod. "That must have been bad, injuring himself in the corn binder."

Reuben agreed. "I was just a boy at the time, but I'll never forget how tore up his arm was. He nearly lost it. The doctors at the hospital were able to do surgery and now years later *Dat* has *gut* use of the arm."

Annie thought of Reuben's father and recalled his scarred arm. It was a blessing that Jonas Miller was left-handed. Still, his concern over how he would manage long term must have been worrisome to him.

"The Lord gives us the strength to handle what we must and the courage to continue in times of great worry," Annie said.

"Amen," *Mam* murmured with a quick glance at her parents. Suddenly, she grinned. "Everyone hungry?" she asked as she ensured that everyone—the men especially—had their food.

After saying a prayer of thanks, they ate and talked and ate some more. In preparation for dessert, Annie stood and collected the dinner plates.

"I heard Rebekkah is seeing someone," *Mam* said.

"Ja," Reuben said. "She's being courted by Caleb Yoder. They plan to marry, and the banns will be posted this Sunday."

"How wonderful!" *Mam* exclaimed. After a short pause, she'd then asked, "And you? Are you courting anyone?"

"Nay. I haven't found the right woman yet."

Mam had risen from the table, gone to the counter and picked up a rich chocolate cake. "You should try a piece of cake." She'd set it in the center of the table. "Annie made it."

Later that night, Annie lay in bed and felt her face redden at the memory of dinner with Reuben. She should tell Jacob. He'd put things into perspective for her. *Ja*, she would tell Jacob of her mother's latest matchmaking attempt and see what he had to say.

But first she had to tell her mother about Levi wanting

to take her for a buggy ride with him, and her dilemma with Barbara. Unless… Annie began to think, and came up with an idea.

"Reuben!" Annie was surprised to see him again so soon. "What are *ya* doing here?"

"*Hallo*, Annie. I wanted to stop by and ask if you are going to the next church Sunday singing."

"I thought I might." Annie stepped off her front porch, carrying a laundry basket of clothes. She headed to the clothesline, dismayed when Reuben followed her.

"Will you consider allowing me to take *ya* home afterward?"

Annie set down her basket and stood. "That is nice of you, Reuben, but that's over a week away. I'm not sure of my plans yet, and I wouldn't want to hold you up."

He nodded, and to her relief, he didn't seem disappointed. "We'll see what happens during the next week. I know 'tis been a while since I came to a singing in your church district. I had a *gut* time when I did." He smiled. Fair-haired and with blue eyes, Reuben Miller was a handsome young man. *Not as handsome as the Lapp brothers*, she thought and then mentally scolded herself. She reminded herself how she wanted to steer clear of attractive men who could break her heart.

"It was a wonderful supper last night, Annie."

Annie bent to pull a green shirt out of the clothes basket. "I'm glad you enjoyed it," she said as she pinned it into place.

"I especially liked the chocolate cake," he said.

"That's kind of you to say." She continued to hang clothes, hoping that he would decide that he should take his leave and return home. "You've got a free day today?"

she asked conversationally as she hung a pair of one of her brother's pants.

"*Nay.* I brought my *dat's* mare for new shoes. Jacob said he could fit her in today."

Annie blinked. "Is she inside already?" Jacob was already here? She hadn't seen him come.

"*Ja*, he's in the shop. He said to arrive early, that he could take Aggie, and so here I am."

Annie was thoughtful, her mind racing with visions of Jacob shoeing the Millers' horse. He was *gut* at the work, just as her father had said he would be. Business had increased since Jacob had come to help in the blacksmithy. With the cooling weather of late autumn, he was bound to be busier than normal as folks brought their animals in for shoes before the onset of winter. She had wanted to talk with him, tell him about last evening, but she doubted he'd have any time for her.

"Annie."

She was startled. *"Ja?"* She blushed, realizing that Reuben must have called her name several times before she'd heard him.

"Did *ya* want coffee while *ya* wait?" she asked politely. "I can bring it to the shop." Then she would have a chance to see Jacob and bring him a cup, as well.

"*Nay*, I'm not much of a coffee drinker."

"Tea, then?"

He moved in too closely, and she shifted away as she continued to hang clothes. *"Nay,"* he said after a brief moment of hesitation. "I'll be heading back to the shop. Jacob's almost done with Aggie. You have a nice day."

Relieved, Annie gave him a genuine smile. "You, too, Reuben." He hadn't mentioned the singing again, and Annie was grateful.

By the time she'd hung all the clothes on the line, Annie saw Reuben leave the shop, leading his father's mare. Her heart gave a thump as Jacob exited the building behind him. She watched them talk a moment before Reuben hitched Aggie on to his buggy. He looked over, saw her watching him and waved before he climbed into the vehicle.

Jacob had briefly gone back into the shop, returning outside in time to see Reuben's wave. Jacob stared at her, and she felt suddenly awkward. She had yet to tell him about her conversation with Levi or about Reuben's presence at dinner last night. She studied Jacob for a long moment while trying to decide if she should approach him now or talk with him later. He took the decision out of her hands when he reentered the shop without a wave or a smile.

Annie fought the urge to cry. *You've got work to do, Annie*, she told herself, trying her best to put Jacob from her mind. He was probably too busy. He didn't have time to talk, not with the increase in work.

As she crossed the yard and climbed the front porch, she heard the approach of another vehicle, a wagon with a team of two horses. Jacob would most definitely be busy today, she realized, and she took heart that he wasn't ignoring her. His mind was simply focused on business matters.

Chapter Ten

Friday evening, Levi arrived in his open courting buggy. He came to the door, and her mother let him in. "I've come for Annie," he said.

"I'm here," Annie announced as she came from the back of the house, and the two went outside. It was a pleasant and clear evening. Annie had told her mother about the buggy ride once the preacher had left after his usual supper visit. Her mother hadn't said much, but the happy gleam in her eyes had spoken volumes.

Mam stepped out onto the porch as Levi helped Annie into the vehicle. Barbara came out and approached cautiously. Seconds later, Levi assisted Barbara, who looked embarrassed as she climbed up. "*Mam* says I'm to be your chaperone," she said solemnly as Levi got in. "Peter wanted to go, but—"

"'Tis fine, Barbara," Annie interrupted before her sister could say more. She had made the suggestion to *Mam* that Barbara come with them.

Levi nodded as if he understood. Preacher or not, they were not betrothed and needed someone to accompany the two of them. He smiled at her as he reached for the reins. "Where shall we go?"

"Wherever you wish," Annie said softly.

With a click of his tongue, he flicked the reins and drove the horse out onto the paved main road. Annie sat back, prepared to enjoy the ride.

Monday morning Joe sat in his wheelchair, watching as the younger man put shoes on Janey, one of the Lapps' horses. "You're doing well, Jacob. I am grateful for all the work you've done for me and my family."

Jacob stopped and flashed Joe a glance. "I've not done anything another man wouldn't have done."

"*Nay*, son," Joe insisted. "No one else has the skill or the knowledge."

Jacob had been surprised to see the older man wheel himself inside the shop earlier this morning. Horseshoe Joe had been getting around with a wooden crutch with his leg brace. Joe's leg must be causing him great pain, he thought with sympathy.

"'Tis nothing," Jacob said. "I've enjoyed the work. I was always fascinated watching you when I was younger." The horse shifted restlessly, and Jacob took a moment to soothe the animal. The sound of his familiar voice did the trick, and the mare settled.

Jacob carefully worked on Janey's right front foot, removing the old shoe and then preparing her hoof before he picked up the new one to compare it with the other. After examining them, he was satisfied with the result. He lifted the animal's hoof, set the shoe and then carefully nailed it into place.

"There you go, girl," he murmured before he started the same process on the left side.

Joe was unusually quiet as Jacob worked. Jacob paused. "Joe, are *you* all right? I can take you back to the *haus*."

The older man smiled. "I'm fine, Jake. Just a bit tired is all. My eldest stopped in to visit last night."

Jacob raised an eyebrow. "Joan?"

Joe nodded, his expression softening. "Haven't seen her, Adam or the *kinner* in months. It was *gut* to see them."

"Are they still here?" Jacob asked as he went back to the task at hand.

"*Nay.* They stayed the night and left early this morning. They're traveling to Delaware, said they wanted to stop and see us before they moved on. They plan to return for a longer visit on their way back."

Jacob smiled as, after finishing the front hooves, he returned to double-check each shoe on Janey's rear hooves. He had replaced them over a month ago, his first attempt since he was a young boy. He'd been grateful that she'd belonged to his family; the animal's trust in him had allowed Jacob to get the job done. His success with the mare had given him the confidence to continue the work. After remembering to lean in to brace the animal, he found the job easier than he'd recalled.

"I'm going to put Janey outside, Joe," he said. "I'll be right back. Did *ya* need me to get you something from the *haus*?"

"Coffee would be *gut*."

Jacob smiled. "I could use a cup myself. I'll see if Miriam can put a pot on."

"If she's busy," Joe said, "ask Annie. She makes a *gut* cup of coffee."

Jacob felt a flutter within his chest at the mention of

Annie. She did make a good cup of coffee. It had been some time since he'd spoken with her. The memory of her and Reuben, talking outside while Annie hung clothes, still stung. Reuben and Annie? He didn't believe Reuben was the right man for her.

"I'll be right back," he said as he led the animal toward the door.

"Ask Annie about her outing with the preacher," Joe called out as Jacob reached the door.

"Levi Stoltzfus?" he asked, experiencing discomfort.

"*Ja*, he came for her Friday evening. Can't say if she's seen him again, but he's due to come by for another meal next week."

Jacob felt his heart ache as he stepped out into the sunny autumn day and glanced toward the house. There was no sign of life outside. He tied Janey to a hitching post and then headed slowly toward the residence, his thoughts in a whirl. He knew Reuben had taken supper with the Zooks, but he hadn't known about Annie and Levi.

I shouldn't be surprised. I did see them talking together. Annie hadn't visited him in the shop lately. He had no idea what Annie was thinking or feeling, and it bothered him.

He went to the back entrance that led into the kitchen. The inside door was open, allowing in the fresh air through the screen. Soon, it would be too cold to enjoy raised windows and open doors. He could smell the delicious scent of baking. His mouth watered. He peered inside and saw Annie opening the oven. She reached in with pot holders and removed what looked to be a breakfast cake, then set it on top of the stove. He didn't want to startle her, so he waited a minute until she moved away from the stove. He lifted his hand and knocked softly.

She turned quickly, saw who it was and smiled. "Jacob! Come in, come in."

"*Hallo*, Annie. Your *vadder* wants coffee."

"Just made a fresh pot." She pulled out two cups and placed them on the counter, before she reached for the vessel on the stove.

Jacob came farther into the kitchen. He enjoyed what he saw. Everything about the room—the warmth and feeling of home, the aromas of fresh coffee, vanilla and cinnamon—spoke of Annie. He swallowed. He promised himself that he would protect his heart, but he'd failed. There were too many wonderful things about her to resist loving her.

He studied her back. The royal blue dress, which brightened her eyes, looked wonderful on her. She wore a cooking apron tied about her neck and waist. He noted the tiny tendrils of golden-blond hair at her nape. He noted every little thing about Horseshoe Joe's daughter. She turned and flashed him a smile that lit up her face. He felt his heart give a little jump before it picked up again at a faster pace.

"I've poured you a cup, as well," she said as she set two on the kitchen table.

He nodded his thanks. "How does your *vadder* like his coffee?"

"Black, lots of sugar. His is the one on the right."

Jacob reached to pull the cups closer. He saw with delight that she had fixed his just the way he preferred, just as she'd made it for him previously. He took a quick sip. As expected, it was delicious.

"Cake?" She placed a hot mat on the table and transferred a baking pan from the counter to the pad. "Fresh out of the oven. Cinnamon-streusel coffee cake."

He sniffed appreciatively. "It smells wonderful."

"I think you'll like it," she said with a smile. "Do you want some?"

He grinned. *"Ja."* He watched as she cut a piece. "And make sure you have a slice for your *vadder.* I don't think he'll like watching me enjoy your cake without his own." He observed as she prepared two generous helpings.

"I'll take these out and come back for the rest." With cups in hand, he turned to leave.

"Jacob."

He halted and glanced back.

"I can carry this out for you. There is something I want to tell you—"

Peter entered the kitchen. "Cake! Can I have a piece?"

"Nay." Annie grinned to show that she was teasing and offered a piece to her brother.

"Hallo, Jake," the boy said as he spied him in the room. "'Tis *gut* to see *ya.* Is my *vadder* in the shop?"

"Ja, I'm heading back there now." Jacob smiled. He liked Annie's younger brother. He was a nice boy, who worked hard on his father's farm. "Annie." He nodded toward the plates Annie had wanted to carry for him. "I'll be back for those." She was busy. There was no need for her to come out to the shop. She opened her mouth as if to say something, glanced quickly at her brother and kept silent.

"I'll bring them out to the shop for you," Peter said.

"I'd appreciate it." Jacob flashed Annie one last glance, then left. As he headed back toward the shop, he was afraid he knew what Annie wished to tell him. About her outing with the preacher.

He couldn't fault Annie's choice; Levi Stoltzfus was a fine man. But he wasn't him. *He* wanted to be the one taking buggy rides with Annie. He forced a smile as he entered the shop. He couldn't let Joe see how upset he was. The idea of Annie with another man was painful to him.

"Joe," he greeted cheerfully as he stepped into the shop, "I've brought your coffee. Peter is bringing us coffee cake."

"Did you visit with Annie?" Joe asked.

Jacob shook his head. "She was too busy to talk."

While she cleaned up the kitchen, Annie thought of Jacob. He'd seemed quiet...too quiet. What was wrong? Their conversation had begun friendly, then suddenly Jacob had seemed in a hurry to get back to the shop. She sighed. She wanted badly to tell him about Levi and Reuben, just as she had with all of the other men her mother had tried to match her with.

She'd done the right thing in asking Barbara to accompany her and Levi as their chaperone. Annie had been silent during the ride, while Levi and Barbara had kept up a steady stream of conversation. They had driven through the country roads, enjoying the scenery and the fall weather. She had observed the preacher with her sister, noting each time Barbara blushed at something Levi said. When the sun had begun to set, Levi had driven the buggy back to the farmhouse. Annie had climbed down from the vehicle and waited to talk with Levi after her sister was done chatting with him. Barbara had ended the conversation and looked sheepish as she passed Annie on her way toward the house.

Levi had approached, his brow furrowed. "Annie—"

"I know, Levi. You don't have to say it. I appreciated the ride, but I think you and my sister are better suited."

"You're not angry?" he asked, looking apologetic.

"*Nay*, why should I be angry? It was a buggy ride. If you like Barbara, ask her to go next time. If you don't," she said softly, "please keep your distance. I don't want my sister hurt."

"I would never hurt Barbara."

"*Gut.*" Annie smiled. "Next time, *Mam* may ask Peter to be your chaperone," she warned.

Levi nodded and then glanced toward the house, where Barbara waited inside the screen door. "May I talk with her before I go?"

Annie had nodded. "I'll send her out."

Now, as she finished tidying the kitchen, her thoughts went to Jacob. She wanted to tell him about her mother's continued matchmaking attempts. She wanted to tell him about Levi and Barbara. She wrapped up some of the cinnamon-streusel cake to take to her grandparents. She thought of her daily chores and knew she had a lot to accomplish. She picked up a broom to sweep the floor and then headed into the gathering room. She heard the kitchen screen door slam against the side of the house.

"Annie!"

Annie returned to the kitchen. "Peter?" She saw his frightened face and felt her chest tighten. "What's happened? What's wrong?"

"'Tis Jacob! He burned himself!"

"How?" she asked. She saw the odd look on her brother's face as he glanced away and then down at his feet. "How bad?" she rephrased the question.

Peter lifted his head, looked at her. "Bad enough," he

admitted. "The burn is on the back of his hand, and it's bright red."

Her heart kicked into high gear. "I'll bring ointment." Annie ran to the medicine cabinet for a tube of B & W Ointment. She returned to the kitchen to find that Peter had disappeared.

Annie paused to consider what else she needed in order to dress Jacob's burn. After grabbing a bowl, she ran to the back room freezer for ice, then hurried to the kitchen for water and a towel before she raced across the yard.

Hissing at the pain, Jacob examined the burn on his hand. "It's red and swelling." And it hurt like fire.

"It looks awful." Peter hovered nearby, alternately pacing and stopping to inspect Jacob's burn. "This is my fault," he cried.

"*Nay*, Peter, I was clumsy."

"But you wouldn't have taken off your gloves if not for me," Peter cried.

"Come away from the anvil, Jacob, and sit down over here," Joe urged. He gestured toward a chair near the worktable. "Annie is on her way. She'll know what to do to help you."

Jacob obeyed and took a seat. Water blisters were forming on the burn. He flexed his hand and hissed at the growing intensity of the nonstop fiery pain. He'd been careless, his thoughts on Annie with Levi Stoltzfus.

Annie burst into the shop, carrying several items. "Jacob! Let me see." Her prayer *kapp* was slightly askew on her head, no doubt the result of her wild dash across the yard. She still wore her quilted cooking apron, and he immediately detected the mingled scents of fresh cinnamon and pure vanilla as she drew near.

Jacob sat and extended his arm. The last thing he needed was for Annie to play nursemaid. He felt a tingling awareness when she took hold of his hand. "It looks worse than it is," he assured her.

"*Nay*, Jacob. You've got a second-degree burn. It is as bad as it looks." Annie studied him with concern. She suddenly took charge in a no-nonsense manner. "I've brought cold water and burn cream." She set a bowl on the table beside him. "Put your hand in this," she said. "More water than ice, but it will help numb the pain."

When he didn't immediately move, she gently took his wrist and eased his burned hand into the dish. Jacob inhaled sharply. The harsh chill felt good against his throbbing, tender skin. He shuddered. But it was the sensation of her fingers about his wrist that most affected him.

Her blue eyes filled with compassion. "I'm sorry," she said. "I know it hurts, but the water is *gut* for it. And it will help clean out the burn." She glanced down, made a sound of dismay and removed her cooking apron.

Jacob kept his hand submerged and watched her. His heart beat a wild tattoo at Annie's closeness. Her scent of home and baked goods was a heady combination for his lovesick heart.

Annie stood patiently while he soaked his hand. She then laid a clean tea towel on the worktable and reached to gently lift his hand from the bowl. "You should come up to the *haus*," she urged as she carefully placed his hand on the towel, palm side down, burn side up. "I can take better care of your injury there."

"I will be fine," he said gruffly.

"After I put on this ointment," she argued, "I'll need

to cover the burn with gauze." She unscrewed the lid off the jar and dipped her finger into the B & W Ointment, which she spread gently over his blistered skin. "I'll need to bandage it."

"*Ja*, Jacob," Joe agreed. "You need to listen to Annie. Go with her up to the *haus* and get that hand taken care of properly. Peter will clean up here. You'll not be doing any more work for a while."

He didn't want to follow her, but he did—for Joe. Having Annie minister to him was bittersweet. As he strode behind her toward the house, Jacob observed her, enjoying the view. He saw the fine curve of her nape beneath the back of her prayer *kapp*, and with an aching heart, he looked away.

Annie waited for him to catch up, and then he walked beside her, aware of her frequent looks of concern.

She stopped at the door, opened it for him to enter. "Sit," she ordered as she moved across the kitchen. He tried not to appear startled when she crouched before him and took his hand. She examined it closely, turning it to inspect it from all angles. She rose to her feet. "I'll do what I can here, Jacob, but you may need to see a doctor."

"*Nay*, I'll—"

"*Ach*, don't you be arguing with me," she said as she washed her hands. Reaching into a cabinet, she withdrew a small box, which she set on the dining table. Millie padded into the room and pushed against her leg. "Not now, Millie. Go lie down," she commanded, and he saw the dog obey and curl up in the corner.

Silently, he watched as Annie opened the box and removed a roll of medicine tape with two packages of sterile gauze.

"You seem to know what you're doing," he said as she

pulled a chair close to his. She captured his hand and gently spread another layer of ointment over the burn. He inhaled sharply, disturbed by her touch.

She didn't seem to notice. Her eyes on his injury, she smiled crookedly. "You don't cook as often as I do without suffering a burn or two from the oven or stove."

She rose and went to the sink to clean the ointment from her fingers. "You must be careful to keep it clean," she instructed as she returned to her seat. "No farm or shop work—nothing that could cause infection in your wound."

She tore open the package of gauze and secured two squares over the wound with the medical tape. He didn't seem to feel the pain as much in Annie's presence.

"I'll take you home," she said, startling him.

He stood abruptly. "I can drive."

She placed a hand on his arm, and he felt the warmth of her fingers through his broadcloth shirt. "*Nay*, your buggy is here, but *you* shouldn't be holding the reins. If you'd prefer, I'll walk to your house and ask one of your brothers to come drive *ya*. Or you can save time and allow me to do it. I'm sure someone there will be happy to bring me back."

"Annie—"

"Please, Jacob," she pleaded. "Let me see *you* home."

He groaned inwardly. The last thing he needed was to be close to Annie Zook in a closed buggy. "Fine. If you insist, then I will go with you."

She flashed him a radiant smile. "Stay here." She got up and pushed in her chair. "I'll tell *Dat*."

He grabbed his hat off the kitchen table. "I will come with you, since the wagon is parked near the shop."

She stared at him a long moment through narrowed

eyes before she nodded. She was silent as he fell into step beside her. He kept quiet; he had nothing to say. As they reached the building, Jacob allowed her to precede him inside. He listened calmly while she explained to her father where she was going.

"I can take him," Peter offered.

"Nay," Joe said, surprising Jacob. "Your sister will drive him. I need you to help me with a few things here." He eyed Jacob with concern. "Watch that hand, Jake. Annie will bring you home. Think about seeing a doctor, *ja?"*

Jacob lifted his uninjured hand. "I will call one in the morning if the burn looks worse."

"Are *ya* ready?" Annie asked.

Jacob didn't want to ride with her, but what other choice did he have? "I will talk with you soon," he told Joe.

"Take care of that hand, Jacob." Joe followed in his wheelchair. Peter was silent as he exited the shop with his father.

Without thought, Jacob started to climb into the vehicle's left side. *"Nay,* Jacob," Annie scolded.

Embarrassed, he managed to grin. She flashed him a look of steel that had him skirting the vehicle to climb up on the other side. He used his good hand to grab hold and hoist himself onto the bench seat. Annie got in next to him and picked up the leathers.

"I'll be right back, *Dat,"* she said.

"Take your time," her father told her. "Make sure Jacob is taken care of. We can manage without you for a while."

Annie looked momentarily startled, but then she smiled and waved as she turned the horse toward the road. Jacob was silent as she steered the horse down the dirt lane and onto the paved main road. The only sounds were the soft thud of each horse hoof and the noise of the metal wagon wheels rolling along.

"You drive well," he said, feeling the need to break the silence. When it was quiet, he was too consumed by thoughts of the woman beside him.

She didn't take her eyes off the way ahead. "Janey is a *gut* horse. Your family has had her a long time. She listens well."

"Ja." Struck silent by her smile, he turned toward the side window opening. "She is a fine animal, and we are glad to have her." Being this close to Annie made him realize how much he cared for her. He was conscious of her quiet strength, her warmth and her pleasing clean scent as she handled the reins. When she'd ministered to his wounded hand at the house earlier, he'd been close to confessing his feelings for her. But he'd kept silent. What would she say if he told her now? He wanted to hold on to this moment, when he almost could believe that she might care. He felt the strongest urge to face her, to touch her hair and tug teasingly on her *kapp* strings. She stirred something within him that urged him to discover a way to keep her in his life and by his side.

Chapter Eleven

As she steered the horse-drawn wagon toward the Lapp farm, Annie was anxiously aware of Jacob's silence. "Your hand hurts."

He appeared startled and then his expression turned wry. "*Ja*, it's throbbing. I'll live."

She turned her attention back to the road. "I'm sorry this happened." She hesitated. "Was it Peter's fault?"

"*Nay.* I became distracted."

"Peter says it's his fault."

"*Nay*, I took off my work glove before he accidentally knocked a table peg off the anvil. I didn't think, and I brushed the back of my hand against the hot metal as I leaned to pick it up."

"Table peg?" She flashed him another glance.

"*Ja.* Rick Martin bought a table from a used furniture dealer. The legs are secured with metal pegs. One was bent and another missing. Rick asked me to make replacements for him." He offered her a pain-filled smile. "It was my fault, not Peter's."

She looked skeptical. "You are a kind man, Jacob Lapp."

He was silent as he stared out of his side of the vehicle. "I don't feel kind."

She frowned. Not kind? She wanted to ask why he felt this way. He obviously didn't know himself well. He was thoughtful, generous and had a good heart. Annie steered the conversation in another direction to distract him from his pain. "I wanted to tell you earlier—before Peter came into the kitchen—Reuben Miller came to dinner the other night."

"I saw him talking with you in the yard," he said quietly.

"He said he came for new horseshoes." Annie waited for his response.

"*Ja*, he did," he said. "The job didn't take long. I replaced the mare's front shoes. Your *vadder* changed out the others last summer."

Annie gave him a look. "My *mudder's* been playing matchmaker again. Reuben was invited to the house as the next in line as my potential husband." She sighed. "I wish she would stop interfering."

"You don't like Reuben?" he asked.

"He is nice enough, but he isn't what I'm looking for."

"*Ja*, you want to marry a church elder."

Annie nodded but kept her eyes on the road ahead of her.

"Levi," he guessed.

"*Nay,*" she murmured. "He likes Barbara."

"Barbara?" He sounded surprised. "I thought you went on an outing with him."

She nodded, surprised that he'd known. "*Ja*, I did, with Barbara as our chaperone." She smiled crookedly. "They had a wonderful time together. It was I who felt like the chaperone."

"I'm sorry," Jacob said.

Annie shrugged. "I'm not. There are other older men in our community."

"Why do you want only an older man?" Jacob asked. "Don't *ya* want someone who'll cherish you?"

She flashed him a look, startled by the intensity of his golden gaze. Cherish? She was hoping for someone who would simply be happy to have her to wife. She would feel blessed to be cherished by her husband, but she doubted that would ever happen.

"Younger men don't want me." Annie felt her face heat. "I can trust an older man."

"What about me?" Jacob asked.

"You?" She became flustered. "What about you?"

"Don't you trust me?"

"I trust you," she hedged, wondering where the conversation was leading. "We are friends—" He shifted in his seat and Annie saw him wince. "I'm sorry. Your hand is hurting you."

"I'm fine," he insisted, but his pale features said otherwise.

The Samuel Lapp farm was several yards ahead. Annie flipped on the buggy's battery-operated turn signal as the vehicle approached the dirt road. She waited for two cars to pass, then when the path was clear, she carefully steered the horse onto the lane that led to their farmhouse. She was glad that conversation had ended. She didn't know why he'd started it.

"I'll ask Eli to take you home," Jacob said as she parked in the barnyard.

"Danki." She glanced his way as he shifted to get out. "Jacob—"

He turned, his brow furrowed. "I'm fine, Annie."

She touched his arm, felt the muscle tighten. "I'm sorry this happened."

One corner of his mouth curved upward as he shrugged. "You don't have to apologize." He held up his bandaged hand. "You're not responsible."

"You will see a doctor?"

"I'll see how it is in the morning. If it looks worse, then, *ja*, I'll see a doctor."

She nodded, satisfied. It was all she could ask of him. "Until then, if you need anything—" She bit her lip. "You'll tell me?" She leaned closer and stared into his eyes. *"Please?"*

He stared back at her, his good hand cradling his injured one. Finally, he broke eye contact. "I'll get my brother Eli." He walked a few feet and then stopped and faced her. "Annie, you said you trust me. I want you to consider something carefully...*me.*"

As Jacob headed toward the house again, Annie climbed out of the vehicle, skirted the buggy and waited outside in the yard. *Him?* Was Jacob actually suggesting that she consider him as someone who could be more than a friend? Had he been serious? Or just teasing her? Now that he had put the idea in her mind, she had trouble dismissing it. They were friends, she reminded herself. Then why did she feel flustered whenever Jacob was near?

She stared at the house, waiting for Eli. Within minutes, Katie Lapp appeared. "Annie!" Jacob's mother called out to her. "Come inside while you wait."

Annie smiled shyly as she climbed the porch steps and entered through the door Katie held open.

"I did the best I could for him," Annie said as she moved into the warmth of Katie's kitchen, "but you may want to check his hand yourself. I'm afraid he'll be stubborn about seeing a doctor."

"I'm sure you did fine, Annie, but if it makes you feel better, I'll examine the burn later." Katie smiled at her as she gestured for Annie to sit down. "Our men can be stubborn creatures."

"*Ja*, and Jacob, I fear, is more stubborn than my *vadder*, who is stubborn as a mule." Annie gasped and covered her mouth, realizing what she'd said, but Jacob's mother chuckled. "I can walk home. 'Tis no trouble, and the day is pleasant outside."

Katie shook her head. "Eli will take you. Jacob went upstairs to get him."

"*Ach*, I don't want to impose."

Katie turned on the stove and put on a kettle. "Will *ya* have tea?"

Annie thought a moment. *Dat* had told her to take her time. "*Ja*, I'd like that."

"*Gut.*" As the water heated on the stove, Jacob's mother reached into the cabinet for cups.

Jacob and Eli entered the kitchen as their mother brewed the tea. "Annie is going to enjoy refreshments before you take her home, Eli. I made you each a cup."

"If *ya* don't mind, *Mam*, I would prefer something cold." Jacob held up his bandaged hand. Annie was conscious that he avoided her gaze. She wanted to pull him aside and ask him if he'd been teasing earlier about considering him as a potential husband instead of someone older.

"How about a root beer?" his mother asked.

"That would be *gut*." Jacob pulled out a chair and saw Eli smile at Annie as he took the seat next to her.

"*Hallo*, Annie," his twin said.

She smiled. "Eli. You have time to take me home?"

"*Ja*. After we enjoy our tea."

"Annie." Katie handed Annie a cup and then extended one toward Eli.

After accepting it from her, Eli prepared the tea the way he liked it. "How is Joe?" he asked.

"*Dat* is fine. Doing better." Annie frowned as she watched Jacob. She had noticed that he'd winced a time or two, although he'd tried hard to hide it. "*Dat* is worried about your brother," she told Eli.

She saw Eli glance at Jacob before returning his attention back to her with a funny look on his face.

Katie took a chilled bottle of root beer out of the refrigerator and handed it to Jacob.

"Where's Hannah?" Annie asked of Katie's youngest child and only daughter.

"She's over at Charlotte's." Katie sat down at the table. "Playing with Ruth Ann."

Jacob lifted his drink with his uninjured hand.

Annie couldn't seem to take her eyes off him as he took a sip and set the glass down on the table. "Jacob—"

He turned and fixed her with a look. "I'm fine, Annie."

Eli raised his eyebrows. "She saw the burn, Jake. Maybe she knows better than you."

"*Ja*, Eli," Annie said. "I think he should see a doctor. He says he is fine, but he's not." She paused. "You said you'd go if your hand appeared worse. Will you go if your *mam* says you should though you may think differently?" she asked him with a quick glance toward his mother.

Jacob sighed. "You'll not rest unless I agree?"

Annie nodded. "If you agree, I won't mention it again."

"Then I agree."

"And I will take a look at it and decide." Katie pushed a plate of lemon squares in Annie's direction.

Annie smiled with satisfaction as she chose one before sliding the plate toward Eli, who sat next to her. Eli took a square and nudged the plate toward Jacob.

Jacob declined the treat and finished his soda. As he set down the empty bottle, he rose. "If you don't mind, I'm going to head upstairs." He addressed Annie. "*Danki* for dressing my burn and bringing me home."

"Even though you didn't want me to drive?" she challenged.

Jacob's cheeks flushed. "*Ja*, even though." He grabbed the empty soda bottle and set it on the counter near the sink. "Eli, I'll talk with you after you take Annie home."

Eli nodded. "I'll see you later."

Annie finished her tea. "I will talk with you again soon, Jacob," she murmured.

Eli put down his empty cup and stood. "Would you like another?"

"*Nay.* I'm ready to go whenever you are."

Katie rose and gathered the teacups. "Let me help wash those," Annie said as Eli went outside to check on the horse.

"*Nay*, you get home to your *dat*. If I know Joe, he'll be worrying about Jacob." She smiled. "I appreciate the way you took care of him today."

"Jacob is a *gut* man. I'm glad I could help him."

"Jacob may seem too serious at times, but he has a pure heart." Katie tied a work apron about her waist.

"He's been kind to my family, helping me after *Dat's* accident, working in the shop to help my *vadder*." She paused. "He is a *gut* friend."

"Annie?" Eli appeared in the doorway. "Ready?"

She nodded. "The tea and lemon squares were delicious."

Katie smiled. "Say *hallo* to your *mudder* and *vadder*."

Annie nodded and then left, following Eli out of the house and into the buggy. Soon, Eli had steered Janey out onto the main road in the direction of Annie's home.

"You're quiet," Eli said after a time.

"Just thoughtful," she answered.

"He'll be fine, Jacob." He exchanged looks with her. "His hand will heal."

Annie inclined her head. "It shouldn't have happened. He said that no one was at fault, but I wonder…"

Eli raised his eyebrows. "Does it matter?"

She sighed. "*Nay*, I suppose not."

Eli drew up on the leathers as a car passed too swiftly. He frowned. "Careless *Englishers* are going to hurt someone seriously one day."

"*Ja.* Lately, it seems that there are more than the usual tourists in Lancaster County."

"Come to enjoy the fall foliage?" Eli asked.

Annie smiled. "Or to get a *gut* look at us Plain folk."

They chatted easily as Eli drove onto the Zooks' dirt lane and into the barnyard.

"I appreciate the ride, Eli," Annie said with a smile before she climbed out of the buggy.

"I'll see you on Sunday, Annie. *Danki* for taking care of Jacob."

Annie felt her face warm at the mention of Jacob's name. "Will you take him to the doctor if he needs it?"

"*Ja.*" Eli tilted his head, then suddenly widened his eyes. "You like him!"

Her heart skipped a beat. "He's my friend."

Eli smiled. "Jacob's a lucky man to have you as his friend."

She felt as if she needed to get away before she said something she shouldn't. "I will see you on Sunday. Will *ya* be going to the youth singing?"

Eli nodded. "*Ja*, I wouldn't miss it." He shifted to face her. "You?"

"I'm thinking about it. I haven't been since before *Dat's* accident." Annie leaned in while she talked with Eli. "It should be fun." She started to walk away, then promptly spun back around. "Did *ya* hear that Rebekkah Miller is betrothed? The banns are being posted today."

"She is?" Eli looked thoughtful. "To whom, do you know?"

"Caleb Yoder."

"The new doctor?" he asked, and Annie nodded. "How did you find out?"

She stood back and brushed something off her apron. "I spoke with Reuben the other day."

Eli looked out the front buggy window before turning to give her a twisted smile. "I used to be sweet on her."

"*Ach*, I'm sorry, Eli," Annie said. "I shouldn't have said anything."

He waved it off as if it were of no consequence. "*Nay*, 'tis fine. It was a long time ago. I haven't seen or spoken with Rebekkah in over a year."

Annie inclined her head. "I should get inside. I appreciate the ride." She stepped away from the vehicle. "I'll see you soon." Then she waved and watched as Eli drove away from the house. Images of Jacob intermingled while his brother Eli's words spun in her head.

Jacob Lapp. He was different than his brother but also the same.

She climbed the front stoop and onto the covered porch. Annie froze as emotion hit her with sudden clarity. Why couldn't she stop thinking about Jacob Lapp? Jacob was a *gut* and caring friend, but he was young and handsome, and she didn't want young and handsome. She wanted—needed—calm, peace and an easy affection. She scowled. By suggesting that she consider him, he had made it impossible for her to ignore him.

Four days after his burn accident, Jacob stood on his front porch, gazing out at the landscape. His hand throbbed, causing him pain. As expected, a huge water blister had risen to cover the injured area. It was only after the blister burst that his mother had suggested that he seek medical help from Jonah Troyer, who gave medical aid to the less serious injuries among the members of their Amish community. Jonah had taken one look at Jacob's hand and frowned.

"You'd best go and see that English doc, Dr. Jamieson," he had told Jacob. "I think you need a prescription. Dr. Jamieson can write you one." And so Jacob had made an appointment with Dr. Jamieson for the next day.

Dr. Jamieson had examined the burn and agreed. "Jonah is right. I'll prescribe an antibiotic cream. Spread it gently over the open burn wound and then keep the burn covered with gauze. Continue to use both until the burn heals."

"When can I go back to work?" Jacob had asked.

Dr. Jamieson had shaken his head. "Stay away from the shop for at least a week. You're going to feel uncomfortable going back too soon. You mustn't do anything to jeopardize the sterile environment of the wound. In other words, Jacob, don't do anything that may cause infection."

Waiting for his family to depart for Sunday church service, Jacob wondered what he was going to do during the coming week. He needed to keep busy. He wasn't allowed to help on the farm, although at this time of year, most of the work was in preparation for next spring's planting. He couldn't work with the animals. He couldn't work in Noah's furniture shop or with Jed for the construction company. Suddenly, the chores he never particularly enjoyed seemed inviting. He wasn't used to being idle, and it didn't sit well with him. In fact, it gave him way too much time to think about Annie and his feelings for her.

Friends, he thought. She said they were friends. If only he were older and had a permanent position…then he'd have a chance with Annie. *Think about me, Annie. Consider me. I can make you happy if only you'll let me.*

Jacob adjusted his Sunday-best black felt hat as he stepped out onto the lawn. He had to decide on his life's path. What were his options? He could work on a farm but not his father's. All monies earned from the Samuel Lapp farm went to provide for his mother and the remaining five siblings, besides him, still living at home.

There was always Noah's furniture shop, but he didn't have his older brother's talent for crafting furniture, and while he could make deliveries for Noah, he couldn't earn a living at it.

He would do anything to show Annie that they were meant to be together. But what if she didn't ever consider him seriously? What if she remained determined to marry a church elder? Someone like Ike King?

His younger brother Daniel burst out of the house and

flew down the porch steps. "We're going to be late for Sunday services!"

"I'm ready. I've been ready," Isaac insisted as he joined them.

"We're all ready," his mother said as she exited the house with their youngest brother, Joseph, and Hannah, their little sister.

"Where's *Dat*?" Eli asked as he came up from the yard. He'd brought around the family buggy.

"He's coming," *Mam* said.

"I'm here," their father said as he pulled the front door shut and locked it. "Let's go." He nodded toward the buggy, parked only a few yards away.

"Aren't you coming, Jacob?" Hannah beamed up at him as she approached and then tugged on his arm.

Jacob smiled at her. Dressed in her Sunday best, she looked adorable. "*Ja*, Hannah. I'm coming."

"*Mam?*" Isaac said. "What about the food?"

"I took it over to Mae's yesterday."

"Let's go," Samuel urged. "We don't want to be late."

They rode in the buggy because they were running behind, and the vehicle was quicker. If they'd left earlier, they could have easily walked. And Jacob's father had heard that it was going to rain this afternoon.

Samuel drove the short distance down their lane and across the road, onto the Amos King property. Several gray family buggies were already parked in the yard when Jacob's father drove in and halted their vehicle.

Were the Zooks here? Jacob glanced about, longing for a glimpse of Annie. As if the Lord had heard his thoughts, Josiah drove the Zook family into the barnyard and pulled up directly next to the Lapps' vehicle.

Jacob spied Annie as she exited the buggy, and his

spirits rose. She didn't see him as she skirted the vehicle to help her father. Annie pulled out Joe's crutches and set them against the buggy's side before she extended a hand toward her father. Josiah came around to help his sister with Joe. Annie handed the crutches to Joe and then reached into the buggy for the food she'd prepared.

Jacob's family had climbed out of their buggy and headed toward the Amos King farmhouse. With eyes for only Annie, Jacob was slow to follow. Annie turned and caught sight of him.

"Jacob." She smiled at him, and heart pumping hard, he waited for her. "How is your hand?" she asked. She sounded breathless.

"Let me carry this for you." He reached for her plate before she had a chance to refuse, and he held it against him with his good hand. They fell into step together as they approached the house. "My hand is healing well." He flashed her glance. "Because of you." He smiled as he caressed her with his gaze. "How is Joe?"

She blinked as if taken aback. "*Dat's* fine." Annie looked pretty in her Sunday-best dark green dress with white cape and apron. Her white head covering, or prayer *kapp*, revealed a glimpse of her golden-blond hair.

"No more buggy rides with any older men?" he asked, watching her carefully.

"*Nay* and no new, prospective husband candidates. Thanks be to God."

"Did you think about what I said?" He watched her carefully.

She grew still. "Said?"

He nodded. "About me."

"Jacob—"

"Jake!" Eli interrupted from inside the house. "Are you coming?"

"*Ja*, in a minute! I'm helping Annie." As they reached the steps, Jacob gestured for Annie to precede him. He saw that she was blushing. He handed her the covered dish. "Annie—" He stopped, looked at her. She looked awkward, dismayed. Now wasn't the time to talk seriously with her. "What did you make?" he asked with a smile. "Whatever is in there smells wonderful."

"You'll have to wait until after Sunday service to find out," she replied. He watched her visibly relax.

"But I carried it all the way up here for you." He pretended to be sad.

"And *ya* handled the weight well," she quipped.

Jacob laughed outright. He couldn't help it; Annie looked so cute with that determined expression on her face and the teasing twinkle in her blue eyes. He felt hopeful. He quieted his laugh to a soft chuckle. Folks were gathering inside the house for church service. He didn't want to draw unwanted attention to himself or Annie.

"I hope that whatever you made is worth waiting for," he said.

"Worth is entirely your opinion and of no consequence to me," she replied crisply. She turned abruptly and marched across the lawn toward the kitchen area of the house.

Amused by her attitude, Jacob watched her stalk off. He grinned.

Anger was better than indifference.

Chapter Twelve

Seated between her mother and sister, Annie listened as Levi Stoltzfus gave the Sunday sermon. He was a good speaker, reminding all about the importance of God in life and about family values. He spoke of the *Ordnung*, the teachings of the Amish faith, and he spoke of it with eloquence.

She became aware of Charlotte King Peachy, Abram's wife, who sat with Abram's five children. Charlotte glanced frequently and with affection toward her husband across the room. He beamed back at her while he attempted to keep focused on Preacher Levi's words.

She wanted a relationship like theirs, Annie thought. A man to love and marry and be a good father to their children.

She sensed someone's regard and turned to discover Ike. The man smiled. Ike was a nice man as well as a good member of the Happiness community. He was also Amos King's younger brother.

She felt the impact of someone else's stare and locked gazes with Jacob Lapp, seated on the bench behind Ike. His tawny gaze was sharp, and he didn't smile. He con-

tinued to gawk at her without expression before returning his attention to the preacher's sermon.

Annie felt her cheeks burning. Pulse thrumming, she
forced her attention back to Ike King. Ike was looking for
a wife and he wanted a family. Ike was older, safe. She
could marry someone like Ike and be happy.

Couldn't she?

She couldn't consider Jacob. It wouldn't be wise. Yet,
she couldn't ignore that she had feelings for the man.

Annie straightened in her seat, unwavering in her decision to put a plan in motion that would keep her on her
determined path. She would talk with Ike, see if he was
interested in walking out with her.

Why would Jacob want a woman who was two years
older and afraid of getting hurt?

She felt her mother's regard, saw her displeasure,
and straightened as she focused on the sermon again.
She joined in loudly as the congregation sang a hymn.
Their chanting voices blended beautifully, and Annie
got caught up in the song. She pushed all of her concerns
away as she prayed to the Lord and asked His help. A
sense of peace overcame her; the Lord's way of showing
her His presence. And she smiled. Everything would be
fine. God would guide her in the right direction. All she
had to do was pray hard and believe.

Church service ended, and Jacob stood on the front
porch leaning against the railing. Seeing Annie again
was like a kick to his midsection. He had put his heart
on the line for her, throwing out the idea that they could
be sweethearts rather than friends. If she had given it any
serious thought, Annie gave no sign.

I should have listened to Eli. His brother had warned him to stay away from the Zook family farm.

There was a singing tonight. Should he go? Annie probably wouldn't attend, not if she planned to marry Ike King. He'd go, have fun and flirt a little with one of the other girls.

He frowned. *As if I could.* He loved Annie too much to even think of spending time with another woman.

At some point he would return to work at the blacksmithy. But he would keep his distance from Annie. If she was interested in a relationship with him, then she would have to make the next move.

"What are you doing out here?" Eli stepped up to lean against the porch railing next to Jacob.

"Just thinking about tonight's singing…"

Eli scowled. "You are planning to go?" He leaned closer to whisper in Jacob's ear. "Or are you going to let Annie Zook stop you from enjoying yourself?" He ran a hand through his blond hair. Like the rest of the men, he removed his hat before attending church. "You need to show Annie that you are fine without her."

"I already decided to go."

Eli's mouth opened and closed. *"Gut,"* he said finally.

Jacob chuckled. "Almost speechless. That's new for you."

"Jacob! Eli!" Amos and Mae King's son John, affectionately called BJ or Big John after Amos's eldest daughter, Sarah, and her husband, Eli, had chosen little John for their baby son. "My *vadder* has been looking for you," BJ said. "He wants to know if you'll help with the church. He wants to move several benches into the other room."

Jacob pushed off the railing, and Eli followed. "Any *gut* food waiting inside for us?" he asked the boy.

"Lots of *gut* food. I've got a hankering for a big help-ing of apple crisp."

Eli smiled as he grabbed hold of the screen door and held it open as they stepped inside. "I've a yearning for a slice of spice cake or a helping of chocolate cream pudding."

With Eli's help, Jacob moved benches into the other room. His thoughts turned to Annie. *I wonder what she made today.* Whatever it was—cake, pie or sheet cookie, it would taste delicious.

Eli's voice interrupted his train of thought. "Let's grab these and take them outside."

Jacob worked with his brother and the two King boys until all the benches were either set up inside or outside in the yard, for those wishing to enjoy the warm au-tumn day.

By the time he and Eli were done, Jacob felt in control of his emotions again. He would go to the singing and would have a good time…without Annie Zook.

Annie rode to the singing with her two brothers. Jo-siah climbed out of the buggy and headed straight for Nancy King, who stood outside waiting for him. Peter lingered as Annie reached into the back of the vehicle to pick up the nearest of two snack platters she'd prepared for the evening.

Her brother was studying the people who chatted out-side the barn. This was Peter's first singing and he had been eager to come. She smiled. "Are you ready?"

Peter rewarded her with a grin. *"Ja."* A buggy arrived bringing more friends. "There's Reuben Miller," he said as he lifted a hand to wave.

"I see him." Annie suddenly remembered Reuben's

offer to take her home. She was startled to realize that she hadn't given the young man any thought since their last encounter over a week and a half ago. Except when she'd spoken of him to Jacob.

"I don't see Rebekkah," Peter noticed.

"You won't," Annie said. "She's betrothed." She handed him the platter.

"*Ach, ja,* I'd forgotten." He accepted the plate of lemon squares. "What about the gingerbread cake?"

"I'll get it." Annie reached to retrieve the gingerbread cake with cream-cheese frosting.

Another buggy pulled in to park on the other side. The Lapp twin brothers stepped out, and Annie watched their approach with her heart thundering in startling awareness of Jacob.

"*Hallo,* Annie," Eli greeted. "Peter, I'm glad to see you here."

Annie locked eyes with Jacob. "Jacob," she said.

Jacob gave her a solemn nod. "Annie."

Eli and Peter chatted as they headed toward the barn. Annie had no choice but to follow, with Jacob accompanying her. She couldn't help but notice how handsome he was. He cut a fine figure in his Sunday best. His black vest and white shirt fit him well as did his black pants with black shoes. The brim of his black felt hat shielded his eyes, but Annie could tell when he was looking at her. It was evening, and the setting sun was beautiful, a fiery orb that had changed the sky to colorful splashes of bright orange interwoven with red. The evening was quiet, and Annie felt the tension between them vibrate in the night air.

"Your hand looks better," she said after desperately searching for something to say.

"*Ja*, 'tis much improved," he said, sounding amused. Jacob had nothing to add to keep up the flow of conversation.

"I need to go," Annie began.

"Annie." The intensity in Jacob's voice stopped her. "*Ja?*"

"We need to talk later. We haven't talked in ages."

Annie nodded. Leaving Jacob's side after they entered the barn together, Annie placed the gingerbread cake with the rest of the snack food.

A long table with chairs had been set up in the barn. Girls were seated on one side and boys on the other. Annie took the first available seat, and to her dismay, Joseph Byler appeared and sat down across from her.

"Hello, Annie," he said with a sloppy smile.

Annie nodded. His presence dampened her enjoyment of the evening. "Joseph."

"Annie!" Reuben Miller stepped into the room and took a seat next to Joseph. "I told *ya* I would come."

She smiled; she couldn't help it. "I take it the banns were posted for Rebekkah and Caleb."

Reuben nodded. "*Ja*, and everyone is happy about the union."

Jacob sat on Joseph's other side. "Joseph," he greeted. He eyed Reuben over Joseph's head. "How are *ya*, Reuben?" He took off his hat and set it on the table, rewarding Annie with a good view of his features. His brown hair shone in the gas-lantern light, and there was a tiny smile playing about his masculine lips.

Her heart beat a rapid tattoo as she compared him to the two other men. Jacob Lapp was easily the most handsome.

Her brother Josiah opened his copy of the *Ausbund*

and led them in the first song. He flashed Nancy a smile before he began to sing his chosen hymn in a deep, confident voice. Eli Lapp joined in, followed by the other young people. Annie couldn't keep her eyes off Jacob as he raised his voice in song, his tone strong, melodic and pleasant.

Caught up in the moment, Annie sang out for God and for the sure joy of it. Jacob captured her attention and Annie was surprised to see his golden eyes fill with warmth as they held gazes and joined voices.

A while later, at Nancy's urging, Josiah called a refreshment break. Anne rose along with the other girls to unwrap the food, while the young men stood to chat and stretch their legs. Nancy had made lemonade, and someone had brought homemade birch beer. Mae King, Nancy's mother, had provided hot tea and coffee as the days were cool and the nights could be downright cold. Soon everyone enjoyed paper plates filled with goodies and the beverage of their choice.

Annie was nursing a cup of hot tea, when Joseph Byler approached.

"Annie," he said, "did you make these brownies?"

Annie shook her head. "Meg Stoltzfus did."

He turned with a frown to eye the snack table, and as he did, Reuben Miller slid into his place in front of Annie.

"Annie," he greeted with a smile. "This is yours. I can tell." He referred to her gingerbread cake.

"How?" Annie asked. She wondered how he'd known.

He grinned. "Because it's the most delicious item on the table." He lowered his voice. "And Peter told me."

Annie laughed.

"May I take *ya* home this evening?" he asked, fulfilling her worst fears.

"I—"

"I'm afraid to disappoint you, but she's riding with me this evening," Jacob said as he joined them.

Annie's heart began to race as soon as she heard Jacob's voice.

Reuben glanced from Jacob to Annie, who didn't refute Jacob's claim. "I see."

"I appreciate the offer, Reuben," Annie said while shooting Jacob a look, "but yes, Jacob will be taking me home."

Joseph Byler, who'd been shifted outside the circle, returned with another snack on his plate. "This one must be yours," he told Annie.

Jacob didn't move, and Annie was stunned by his desire to linger.

Sensing Joseph's confusion, she glanced at his plate. "*Ja*, I made that one."

Joseph glanced toward Jacob and frowned as Jacob shifted closer to Annie's side. The young man widened his eyes and scurried away.

"So, you'll be taking me home, will you?" she said softly.

"You wanted to be rescued, didn't *ya*?" He took a bite of a lemon square. "These are delicious, Annie," he said, sounding sincere. "You are an excellent cook and baker." He lowered his voice conspiratorially. "And your *mudder* didn't have to point it out to me. I just knew."

Annie laughed, and the earlier awkwardness between them suddenly vanished. "I'm glad you like them." Reuben had already moved on to talk to Meg Stoltzfus. Joseph, on the other hand, continued to watch her from a distance, with a pouting look on his face.

Jacob followed the direction of her gaze. "He's not happy."

"Nay." She gave Jacob a crooked smile. "He doesn't take a hint well."

"I can't speak for Joseph. He is a determined man, but I think he is harmless. Eventually he'll get the hint. You mustn't worry too much about him."

"And how many times will you have to rescue me from him before he'll understand that I'm just not interested in him?"

"If I'm not available, you can ask someone else to rescue you, like Eli or Ike King," he said softly.

Annie felt keen disappointment. "I'm sorry. I didn't mean to impose."

Jacob narrowed his eyes. "I offered to take you home and you accepted. How is that an imposition?"

"It's not?" She waited with a wildly beating heart for his answer.

"Nay, taking you home can never be an imposition," he said, and Annie felt joy at his words. "After all, we're friends, aren't we?" He shot a look over his shoulder. "'Tis time to go back inside."

She nodded and set down her teacup. *Friends*, she thought. He *had* been teasing her when he'd suggested a possible deeper relationship between them. When she headed back inside, she was surprised to find that Jacob had waited for her.

She resumed her seat in the other room and was startled when Jacob took the chair directly across from her. Joseph frowned and shifted to the seat that Jacob had vacated earlier. Jacob smiled at her, and Annie knew a warmth and pleasure she'd never felt with his older brother Jed. When Jacob raised an eyebrow at her, she felt her heart soar. She wondered what it would be like to hold hands with him, then scolded herself for foolishly entertaining the thought. She blushed when she saw Jacob eyeing her with curiosity.

The singing resumed with Peter's choice of hymn. As her brother began to sing, Annie watched Jacob, loving the way he'd made her feel, recalling all the wonderful things he'd done for her and her family. She had a sudden mental image of living with him as man and wife. *What am I doing?* Setting herself up for heartbreak, she thought.

The evening passed quickly, and soon everyone rose to leave. A few of the young men and women coupled up and walked out into the night together. Annie headed out the door alone, disappointed that Jacob had gone outside without her. Still, she was grateful for the reprieve. She was confused, wanting one thing but afraid of what could happen if she gave in.

The night was chilly, and Annie hugged herself with her arms as she waited and wondered if Jacob had forgotten her.

Josiah approached. "Annie, I'm going to stay awhile with Nancy," he said. "Will *ya* be able to get a ride home?"

She smiled. "I have a ride." Josiah looked surprised but pleased, yet his curiosity about whom she was referring to wasn't stronger than his desire to return to Nancy.

"Are you ready?" Jacob appeared out of nowhere, startling her, causing her heart to jump.

She nodded. Following him, Annie anticipated the ride home with excitement. She knew it was wrong to put her heart at risk, but she couldn't help it. It was one night; surely, she could enjoy one night in Jacob Lapp's company and still keep her heart intact.

Chapter Thirteen

Jacob gestured for Annie to precede him as they headed toward his family's market wagon. His brother Eli and Mary Hershberger, Annie's cousin, were already in the open wagon bed along with Annie's youngest brother, Peter.

He felt Annie hesitate before continuing, almost as if she was startled to learn that others would be riding home with them. He recalled the way Annie had laughed and spoken with Ike King earlier in the day and decided that he was mistaken, especially after she'd greeted the occupants of the wagon cheerfully.

He followed her to the passenger side of the vehicle's front bench seat and extended his hand to assist her up. She looked at him for a heartbeat, before she placed her fingers within his grasp. As he helped her onto the bench, Jacob was not unaffected by the warmth of her small hand within his. He drew a sharp breath as he released his grip and hurried to the other side, where he climbed in. Emotion slammed in his chest. He wanted to take her in his arms and whirl her away to a place where they could be alone. He was conscious of Annie beside him as he picked up the reins and spurred the horse on.

He heard conversation and laughter from the back of the wagon. Annie's brother Peter needed a ride, and Eli had offered to take him home. They arrived at the Hershberger farm first, and Jacob pulled into the barnyard and waited as Eli walked Mary Hershberger to her door. He wondered what Annie was thinking as she watched Eli and Mary before turning to stare straight ahead.

"You look lovely tonight," he said softly. There was enough moonlight for him to see her. The sight of her stole his breath away.

Annie shot him a glance in the darkness. She was quiet a moment. "You're just being kind."

"I wasn't being kind, Annie," he admitted. His fingers reached for hers. She jumped at his touch, as if startled, and he quickly withdrew his hand.

"Jacob?" she whispered.

He turned, stared at her, saw the look in her eyes and was tempted to reach for her hand again. But he didn't, for he saw indecision and dismay in her expression. He shrugged and smiled at her instead. "It's all right, Annie." He heard her sigh and wondered what she was thinking.

Soon, his brother had returned. Eli hopped into the back of the wagon, and Jacob steered the horse back to the main road and on toward the Joseph Zook farm.

"How did you like your first singing, Pete?" Eli asked.

"It was fun." Jacob couldn't see Peter's face, but he could imagine the boy's delight. "I like Meg Hostetler," he confessed.

"She's our cousin," Eli said.

"She's a nice girl," Peter replied.

"*Ja*, and don't *ya* forget it," Eli warned, but Jacob could hear laughter in his brother's voice.

Peter was silent for a moment, as if taking Eli's warning seriously. "I won't."

Reaching the road to the Zook farmhouse, Jacob turned on the battery-operated turn signal and steered the horse left onto the dirt lane. He wanted to kiss her, he thought. If only they were alone...

He reined in the horse in the barnyard and sat still for several seconds. Then he jumped down from the vehicle, walked around the wagon to Annie's side and offered his hand to her. As he waited a heartbeat, Jacob remembered another time when he'd offered her his hand and she'd chosen to ignore his help. This time, to his delight, she accepted it, and he enjoyed the feeling of holding her hand. There was warmth where they touched. Jacob experienced tightness in his chest when Annie gave him a tremulous smile. He released her fingers as her brother scrambled out of the back of the wagon.

"I appreciate the ride," Peter said before he hurried inside the house and shut the door.

Eli climbed from the back of the wagon onto the front seat as Jacob accompanied Annie to her door.

"I didn't get a chance to tell you," Jacob said huskily, "but I wanted to be alone with you tonight."

He felt her surprise and wondered if he should have kept his mouth shut. But then she smiled and her blue eyes shone in the moonlight and the golden glow from the lamplight glimmering from inside the house, through the windows.

"You did?" He saw her glance toward the wagon and Eli, who waited patiently up front.

He nodded, reached for her hand again. He rubbed his thumb over her soft skin. "We need to talk—"

"Jacob—"

He leaned in and kissed her, catching her off guard.

"Jacob…"

"Annie?" Her sister Barbara stood just inside the doorway.

Annie stepped back, out of reach, and Jacob wondered if Barbara had witnessed their kiss. "I'll be inside in a minute."

He inwardly scolded himself for wanting to spend more time with her. "I should say *gut* night, Annie."

"Jacob," she whispered. She stared at him a moment and then leaned forward.

Jacob saw the longing in her blue gaze and started to reach for her.

"Annie," Barbara called.

"I have to go." Her eyes sparkled in the lantern light. "*Gut* night, Jacob," she murmured. Then she disappeared into the house, without looking back.

Jacob returned to the wagon, where his brother waited with a knowing look.

"You love her," Eli accused.

Jacob sighed. "We're just friends."

"But you want to be more."

He shrugged as he pulled the brim of his hat down low. "I'll get over it." His heart thumped hard as he recalled the sweet taste of her lips and the way she'd hovered as if she wanted him to kiss her again.

Eli shook his head as he picked up the leathers. "I think not, brother," he said, and he drove the horse toward home.

"What's between you and Mary Hershberger?" Jacob asked Eli.

"Nothing. We were just having a *gut* time. Mary has her heart set on someone else."

Jacob made a noise of disbelief. "And she told you this?"

Eli grinned at him. "*Nay*, but I can tell. Didn't ya see how she was watching Joseph this evening?"

"Joseph Byler?" Jacob was surprised.

"*Ja.*"

He laughed. Jacob couldn't help himself. Joseph liked Annie, but Mary Hershberger liked Joseph, while he liked Annie, who liked... Ike King. *Or maybe not.* There had been a flash of something in her blue eyes, her response to his quick kiss, before she'd gone into the house, that made him wonder.

"And you?" Jacob asked. "Have you got your heart set on anyone in particular?"

Eli shook his head. "I'm in no hurry to find a sweet-heart. 'Tis more fun to watch the drama of you and Annie."

He didn't think Eli had seen their kiss. It had been dark, and Jacob had made it a quick one. "There is no drama between Annie and me."

Eli looked unconvinced. "If you say so, *bruder*."

Inside the house, through the window, Annie watched Jacob and Eli drive off in the wagon. Her lips still tingled from his surprising kiss. *Why did he kiss me?* After a kiss like that, how was she to remember all the reasons why she'd wanted to avoid him?

Jacob had stepped in this evening to prevent Reuben or Joseph from taking her home. It was as if he'd read her mind and suddenly he'd been there to rescue her. She knew he had helped out of friendship. Though that kiss was more than friendly…

Annie left the window and went upstairs to her room. Barbara had gone up to bed, and she was eager to speak with her. Levi Stoltzfus had come to dinner again, and Barbara had chosen to stay home to spend time with him.

"How did things go?" Annie asked Barbara as she started to undress.

Barbara was quiet. "You're not mad that I'm seeing him?"

Annie stopped and stared. "Why should I be? I can tell that he cares for you."

"You can?" Barbara sounded pleased.

"*Ja*, he is a *gut* man, and I think you and he will do well together."

"I'm glad you feel that way." Barbara moved to sit up against the headboard. "Levi and I went for a walk after dinner."

Annie widened her eyes. "You did?" She took off her prayer *kapp* and unpinned her long hair.

A soft smile played about his lips. "*Ja*, and *Mam* didn't mind. She and *Dat* said I could go with him." Barbara sighed dreamily. "We went through the yard and then across the fields. The moon was bright, and I could see his face." Barbara ran fingers through her long dark unbound hair. "He is so handsome. And he seemed to enjoy himself." She sighed. "I loved every minute with him."

"You love him." Annie smiled as she pulled back the quilt and climbed into bed beside her sister.

She sensed Barbara's surprise, but her voice was soft as she said, "*Ja*."

"That's *gut*!" Annie assured her.

"You must think me foolish," Barbara said. "I fell for David, and now it's only been a little over a month, and I've fallen in love with Levi Stoltzfus." She paused. "But this feels different."

"I don't think you foolish at all," Annie assured her. "You have known Levi your entire life. You know who he is and the type of man he's become." She climbed into bed next to Barbara. "David Byler was just an infatuation. By your own admission, he was a *gut*-looking boy, and you were flattered by his attention. He lives in New Wilmington while you belong here. Levi is here—why shouldn't you allow yourself to love him?"

"I can't be sure he loves me," Barbara said, "or if he is just being nice."

"Enjoy your time with him, and you'll know. Whatever happens, I want you to be happy."

"Even if Levi Stoltzfus is no long available?"

Annie chuckled as she slid down under the bed quilt and stared at the ceiling. "I want to marry an older man. But did I say it has to be Levi?" She met Barbara's gaze. "*Nay*, it was *Mam's* idea to encourage him in my direction."

"I could be happy spending my whole life with him," Barbara said. She blew out the candle, then settled in next to Annie. "I hope you find someone soon."

Annie sighed. "What will be, will be. I can't know God's will until He shows it to me. I'll be fine. You worry about yourself and stop fretting over my future."

"I love you, Annie," Barbara whispered into the dark.

"I love you, Barbara. *Gut* night." While she drifted off to sleep, Annie thought of Jacob, knowing that she shouldn't be giving advice to others when she couldn't make up her mind about her own future.

* * *

"Are you heading to the Zooks'?" Eli asked as he worked alongside Jacob in the barn.

"*Nay.* Maybe later this afternoon." His hand was bothering him. Although it was healing, he still kept it covered. The large blister formed by the second-degree burn had popped, and the skin was still tender, but the wound itself looked much better.

"What about Joe?" his brother asked as he mucked out the stable.

Jacob filled a feed pail for Janey and set it within her reach. He checked to make sure she had water and then moved on to the other horses.

"Joe knows I'll be back eventually. He's the one who wanted to make sure my hand was healed properly before starting back to work."

"But it's not your hand that's keeping you away now," Eli said with the keen sense of knowing his brother well. "It's Annie."

"She can't keep me from helping Joe." Jacob finished with the horses and moved to feed *Mam's* chickens. His brother had it right. It was Annie who made him reluctant to return. He had kissed her, and now he was afraid that in the end, he'd be left alone as she chose to wed Ike King.

Finished with one stall, Eli moved on to the next one. "Why don't you just tell her how you feel?"

Jacob watched his brother's progress. "You missed something," he said with amusement.

"You're enjoying this, aren't you?" Eli glared with feigned anger at his brother, who was older by four minutes. "You get the easy chores while I handle this—" He gestured toward the wheelbarrow that held horse manure.

"I can't risk getting my hand dirty."

"You're avoiding an answer," Eli said.

"Annie Zook has her heart set on marrying someone like Ike King. The woman can't seem to make up her mind," Jacob said.

"But she doesn't know how long you've had feelings for her. What if she likes you more than she's let on?" Eli said. Finished with the stalls, he lifted the handles of the wheelbarrow and pushed it outside. Jacob followed behind, a bucket of chicken feed in his uninjured hand.

Jacob dipped his fingers into the grain and tossed it onto the ground, among the fowl. The birds clucked and moved about excitedly before they pecked at their meal.

Annie had been too surprised to kiss him back last night, but he feared he was mistaken in that she wanted to. "She does like me," Jacob admitted, "as a friend."

"A *gut* friend." Eli swatted a fly on his neck.

"*Ja*, perhaps." Jacob threw feed in another direction and the chickens found their way to the newly tossed grain. "But sometimes being a friend isn't enough."

Eli sighed. "So you hope your feelings will go away."

Jacob had gone back and forth in his mind about whether or not he should continue to pursue Annie. He wanted to be with her. But he had no idea if she'd changed her plans. What if she still wanted to marry an older man?

"Why not go after her? What if she's changed her mind and wants someone like you?" Eli went to dump the refuse in a designated area.

Should he try? Should he confront her, tell her of his feelings, risk all in the hope that she might return his love?

Eli returned with the empty wheelbarrow. "Are you going to Joe's this afternoon or not?"

"I don't know." Something inside urged him to go,

while another side of him caused him to hesitate. "I'm still deciding."

"Think about going. If you see Annie, talk with her. If you don't, you'll regret that you missed an opportunity to win her love."

After Eli left, Jacob put away the empty chicken-feed bucket and headed toward the house. He could go to the blacksmith shop to work. He wouldn't let Joe down, no matter how difficult circumstances might become for him. *Annie*, he thought. He wanted to see her, talk with her…and reach across a bench seat in the dark to capture her hand.

Chapter Fourteen

"*Mam!* I'm going to take Jacob breakfast!" Annie called as she headed toward the door with a thermos and a covered plate of food.

"That's fine, Annie," *Mam* said as she came out of the gathering room with corn broom in hand. "Don't be long. We've got a lot to do today."

"I won't be," she promised. Annie found she was eager to see Jacob. Had she imagined the attraction between them? Or had she simply dreamed of their kiss? She hurried across the yard, the jug in one hand, a plate of sticky buns in the other and a smile on her face. When she reached the shop, she experienced a tremor of excitement.

"Jacob?" she called as she opened the door to the building.

The shop was quiet, too quiet. Annie frowned. There was no light inside the building, no ring of steel against iron.

"Jacob?" she said hesitantly. She moved to stand in the inner doorway and stared inside. Everything was as neat as a pin, just as Peter and *Dat* had left it after Jacob's accident.

Where was Jacob? He had been well enough to attend the singing. And he'd offered his hand to help her onto the wagon. She became concerned. Had he done too much yesterday? Had he reinjured his hand?

Where is he? She longed to see him in his leather apron, heating metal until it glowed red, raising the tongs to inspect the fiery red piece before setting it on the anvil to hammer into shape. She recalled how he looked, his eyes narrowed as he concentrated on the task, the movement of his forearms as he brought down the hammer again and again, fired up the metal and repeated the process. She felt an odd feeling in her chest at the mental image.

Annie left the thermos on the worktable in case Jacob came later. She eyed the plate of sticky buns and decided it would be fine to leave them, too. As she left the shop and headed back toward the house, she felt a rush of disappointment. *Mam* said that they had much to do today. It was just as well that Jacob wasn't here, for she had no time to visit with him this morning.

What if he regretted kissing her? she thought. What if he'd simply tried to prove a point? All the more reason for her to avoid him.

Annie walked slowly back to the house, wondering why it felt as if the sunshine and joy had been stolen from her day. She had to stop thinking the worst. She would see and talk with Jacob another day. She'd have to be satisfied with that. She picked up her pace and ran toward the porch steps. "*Mam!* I'm back! What would you like me to do first?"

There was no one around when Jacob arrived at Horseshoe Joe's. His brother had needed to run errands in town, so Eli had brought him with the promise to return for him later.

There was no sign of anyone in the yard, no sign of movement in the farmhouse windows. He entered the shop and pushed open a window to allow the sunlight inside. Then, he checked the work ledger to see what needed to be done. William Mast—handsaw repair. Bob Whittier—metal coat hooks.

He continued down the list. Arlin Stoltzfus requested that he make some shepherd's hooks, like *Englishers* liked to use in their front yards, on which to hang flower pots or wind chimes. The cold weather was an impending threat, and several neighbors had appointments for him to replace their horses' and mules' shoes.

He glanced toward the vise mounted on one end of the worktable. As he took down his leather apron, he caught sight of a thermos and a plate of sticky buns. *Annie.* He smiled. He wasn't ready to see her yet, but it was comforting to know that she cared enough to bring him breakfast. Laying the apron across the top of the worktable, he paused to pour himself a cup of coffee. After a few slow sips, he sighed appreciatively. The woman always remembered how he liked it best. The plate of sticky buns tempted him, making his mouth water, for he had eaten breakfast hours ago before helping his brothers around the farm. One delicious bite of the bun led to another until he had finished the first and started on a second one. Wouldn't it be wonderful if he had her in his life always! Then he scolded himself for being distracted by her.

Forcing her from his mind, Jacob focused on the work. He donned his apron and pulled on gloves to protect his hands. As canvas and leather brushed his burn injury, he winced, but then the pain passed and he was ready to begin. He grabbed solid iron pieces from a shelf and set them on the worktable. Then he reached for a pair of recently purchased safety glasses and put them on. He readied the forge, grabbed his metal tongs and cross-peen hammer and went to work.

"Annie!" *Mam's* voice came from the bottom of the stairs.

"Ja?" Annie left her brothers' bedroom to look down at her from the top landing. "Do you need me?"

"I'd like you and your sister to run an errand for me."

"I'll be right down." Annie returned to the bedroom and grabbed the sheets she'd stripped off the two beds.

Mam and Barbara were in the kitchen when Annie came downstairs. *Mam* stood near the stove, ladling homemade soup into a large bowl. When she was done, she turned to her daughters. "I'd like you to take this chicken soup over to Ike King."

Annie exchanged glances with her sister. "Is he ill?" she asked.

Mam nodded. "Josie stopped by on her way to Whittier's Store. She said he has stomach pains." She worked as she talked, withdrawing a sleeve of saltines from the pantry and setting them near the soup bowl.

"Do you think we should bring him chamomile tea?" Barbara suggested. "He may want a cup to settle his stomach."

"That's a fine idea, Barbara," *Mam* said.

Annie pitched in to gather things to take to Ike. Her mother's concern for him alleviated the fear that this was a way for *Mam* to get her into Ike's company. She didn't think her mother was trying to make her a match—this time.

When she was done preparing Ike's care package, *Mam* gave Barbara a plastic bag with the crackers, one of her home remedies for stomachaches and the chamomile tea.

"Annie, you take the soup," *Mam* instructed. "Barbara, put some paper bowls in the bag so there will be no dirty dishes to wash."

Soon, the sisters were in the buggy, with Annie steering the horse toward Ike King's farm. They arrived within minutes. Annie parked their vehicle in Ike's barnyard, and the sisters climbed out.

"Shall we knock or just call out?" Barbara asked as they approached the house.

"Why not do both?" Annie shifted the bowl of soup to one arm as she climbed the porch steps. She tapped lightly on the wooden door. "It's a big place," she commented. Ike's home was an impressive two-story whitewashed brick farmhouse.

Annie rapped on the door again. "Ike?" When there was no response, she grew concerned. She knocked harder. *"Ike?"*

"What do we do if he doesn't answer?" Barbara peered inside a window. "I don't see him."

Annie thought a moment. "If he doesn't come, we'll go around to the back. He might have fallen asleep in a chair."

"Let's try again," Barbara suggested. This time she knocked. *"Ike!"*

Finally, they heard movement inside and then the door opened. Ike stood on the threshold, looking ill and with his hair mussed up as if he'd run his fingers through it. He appeared disoriented at first, and his eyes widened as realization dawned. "Annie!" he said. "Barbara."

"We heard you were feeling poorly," Annie explained with a sympathetic smile. "We've brought soup and crackers and some chamomile tea to settle your stomach. *Mam* sent some of her bellyache medicine."

"Danki." He moved aside to allow them to enter. Suddenly, he gasped, "I'm sorry, I have to—" And he ran out of the room.

Annie set the soup on his kitchen counter while Barbara took items out of the paper bag.

Minutes later, Ike returned, looking green in the face. His eyes had a glassy look to them as he stood teetering on unsteady legs.

"Sit down, Ike," Anne urged. "Would you like some chicken soup?" She held up *Mam's* bowl.

Ike agreed, and Annie went to work heating it. After Ike ate and returned to rest on the sofa in his gathering room, Annie and Barbara left. Once home, Annie went inside the farmhouse while Barbara headed toward the clothesline to check on the garments they'd hung earlier.

Peter was at the kitchen table when Annie walked in. "Where have you been?" he asked as he munched on a cookie.

"Ike King's. He's ill, and *Mam* wanted him to have some of her chicken soup.

Her brother set his glass down after taking a drink of milk. "He didn't look sick yesterday," he said as he reached for another cookie.

"He's sick today. He looks awful." Annie grabbed Peter's now empty glass and held it up. "More?"

He nodded. She picked up the jug from the counter when she spied the thermos sitting in the dish drainer. "Did you bring this in from *Dat's* shop?" she asked.

"*Nay.* Jacob brought it before he left earlier. He said the coffee—and the sticky buns—were *gut.*"

"Jacob was here?" Recalling his kiss, Annie felt a short burst of joy but then was disappointed when she realized that he'd left and she missed him. "Is he coming tomorrow?" she asked casually as she handed her brother his milk.

Peter shrugged as he drank from his glass. "He didn't say."

Annie stared out the kitchen window. He'd kissed her. It could mean nothing. Handsome young men were always trying to catch women off guard.

She frowned. Kiss or not, handsome young men like Jacob were not in her plans, while someone like Ike would be the husband she needed. But was Ike really what she wanted? Or did she want Jacob?

She recalled Jacob's golden gaze, his warm smile, the feelings she had whenever he was near. Annie hugged herself with her arms. She had done the unthinkable. She had fallen in love with Jacob Lapp, and there was nothing she could do to stop it. *Except to walk away, keep to the plan and marry someone like Ike.*

Two days later...

"Annie." Ike stood a few feet away from the clothesline where Annie worked hanging laundry.

"Ike!" Surprised to see him, she faced him with a smile. "You're looking well."

"I'm feeling better." Ike was an attractive man in his late thirties with sandy-brown hair and a matching beard that edged along the line of his chin. His pale blue eyes twinkled with good health. "It was *gut* of you to bring me soup."

"*Mam* made it." She secured her brother's shirt on the rope with clothespins. "Have you brought work for Jacob?"

"*Nay*, I've brought back your *mudder's* dish. The chicken soup was delicious. It made me feel better."

"I'm glad to hear it." She faced him, squinted against the sun, then held her hand up to shield her eyes. "*Mam* is a wonderful cook."

"So are you," he said with a small smile. "I've tasted your cakes and pies."

Annie felt her face turn warm. "My sister can cook, as well."

He glanced toward the house. "Where is Barbara?" he asked, and Annie was relieved at the switch in the topic of conversation.

"Inside. Why don't you go in for a visit? My *mudder* will make you tea and give you some fresh-baked cookies."

Ike appraised her with an intensity that gave her pause. "And you?" His voice was soft. "Will you be coming up to the *haus*?"

"*Ja*, as soon as I finish here."

"Then I will see you when you are done." Ike smiled at her and then headed toward the farmhouse.

Annie went back to hanging clothes. When she was done, she picked up the laundry basket and strode toward the house. She stopped suddenly and changed directions, moving toward her father's blacksmith shop, her thoughts now focused on Jacob Lapp.

She hadn't seen him this morning. In fact, she hadn't

seen them since he'd kissed her the night of the singing. He was avoiding her. Why?

Because he regretted the kiss and their time together? She needed to know.

Again Annie halted and turned back to the house. Why was she chasing Jacob, a man who clearly bemoaned his time with her, when there was Ike—a *gut*, hardworking, caring man—waiting in the house for her?

She retraced her steps until she reached the back porch. As she pushed the door inward, she could hear Ike and *Mam* talking. Ike's voice was easily recognizable from the kitchen.

Annie sighed. The sound of his voice might not incite butterflies in her stomach or make her breath catch, like Jacob's did, but it was kind and gentle and she was drawn to the sound. She set the basket near the bottom of the stairs and went to the kitchen. *"Hallo,"* she greeted with a smile. Ike, Barbara, *Mam* and *Dat* were seated at the table, each with a steaming cup of tea in front of them.

She crossed the room to take out a cup for herself. "What's that delicious aroma?" she asked.

"Cinnamon rolls," *Mam* said. "I'm warming the buns you made this morning."

"They smell wonderful." Ike flashed Annie an appreciative smile.

"I'm ready for tea," Annie said. "Does anyone want another cup?" She ignored her mother's pleased look.

"I'll have another," Ike said.

When he entered the Zook farmhouse, Jacob heard Annie's laughter coming from the kitchen. Enjoying the delightful sound, he made his way toward the back of the house. Whenever he wasn't with her, he missed her. He anticipated her smile, longed for her response the next time he held her more properly in his arms and kissed her.

"*Gut* morning!" he said with a smile as he entered the kitchen. He became the focus of four pairs of eyes. He stopped abruptly. He was surprised to see Ike King seated next to Annie at the table. His chest tightened. He nodded at Ike. "*Hallo.*"

"Jacob." At least Horseshoe Joe looked pleased to see him. "Are you hungry?"

"*Nay,* but I'll take a glass of water." He sought Miriam's permission. "May I?"

She smiled. "*Ja,* of course."

Annie started to rise. "I'll get it."

Jacob held up his hand to stop her. "I know where everything is." The conversation resumed behind him as he reached into a kitchen cabinet and withdrew a glass. He filled the tumbler with water from the faucet. When he was done, he turned and leaned back against the cabinet as he lifted the glass to his lips. He took note of the gathering, his attention returning to Annie often.

"This is delicious," Ike said after he'd taken a bite of a cinnamon bun.

Annie avoided his glance. "That's kind of you to say."

"Annie is a wonderful cook," Jacob said pleasantly, trying to draw her attention. "Everything she makes comes out perfectly. You should taste her homemade bread."

Jacob was amused when her eyes shot daggers at him. "Not only is she a *gut* cook but she is modest about it. She will make some lucky man a fine wife." He couldn't help stirring things up a bit. Annie was livid, but Ike appeared pleased. Annie was angry, so she couldn't be indifferent to him.

"I get coffee and breakfast from her whenever I come to work—at least most of the time. Annie doesn't always know whether or not I'm working."

Ike looked concerned. "That's right. You injured your hand. Is it better?"

Jacob captured Annie's gaze and fought to keep it. "My hand is healing," he said. He drank the last of the water and then set the glass in the dish basin. "I should get back." He turned to Annie. "We need to talk later."

"You'll be coming for lunch?" Joe asked, speaking up after being unusually quiet.

"*Danki*, but *nay*. I'll finish in the shop and then head home." He crossed the room to the nearest exit. "I'll see you on Sunday if not before. Miriam, *Mam* said to tell you that she'll bring roast beef on Sunday." This Sunday was visiting day. Friends and family would gather at the Zooks for a meal and conversation. The children—young and old—would play games outside as long as the weather held and didn't suddenly turn cold.

Jacob heard his pulse pounding in his ears as he left the house and continued toward the shop. What if Annie decided to marry Ike King? She certainly looked cozy seated next to him at the kitchen table. He suddenly felt unsure. Annie's anger with him could be just that—anger.

He released a shuddering breath. The memory of her and Ike's shared laughter stung. Seeing them together made his chest tighten and his thoughts churn.

If Ike is the man you want, Annie Zook, then I wish you well.

"*Jacob!*" Annie came out of the house and approached him. With heart beating hard, he waited for her.

When he saw the look on her face, he raised an eyebrow. "*Ja?*"

She scowled up at him. "What was that about?"

He regarded her with amusement. "What was what about?"

"You know. You were playing matchmaker, telling Ike that I'd make some man a wonderful wife. Why? You know I hate that."

He saw her eyes fill and his heart gave a lurch, although he knew her tears were of anger, not sadness. "You wanted a man like Ike to wed. I thought I'd help by telling the truth."

"By trying to sell me with fancy words and too much praise for my cooking?" she challenged.

"Annie—"

"I didn't appreciate it, Jacob. If I'm meant to marry Ike, then it will be God's will and mine. Not *Mam's* and yours!" She turned then and stomped toward the house.

"Annie!" he called out. She froze in her tracks but didn't turn around. "'Tis *not* my will that you marry Ike," he told her.

She turned and stared at him. "What *do* you want, Jacob?" The memory of their shared kiss hung in the air between them. When he didn't immediately answer, Annie sighed. "I should get back."

Watching her leave, he felt an overwhelming surge of love. She was always beautiful to him, but she never looked more so than with fire in her blue eyes and her hands planted firmly on her hips. He wanted to follow her, take her into his arms and kiss her until she was breathless.

"Annie!" he called as she climbed the porch steps, but she didn't stop. She disappeared inside, leaving him yearning for her company and her love, and regretting that he'd kissed her, then stayed away.

Jacob returned to the shop and went to work, but he had trouble concentrating. After dropping the hot piece of metal three times, he set the unfinished object on the worktable and put away his tools. Then he left the shop and Horseshoe Joe's farm. He needed to think, to put distance between him and Annie Zook—and quickly.

Chapter Fifteen

"Annie, did you wash the kitchen curtains?" *Mam* asked the following Friday.

"*Ja, Mam*. And hung them on the line." Annie smiled. "And I dusted all of the furniture, and Barbara did the floors," she said, anticipating her mother's next question. Her mother and sister and she were preparing for this visiting Sunday's company.

Annie could tell that her mother was running a list of chores through her mind. She approached, put a hand on her shoulder. "*Mam*, what's wrong? You know that we're always more than ready whenever we host visiting Sunday. It's not as if our entire church community will be visiting. Only some of our closest friends and neighbors."

Mam sighed and rubbed a hand across her eyes. She appeared worried as she met Annie's gaze. "I'm concerned about your *grossmudder*. She hasn't been herself again lately. Earlier this morning, she fell."

Annie became alarmed. "Did she hurt herself?"

"She's bruised and sore. I fear she is failing again." *Mam* captured Annie's hand with her own. "I think she needs to see a doctor."

An *Englisher*, Annie thought. After her father's accident, her mother would be as worried about the expense of the doctor's visit as she was concerned about *Grossmudder's* health.

"Things will be fine," she told her mother. "The Lord will watch over *Grossmudder* and all of us."

Mam's expression softened. "Annie, you are a joy to me," she said. "All of you *kinner* are." She squeezed Annie's hand and then released it. "But you have been the strength in this family since your *vadder's* accident. I shudder to think what might have happened if not for your quick thinking after he fell."

Annie waved away the praise. "I ran for help. It was Jacob Lapp who got *Dat* the help he needed." *Jacob*. She hadn't seen him since he'd come into the house when Ike King had stopped by to return her mother's soup bowl. Had he worked in the shop yesterday?

Did she care? In truth, she was still angry with him. He had embarrassed her in front of Ike, much as her mother had done with Joseph, Levi and Reuben. And he'd kissed her simply because she was there and available. That's what hurt the most. That he could so easily play with her emotions and then dismiss her.

Anger is a sin. She said a silent prayer, asking for the Lord's forgiveness, seeking His guidance with Jacob.

Her thoughts turned to Barbara and Levi. She and Barbara had encountered Levi in town when they'd run an errand for *Mam*. She had made all of the purchases while her sister and Levi had spent a few precious moments together. Recalling her sister's expression during the ride home, Annie grinned.

Her mother, she realized, was studying her carefully. "Why are you grinning?"

"Barbara and I saw Levi Stoltzfus in the store yesterday. I'm remembering how happy Barbara looked on the way home."

Mam looked pleased. "Levi is *gut* for your sister."

Annie nodded. *And me? Who is the man for me?* "About *Grossmudder*, I think we should bring her here."

"She'll want to clean *haus* with us," *Mam* warned as she rubbed her temple.

"The *haus* is clean," she reminded her. "She can arrange the desserts on plates for us."

Her mother smiled. "That's a wonderful idea." She paused. "Annie—" *Mam* added as Annie opened the back screen door.

She halted and faced her. *"Ja, Mam?"*

"Jacob Lapp is a *fine, young* man," her mother said, surprising her.

"He's been *kind* to all of us."

"And you especially," she said softly.

Annie felt a flash of heat. "He's just a friend."

"Ja. A friend." Her brow furrowed as *Mam* looked contemplative.

Annie sensed her concern. *"Ja*, he is." *Was*, she thought. And she was foolish enough to want him to be more. She released a breath. "Ike King will be coming tomorrow. He, too, is a *gut* man."

"It was kind of him to return my soup bowl before Sunday," *Mam* said.

"Ja," Annie agreed as she continued on. "I'll be right back with *Grossmudder*."

As she walked the distance between the main farmhouse and the *dawdi haus*, Annie thought of Jacob Lapp. Her mother suspected that there might be something more than friendship between her and Jacob. How wrong could she be? Jacob had been right when he'd told her that her mother wouldn't approve of him as anything more than her friend. *Mam* saw Jacob only as a man without the financial means to support a wife and family.

Annie swallowed hard. He had asked if she trusted him. She had trusted him, but no more. He had played with her affections and then…nothing.

If only things were different… She released a small sob as she reached the *grosseldre's* house. Annie paused on the front steps to wipe her eyes. After several deep breaths, she stood up straight, then knocked on her *grossmudder's* door.

"Annie says she likes Ike, but I'm beginning to think she prefers Jacob." Miriam Zook looked worried as she confided in her husband.

Horseshoe Joe shrugged. "What's wrong with Jacob?" He rose from his chair and noted that his previously injured leg felt stronger. "Jake is a *hard-working, young* man who loves our daughter, and Ike— Well, he is a kind man, but he is too old for Annie."

"But she wants an older husband." His wife reached out to steady him.

Joe shook his head. "I need to learn to get around on my own, Miriam." When his wife nodded and stepped back as if stung, Joe softened his expression and his tone. "'Tis not that I don't need you, but I need to do this by myself." He gazed at her lovingly. There was no one else in the house at the moment, a rare thing when parents had teenage and older children who lived with them.

Miriam smiled and walked with him as he hobbled to the kitchen.

"Does Annie really want an older man? Or does she

want young Jacob?" Joe asked as they entered the room. "She can't want both."

"She needs someone who can take care of her." She put the coffeepot on the stove to heat. "Jacob cannot provide for her."

Joe lowered himself gingerly into a kitchen chair and watched her work. "You underestimate him, Miriam. He is a Lapp, after all."

She set out two cups and waited by the table for the coffee to percolate. "Ike has a *haus* and farmland, and he needs a wife and a family. Annie would be *gut* for him," she insisted.

Joe grabbed her arm as she moved toward the counter. "But will Ike be *gut* for Annie? Would she truly be happy as his wife?" He released her and she stared at him. "She doesn't look at Ike the way you gaze at me, dearest."

She scowled, although she seemed pleased by his endearment. "She will learn to love him." She reached for the sugar and then fetched the cream from the refrigerator.

"And that is what you want for her? Someone she must *learn* to love?" He sighed. "Annie is afraid to love. Whether or not the man is older makes no difference. If she loves again, she will be hurt if things don't work out as they should."

"What would you have me do?" she asked.

"Allow things to take their natural course. If Annie is meant to be with Ike, then so shall she be. If she wants Jacob, then let God's will be done."

As his wife poured his coffee, Joe hoped that Miriam would stop interfering in his middle daughter's love life. Jacob had become a fine man, and Joe loved him as one of his own. He'd cautioned his wife about playing matchmaker to any of their children, but that didn't mean he couldn't ask the Lord for a little help. Jacob and Annie had barely spoken to each other. That had to change soon.

While he drank his coffee and enjoyed time alone with his wife, Joe pushed an idea to the back of his mind. Later, after supper, Joe stepped outside for a breath of fresh air. Soon, the winter weather would set in, and they would be locked inside the warmth of the house except for those times when farm chores drove them into the bitter cold.

November was the month of weddings. He would enjoy seeing Annie happily wed, but to only one man. Jacob Lapp.

His leg pained him, a sure sign that it was going to rain or that a full moon was imminent. Joe moved from the porch railing and limped over to sit on a rocker. *Weather is about to change*, he thought.

"Lord, what do You think?" he said. "Could You help me make two young people happy?"

Joe knew with certainty that Jacob Lapp was in love with Annie, despite the fact that Jacob had gone out of his way to avoid her in recent days. And somehow he knew that Annie loved Jake, despite her willingness to spend time with Ike King.

When it came down to it, if Ike proposed, would Annie accept and follow through?

Joe put it all in God's hands.

On Sunday morning, Annie came out of the house as the first visitors arrived. She smiled at her father, who sat on a porch rocker watching as a buggy pulled into the yard. "'Tis a lovely day," she said.

"*Ja.* Hope the weather holds out. Hard to tell with the way this leg is hurting me."

Annie frowned. "Do you need a pain pill?"

"You know I don't like to take pills. I had to after the surgery, but this—" He rubbed along the area of the repaired bone. "I can deal with this ache. Might have to learn to live with it. Only the Lord knows if it will fade in time."

"*Dat,*" Annie said with concern, "it will get better, I'm sure of it."

Joe regarded her with affection as he reached over to pet Millie, who rested near his chair. "If you're sure of it, then I believe." He jerked his head in the direction of the Hershbergers—Annie's aunt and cousins—who had left their buggy and were approaching the house. "You'd best put Millie upstairs," he said, and Annie hurried to obey, returning in time to greet her aunt and cousins.

Her Aunt Alta was a *gut* soul, but at times, she could be trying, Annie thought. She didn't always think before she spoke and when that happened, someone's feelings were often unintentionally hurt.

"Alta," *Dat* greeted as Annie waved her cousins inside. Neither daughter was wed or being courted. Annie wondered with amusement if the men who liked her cousins feared having Alta as a mother-in-law. "*Mam* has tea and coffee ready. Would you like a cup?"

"I'll have coffee," Mary said.

"Make that two," Sally replied.

Annie looked at her cousins and thought how much they resembled their mother, as Alta might have been when, as a young girl, she'd fallen in love with *Mam's* brother John. From what her *grossmudder* told her, Alta's love for John had made her breathtakingly lovely in her joy. But after John died tragically at the young age of twenty-eight, Alta had been devastated. She had gone into mourning, from which she nearly hadn't emerged. It was only the fact that her two fatherless daughters had desperately needed her that Alta had pulled herself from the depths of despair and gone on to care for them with love and affection. The loss of her husband had stolen something vital in Alta's life. She had not remarried and had become a busybody, eager to gossip about neighbors and friends. The nattering wasn't malicious, not intentionally, Annie thought, but everyone knew not to tell Alta anything in confidence.

Annie smiled inwardly as she gave coffee to each of her cousins. On the other hand, if there was news that someone was eager to share, Alta was the one to tell, for then everyone in Happiness would know within forty-eight hours.

"Do you know who's coming today?" Mary asked. She sipped from her coffee as she waited for Annie's reply.

"The Kings, the Lapps and the Bylers," Annie began. "*Ach*, and the Masts and the Troyers." Annie tried to think of who else had promised to visit, but couldn't recall.

"Will the preacher come?" Sally asked.

"*Ja.*" Of that, Annie had no doubt, especially when she thought of the last time she'd seen Barbara and Levi Stoltzfus together. She didn't believe that Levi would pass up an opportunity to spend time with her sister.

"Why don't we go outside while the weather is still warm?" Annie suggested.

After agreeing, Sally and Mary took their coffee and followed Annie out onto the covered front porch. A large family buggy had parked next to the Hershbergers, and

Abram and Charlotte Peachy along with their children stepped out.

"Ach, ja!" Annie exclaimed. "And the Abram Peachys."

Sally grinned. "Obviously."

Another gray buggy pulled up in the yard. "Isn't that Ike King?" Mary said.

Annie nodded when the kind man took notice of her and waved. "Excuse me, cousins," she said, forcing herself to greet him with a smile. *"Hallo,* Ike."

Samuel Lapp drove his family buggy down the dirt lane toward the Joseph Zook farmhouse. "Do we have everyone?"

"A little late to ask, don't ya think, *Dat?"* Eli sounded amused. "We're already here."

As his mother and siblings chuckled, Jacob exchanged smiles with his twin brother. His amusement promptly faded as he recalled seeing Annie with Ike King, laughing and talking in Miriam's kitchen the other day. Seeing Ike sitting so comfortably at the table had made him realize that Annie might have found her match.

The teasing comments between his family members continued, but Jacob was lost in his own thoughts. Eli tapped him on the shoulder through the open window. Jacob was surprised to realize that everyone had left the vehicle except him.

Eli eyed him with a frown. "What is wrong?"

Jacob shook his head. "I shouldn't be here."

"Annie." His brother sighed. "I told you it was dangerous for you to be in her company. You love her, and now you're hurting. What has she done now?"

He paused. "She's decided on Ike King."

Eli raised his eyebrows. "Amos's brother?" He gestured toward the door, reminding Jacob that he needed to get out of the buggy.

Jacob took the hint and climbed down. "*Ja*, Amos's brother. A *widower*."

"I find it difficult to believe." Eli started toward the house, and reluctantly, Jacob fell into step with him.

"Believe it," Jacob said. "I've seen them together—more than once."

Eli shrugged. "You've seen me with Mary Hershberger, and there is nothing between us."

Jacob felt as if his feet were made of lead as he continued on. "Mary is not interested in you. She likes Joseph Byler, and you know that. Ike *is* interested in Annie Zook, and Annie seems to be comfortable with him. She wants to marry an older man."

Eli was shaking his head. "*Nay*, I think not."

"You wait and see for yourself," Jacob challenged him. "I know Annie Zook."

"How often have you seen her since you hurt your hand?" Eli asked.

"The past couple of times I worked, she never once came out to talk or visit."

"You haven't exactly encouraged her."

Jacob readjusted his hat. "I kissed her."

"You *what*?"

"It happened after the singing. The time seemed right, but then it all went wrong."

"What did she say afterward?" Eli asked.

Jacob frowned. "Nothing. We didn't have a chance to discuss it."

"You kissed her and then stayed away? That was foolish, Jake." His twin knew him too well.

"I know." He spied a group of men in the side yard and switched directions. Eli followed his lead. "But it's too late now."

"Is it? You love this woman, but you avoid her after one kiss. What are you waiting for? To be miserable after she marries someone else?"

The thought of Annie marrying Ike made Jacob sick inside. "I can't tell her. I missed my chance." He felt as if he were twelve again and heartbroken after having learned that Annie was in love with Jedidiah, his eldest brother. "If I'm wrong about her feelings for Ike, I'll know soon enough and then I'll tell her how I feel. If I'm right, I'll keep my distance. I want her to be happy, even if it means losing her."

"You're a fool, Jacob."

A fool for Annie, Jacob thought. "Wait until you fall in love, Eli. Until then, don't judge me."

Eli halted, put a hand on Jacob's shoulder. "I'm not judging you, Jake. I want you to be happy with her. It frustrates me that you won't do anything, and I can't help you."

Jacob gave him a wry smile. "I'm sorry, Eli. I'm not myself."

"*Ja*, you are, and I admire you for it. You think I don't want a wife of my own? A home? A family? I want all of those things, but I'm not ready yet."

"When you meet the right woman, you'll be ready," Jacob said with conviction.

His brother grinned at him. "Then what are *you* waiting for?"

As they joined the men, the back door to the farmhouse opened and Annie Zook stepped outside with Ike

King. Jacob elbowed his brother, nodded in the couple's direction.

Eli frowned. "Maybe it's not as it seems."

Jacob felt a burning in his stomach. "And maybe it is." He couldn't tear his gaze away. Annie happened to glance over in his direction, and their gazes locked a moment before she looked away.

"There's *Dat*," Eli said, grabbing hold of his arm. "Let's join him and the others. It looks like we'll be dining outside today since the weather has taken a delightful turn."

He knew his brother was trying to distract him. Jacob tore his gaze away, feeling battered and bruised. His heart was aching. How could he have allowed it to happen?

Because love just happens. Love was a gift from God, which should be cherished for all the small, memorable moments he'd enjoyed with Annie, even if he wasn't meant to have her for a lifetime, as his wife.

"Come on, Jake," Eli urged.

He hadn't realized that he'd hesitated. Jacob nodded and continued on.

Eli looked at him with concern. "You will find some other woman to make you happy."

But would he? Jacob didn't think so. He believed he'd never love anyone as much as he loved Annie. If he didn't act now, he would lose all hope of having her. He had to do something, but what?

Chapter Sixteen

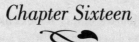

"I'd like to take you around my property sometime," Ike said as he accompanied Annie outside. "Show you my *haus*. You've seen the kitchen. I'd like you to see the rest of it."

Annie looked at him. "And Barbara?"

His hesitation was barely visible, but Annie noticed. "*Ja*, Barbara, too." He softened his tone. "But it is *you* I want to have see everything."

Ike's words gave her a jolt. The man apparently was interested in her, and she should be happy, for he was the kind of man who would make her a good husband, yet...

Her thoughts turned to Jacob Lapp. Could she settle for Ike if her heart belonged to Jacob? Ike was still talking, telling her about all the things he wanted her to see. Annie nodded, smiled and barely heard him as she looked over at Jacob, who had captured her attention. Jacob Lapp walked with his brother Eli toward the gathering of men. He turned and they locked gazes. Annie felt a rush of heat. Embarrassed to be caught staring, she could only imagine the look in the man's bright eyes.

"And I wanted your opinion on a new mare I purchased…" Ike said, but Annie was distracted by Jacob. "…I know you will have much to do in the *haus*."

Annie stiffened. "I will have to check with *Mam*," she said, "I have my chores to do."

Ike looked puzzled. "*Ja*. I know you do a lot in your family's *haus*. I wouldn't ask you to neglect your chores." He regarded her closely and frowned. "Annie, aren't you well?"

She felt an overwhelming burst of relief. He hadn't been talking about her working in *his* house. If that was the case, then she would have panicked—it would have been happening all too soon.

She saw Jacob and Eli Lapp had joined the men. Her heart skipped a beat. Jacob was deep in conversation with his father and brother. Abram Peachy and Amos King, Abram's father-in-law and Ike's brother, approached and joined in the conversation.

As if following the direction of her gaze, Ike said, "I'll leave you to the women. I will visit with the men."

Annie nodded, relieved to see him go, when only a short while ago, she'd been glad to welcome him. She should be enjoying every moment spent in Ike's company, but she found herself distracted, her thoughts returning again and again to the younger man with dark hair and golden eyes, the man who had kissed her and made her fall in love.

"Annie!" her mother's voice called from the doorway.

"Coming, *Mam*!" She ran inside, glad to have something to do to take her mind off Ike King and Jacob Lapp. Why couldn't she stop thinking of Jacob when her goal of finding an older sweetheart was within reach?

The kitchen was filled with women as Annie stepped into the room.

"I thought we could eat outside," *Mam* told her, "but your *dat's* leg has been hurting." She smiled. "He's become a *gut* weather forecaster. He said it will rain or there will be a full moon."

"Ja," Aunt Alta said, "my hip has been bothering me. It will rain."

Annie greeted the women. When she approached Charlotte, the young woman smiled and introduced Martha Schrock, her brother-in-law Eli's cousin.

"She has come to visit from Indiana," Charlotte said.

Annie smiled and welcomed Martha, a dark-haired, unmarried woman in her mid-twenties. She was a plain woman without a husband, according to Aunt Alta. *Will I be like her if I don't marry Ike?* "You're staying with Sarah and Eli."

"Ja," Martha said. "I haven't seen Eli since he was a boy. I am enjoying my time here."

As she carried on a conversation with the woman, Annie recognized God's light in her. She might be plain, but there was something about her brown eyes, her warm smile and her ability to listen. Martha looked and paid attention to her as if she were the only one in the room.

"I'm glad you could be here today," Annie said.

"Danki," Martha replied.

When her mother called to her from the gathering room, Annie gave Martha a look of apology. "Coming," she called. "No doubt she wants me to set up a table so we can put out the food."

"May I help?" Martha seemed eager for something to do.

"That would be wonderful." Annie entered the room with Martha.

"There you are," *Mam* said. "*Gut. Hallo*, Martha, have you come to help?"

Martha nodded, and Annie's mother quickly instructed where she wanted the furniture arranged. With Martha's help, Annie shifted a table to another area of the room. "I hope it is not too heavy."

Martha smiled. *"Nay."* After they set it down, the woman held up her hands. They were large hands for a woman, and clearly she had done her share of hard work.

"Let's get the other one," Annie said.

Martha nodded. When the tables were in their proper place, according to *Mam*, Annie smiled and said, "Let's get something to drink before we put out the food." Martha agreed as she trailed her back into the kitchen.

Annie and the other women had put out all the food when the men arrived to eat first, as was custom on Sundays. If they had chosen to dine outside, then families might have sat down together. They had shared tables on Church and visiting Sundays before. It was up to the preacher, and since Levi Stoltzfus said nothing about relaxing the custom this Sunday, Annie, Martha and the other women, along with the children, waited for their turn.

Annie became aware of Jacob as he entered the room. He captured her gaze as he walked by. "Annie," he said, but Annie noticed that he didn't smile.

She felt a tightening in her throat as she whispered, "Jacob."

Ike King, on the other hand, grinned at her as he passed by her to take his seat. Conscious of Jacob and Ike, Annie left the gathering room with its makeshift bench tables and bench seats. In the kitchen, Katie Lapp and her two daughters-in-law, Sarah and Rachel, were enjoying a cup of tea while they waited for the men to finish.

"I prefer it when we all eat together," Katie said, and the other women agreed.

Jacob's young sister, Hannah, burst into the kitchen. She and the other children had been outside, playing in the yard. "*Mam*, is it almost time to eat?"

"*Ja*, Hannah, but you must be patient," Katie said. She glanced past her daughter to the window. "Where are your *bruders*?"

"Daniel and Isaac are inside with *Dat*," she said. "Joseph is outside with me."

Katie's lips twitched. "Will you tell Joseph to come inside?"

Hannah's golden head nodded vigorously.

"Are Will and Elam outside?" Josie asked of her two young sons.

"*Ja*. I can get them, too," Hannah said.

Josie exchanged smiles with Katie as the child ran back to round up her playmates. "She is growing fast, Katie."

Annie agreed. She longed to have a child like Hannah, wanted to have a large number of them.

Her thoughts returned to Ike and Jacob. Ike liked her. Should she allow him to court her if he asked?

It was Jacob who made her feel alive. She imagined him holding their child, and pictured him running in the yard, chasing their *kinner*. The image was wonderful—and out of her reach. What was she doing with Ike King?

She frowned. *Because I don't know what Jacob's intentions are?*

Her mother broke into her thoughts. "Annie, would

you check to see if your *dat* or any of the men need anything?"

"Ja, Mam." Annie headed toward the gathering room, thoughts of Jacob whirling in her head.

"Do *ya* mind if I come?" Martha asked shyly.

"Not at all." Annie moved aside to allow her room.

The men had finished eating and were starting to rise from the tables.

"Is there anything else you need?" Annie asked. "Dessert? Or would you like it later?" Most of the men chose to wait.

Ike King approached with a smile. "Annie, the meal was delicious."

"I'm glad you enjoyed it." Annie felt slightly uncomfortable with his praise. She pulled Martha forward and introduced her. "She's Eli Schrock's cousin."

Ike inclined his head and offered her a smile. *"Hallo.* A pleasure to meet you."

Martha beamed.

Annie left Ike and Martha to talk, and moved to pick up dishes and plates and ready the dining area for the women and younger children.

She was engrossed in the task and didn't realize that someone had approached from behind. Then she felt an odd tingling at the base of her neck, and she turned. Jacob Lapp stood a few feet away, watching her.

"Jacob!" she gasped.

"Annie." His voice was quiet, his expression unreadable. "Are you angry with me?"

She stilled for a moment, then shook her head.

He raised an eyebrow. "I saw you with Ike again." He gave her a crooked smile. "Are you going to marry him?"

Annie felt flustered. She loved Jacob and fought to

hide it. She wanted to tell him, but she was afraid. She'd never felt this way before—not with Jedidiah and certainly not with Ike. "Ike is a nice man."

Jacob nodded. He turned toward a window to watch the children playing in the yard. Annie couldn't keep her eyes off him. The sight of him stole her breath. He wore his Sunday best and his long-sleeved white shirt emphasized his arms, reminding her of the way they moved as he worked in her father's shop. He was taller than her, but not too tall. She couldn't tell by his features what he was thinking.

"Ike is kind," Jacob finally said. He hesitated, turned from the window to face her. "But is he truly the man for you?"

She looked down, afraid to answer him lest he see the truth of her feelings for him in her eyes. Her attention focused on his injured hand. The burned area was healed but still red. "Your burn looks better." She had the strong urge to gently take hold of his hand, smooth her finger over the scar. When Jacob didn't answer, Annie looked up and found him studying her curiously. His intense gaze gave her goose bumps. "Do I have a mark on my nose?" she asked.

His lips twitched. *"Nay."* His gaze caressed her face. "You didn't answer my question about Ike."

She raised her chin. "And I'm not going to."

He sighed and glanced out the window. "I should go. Eli is waiting for me." He faced her. "Annie, I want you to know that I am happy for you. I wish you and Ike all the best," he said.

Nay, she cried silently. *I don't want Ike. I want you!* Her sister had said, *Why don't you tell him?* Barbara was right. What did she have to lose?

"Jacob!" He was at the door when she called out. He stopped and turned, his expression closed off. She shook her head, afraid to continue. There were others around; this wasn't the time or place. "I will call you when dessert is ready."

His brow cleared, but his expression didn't soften. He continued outside to join his brother, and Annie watched him with tears in her eyes but made no attempt to stop him. She crossed through the house to the front porch. Her father was seated on a rocker, rubbing his sore leg.

"*Dat*, what are you doing out here by yourself?"

He gestured for her to sit on the rocking chair next to his. "I needed to rest this leg." He looked at the clear sky. "I still think it's going to rain." He turned back to her, and Annie blushed. Could he tell she'd been crying? Would he ask why?

If he'd noticed, he didn't say as he gazed out over the barnyard. "Can I get you anything?"

"*Nay.*" He sighed.

Jacob and Eli came into their line of vision as they walked to their buggy. Watching Jacob, Annie drew a sharp breath. She sensed when her father looked at her, and she smiled as she faced him. He didn't need to know that she'd foolishly fallen in love with Jacob Lapp.

She pretended indifference as Jacob stood near the family buggy while Eli reached into the back and pulled out a ball. Eli held it up and shouted. Suddenly, a group of children came barreling toward him from the side yard.

Eli laughed and ran while calling out to his twin. He tossed the ball to Jacob, and as he reached for it, Jacob fell. The children piled on top of him. Annie gasped, but her father only chuckled. Soon, children were tossed this way and that as Jacob rose with ball still clutched under his arm.

There were shouts of glee and laughter as the children chased Jacob around the yard. He shouted for his older brother Noah to join in. Soon, all the older Lapp siblings were involved in playing catch over the children's heads. Jacob caught the ball and pretended to drop it. When his youngest brother Joseph grabbed it, Jacob picked up the little boy and threatened to toss Joseph with the ball while he ran. The little boy's giggles were sweet to Annie's ears.

Annie smiled as she watched them. Seeing Jacob having fun with the children, hearing his laughter made her think of things she wanted but couldn't have. Jacob as her husband playing with their children, flashing her smiles of love and joy whenever he glanced toward her, which was often.

Disturbed by her thoughts, she concentrated on the good time before her. She laughed at some of Jacob's antics, gasped when a group of youngsters shoved him to the ground.

"They are having fun," Joe said. "If it wasn't for this leg, I'd join them."

Annie looked at him with surprise. "You would?"

Joe nodded. *"Ja."* He paused as if choosing his words carefully, "Annie, Ike King—"

She stiffened. "What about him?"

"He's headed this way." *Dat* held her glance. "There is something I need to show you in the shop. Do you want to talk with him first?"

"Now?" she asked with raised eyebrows.

"Ja." Her father rose and reached for his cane. "But we can go later if you need time with Ike."

Annie noted Ike's purposeful strides as he crossed the

yard. She didn't particularly want to talk with him right now. She met her father's gaze. "I'll go with you." Her father looked pleased. "I'll tell *Mam*."

Dat shook his head. "*Nay*, no need. She's busy with her friends." He rose and took several steps on his sore leg, grimacing with each one.

"Wait here," she told him.

"Annie—"

"I'll be right back." She hurried inside for his wheel-chair. When she returned, she found her father talking with Ike.

Looking pleased at her approach, Ike smiled. "I told your *dat* about our scheduled ride through my property."

Had they scheduled a ride? Annie glanced from Ike to her father, then back to Ike. Her father's expression hid his thoughts. "Ike, *Dat* needs me right now," she said. "Can we talk later?"

Ike blinked. "*Ja*, of course." Then he smiled. "When you are done, come and find me."

"Why did you bring that?" *Dat* asked of the wheel-chair.

Annie maneuvered the chair so that he could sit down. "You're in pain, and I thought you should rest your leg awhile longer."

Without argument, he sat in the wheelchair. "Let's go before someone else delays us. I want to get back in time to watch the children play horseshoes."

Annie noted the game's pegs some distance away from each other on the lawn. She pushed her father across the yard until they reached the shop, where she left the wheel-chair to open the door. When she returned to guide him inside, her father raised a hand to stop her. "I can man-age," he said. He pushed himself into the smithy.

"Would you please open up the back window? The day is nice enough, and for now there is plenty of light."

Annie obeyed, then waited for further instructions.

Her father gestured toward a shelf. "The notebook. Would you get it for me?"

Annie reached for the book and silently handed it to him. "Is something wrong?

"*Nay*, daughter." He opened the book and smiled up at her. "Everything is right. Come around. I want to show you this."

Annie frowned as she shifted to his side. "What is it?"

"A listing of all the work that Jacob has done while I've been recovering. Since he stepped in to help, business at the blacksmithy has been better than ever."

At the mention of Jacob, Annie felt warmth skitter across her skin. "He has done well for you. That is *gut*," she said, trying not to give away her thoughts.

"*Ja.* So well that I am going to ask him if he will stay and work with me. Jacob seems to enjoy it, and I like having him here."

Annie struggled to hide a rush of heat brought on by his name. "You want him to work here permanently?"

Her father watched her closely. "*Ja.*" He gestured about the shop. "It looks organized, doesn't it? He leaves it as neat as a pin when he's done. I like that. And the business is profitable. Josiah has never been interested in blacksmithing. And Peter? It's hard to tell, but Jacob— he wanted to learn from early on."

Feeling restless, Annie wandered about, touching tools and work spaces—the table, vise and anvil. Everywhere she looked, she saw not only her father working here but now Jacob, moving about the shop, working with fire and metal.

"Have you asked him yet?" she said, feeling shaky.

"Nay." He smiled. "I wanted your opinion first."

Annie widened her gaze. "Mine? Why?"

"I value your judgment."

She was so stunned she couldn't answer him. It was unusual that a father would value his daughter's thoughts. She was pleased that he felt this way. She considered her father's decision. If *Dat* believed that Jacob should stay on, then who was she to say *nay*?

"If you think Jacob should stay, then I think he should," she said.

Her father sighed and maneuvered himself out of the chair, grimaced then sat again. "Annie."

"Ja, Dat?"

"Ike King is interested in you. I believe he sees you as his future wife."

"He's a nice man," she said carefully.

"But do you want to marry him?"

Annie didn't want to answer, but she knew she must. "He is the kind of man I'd hoped to marry."

"So you will agree to become his wife?"

Annie opened her mouth and then closed it. She thought of her love for Jacob, and she began to cry. "Why is this so hard? Ike is the man I *should* marry, but—"

"You're in love with Jacob Lapp," her father said quietly.

Startled, she stared at him. *"Ja,"* she whispered. "Is my love for him that obvious?" She sniffed and wiped her eyes. *"Dat,* how can I continue to love a man who has no interest in me? I thought if I avoided handsome men, I'd be safe, but I can't help loving Jacob—"

Her father smiled and patted her arm. "There is nothing wrong with loving Jacob."

She nodded, her eyes overflowing. "Except that he doesn't return my love. It's like Jed all over again. Will I ever learn? Only I love Jacob more than anything, more than I ever loved Jedidiah."

"Why not tell him?" *Dat* asked.

"*Nay!* I can't. I don't want to be hurt again. And it is not up to a woman to tell a man she loves him…not when he hasn't told her of his love."

Her father sighed. "You and Jacob are both stubborn as mules." He rose from his wheelchair and hobbled over to a wall cabinet where he kept supplies and specially crafted tools. Stretching to the top shelf with a loud groan, he grabbed something and took it down.

"Here," he said as he extended the metal box to her.

"What is it?"

"Take a look."

Annie took the box out of her father's hands. She turned to study it from every side. "It looks like it was made in the shop." Baffled, she met her *dat's* gaze. "It's pretty. Why did you want me to see it?"

The container was crudely made but there was something endearing about it. It was lovely but it didn't appear to have been made by him recently. She softened her expression. "You made this for *Mam* when you were younger?" She felt warmth inside at the love her father must have felt for her mother at such a young age to have made such a gift.

"*Nay.* Take a look on the bottom," her father instructed.

Annie carefully turned it over, saw that something had been scratched into the surface—"Jacob and Annie," inside the shape of a heart.

Annie felt an overwhelming rush of feeling. "Jacob made this for me?" she whispered.

Her father smiled. "*Ja.* When he was younger. Jacob made that during the months he worked in the shop with me."

Annie clutched the box to her breast. "I don't understand."

"How can you marry Ike when you love Jacob?"

Tears filling her eyes again, Annie shook her head. "I can't. How can I marry without love?" she sobbed. "I love Jacob, but I don't know how he really feels about me." She drew a shuddering breath. "I thought that maybe he cared, but then…something happened." *His kiss.* "And suddenly he was avoiding me. He once asked if I trusted him, and I did, but then he changed, and I didn't know what to think."

"Jacob is trustworthy. Why don't you talk with him?" her father said. "Show him the box. See what he says." He captured her hand. "Maybe he is as unsure of you as you are of him. Annie, don't wait. Do it now."

Should she risk all and talk with him? What if he didn't love her? *What if he does?* She'd be foolish if she did nothing. "I'll talk with him," she promised.

"Thanks be to God," she thought she heard her father murmur as she left the shop.

Chapter Seventeen

Annie saw Jacob purposefully striding in her direction as she exited the barn into the autumn sunshine. She saw his determined look and grew concerned.

"Annie!" he called as he crossed the yard. "We need to talk!"

She lifted a hand and waved. "Jacob!"

She heard a child's wild cry and saw a horseshoe flying toward Jacob. It happened so fast there was nothing she could do but watch as the curved piece of metal connected with the back of Jacob's head. The thud against his flesh propelled her forward. She screamed and ran to him.

"Jacob!" Crouching beside him, she cupped his face. "Jacob? Talk to me. Are you all right?" She leaned closer, felt his breath fan her cheek and knew the tiniest bit of relief.

"Jacob," she urged, "you're scaring me. We do need to talk."

His eyelashes flickered.

"Annie." Eli stood behind her. "Is he all right?"

She looked up with tears in her eyes. "I don't know!

He has to be! There is something important I need to tell him, that I love him—" She glanced back as Jacob's eyes opened. He moaned softly and attempted to sit up. She reached to help him, feeling the strength of muscle beneath his shirtsleeve.

"I'm all right." Upright now, he grabbed her hand. "What do you need to tell me?" he asked hoarsely.

Feeling suddenly shy, Annie stood. Grabbing the box from the ground, she hid it against her back. What if her father was wrong?

But what if he was right?

"Eli," she heard him say, "help me up. Annie and I have to talk."

Annie shot him a glance. "Jacob—"

He stood, grimacing, but there was a look in his glazed golden eyes that set her heart racing. Jacob held out his hand to her. "Walk with me," he said. She saw him studying her intently. His expression changed as if he'd read her face and liked what he saw.

"Jacob, we shouldn't. You're hurt." Nervous, she backed away.

"Annie, *please*."

She saw the panic in his handsome face, and she relented and took his hand. As his fingers entwined with hers, she experienced a feeling of joy like no other. "Where do you want to go?" she asked huskily.

"Anywhere we can be alone."

Her heart skipped a beat. She nodded toward the fields. "We can walk the farm." She glanced over her shoulder. Her father had wheeled himself back to the gathering. They locked eyes, and she saw his pleased smile.

She and Jacob walked without talking for a time. The

air felt thick with anticipation. Annie waited for Jacob to speak, and when he didn't, she wondered what to say.

"What are you carrying?" Jacob asked after a long moment of silence, referring to the object she had in her other hand.

Annie frowned, realized that she still held the box. She didn't want to pull away. She liked the feel of their hands touching. She stopped, faced him, let go of his hand, but she didn't immediately show him the box. "Jacob, the others will have plenty to say about us walking off alone together."

"Annie, tell me," he asked urgently. "Do you love me?" His golden eyes burned. "Enough to marry me? Or do you still want Ike?"

She inhaled sharply. *Marry him?* She closed her eyes and wondered if she was dreaming. "Jacob, I—"

"What is that behind your back?" His voice was soft, tender. "Show me." She was disarmed by his expression and quiet tone. "Annie?" He gazed at her with his beautiful tawny eyes in a face so handsome that he stole her breath.

She hesitated, then showed him the metal box.

Jacob looked stunned. "Where did you find that?"

"*Dat* gave it to me." His expression worried her. "He took it out of the shop cabinet."

She saw deep emotion contort his expression. "I thought I'd tossed it away."

"Jacob…" she began.

"*Nay,*" he said in a strangled voice. "Do you know what that is?" He turned and moved away.

Annie felt his pain as she crossed the distance between them. "It's a beautiful box," she whispered. "A gift from a young boy to a young girl, who had no idea how he felt about her." She was stunned by the knowledge that Jacob had spent hours as a youth, firing and hammering metal into this precious box for her. She placed a hand on his shoulder. She felt his tremor before he jerked away.

"I was young," he said bitterly, "and I adored you."

"Jacob—" Her heart tripped hard.

"And now you know how I feel."

Annie inhaled sharply. "I love you, Jacob," she whispered.

"Don't marry Ike, Annie. He can't make you happy." Jacob cupped her face. Holding her steady, he kissed her with pent-up feeling.

Annie, her pulse racing wildly now, felt his lips against her mouth and reeled with love for him. When he pulled away, she gazed up with raised eyebrows. Hadn't he heard what she'd admitted? "Jacob—"

"Ike can't—and never will—love you as much as I do."

Annie's heart beat with joy. "And that's why you kissed me?" she asked.

"You truly love me?" he said at the same time, apparently just realizing what she'd said.

Jacob gazed at the woman before him and longed to take her into his arms and prove to her that he would be a better husband than Ike or anyone. Hadn't he loved her since he was twelve? He had fought his feelings, shoved them to the back of his mind after she'd become his older brother Jed's sweetheart. He had known for years that she'd loved Jedidiah with all the passion of a young girl's heart, even before Jed had taken notice of her. But now that she was a woman, and he no longer a boy but a man, they could make it work if they both wanted it.

She didn't say anything at first as she inspected the box, turning it over to read the silly inscription he'd scratched into the metal bottom with a forged nail.

"I don't think anyone has ever made anything more lovely for me," she murmured as she looked up and met his gaze. "And to think that I never knew how you felt."

There was nothing mocking or teasing him about the box, no hint of rejection in her pretty blue eyes. She extended the container toward him, and when he reached for it, Annie grabbed his hand and pulled him close. The keepsake fell to the ground as she cupped his face and pressed her lips against his mouth.

"Jacob Lapp, what am I going to do with you?" she whispered.

Jacob stared at her, swallowed. "Love me?" he suggested hoarsely.

"I do." Annie smiled, warmth radiating from her in thick waves. "Jacob, I can't marry Ike King, even if he asks."

"Why?"

"Because he isn't you." She reached for his hand, raised it to examine the burn. "I was sorry when you hurt yourself. I wanted badly to make it feel better, but there was only so much I could do."

Jacob gazed at her bright face, wondering if he'd heard right when she'd said that she loved him. Had he been dreaming?

"Annie—"

"I love you, Jacob," she said, "and I know now that you love me."

Jacob smiled. "Only as much as a man can love a woman and more." He saw her eyes fill with tears. He frowned. "Annie, what's wrong?"

"I didn't understand. You kissed me and then avoided me."

He nodded as he settled his hands on her shoulders, as his gaze roamed over her lovely face, enjoying every glorious inch of it. She was everything to him. "I was afraid to hope," he admitted. "I wanted more from you, but you seemed determined to stick to your plan."

He heard her sigh.

He lifted a hand from her shoulder to caress her cheek. "Annie Zook, I want to court you and marry you." He frowned. "You will marry me?" She nodded, and he continued, "I don't have much to offer you now. But I will. I'll find a job quickly. I don't want to be apart from you any longer than necessary."

"I'll wait for as long as you need," she promised. "At least now, we know how we feel about each other." She looked as if she had something to say, but then she bit her lip instead. "Jacob, I think we should get back, although I would like nothing more than to be alone with you." He released her and she stepped back.

"Your *dat*—"

"Guessed we love each other." Annie grinned, and Jacob felt the sunshine warmth of her smile.

Walking with her by his side as they approached the house, Jacob felt the true power of God's blessings.

Annie halted suddenly. "Ike," she said.

"Do you want me to talk with him?" he asked. The day had turned cloudy. It looked as if it would rain.

"*Nay*, I should be the one to talk with him," she replied, glancing toward the farmhouse.

Ike was on the front porch talking with Horseshoe Joe.

A drop of moisture fell from the sky, hitting Annie on the nose. Annie glanced toward the darkening clouds. "*Dat* was right. He said it would rain." Her smile for him held love. "The shop window," she said and frowned. "What if *Dat* left it open?"

He touched her arm. "I'll go check," he said. His gaze fell on Ike. "I'll be right back. Wait for me before you go up the house?"

"Ja." She appeared uneasy, as if she dreaded her confrontation with Ike King.

She was still standing where he'd left her when he returned.

"Things will be fine, Annie."

She sighed. "We both know what it's like to be hurt by someone. Ike and I weren't courting, but…"

Jacob focused his gaze on Ike and what he saw made him smile. "Ike will be fine. Look. He seems to have found someone who appears to be fascinated by him." He gestured toward Ike and the woman, who were deep in conversation. Jacob beamed a smile at Annie. "Isn't that Martha Shrock?"

"Ja." Annie returned his grin. "So it is. And she is perfect for Ike."

"Let's go. I need to speak with your *vadder.*" He captured her hand, gave it a gentle squeeze, before he released it.

"I had no idea that you loved me," she whispered as if she still couldn't believe her good fortune as they walked toward the house.

"I didn't realize how affected you were by my kiss," he echoed. He grinned teasingly.

Annie's smile was warm, loving and joyful. "It was a kiss, nothing more."

He accepted her challenge. "You'd better be prepared for more of my kisses—and to marry me."

Annie beamed at him. "I'll marry you and love you forever."

He felt shaky at her declaration of love. He'd never expected to be given such a gift from Annie. Joe Zook rolled down his wheelchair ramp and into the yard.

"There's your *dat*," he said. He grabbed Annie's hand, not caring if everyone saw or what they might think. He loved Annie, and that's all that mattered. "I need to talk with him."

"I think he has something he wants to tell you, too," Annie said. Then, laughing, she ran to keep up with him when he hurried to talk with her father, and the joy in Jacob's heart filled to overflowing.

A while later, Annie asked, "Did my *vadder* talk with you?" She offered a tentative smile.

He nodded. *"Ja."* His expression gave nothing away.

Annie felt a sniggle of concern. "And?"

Jacob grinned suddenly, grabbed her about the waist and spun her around, with his laughter bubbling up to the surface. "I'll be staying to work at the blacksmithy!"

Annie felt breathless as he set her down. "You don't mind?" She stepped back and straightened her prayer *kapp*.

"Nay! I love the work." He gazed lovingly into her blue eyes as he ran his finger over her cheek and chin. "I love you, Anna Marie Zook."

The warmth in his expression, his words, melted her heart. "I love you, Jacob Lapp." She hesitated. "I didn't know how you'd feel about *Dat's* offer of a job. 'Tis not that we must wed in a hurry."

He scowled at her. "Why not wed in a hurry?"

"I—" The teasing gleam in his golden eyes made her giggle.

"I want to marry you now," he said earnestly.

She raised her eyebrows. "Now?"

"As soon as can be arranged."

"Will you marry me this November? I know we haven't courted long."

"I have known you for most of my life. I've been ready to marry you, Jacob, since I first realized I loved you. We should tell our parents—"

"No need to tell yours," Jacob said. "I've asked and been given permission by your parents to court and marry their daughter."

He opened his arms and she slipped into the haven of his embrace. He hugged her close, and Annie knew that her prayers had been answered in the best way possible.

"Where will we live?" she asked.

Jacob smiled. "I have an idea, but I can't tell you yet."

"As long as we're together, I'll be happy," she said. "Will you?"

"*Ja*, Jacob Lapp. You make me very happy."

Epilogue

September, a year later

Annie watched as her husband chased the little girl around the yard until he caught her. Jacob lifted the toddler high, and she giggled. He set her down, and she stumbled away from him laughing. Annie chuckled as she watched Jacob give chase and capture her all over again, much to the child's delight.

"You're going to tire her out before lunch," Annie called out.

"You'll eat before you nap, won't ya, Rachel?" Jacob asked the little girl. He bent down as if to hear the child's whisper. "She said she'll eat and then sleep," he assured his wife.

"But Joan will be coming for her soon." Annie cradled her large belly as she rose from a wooden chair out on the lawn behind their new home. They had lived in the schoolhouse until their house was finished. "She'll expect our niece to have eaten." Her sister and her husband had moved back to Lancaster County, much to the family's delight.

Jacob pouted. Annie laughed as she waddled in his direction. He stood still, his expression warming as he watched her approach. "You look more beautiful every day," he murmured.

Annie beamed at him. "I grow bigger every day."

"Ja," Jacob agreed, "but I couldn't be happier." He placed a hand on her belly. "He moved!" he exclaimed with delight.

She chuckled. "Thank the Lord," she said.

"You've made me happy, Annie, happier than I could have ever imagined." He frowned suddenly as he looked for his niece. When he found her, he grinned and pointed. "I think Rachel decided to take her nap *before* lunch."

Following his direction, Annie saw her little niece curled up on the grass with her eyes closed. "So she did." She smiled affectionately at Jacob. "Do you want to carry her inside or should I?"

He raised his eyebrows. "Not in your condition."

Amused, she watched him tenderly pick up their niece. Jacob had confided that he wanted as many children as she. This wasn't the time, she decided, to remind him that there would be occasions when she'd be large with child, with a little one on her hip. *Jacob, my wonderful husband, will be a* gut vadder. He had made her world complete.

Inside the house, he placed the little girl on their bed. He rose and then met her gaze. "Annie?"

"I love you, Jacob. I'll love you forever."

His golden eyes glowed as he slipped his arms around her. "I love you, Annie, and I will love you beyond my last breath."

* * * * *

BURIED SINS

Marta Perry

This story is dedicated to my Love Inspired sisters,
with thanks for your support.
And, as always, to Brian with much love.

Draw near to God, and God will draw near to you.
—*James* 4:8

Chapter One

She was being followed. Caroline Hampton pulled her wool jacket around her, fingers tight on the Navajo embroidery, but even that couldn't dissipate the chill that worked its way down her spine.

Santa Fe could be cold in early March, but the shiver that touched her had nothing to do with the temperature. She detoured around the tour group in front of the central monument of the plaza. Ordinarily, she might stop there to do a little people-watching, her fingers itching for a pad and a charcoal to capture the scene. But not when she felt that inimical gaze upon her.

Evading a vendor determined to sell her a *carnita,* she hurried across the square, only half her attention on the colors, movement and excitement that she loved about the old city. She was letting her active imagination run wild; that was all. This persistent sense that someone watched her was some odd aftereffect of shock and grief.

She stopped at a magazine stand, picking up a newspaper and pretending to study it as she used it for a screen to survey the crowd. There, see? No one was paying any attention to her, or at least, no more attention than her tousled mass of red curls and artistic flair with clothing usually merited. Everything was fine—

Her heart thudded, loud in her ears. Everything was not fine. The man had stopped at a flower stand but his gaze was fixed on her, not on the mixed bouquet the vendor thrust at him. Short, stocky, probably in his forties, dressed in the casual Western style that was so common here—he looked like a hundred other men in the plaza at this moment.

But he wasn't. She'd spotted him before—when she was leaving the gallery after work, when she returned to the apartment she and Tony had shared overlooking the river.

This wasn't grief, or an overactive imagination. This was real.

She shoved the newspaper back on the rack, hurrying toward the Palace of the Governors. It was bustling with tourists, its entrance turned into a maze by the Native American craftspeople who spread their wares there. She'd lose him in the crowd; she'd go back to the gallery....

But he'd been at the gallery. He knew where she worked, where she lived. The chill deepened. Her fingers touched the cell phone that was tucked inside the top pocket of her leather shoulder bag. Call the police?

Her stomach seemed to turn at that, emerging memories of the moment they'd arrived at her apartment door to tell her that her husband was dead. To ask her questions she couldn't answer about Tony Gibson.

She wound her way among the craftspeople, nodding to some of the regulars. Ask them for help? But what could they do? They'd want to call the police.

The knot in her stomach tightened as her mind skirted

the older, darker memory that lurked like a snake in the recesses of her mind. She wouldn't think of that, wouldn't let herself remember—

She risked a quick look around. The man was no longer in sight. The tour group, apparently released by their guide, flooded to the crafts vendors on a tide of enthusiasm, swamping everything in their path.

All right. She'd slip around the Museum of Fine Arts and make her way to the city lot where she'd left her car. It would be fine. She rounded the corner.

The man stepped from a doorway to grab her arm.

Caroline took breath to scream, jerking against his grip, trying to remember the proper response from the self-defense class she'd taken last winter.

"You don't want to scream." His voice was pitched low enough to hide under the chatter of the passing crowd. Cold eyes, small and black as two ripe olives, narrowed. "Think of all the questions you'd have to answer about Tony if you did."

"Tony." Her mind seemed to skip a beat, then settle on the name. "What do you have to do with my husband? What do you want?"

"Just the answers to a couple of questions." He smiled, nodded, as if they were two acquaintances who'd happened to meet on the street. "We can stay here in full view of the crowds." The smile had an edge, like the faint scar that crossed his cheek. "Then you'll feel safe."

She summoned courage. Act as if you're in control, even if you're not. "Or you can beat it before I decide to scream."

She yanked at her arm. A swift kick to his shins might do it—too bad she didn't have heels on today. She'd—

"Just answer me one thing." His tone turned to gravel,

and his fingers twisted her wrist, the stab of pain shocking her. "Where is Tony Gibson?"

She could only stare at him. "Tony? Tony's dead."

Fresh grief gripped her heart on the words. The fact that Tony hadn't been the man she thought him, had lied from the first moment they'd met—none of that could alter the fact that she grieved for him.

Incredibly, the man smiled. "Nice try. Where is he?" The fingers twisted again on her wrist—her right hand, she'd never be able to finish the project she was working on if he broke it, she—

Think. Focus. She'd pray, but God had deserted her a long time ago.

"I'm telling you the truth. Tony died over two weeks ago. His car went off the road up in the Sangre de Cristo Mountains. Check the papers if you don't believe me. They covered the story."

With a photograph showing the burned-out car that was all that was left of her month-long marriage.

"I saw it. A handy accident is a nice out for a man who'd made Santa Fe too hot to hold him." He sounded almost admiring. "Maybe the others will even buy that. Not me." He leaned closer, and she fought not to show her fear. "Your husband owes me a hundred thousand. I want it. All of it. From him. Or from you."

He released her so suddenly that she nearly fell. She stumbled back a step, rubbing her wrist, trying to find the words that would convince this madman that Tony was dead and that she could no more produce a hundred thousand dollars than she could fly.

"Tell Tony." He moved away, raising his hand in a casual goodbye. "Tell him I'll be in touch."

Before she could speak he was gone, melting away

in the crowd of camera-laden tourists who rounded the corner. She stood, letting them flow past her, forcing her mind to work.

Run. That was all it would say. *That's what you do in a situation like this. You run, you find a new place, you start over.*

As she had when she'd come to Santa Fe. As she always did. She shoved the strap of her bag back on her shoulder and walked quickly in the direction of the car park. She could go north, head for Colorado, get lost in Denver. Or west to LA.

An image formed in her mind, startling her—peaceful green fields dotted with white barns, farmhouses, silos. Gray Amish buggies rattling along narrow roads.

She had a choice. For the first time in years she had a choice. She could choose to run home.

Zachary Burkhalter, Chief of Police, pulled the squad car into his favorite place to watch for drivers speeding through his town. The hardware store shielded him from the view of anyone coming east who was inclined to think the residents of tiny Churchville, Pennsylvania, weren't serious about the twenty-five-miles-per-hour speed limit.

They'd be wrong. One of his charges from the township supervisors was to make sure this isolated section of Lancaster County didn't become a speedway for tourists who were eager to catch a sixty-mile-per-hour glimpse of an Amish wagon or a farmer in black pants and straw hat plowing his field behind a team of horses.

No favors, no leeway, just the law. That was what Zach preferred—a nice, clean-cut line to enforce, with none of the gray fuzziness that so often marred human relationships.

Ruthie, with her mop of brown curls and her huge brown eyes, popped into his head as surely as if she were sitting there. She was almost six now, the light God had brought into his life, and he knew that sooner or later she'd start asking questions about how her parents died. He'd rehearsed his answers a thousand times, but he still wasn't sure they were right. He didn't like not being sure.

A blur of red whizzing past brought his attention back to the present. With something like relief at the distraction, he pulled out onto Main Street in a spray of gravel. He didn't even need to touch the radar for that one. Where did the driver think she was going in such a hurry?

He gave a tiny blare on the siren, saw the woman's head turn as she glanced at the rearview mirror. She flipped on the turn signal and slowed to pull off the road.

He drew up behind her, taking his time. New Mexico license plates—now, there was something you didn't see in Pennsylvania every day. For some reason the image stirred a vague response in his mind, but he couldn't quite place it.

Never mind. It would come. He got out, automatically checking the red compact for anything out of place.

The woman's hair matched her car, swinging past her shoulders in a tangle of curls. She had rolled down the driver's-side window by the time he neared it. Her long fingers tapped on the side mirror, as if she had places to go and people to see, and a silver bangle slid along her left wrist with the movement.

Memorable, that's what she was. He sorted through the computer banks in his mind, filled with all the data anyone could want about his township, and came up with the answer. Caroline Hampton, youngest of the Hampton sisters who owned the Three Sisters Inn, just down the road. The one who lived in New Mexico.

"I wasn't speeding, was I?" She looked up at him, green eyes wide.

So apparently they were going to start with innocence. "I'm afraid you were, ma'am. Can I see your license and registration, please?"

She grabbed the oversize leather bag on the seat next to her and began rummaging through it, her movements quick, almost jerky. Irritation, because he'd caught her speeding? Somehow he didn't think that was it.

So Caroline Hampton had come home again. She'd been at the inn at Christmas. They hadn't been introduced, but he remembered her. Any man would—that wild mane of red curls; the slim, lithe figure; the green eyes that at the moment looked rather stormy.

"Here." She snapped the word as she held out the cards.

His hand almost brushed hers when he took them. And *there* was the thing that set his intuition on alert— her almost infinitesimal recoil from the sleeve of his uniform jacket.

Sometimes perfectly innocent people reacted as if they were serial killers when confronted by the police. It wasn't unusual, but it was something to note.

"How fast was I going? Surely not that much over the speed limit." She tried a smile, but he had the feeling her heart wasn't in it. "I'm afraid I didn't see the sign."

Amusement touched him at the effort. He didn't let it show, of course. He had the official poker face down pat, but even if he hadn't, generations of his Pennsylvania Dutch forebears had ensured that his stolid expression didn't give away much.

"The speed limit drops to twenty-five when you enter Churchville, Ms. Hampton."

Funny. In spite of some superficial resemblance, she wasn't much like her sisters. Andrea, the efficient businesswoman; Rachel, the gentle nurturer. He'd come to know them over the past year, to consider them acquaintances, if not close enough to be friends.

"You know who I am." Those jewel-like green eyes surveyed him warily.

He nodded. "I know your grandmother. And your sisters."

No, Caroline Hampton was a different creature. Jeans, leather boots, chunky turquoise jewelry that spilled out over the cream shirt she wore—she definitely belonged someplace other than this quiet Pennsylvania Dutch backwater.

"I'm on my way to see my grandmother. I guess I got a little too eager." The smile was a bit more assured, as if now that they'd touched common ground, she had a bit of leverage.

He ripped off the ticket and handed it to her. "I'm sure Mrs. Unger would prefer that you arrived in one piece."

The flash of anger in those green eyes was expected. What wasn't expected was something that moved beneath it—some vulnerability in the generous mouth, some hint of…what?

Fear? Why would the likes of Caroline Hampton be afraid of a hick township cop?

For a moment she held the ticket in her left hand, motionless. Then she turned to stuff it in her handbag. The movement to grasp the bag shoved up her right sleeve.

Bruises, dark and angry, even though they'd begun to turn color, marred the fair skin.

"Can I go now?"

He nodded. "Drive safely."

There was no reason to hold her, no excuse to inquire into the fear she was hiding or the marks of someone's hand on her wrist. He stepped back and watched her pull out onto the road with exaggerated caution.

No reason to interfere, but somehow he had the feeling Caroline Hampton wasn't there on an ordinary visit.

"Thank you, Grams." Caroline took the delicate china cup filled with a straw-colored brew.

Chamomile tea was Grams's solution to every ill. Declaring Caroline looked tired, she'd decided that was just what she needed.

The entrance of Emma Zook, Grams's Amish housekeeper, with a laden tray looked a little more promising. One of Emma's hearty sandwiches and a slab of her shoofly pie would do more to revive her than tea.

Rachel hurried to clear the low table in front of the sofa, giving Emma a place to deposit the tray. Since Rachel, her two-years-older sister, and Grams had turned the Unger mansion into a bed-and-breakfast inn, the room that had once been Grandfather's library was now converted into a sort of all-purpose office and family room.

The walls were still lined with books, and Grandfather's portrait presided over the mantel, but the desk held a new computer system. Magazines devoted to country living overflowed a handmade basket near the hearth, and Grams's knitting filled one beside her chair.

Caroline took a huge bite of chicken salad on what had to be fresh-baked whole wheat bread. "Thank you, Emma," she murmured around the mouthful. "This is wonderful."

Emma nodded in satisfaction. "You eat. You're too skinny."

That surprised a laugh out of her. "Most women I know would consider that a compliment."

Emma sniffed, leaving no doubt of her opinion of that, and headed back toward the kitchen and the new loaf of bread she no doubt had rising on the back of the stove.

Grams's blue eyes, still sharp despite her seventy-some years, rested on her in a considering way. "Emma's right. You don't look as well as you should. Is something wrong?"

Since there was no way she could tell just part of the story, she couldn't tell any of it. "I'm fine. Just tired from the trip, that's all. It's good to be here."

"If you'd let us know, I'd have had a room ready." Rachel was ever the innkeeper. "Never mind. It's just good to have you home."

Now was not the moment to point out that this hadn't been home to her since she was six. After beginning her prodigal-daughter return with an encounter with the police, she was just relieved things were going so well with her grandmother and sister.

Her mind cringed away from that moment when she'd heard the wail of the siren. It was not the local cop's fault, obviously, that the sound still had a power to evoke frightening memories. Still, he hadn't needed to give her a ticket. He could have just warned her.

Pay the two dollars, as the old joke went. Just pay the fine, which was likely to be considerably more than that, and forget the whole thing.

Barney, Grams's sheltie, pressed at her knee, and she broke off a tiny piece of sandwich for him and then stroked the silky head. Tiredness was settling, bone deep.

She hadn't stopped for more than a few hours all the way back, pushed onward by a panic she'd only just managed to control. That was probably why she'd been speeding when she hit the Churchville village limits—that unreasoning need to be here.

She glanced across the table at Rachel, who was curled up in an armchair, nibbling on a snickerdoodle. Neither she nor Grams had asked the question that must be burning in their minds: Why had she come?

She ought to have created some reasonable explanation during that long trip, but she hadn't. How could she begin? They didn't even know she'd gotten married.

It had seemed like such a sweet idea when Tony proposed it—to wait until they had time to make the trip east and then tell both her family and his in person about their marriage. He'd said his people lived in Philadelphia. Was that true, or was it a mirage, like so much of what he'd told her?

As it had turned out, it was just as well that her family didn't know. If they did, it would be one more reason for them to look at her with the faintly pitying, faintly censoring expression they so often wore.

Poor Caro, the one who's always in trouble. Poor Caro, the one who can't seem to get her life together.

"You look beat," Rachel said, getting up abruptly. "We can catch up on things later. I'll make up a room so you can get settled and take a nap if you want."

Grams stopped her with a slight gesture. "It occurred to me that Caroline might want to have Cal's apartment. Now that he and Andrea are living over in New Holland, it's just standing empty."

Rachel stared at her. "But…won't she want to be in the

house? Why would she want to be out in the barn apartment by herself?"

When she'd been here at Christmas, Caro had seen the apartment her older sister's husband had built in one end of the barn where he'd started his carpentry business. It was simple and uncluttered, with a skylight that would give her plenty of natural light for painting. As she so often did, Grams had known exactly what she needed.

"It would be perfect." She interrupted Rachel's argument about her quarters ruthlessly. "Grams, you're a genius. I'd love to have the apartment. If you're sure—I mean, you could rent it to someone else."

"Nonsense." Grams's smile warmed her heart. "It's yours. I thought it would suit you."

Rachel still looked troubled at the idea, but she nodded. "Well, fine, then. It's clean and ready. I'll help you move your things in."

"Great." It seemed to be a done deal. She'd gone from mindless running to having a home. The thought was oddly disorienting.

Had she really been thinking rationally when she'd packed up what she could fit in the car, arranged to ship the rest, written a note to her boss at the gallery and fled Santa Fe without a backward glance? What would Rachel think if she knew? Or worse, Andrea, the oldest of the three of them, with her sensible, businesslike approach to every problem?

She couldn't explain it, even to herself. She'd just known she couldn't stay there any longer. The urge to run was too strong. The frightening encounter in the plaza had tipped her over the edge, but the need to leave had been building since before Tony's death—probably from the moment she'd realized she'd married a man she didn't really know.

She could only be grateful Grams and Rachel hadn't asked for explanations. She didn't think she could lie to Grams, certainly not under Grandfather's judicious eyes, staring wisely from the portrait. Maybe, somehow, after a little rest, she could figure out what part of the truth she could bear to tell.

The doorbell chimed, startling her. Rachel, already on her feet, headed for the hallway, muttering something about not having any reservations for today.

A low rumble of voices, the sound of footsteps in the hallway. She set down her cup and rose, something in her already steeling. It couldn't be anything to do with her, could it?

The cop—the one who'd stopped her earlier—paused for a moment in the doorway and then came toward them.

"Chief Burkhalter wants to see Caro." Rachel, behind him, looked perplexed. "What…"

She forced a smile. "The chief has already given me a speeding ticket today. Maybe he wants to make sure I'm going to pay up."

Slate-gray eyes in a lean, strong-boned face studied her. "I'm not worried about that, Ms. Hampton." He took a step toward her, and she forced herself not to move back. "Fact is, I've had a call inquiring about you. A call from the Santa Fe Police Department."

Chapter Two

Zach was aware of the sudden silence that greeted his words. The room was so still he could hear the tick of the mantel clock and the thud of the dog's tail against the Oriental carpet.

But there was nothing peaceful about it. Tension flowed from Caroline Hampton. And, to a lesser extent, from her sister and grandmother.

It was a shame they were here, but there wasn't much he could do about that. If he'd come to the door and asked to speak to Caroline privately, it would only have raised more questions.

The plain fact was that something was going on with this woman, and if it had to do with the law, it was his responsibility. And he knew there was something, would have known it even if not for that call from the Santa Fe P.D. He could see it in those brilliant green eyes, read it in the tense lines of her body.

"I can't imagine why you'd hear from the Santa Fe police about me. Did I leave behind an unpaid parking ticket?"

He had to admire, in a detached way, the effort it had taken her to produce that light tone.

"Not that I know of." He was willing to pull out the tension just a little longer in the hope that she'd come out with something that wasn't quite so guarded.

"I don't understand." Katherine Unger sat bolt upright in her chair, chin held high. He'd never met anyone who had the aristocratic manner down any better than she did. "Why on earth would the police be interested in Caroline?"

The words might have sounded demanding. But there was a sense of fragility underneath that made it clear he couldn't prolong this.

"Apparently your granddaughter left Santa Fe without telling her friends where she was going. They're worried about her."

Caroline's eyes narrowed. "Are you saying someone reported me missing?"

"Raised an inquiry is more like it. The police department down there was willing to make a few phone calls to allay the woman's fears." He made a play of taking his notebook out and consulting it, although he remembered perfectly well. "Ms. Francine Carrington. I gathered hers was a name that made the police sit up and take notice."

"Caroline, wasn't that your employer at the gallery?" Mrs. Unger glanced from her granddaughter to him. "My granddaughter had a position at one of the finest galleries dedicated to Southwestern art in the state."

She nodded stiffly. "Francine was my boss. And my friend."

"Well, then, why didn't you tell her where you were going?" Rachel looked puzzled. Obviously, that was what she'd have done under the circumstances.

"Because—" Caroline snapped the word and then seemed to draw rein on her anger. "I left a letter of resignation for her, planning to call her once I got here. I certainly didn't expect her to be so worried that she'd call the police."

So she'd left what was apparently a good, successful life at a moment's notice. In his experience, people didn't do that without a powerful reason.

"Apparently she told the officer she spoke with that you'd been despondent over the recent death of your husband. She—"

A sharp, indrawn breath from Mrs. Unger, a murmured exclamation from Rachel. And an expression of unadulterated fury from Caroline. Apparently he'd spilled a secret.

"Husband?" Mrs. Unger caught her breath. "Caro, what is he talking about? Does he have you confused with someone else?"

Shooting him a look that would drop a charging bull, Caroline crossed the room and knelt next to her grandmother's chair.

"I'm sorry, Grams. Sorry I didn't tell you. Tony and I planned to make a trip east this spring, and we were going to surprise you. But he—" She stopped, her voice choking, and then cleared her throat and went on. "He was killed in an accident a few weeks ago."

It was his turn to clear his throat. "I apologize. I thought you knew all about it, or I wouldn't have blurted it out that way."

Caroline stood, her hand clasped in her grandmother's. She had herself under control now, and again he found himself admiring the effort it took her. "I intended to tell my family when I got here, but I haven't had the chance."

"I understand." But he didn't, and he suspected Mrs. Unger didn't, either.

"I'm sorry that I worried Mrs. Carrington. I'll give her a call and let her know I'm all right."

There was more to it than that. He sensed it, and he'd learned a long time ago to trust that instinct where people were concerned. Caroline Hampton was hiding something.

She'd left Santa Fe in such a rush that she hadn't even talked to the people closest to her. That wasn't a trip. It was flight.

"I'll be in touch with the department in Santa Fe, then. Let them know you're fine and with your family."

She nodded, eyes wary. "Thank you."

And that was just what worried him, he realized as he headed out the door. Her family.

Mrs. Unger had welcomed her granddaughter with open arms, as was only natural. But from everything he'd heard, she didn't know a lot about the life Caroline had been living in recent years.

It was entirely possible that Caroline Hampton had brought trouble home with her. Someone ought to keep an unbiased eye on her, and it looked as if that someone was him.

Caroline woke up all at once, with none of the usual easy transition from dreams to morning. Maybe because it wasn't morning. She stared at the ceiling in the pitch-black, clutching the edge of the Amish quilt that covered the queen-size bed in the loft of the apartment, and willed her heart to stop pounding.

She'd been doing this for so many weeks that it had almost begun to seem normal—waking suddenly, panic-stricken, with the sense that something threatened her out there, in the dark. Nothing. There was nothing. There was never anything other than her own haunted memories to threaten her.

She rolled over to catch a glimpse of the bedside clock. Four in the morning. Well, it served her right for getting onto such a crazy schedule. As it was, she'd slept twelve hours straight after that encounter with the cop and the endless explanations to Grams after the man had finally left.

Much as she'd like to blame every problem in her life on Zachary Burkhalter, she really couldn't in all honesty do that. And it wasn't his fault that just seeing him sent her mind spinning back crazily through the years, so that she was again a scared sixteen-year-old, alone, under arrest, at the mercy of— *No.* She jerked her thoughts under control. She didn't think about that ugly time any longer. She wasn't a helpless teenager, deserted by her mother, thrust into the relentless clutches of the law. She was a grown woman, capable of managing on her own. And if she couldn't sleep, she could at least think about something positive.

She shoved pillows up against the oak headboard and sat up in bed. Her new brother-in-law was certainly talented. Most of the furniture in the apartment, as well as the barn apartment itself, had been built by him. Since so much of the furniture was built-in, he'd left it here, and she was the beneficiary.

She couldn't blame Burkhalter, she couldn't blame the comfortable bed, and it was pointless even to blame the stress of the trip. She hadn't slept well in months, maybe since the day she'd met Tony Gibson.

She'd been working on a display of Zuni Pueblo Indian jewelry for the gallery, repairing the threading of the delicate pieces of silver and turquoise, set up at a worktable in the rear of the main showroom. That had been Francine's idea, and Francine had a sharp eye for anything that would draw people into the Carrington Gallery.

As usual, there was a cluster of schoolkids, accompanied by a teacher, and a few retirement-age tourists, in pairs for the most part, cameras around their necks. She'd already answered the routine questions—what did the designs mean, how valuable was the turquoise, did the Pueblo people still make it and, from the tourists, where could they buy a piece.

She gave her spiel, her hands steady at the delicate work as a result of long training. Eyes on her—she was always hypersensitive to the feeling of eyes on her—but she wouldn't let it disrupt her concentration.

The group wandered on to look at something else eventually. Except for one person. He stood in front of the table, close enough to cast a long shadow over the jewelry pieces laid out in front of her.

"Did you have another question?" She'd been aware of him the entire time, of course. Any woman would be. Tall, dark, with eyes like brown velvet and black hair with a tendency to curl. An elegant, chiseled face that seemed to put him a cut above the rest of the crowd. Even his clothing—well-cut flannel slacks, a dress shirt open at the neck, a flash of gold at his throat—was a touch sophisticated for Santa Fe.

"I was just enjoying watching you." His voice was light, assured, maybe a little teasing.

"Most people like seeing how the jewelry is put together." She wasn't averse to a little flirting, if that was what he had in mind.

"They were watching the jewelry," he said. "I was watching you."

She looked up into those soulful eyes and felt a definite flutter of interest. "If you want to learn about Zuni Pueblo jewelry," she began.

"I'd rather learn about C. Hampton," he said, reading her name badge. "What does the *C* stand for? Celeste? Christina? Catherine?"

"Caroline. Caro, for short. And you are?"

"Anthony Gibson. Tony, for short." He extended his hand, and she slid hers into it with the pleasurable sense that something good was beginning.

"It's nice to meet you, Tony."

He held her hand between both of his. "Not nearly as nice as the reverse." He glanced at the gold watch on his wrist. "I have a meeting with Ms. Carrington about the Carrington Foundation charity drive. Shouldn't take more than half an hour. Might you be ready for coffee or lunch by then?"

"I might."

"I'll see you then."

He'd walked away toward the stairs, his figure slim, elegant and cool against the crowd of tourists who'd just come in. Well, she'd thought. Something could come of this.

Something had, she thought now, shoving the quilt back and getting out of bed, toes curling into the rag rug that covered the oak planks of the flooring. It just hadn't been something nice.

She would not stay in bed. If there was one thing she'd learned in the weeks of her disillusionment about her marriage, the weeks of grief, it was that at four o'clock in the morning, thoughts were better faced upright.

She pulled her robe around her body, tying it snugly. She wouldn't go back to sleep now in any event, so she may as well finish the unpacking she'd been too tired to do earlier. She slung one of the suitcases on the bed and began taking things out, methodically filling the drawers of the tall oak dresser that stood on one side of the bed. The loft was small, but the design of closets and chests gave plenty of storage.

Storage for more than she'd brought with her, actually. She'd packed in such a rush that it was a wonder she even had matching socks. Anything she hadn't had room for had been picked up by the moving company for shipment here. When it arrived, she would figure out what to keep and what to get rid of.

Especially Tony's things. Maybe having them out of her life would help her adjust.

She paused, hands full of T-shirts. When had it begun, that sense that all was not right with Tony? Was it as early as their impulsive elopement, when his credit card hadn't worked, and they'd had to use hers? It had grown gradually over the weeks, fueled by the phone calls in the middle of the night, the money that vanished from her checking account, to be replaced a day or two later with only a plausible excuse.

The fear had solidified the evening she'd answered his cell phone while he was in the shower. He'd exploded from the bathroom, dripping and furious, to snatch it from her hands. She'd never seen him like that—had hoped never to again.

Yet she'd seen it once again on the night she'd confronted him, the day she'd realized that her savings account had been wiped out. She still cringed, sick inside, at the thought of the quarrel that followed. She'd always thought she was good in an argument, but she'd never fought the way Tony had, with cold, icy, acid-filled comments that left her humiliated and defenseless.

Then he'd gone, and in the morning the police had come to say he was dead.

She dropped a stack of sweaters on the bed and shoved her hands back through her unruly mop. This was no good. The bad memories were pursuing her even when she had her hands occupied.

She'd go downstairs, make some coffee, see what Rachel had tucked into the refrigerator. She'd feel better once she had some food inside her, able to face the day and figure out where her life was going now.

Shoving her feet into slippers, she started down the open stairway that led into the great room that filled the whole ground-level space. Kitchen flowed into dining area and living room, with its massive leather couch in front of a fieldstone hearth.

She'd start a fire in the fireplace one evening. She'd put some of her own books on the shelves and set up a work table under the skylight. She'd make it hers, in a sense.

She went quickly into the galley kitchen, finding everything close at hand, and measured coffee into the maker that sat on the counter. The familiar, homey movements steadied her. She was safe here. She could take as much time as she needed to plan. There was no hurry.

A loaf of Emma's fruit-and-nut bread rested on the cutting board. She sliced off a couple of thick pieces and popped them in the toaster. She had family. Maybe she'd needed this reminder. She had people who cared what happened to her.

She could forget that sense of being watched that had

dogged her since Tony's death. She shivered a little, pulling her robe more tightly around her while she waited for the toast and coffee. She'd confided that in only one person, telling Francine about her urge to give up the apartment, get rid of Tony's things, try to go back to the way she'd been before she met him.

Her boss had been comforting and sympathetic, probably the more so because it hadn't been that many months since she'd lost her own husband.

"I know what I was like after Garner's death," she'd said, flicking a strand of ash-blond hair back with a perfectly manicured nail. "I could hardly stand to stay in that big house at night by myself. Jumping at every sound." She'd nodded wisely. "But what you need is stability. All the grief counselors say that. Don't make any big changes in your life, just give yourself time to heal. And remember, I'm always here for you."

Caro smiled faintly as the toast popped up and busied herself buttering it and pouring coffee into a thick, white mug. Dear Francine. She probably didn't think of herself as the nurturing type, but she'd certainly tried her best to help Caro through a difficult time.

The smile wavered. Except that their situations weren't quite the same. Garner had died peacefully in his bed of a heart attack that was not unexpected. Tony had plunged off a mountain road after a furious quarrel with his wife, leaving behind more unanswered questions than she could begin to count.

And it hadn't been grief or an overactive imagination. Someone had been watching her. She shivered at the thought of that encounter in the plaza. Someone who claimed Tony owed him an impossible amount of money. Someone who claimed Tony was alive.

She hadn't told Francine about that incident. She would the next time they talked. Francine had known Tony longer than she had. She might have some insight that eluded her.

Something tapped on the living room window. She jerked around so abruptly that coffee sloshed out of the mug onto the granite countertop. She pressed her hand down on the cool counter, staring.

Nothing but blackness beyond the window. The security lights that illuminated the back of the inn didn't extend around the corner of the barn.

A branch, probably, from the forsythia bush she'd noticed budding near the building. The wind had blown it against the glass.

Except that there was no wind. Her senses, seeming preternaturally alert, strained to identify any unusual sound. Useless. To her, all the sounds here were unfamiliar.

Something tapped again, jolting her heartbeat up a notch. The building could make dozens of noises for all she knew. And everything was locked up. Rachel had shown her, when she'd helped bring her things in, still worried at the idea of her staying alone. But even Rachel hadn't anticipated fear, just loneliness.

How do you know that's not what it is? You're hearing things, imagining things, out of stress, grief, even guilt. Especially guilt. Tony might be alive today if that quarrel hadn't sent him raging out onto the mountain road.

She shoved that thought away with something like panic. She would not think that, could not believe that.

Setting the mug on the countertop, she turned to the window. The only reasonable thing to do was to check and see if something was there. And she was going to be reasonable, remember? No more impulsive actions. Just look where that had gotten her.

She walked steadily across to the window and peered out. Her eyes had grown accustomed to the darkness, or maybe that was the first light of dawn. She could see the outline of the forsythia branches, delicate gray against black, like a Chinese pen-and-ink drawing.

Her fingers longed for a drawing pencil. Or a charcoal, that would be better. She leaned forward, trying to fix the image in her mind.

Something, some sound or brush of movement alerted her. She stumbled back a step. Something man-sized moved beyond the window. For an instant, she saw a hand, fingers widespread, dark and blurry as if it were enclosed in a glove, press against the pane.

Then it was gone, and she was alone, heart pounding in deep, sickening thuds.

She ran back across the room, fingers fumbling in her handbag for her cell phone. Call—

Who would she call? Grams or Rachel? She could hardly ask them to come save her from whatever lurked outside.

The police? Her finger hovered over the numbers. If she dialed 911, would Zachary Burkhalter answer the phone?

The man was already suspicious of her. That wouldn't keep him from doing his job, she supposed. It wasn't his fault that she feared the police nearly as much as she feared the something that had pressed against the window.

She took a breath. Think. The apartment was locked, and already the first light of dawn stained the sky. She had the cell phone in her hand. He…it…couldn't possi-

bly get in, at least not without making so much noise that
she'd have time to call for help.

The panic was fading, the image with it. It had been so
fast—was she even sure that's what she'd seen? And if she
wasn't sure, how did she explain that to a skeptical cop?

Clutching the phone in one hand, she snapped off the
light. Safer in the dark. If someone were outside, now he
couldn't look in and see her. She crept quickly toward
the stairs, listening for any sound.

Upstairs, she pulled the quilt from the bed and huddled
in the chair at the window, peering out like a sentinel.
She stayed there until sunrise flooded the countryside
with light, until she could see black-clad figures moving
around the barn of the Zook farm in the distance.

Chapter Three

In the light of day, sitting in the sunny breakfast room at the inn across from her sister, Caroline decided that her fears had been ridiculous. Already the images that had frightened her were blurring in her mind.

The figure—maybe a branch moving, casting shadows. What she'd thought was a gloved hand could well have been a leaf, blown to stick against the windowpane for a moment and then flutter to the ground. There were plenty of last year's maple leaves left in the hedgerow to be the culprit. Her overactive, middle-of-the-night imagination had done the rest.

"Thanks." She lifted the coffee mug her sister had just refilled. "I need an extra tank of coffee this morning, I think."

"Did you sleep straight through?" Rachel looked up from her cheese omelet, face concerned. "You looked as if you could barely stay on your feet. Grams wanted to wake you for supper, but I thought you'd be better for the sleep."

"You were right." If not for what happened when she

woke up, but that wasn't Rachel's doing. Besides, she'd just decided it was imagination, hadn't she?

She'd looked in the flower bed when she went outside this morning. Crocuses were blooming, and tulips had poked inquisitive heads above the ground. The forsythia branches, so eerie in the night, were ready to burst into bloom. There had been no footprints in the mulch, nothing to indicate that anyone had stood there, looking in.

She'd clipped some sprigs of the forsythia, brought them inside and put them in a glass on the breakfast bar as a defiant gesture toward the terrors of the night.

She put a forkful of omelet in her mouth, savoring the flavor. "Wonderful. Your guests must demand seconds all the time. Did Grams eat already?" She glanced toward the chair at the head of the table.

"Emma thought she looked tired and insisted she have her breakfast in bed. When Emma makes up her mind, not even Grams can hold out."

She put down her fork. "Was she that upset because of me?" Because of all the things Caro hadn't told her?

"Don't be silly." Rachel looked genuinely surprised. "She's delighted to have you here. So am I. And Andrea. No, it's just Emma's idea of what's right. You'll see. When people are here, Grams is the perfect hostess, and no one could keep her in bed then."

"It's going well, is it?" Rachel and Grams had started the inn in the historic Unger mansion at the beginning of last summer on something of a shoestring, but they seemed to be happy with how things were going.

"Very well." Rachel's eyes sparkled. "I know people thought this was a foolish decision, but I've never been happier. Being a chef in someone else's restaurant can't hold a candle to living here, working with Grams and being my own boss."

"And then there's Tyler to make you even happier." Her sister was lucky. She'd found both the work that was perfect for her and the man of her dreams. "How is it working out, with him in Baltimore during the week?"

"Not bad." Rachel's gentle face glowed when she spoke of her architect fiancé. "Right now he's in Chicago, but usually he works from here a couple of days a week, while his partner handles things at the office."

"I'm glad for you." Caro reached out to clasp her sister's hand. Rachel deserved her happily-ever-after. She just couldn't help feeling a little lonely in the face of all that happiness.

Rachel squeezed her hand. "I shouldn't be babbling about how lucky I am when you've had such a terrible loss."

"It's all right." What else could she say? Rachel didn't know that the real loss was the discovery that Tony had lied to her, cheated her and then abandoned her in the most final way possible.

That was what happened when you trusted someone. She'd learned that lesson a long time ago. Too bad she'd had to have a refresher course.

She *could* tell Rachel all of it. Rachel would try to understand. She'd be loving and sympathetic, because that was her nature. But underneath, she'd be thinking that poor Caro had blown it again.

It was far better to avoid that as long as possible. She didn't need to lean on her sister. It was safer to rely on no one but herself.

She took a last sip of the cooling coffee and rose. "I'm

going to drive down to the grocery store to pick up a few things. Do you need anything?"

Rachel seemed to make a mental inventory. "Actually, you could pick up a bottle of vanilla and a tin of cinnamon for me. Otherwise, I think I'm set. Just put everything on the inn account. Your stuff, too."

"You don't need—"

"Don't argue." Rachel was unusually firm. "If you were staying in the house, you wouldn't think twice about that."

She nodded reluctantly. There was independence, and then there was the fact that her bills were coming due with no money in her bank account, thanks to Tony. *What did you do with it all, Tony?*

She felt a flicker of panic. How could she have been so wrong about him?

Main Street was quiet enough on a Tuesday morning in March that he could patrol it in his sleep. Zach automatically eyeballed the businesses that were closed during the week, making sure everything looked all right. They'd open on the weekends, when the tourists arrived.

The tourist flow would be small awhile yet, and his township police force was correspondingly small. Come summer, they'd add a few part-timers, usually earnest young college students who were majoring in criminal justice.

He enjoyed this quiet time. He liked to be able to spend his evenings at home, playing board games or working puzzles with Ruth, listening to the soft voices of his parents in the kitchen as they did the dishes.

Families were a blessing, but worry went along with that. Look at Caroline Hampton, coming home to her grandmother with who-knows-what in her background. No matter how you looked at it, that was an odd story, what with her not telling her family she was married, let alone that her husband died. The sort of odd story that made a curious cop want to know what lay behind it.

He'd poked a bit, when he'd called the Santa Fe P.D. back to let them know that the lost sheep was fine. The officer he'd spoken with had been guarded, which just increased his curiosity.

It might have been the city cop's natural derision for a rural cop, or something more. In any event, the man had said that there was no reason to think the death of Tony Gibson was anything but an accident.

And that way of phrasing it said to him that someone, at least, had wondered.

He slowed, noticing the red compact pulled to the curb, then a quick figure sliding out. Caroline Hampton was headed into Snyder's Grocery. Maybe it was time for his morning cup of coffee. He pulled into the gravel lot next to the store.

When he got inside, Etta Snyder gave him a wave from behind the counter. "Usual coffee, Chief?"

"Sounds good."

Caroline's face had been animated in conversation, but he saw that by-now-familiar jolt of something that might have been fear at the sight of him. It could be dislike, but he had the feeling it went deeper than that.

She cut off something she was saying to the only other customer in the shop—tall guy, midthirties, chinos and windbreaker, slung round with cameras. He'd peg him as a tourist, except that tourists didn't usually travel in the single-male variety, and the cameras looked a little too professional for amateur snapshots.

"Here's the person who can answer your questions," she said, taking a step toward the counter. "Chief Burkhalter knows all about everything when it comes to his township."

He decided to ignore the probable sarcasm in the comment, turning to the stranger. "Something I can help you with?"

The guy looked as if he found him a poor substitute for a gorgeous redhead, but he rallied. "Jason Tenley, Chief. I was just wondering what the etiquette is for getting photos of the Amish. I'm working on a magazine photo story, and—"

"There isn't any," he said bluntly. He'd think any professional photographer would have found that out before coming. "Adult Amish don't want their photographs taken, and it would be an invasion of privacy to do so."

"What about from behind? Or from a distance?"

The guy was certainly enthusiastic enough. "You can ask, but the answer may still be no. Sometimes they'll allow pictures of the children, but again, you'll have to ask."

"And you'd better listen, or the chief might have to give you a ticket." Caroline, turning toward them, seemed to have regained her spunk along with her purchases.

"That's only for speeding," he said gravely. "Although I've been known to ticket for blocking public access, when some outsider tried to take photos of an Amish funeral."

"I'll remember that." The photographer didn't act as if the prospect was going to deter him.

Caroline seemed ready to leave, but they stood in front of the doorway, and he suspected she didn't want to have to ask him to move. Instead she sauntered to the bulletin board and stood staring at it.

"Well, thanks for your help." Tenley glanced at Caroline hopefully. "Goodbye, Ms. Hampton. I hope I'll see you again while I'm here."

She gave him a noncommittal nod, her attention still focused on the bulletin board.

Tenley went out, the bell jingling, and Zach moved over to stand behind Caroline at the bulletin board.

"What are you looking for? The mixed-breed puppies, or that convertible sofa bed? I should warn you that the puppies' parentage is very uncertain, and the sofa bed is one that the Muller kid had at his college apartment."

"You really do know everything about everyone, don't you?" That didn't sound as if she found it admirable. "Neither, but I've found something else I need." She tore off a strip of paper with information about the upcoming craft show at the grange hall.

She turned to go, and he stopped her with a light touch on her arm. She froze.

"I wanted to tell you that I'm sorry for bringing up your husband's death in front of your grandmother. I shouldn't have assumed she already knew about it."

"It doesn't matter." She seemed to force the words out. "I was about to tell her, anyway. If you'll excuse me—" She looked pointedly at his hand on her arm.

He let go, stepping back. *What would you do if I asked you why you're so afraid of me, Caroline? How would you answer that?*

It wasn't a question he could ask, but he wondered. He really did wonder.

Caroline drove straight to the barn by way of the narrow lane that ran along the hedgerow. She pulled up to the gravel parking space near the apartment door and began to unload. She would put her own perishables away before running the vanilla and cinnamon over to Rachel at the house. Maybe by then she'd have controlled her temper at running into Chief Burkhalter once again.

Arms filled with grocery bags, she shoved the car door shut with her hip. And turned at the sound of another vehicle coming up the lane behind her.

It was with a sense almost of resignation that she saw the township police car driving toward her. Resignation was dangerous, though. This persistence of Burkhalter's was unsettling and unwelcome. She'd dealt with enough lately, and she didn't want to have to cope with an overly inquisitive country cop.

She leaned against the car, clutching the grocery bags, and waited while he pulled up behind her, got out and walked toward her with that deceptively easy stride of his. If he were anyone else, she might enjoy watching that lean, long-limbed grace. But he wasn't just anyone. He was a cop who'd been spending far too much time snooping into her business.

Her fingers tightened on the bags. "Why are you following me around? Police harassment—"

His eyebrows, a shade darker than his sandy hair, lifted slightly. "Etta Snyder would be surprised at the accusation, since she sent me after you." He held up the tin of cinnamon. "She thought you might need this."

Her cheeks were probably as red as her hair. "I'm sorry. I thought—" Well, maybe it was better not to go into what she'd thought. "Thank you. That's for my sister, and she'll appreciate it." She hesitated, realizing that probably wasn't enough of an apology. "I am sorry. I shouldn't have jumped to conclusions about you."

Those gray eyes of his didn't give anything away. "No problem. Let me give you a hand with the bags."

Before she could object, he'd taken the grocery bags from her. Snatching them back would only make her look foolish, so instead she fished in her purse for the key.

She was very aware of him following her to the door. Knowing his gaze was on her. The combination of cop and attractive, confident male was disturbing.

"Does Etta often turn you into a grocery deliveryman? I'd think police work would be enough to keep you busy, even in a quiet place like this."

"You haven't been here on a busy Saturday in tourist season if you find it quiet," he said. "Dropping off something you forgot at the store is just being neighborly."

Neighborly. She didn't think she was destined to be neighborly with the local cop. She reached the door, key extended. The door stood ajar. Panic froze her to the spot.

"What is it?" His tone was sharp.

She gestured mutely toward the door. "I locked it when I left." Her voice was breathless. "Someone's in there."

"It doesn't look as if it was broken into. Anyone else have a key?"

She took a breath, trying to shake off the sense of dread that had dogged her in Santa Fe. She was being ridiculous.

"Of course. You're right." Her voice was still too high. "Rachel has a key. She might have brought something over from the house. I'm being stupid."

She stepped forward and ran into an arm that was the approximate strength of a steel bar.

"Probably it's one of the family." His voice was casual, but his expression seemed to have solidified in some way, and his eyes were intent. "But let's play it safe. You stay here." It was a command, not a request.

She opened her mouth to protest and then closed it again. He was right.

He put the bags down and pushed the door open gently with his elbow. She wrapped her arms around herself, chilled in spite of the warmth of the sunshine.

No one would be there who shouldn't be. The things that had troubled her after Tony's death were far away, in a different world, a different life. They couldn't affect her here.

Zach's footsteps sounded on the plank floor, softened when he crossed the braided rugs. She could follow his progress with her ears. First the living room, then the adjoining dining area, then around the breakfast bar into the kitchen. That sound was the door to the laundry room; that, the door to the pantry.

When she heard him mounting the stairs to the loft, she could stand it no longer. She sidled inside. It wouldn't take him long to look around the loft bedroom. Had she made her bed before she left? She hoped so.

Then he was coming back down, frowning at her. "I thought you were going to stay outside."

"This is my home." Brave words, but she wasn't feeling particularly brave.

"There aren't any obvious signs of a break-in. Maybe you'd better check upstairs for any money or valuables you have with you."

She hurried up the steps, brushing against him as she did so, and was a little startled by the wave of awareness that went through her.

She had made the bed, and thank goodness nothing embarrassingly personal was lying out in plain sight. Although Grams would probably find it embarrassing that she'd left things half-unpacked. Grams was a great one for finishing anything you started.

In a moment she was starting back down. "I don't see anything missing upstairs. I was in the middle of unpacking, so it's a bit hard to tell."

And the truth was that neatness had never been her strong suit. Or even a virtue, as far as she was concerned.

Zach stood at the worktable she'd pulled out from the wall, staring at the cartons that held her supplies for jewelry making. She'd wanted those things with her, because it was both a vocation and avocation. Or it would be, if she could ever find a way to make enough money to live on. She patted her pocket, where she'd tucked the information about the local craft show.

He held up a box that contained the supply of turquoise she'd brought. "This must be valuable, isn't it?"

"Fairly. I don't have any really expensive stones. I've been experimenting with variations on some traditional Zuni designs in silver and turquoise." She touched a stone, tracing its striations with the tip of her finger, longing to lose herself in working with it.

"I doubt anybody's been in here with the intent to rob you, or they'd have gone for the obvious."

She nodded, reassured. "Thank you. I—well, I'm glad you were here. I probably overreacted for a moment."

He shrugged, broad shoulders moving under the gray uniform shirt. "A break-in didn't seem likely, but we have our share of sneak thieves, like most places. It's always better to be cautious." His voice had softened, as if he spoke to a friend. "And you've been through a rough time with your husband dying so suddenly."

The sympathy in his voice brought a spurt of tears

to her eyes. He was being kind, and she never expected kindness from someone in a uniform.

"We quarreled." The words she hadn't spoken to anyone here just seemed to fall out of her mouth. "We had a fight, and he drove off mad. And in the morning they came to tell me he was dead."

Strong fingers closed over hers, warming her. "It was not your fault. Survivors always think that if they'd done something differently, their loved one wouldn't have died. Don't let yourself fall into that trap."

He had a strength that seemed contagious. She could almost feel it flowing into her. Or maybe she was starting to see him as a man instead of a cop.

"Thank you." She turned away, willing herself to composure. "I appreciate your kindness."

"Plenty of people around here are ready to be neighborly. Just give them a chance."

She nodded, shoving her hair back from her face. Something lay on the breakfast bar—a white sheet of paper that looked as if it had been crumpled and spread flat again. She took a step toward it, recognizing that it was something out of place even before she reached the counter.

She stopped, staring down at the paper, unwilling to touch it. She couldn't seem to take a breath.

"What is it?" Zach covered the space between them in a couple of long strides. "What's wrong?"

She turned, feeling as if she moved all in one piece, like a wooden doll. "That letter." She took a breath, fighting down the rising panic. "Someone has been in here."

Zach grasped her arm, leaning past her to look at the paper without touching it. "Why do you say that?" His tone was neutral, professional again.

"It's a letter my husband wrote to me. I threw it away before I left Santa Fe. Someone came into the house and left it here for me."

Chapter Four

Zach took a moment before responding. Was this hysteria? Caroline was upset, but she didn't seem irrational, no matter how odd her reaction to that letter.

"Are you sure about that?" Careful, keep your voice neutral, don't jump to conclusions. Getting at the truth was a major part of his job, and he didn't do that by prejudging any situation.

He pulled a pen from his pocket, using the end of it to turn the paper and pull it toward them. "Take a closer look and—"

Before he could finish, she'd snatched up the letter, adding her fingerprints to whatever was already on it. Still, even if what she said was true, returning a letter that belonged to her to begin with probably wasn't a crime.

"I know what I'm talking about." Her voice was tight, and her fingers, when she grasped the letter, showed as white as the paper.

A highly strung person might imagine things after a tragic loss. Her actions in leaving Santa Fe so abruptly weren't what he'd call normal, but she might have reasons no one here knew about. That was what worried him. As well, there were those bruises he'd seen on her arms.

"Isn't it possible this was among the things you brought with you? It could have fallen out when you were unpacking." He glanced toward the stack of boxes that overflowed one of the armchairs. "Maybe Emma or your sister came in, tidying things up, found it and put it there."

That generous mouth set in a firm line, and she shook her head. "They couldn't find something I didn't bring."

Stubborn, and the type to flare up at opposition. Well, she hadn't known stubborn until she'd met a Burkhalter. He could be as persistent as a cat at a mouse hole if necessary. His fingers itched to take the letter and find out what had her so upset about it.

"How can you be so sure it's the same one?"

"Look at it," she commanded. She thrust the paper into his hands, just where he wanted it. "You can see the marks where I crumpled it up before I threw it away."

She was right. The marks were visible, even though the paper had been smoothed out before it was put on the counter. He read quickly, before she could snatch it away again, not that there was much to read—just a single page, written in a sprawling, confident hand. A love note.

Caroline grabbed it. "I wasn't asking you to read it."

"Not many men write love notes anymore, I'd think. Too easy to e-mail or text message instead." And not many women would throw such a message away, especially when the sender had just died. "He must have been thoughtful."

Her expressive face tightened. "Tony could be very charming."

That was the kind of word that could be either praise or censure. "How long were you married?"

She turned away, as if she didn't want him to see her face. "Just over a month."

At that point most couples were still in the honeymoon-glow period. "I'm sorry. That's rough."

She swung back again, temper flaring in her eyes. "You obviously think I'm imagining things. I assure you, grief hasn't made me start to hallucinate. I threw the letter away in Santa Fe. It reappeared here. Now that's real, not imagination, whatever you may think."

"Okay." He leaned back against the granite countertop, taking his time answering. "Question is, do you want to file a complaint about someone entering your apartment?"

"You said the door hadn't been forced." She frowned, the quick anger fading. "I know I locked it when I left."

"The windows are all securely closed now, with the locks snapped." A sensible precaution when no one had been living here, especially since the entrance to the apartment wasn't visible from the main house. "Let's take another look at the door."

He crossed to the entry, and she followed him. He bent to study the lock, moving the door carefully by its edge. The metalwork of the lock was new enough to be still shiny, and no scratches marred its surface.

"I don't see any signs the lock has been picked or forced."

"So only someone with a key could get in."

He shrugged. "Unless it wasn't locked. Easy enough to forget to double check it."

"I suppose." But she didn't sound convinced.

"Look, if you want to file a complaint—"

"No." She backed away from that. "I don't. As you said, there could be some rational explanation."

He studied her face for a moment. "You're not convinced." He wasn't too happy about the situation himself, but he didn't see what else he could do.

Caroline raked her fingers back through that mane of hair, turquoise and silver earrings swinging at the movement. "I'll talk to Emma and my sister. Find out if either of them was in here this afternoon. If not—" She shrugged, eyes clouded. "If not, I guess it's just one of those little mysteries that happen sometimes."

He didn't like mysteries of any size. And he was about to take a step beyond normal police procedure.

"You know, if you were to tell me what made you leave Santa Fe in such a hurry, I might be able to help you."

Her eyes met his for an instant—wide, startled, a little frightened. "How did—"

She stopped, and he could almost see her struggle, wanting to speak. Not trusting him. Or having a good reason why she couldn't trust whatever it was to a cop.

"I don't know what you mean." Her voice was flat and unconvincing.

"Neither of us believes that," he said quietly. "I can understand that you don't want to talk to me about your private life, but talk to one of your sisters. Or move into the house, where there are people around all the time."

"I'd rather stay here."

He let the silence stretch, but she had herself under control now. She didn't speak. And he couldn't help her if she wasn't honest with him.

"If you want me, you know how to reach me." He stepped out onto the flagstone that served as a walk.

She summoned a smile, holding the door to close it as if he'd been any ordinary visitor. "Yes. Thank you."

She might change her mind. Decide to tell him about it. But he suspected he was the last person she'd choose to confide in. He just hoped Caroline's secrets weren't going to land her in a mess of trouble.

They were eating dinner around the long table in the breakfast room, but Rachel had made it both festive and formal with white linens, flowers and Grams's Bavarian china. Caroline discovered that the sense of being welcomed home was a bit disconcerting. Nice to know they considered her arrival a cause for celebration, but at the same time, that welcome seemed to call for a response from her that she wasn't sure she was ready to make.

Depend on yourself. That was what life had taught her. Rachel and Andrea were her sisters, but they hadn't lived under the same roof since she was fifteen—longer than that with Andrea. They'd left their mother's erratic existence as soon as they could, as she had.

Andrea and Rachel had left conventionally for college. She was the only one who'd gotten out by way of a correctional facility.

"Great roast, Rachel." Cal, Andrea's husband of four months, leaned back in his chair with satisfaction. "You are one inspired cook. You ought to give the guests breakfast, lunch and dinner."

"No, thanks." Rachel flushed with pleasure at the compliment. "We have enough to do as it is. I'll save my favorite dinner recipes for family."

Andrea nudged her husband. "Haven't I mentioned to you that it's not the wisest thing to praise someone else's cooking more than you praise your wife's?"

"You make the best tuna fish sandwiches this side of the Mississippi," he said, leaning over to kiss her cheek.

Andrea tapped his face lightly with her fingers, eyes sparkling in the glow of the candles. "Sweet-talking will only get you more tuna fish," she warned.

Caro's gaze crossed with Grams's, and she saw an amusement there that was reflected in her own. Marriage had taken away some of Andrea's sharp edges. She'd always be the businesslike one of the family, but Cal had softened the crispness that used to put people off a bit. You could even see the difference in the way she looked, with her blond hair soft around her face and wearing slacks and a sweater instead of her usual blazer.

Had she and Tony ever looked at each other with that incandescent glow? If so, it had been an illusion.

Cal tore his smiling gaze away from his wife. "How do you like the apartment, Caroline? If you find anything wrong, all you have to do is give me a shout."

"Everything seems to work fine." *Except for the fact that someone got in while I was out.* She wasn't sure she wanted to tell them that, wanted to have them look at her the way Zach Burkhalter had, with that doubt in their eyes. "You're obviously a good craftsman."

"He is that," Andrea said. "You have to come over to our new house, so you can see how we've fixed it up. Cal built my accounting office on one end, and his workshop and showroom are in a separate building in the back."

"I'd like to." She could hardly say anything else.

How would they react if she asked how many keys to the barn apartment were floating around in possession of who-knew-who? Would they think she was afraid—the baby sister who couldn't manage on her own?

This was ridiculous. She was a grown woman who'd

been taking care of herself for years. There was just something about being back at her grandmother's table that made her feel like a child again.

"You fix up the apartment to suit yourself," Cal said. "That's only right. Maybe I ought to put up a few more outside lights." He nodded toward the wall of windows that overlooked the gardens, lit up now by the security lights on the outbuildings.

More lighting sounded like a comforting idea. "Thanks. I'm careful to lock up, but it would be nice to be able to see a bit farther outside at night."

"Why? Is anything wrong?" Andrea, sharp as ever, jumped on that immediately.

"No. Nothing."

They were family, she argued with herself. She could tell them. Except that she couldn't tell them just a piece of her troubles—she'd have to expose the whole sorry story.

"When you asked if I'd been in the apartment earlier—was it because something happened?" Rachel's voice was troubled.

Andrea's gaze whipped round to her. "You thought someone had been in there?"

"It was nothing." She should have remembered that you could never get away with half truths with Andrea. She'd always taken her role as oldest sister seriously. Far more seriously than Mom had taken motherhood, in fact.

"You had better tell us, Caroline." Grams sat very straight in the chair at the head of the table.

She began to feel like a sulky child, being told to behave by her elders. "It wasn't anything serious. I found the door ajar when I came home from the store, and I was sure I'd locked it when I left."

"You probably forgot." Andrea's response had echoes

of childhood—of Andrea bringing the lunch she'd forgotten to school or picking up the jacket she'd left at a friend's house. *When are you going to be more responsible, Caro?*

"I didn't forget." She could hear the edge in her voice. "I've been living on my own in the city for years, and it's second nature to lock up."

"Even so—"

It looked as if Cal nudged his wife under the table to shut her up. "To tell the truth, I seldom locked up when I lived there. The latch is probably sticking. I'll stop by in the morning and take care of it."

"You don't need—" she began.

Cal shook his head decisively. "I'll come by."

His tone didn't leave room for argument, so she just nodded. Apparently Andrea had found herself a man who was as strong-willed as she was.

The entrance of Emma from the kitchen put an end to anything else Andrea might have had to say. Emma placed a platter in front of Caroline. One look, one sniff of the delectable aroma, and she knew what it was.

"Emma, your peaches-and-cream cake. That was always my favorite."

"I remember, *ja.*" Emma's round face beamed with pleasure. "You'd come into the kitchen and tease me to make it when you were no more than three."

For an instant she was back in that warm kitchen, leaning against Emma's full skirt, feeling the comfort of Emma's hand on her shoulder, the soft cadence of her speech, the sense that the kitchen was a refuge from tension she didn't understand elsewhere in the house.

"I did, didn't I?" It took an effort to speak around the lump in her throat.

"You'll have a big piece." Emma cut an enormous slab and put it on a flowered dessert plate. "And there is a bowl of whipping cream that I brought from the farm this morning to top it."

Funny. Cal and Emma, the two outsiders, were the ones who made her feel most at home.

But not even their intervention could change the way the others were looking at her. Wondering. Waiting to say it. Poor Caro, always needing to be bailed out. Poor Caro, in trouble again.

"I'm sure we'll find something up here that you can use for your booth for the craft show." Rachel led the way into the attic the next day. She'd been quick to offer her help when she learned that Caroline planned to sell some of her jewelry at the show. "As far as I can tell, no one has thrown anything away in the history of Unger House. They just put it in the attic."

"I see what you mean." She'd forgotten, if she'd ever known, how huge the connecting attics were, and how stuffed with furniture, boxes, trunks and some objects that defied classification. She picked up an odd-looking metal object with a handle. "What on earth is this?"

Rachel grinned. "A cherry pitter. See what I mean?"

"I see that I wouldn't want to be the one to sort all this out."

"We'll keep that in mind." Rachel worked her way purposefully through a maze of trunks. "I'd vote for Andrea, myself. She's the organized one."

"I doubt she'd appreciate that." She followed Rachel, wondering a little at how easy she was finding it to talk to her sister. The years when their lives had gone in separate directions seemed to have telescoped together.

"Here's the screen I was talking about." Rachel pulled a triple folding screen out from behind a dusty dress form. "This would do for a backdrop, and then you could use one of the folding tables to display your jewelry."

"It's pretty dark. I'd like to find something a little brighter to draw people's attention." She hefted the screen. At least it was easily movable. She'd left most of her craft-show things to be shipped with the apartment's contents, and who knew when the moving company would finally get them here?

"I know just the thing. There are loads of handmade quilts stored in trunks. Throw one of them over the screen, and you've got instant color."

"That would work." It was nice to have Rachel so willing to support her.

Rachel lifted the lid of the nearest trunk. "By the way, did you ever get in touch with your friend in Santa Fe? The one who was worried about you?"

And that was the flip side of support. You owed someone else an explanation of your actions.

"Yes, we had a long talk. I should have called her sooner."

She hadn't, because she hadn't been especially eager to listen to Francine, who had been appalled that Caro had, as she put it, run away.

Well, what else would you call it? That's what you do. You run away when things turn sour. She'd run from home. She'd packed up and left every time a relationship went bad or a job failed. That was always the default action. Leave.

Rachel, burrowing into the trunk, didn't respond, leaving her free to mull over that conversation with Francine. She'd told Francine what she hadn't told her family—

about the man who'd accosted her in the plaza, his demands, his conviction that Tony was still alive.

Surprisingly, Francine hadn't rejected that instantly.

"Honestly, Caro, I can't say I knew Tony all that well." She'd sounded troubled. "We worked on a couple of charity events together, and I knew basically what everyone else did—that he was smart, charming, well connected. As for any problems...well, did you think he might have been gambling?"

"That would be an explanation, wouldn't it?" She'd felt her way, trying that on for size. "I never saw any proof, one way or the other."

It was on the tip of her tongue to tell Francine about the disappearance of her own money, but something held her back. Loyalty, maybe, after the wedding promises she'd made. Or just because it revealed how stupid she'd been.

"One thing I'm sure of," Francine said. "If Tony did fake his death in some bizarre need to get out of a difficult situation, he'd find some way to let you know he's still alive. You can be sure of that."

She hadn't found that as comforting as Francine had obviously intended. How could she?

"Caroline." Rachel's voice suggested that she'd said Caro's name several times. "Where are you? You look a thousand miles away." Her expression changed. "I'm sorry. Were you thinking about your husband?"

"Yes, I guess I was." But her thoughts hadn't been what Rachel probably imagined. She went to help her lift a sheet-wrapped bundle from a trunk. "I'm all right. Really." Her mind flicked back to that conversation over the dinner table. "No matter what Andrea might think."

"Oh, honey, Andrea didn't mean that the way it sounded. Don't be mad at her."

"I'm not." She found herself smiling. "You were always the buffer, weren't you? Sometimes you'd side with me, sometimes with Andrea, but usually you were the peacemaker."

"Well, somebody had to be." Smiling back, Rachel began unwrapping the sheet.

The urge to confide in Rachel swept over her, so strong it startled her. She could tell Rachel, because Rachel had always been the understanding one.

But it wasn't fair to ask Rachel to keep her secrets. And she wasn't ready to risk trusting anyone with her troubles and mistakes.

"There." Rachel unrolled the quilt, exposing the vibrant colors of the design. "It's a Log Cabin quilt, one of the ones Emma's mother made, I think."

"It's beautiful." She touched the edge carefully, aware of the damage skin oils could do to aged fabric. "If you're sure you don't mind—"

"It's as much yours as mine," Rachel said. "There might be something you'd like better, though." She pulled out the next bundle, this one wrapped in a yellowing linen sheet. "Goodness, this is really an old one." She squinted at a faded note pinned to the fabric. "According to this, it was made by Grandfather's grandmother in 1856."

"It should be on display, not stored away." The sheet fell back, exposing the quilt. She frowned. "That's an unusual design, isn't it?"

Rachel pointed to the triangles that soared up the fabric. "Flying geese, combined with a star. I don't know enough about antique quilts to have any idea." She folded the sheet back over it.

Caro felt an almost physical pang as the quilt disappeared from view. To actually hold something that had been made by an ancestress almost 150 years ago—had she been as captivated by color and pattern as Caro was? Had she lost herself in her work, too?

"Well, it certainly needs to be better preserved than it is. If you don't mind, I'll see if I can find out how it should be kept."

"Be my guest. That's more your domain than mine." Rachel laid the bundle gently back in the trunk.

Taking the Log Cabin quilt, Caroline stood, stretching. "I'll run this down first and then come back and help carry the—"

Her words died as she passed the attic window. She hadn't realized that from this height she could see over the outbuildings to the barn, even to the walk that curved around to the door of her apartment. And to the flash of movement on that walk.

"Someone's out there." She grabbed Rachel's arm, her heart thudding. He was back. The person who'd been in the apartment was back.

"Who? What?" Rachel followed her gaze. "I don't see anyone."

"Someone was there, by the apartment. I'm not imagining things, and I'll prove it." She thrust the quilt into Rachel's arms and rushed toward the stairs.

Chapter Five

"I told you not to call him." Caroline glanced from the police car that was bumping down the rutted lane to the barn to her sister.

Rachel looked guilty but determined. "If someone's been prowling around your apartment, it's a matter for the police. I know you had a bad experience—"

"That has nothing to do with it." Rachel didn't know just how bad that experience had been, and she had no intention of telling her. "I suppose it won't hurt to talk to the man, but there's nothing he can do."

Zach Burkhalter slid out of the police car, probably in time to hear what she said. Or, if not, he was quick enough to guess at the conversation based on their expressions. He came toward them with that deceptively casual-looking stride.

"You reported a prowler, Rachel?" He glanced from Rachel to her, as if measuring their responses.

"My sister was the one who saw him. She'll tell you all about it." Rachel turned away, as if leaving.

"Wait a minute." Caro grabbed her arm. She was the

one who'd called the man. At least she could stick around for moral support. "You're not going."

Rachel pulled free. "I'd better get back to the house and tell Grams everything is okay. Unless you want to have her out here, that is?"

"Of course not." That was hardly something she could argue, but her sister was going to hear about this later.

"Just tell Zach what you saw. You can trust him. He's one of the good guys." Rachel turned and hurried off around the corner of the barn toward the house.

Caro glanced at the police chief, catching a bemused expression on his face. "You look surprised. Didn't you know my sister thought that about you?"

He shrugged. "Plenty of people don't have good opinions of cops. Like you."

The words dismayed her. Was she really that obvious? "I don't know what you mean."

"Ms. Hampton, I suspect you'd be about as happy to see a snake on your doorstep as to see me. But your sister called me to report a prowler, so I'm here."

She would definitely pay Rachel back for this one. "You'd better come in, but I don't know what you can do."

"Why don't you let me figure that one out."

He followed her inside, and the apartment immediately felt smaller than it should. A police chief, even one in a place as small as Churchville, probably found that air of command useful. She just found it unsettling.

She gestured toward the leather couch and sat down opposite him on the bentwood rocker. "There isn't much to tell. Rachel and I were up in the attic of the house, and I glanced out the window. I hadn't realized that you could see the barn clearly from that height. I saw—"

She hesitated. Had she seen enough to be sure?

"Go ahead." He leaned forward. "Just tell it the way you saw it, without second-guessing."

She nodded. That was exactly what she'd been doing. "I could see the end of the walk that leads to the apartment door. I had a quick glimpse of a figure heading toward the door, but he was out of sight almost before it registered."

"Male?"

She closed her eyes, visualizing. "I said 'he' but I'm not sure. It was just an impression of a human figure, probably male, wearing something dark—maybe a jacket."

The face of the man in the plaza came back to her. He'd worn a denim jacket. Would that have looked dark from a distance?

"Did you see anything else? A vehicle, maybe?"

"No. I ran down the stairs, hoping I could get a look at him. But the dog started to bark, and that could have alerted him. By the time Rachel and I got here, there was no one in sight. And before you ask, it doesn't look as if anyone got inside." She shrugged. "I told you it was a wild-goose chase. That was why I didn't want Rachel to call."

He seemed to have a face designed for expressing doubt. "Did you hear a car when you were running out here?"

"I don't think so." She frowned. "There was traffic going by on the road, but I don't think I heard anything any closer. You're thinking that if there really was a prowler, he'd have had to come in a vehicle."

He seemed to suppress a sigh. "Ms. Hampton, maybe you shouldn't be so quick to assume you know what I'm thinking."

There didn't seem to be anything to say to that. "You seem to be on a first-name basis with my sister."

His gray eyes seemed to lighten with his smile. "I've known her a bit longer. And what I was thinking was that it's not a wild-goose chase if you believe you saw someone who shouldn't be here."

She looked down at her hands, clasped in her lap. "All right. Thank you."

"Still, it makes me wonder." His voice was as easy as if they talked about the weather. "What makes you so quick to decide someone's been prowling around?"

Her hands twisted, tight against each other. He thought he'd boxed her in. "Anyone would think that if—"

He was shaking his head. "You're afraid of something. You don't want to talk about it, but you are."

"That's ridiculous." She forced herself to meet his eyes. "I'm not afraid."

"You left Santa Fe in such a hurry that you didn't even tell your friends where you were going. That looks a lot like running. And if someone's been prowling around here, maybe you had a good reason to run."

She couldn't seem to come up with any rational explanation that would satisfy him and send him away.

He leaned toward her, and she stiffened to keep from pulling back. "Caroline, if you're in trouble, the best thing you can do is tell me about it. Because sooner or later I'll find out what's going on, and it would be better coming from you than from someone else."

She wanted to deny it, but she couldn't. She seemed to be poised on the edge of a high dive, ready to plunge into the unknown. "Someone threatened me."

"When? Where?" He didn't raise his voice, but she felt the demand in it.

"In Santa Fe." She pressed her hand to her head. "The day before I left there. He'd been following me, and I kept telling myself it was my imagination, but then he grabbed my arm." Something seemed to quake inside her.

Zach reached out, brushing the sleeve of her shirt back. "He left marks."

She looked down at the bruises, faint and yellow now.

"Did you know him?"

"No. I'd never seen him before I noticed him outside the gallery where I worked. And later outside my apartment building."

"So this man you didn't know accosted you. Why didn't you yell for help? Call the police?"

That was what a normal person would do, she supposed. "Because of what he asked me." She took a breath, feeling as if she hadn't inhaled for several minutes. "He wanted to know where Tony was. My husband. And he'd been dead for over two weeks."

"If he didn't know—"

She shook her head. "He knew about the accident. He said that faking your own death was a good thing to do if Santa Fe was getting too hot for you. And that other people might believe it, but he didn't."

"That took you by surprise?"

She stared at him. "Of course it did. My husband was dead. The police told me—showed me pictures of the burned-out car." She had to force the rest of it out. "The fire—there wasn't much left, but I had a funeral."

His face didn't give anything away. He might believe her. Or he might be thinking she was crazy.

"This man. What did he want?"

"He said Tony owed him a hundred thousand dollars."

She closed her eyes for a moment. "He wanted it. From Tony or from me."

"Why did your husband owe him the money?" He was relentless. Of course he would be. He was a cop.

"I don't know that he did. I don't know anything about it. I just knew the man scared me and I wanted to get away." She lifted her hands. "I can't tell you what I don't know, any more than I could have told him."

"Okay." He touched her hand in a brief gesture of… what? Sympathy? Or did he just want to calm her enough to get more answers? "Was your husband a gambler?"

"I don't know." She thought of the missing money. If she told him, it would lend credence to the gambling theory.

But she couldn't. She didn't want him, or anyone, to know just what a sham her marriage had been. "I suppose that makes sense. I can't think of any other way he could owe that much."

Zach leaned back, giving her a little breathing room. "So this guy scared you. And instead of going to the police or your friends, you left."

At least he hadn't said "ran away." She met his eyes. "I have family here. With my husband dead, I wanted to be with them."

"I can understand that." But his eyes held a reservation. "So, this man. You're an artist. Can you draw his face?"

She blinked at the sudden change of subject when she'd expected more questions about Tony, more about why she'd left. "I did a sketch right after it happened, but then I tore it up. I'll do another. Would that help?"

"It can't hurt. I can fax it to the authorities in Santa

Fe, see what they can come up with. If he's in my territory, I want to know it."

"You think he's the one who got into the apartment." She hadn't expected him to agree with her. "How could he have had access to that letter?"

He shrugged. "The letter might somehow have gotten into the things you packed."

"Or he might have searched the apartment in Santa Fe. Found it in the trash." That made sense. "He'd been outside the building. I saw him."

"Possible." His tone didn't give her a clue as to whether he believed her or not. "About that sketch?"

The thought of him watching over her shoulder while she drew that face tightened her nerves. "I'll work on it and drop it off at your office later this afternoon."

"Fine." He rose. "But you don't need to bring it to me. I'll stop by for it."

If she argued, it would sound as if having him here bothered her. It did, but she'd rather he didn't know.

Of course, he'd probably figured it out already.

"All right." She stood, too, walking him to the door as if he were any ordinary visitor. "Thank you."

"Just one other thing." He paused, holding the door.

She looked at him, eyebrows lifting.

"What he said about your husband. Do you think your husband is still alive, Caroline?"

"No." The word was out, harsh and emphatic, before she thought. She took a breath. "No, I don't."

Zach nodded. Then he stepped outside and closed the door behind him.

Caroline spread a length of black velvet over the metal folding table Rachel had unearthed for her to use at the craft show. All around her, the cement block fire hall echoed with the clatter and chatter of a hundred-plus crafters getting ready for the event. The doors opened at nine, and everyone wanted to be ready.

The aroma of coffee floated from the food stand at the end of the row. Maybe, once she was set up, she could ask the stall holder next to her to watch the stand while she went for a quart or two of caffeine.

She smoothed out the cloth with her palms and bent to retrieve the first box of jewelry. Silly, maybe, but being here made her feel at home. Veterans of craft shows were a friendly bunch, and Caro had found that no matter what they made, they shared a common bond.

That love of creating something beautiful with your hands was hard to describe but very real. She might not personally understand the drive to make, for instance, the ruffled toilet paper covers that the stand across the walkway offered, but she did know the pleasure of creation.

She began laying out an assortment of turquoise and silver bracelets and necklaces, loving the way they glowed against the black velvet.

"Those are gorgeous." The basket weaver in the next booth leaned over to have a closer look. "I just might end up spending more than I make today. Where did you learn to work with turquoise? Not around here."

Caro shook her head. "Out West. Santa Fe, mostly. The Zunis do some amazing work with silver and turquoise."

"Gorgeous," the woman said again, then grinned and held out her hand. "Karen Burkhalter. Welcome. This is your first time here, isn't it?"

"Yes." She returned a firm grip. Blond hair, hazel eyes, an open, friendly face with a turned-up nose—the woman was probably about her age, she'd guess, with the engaging air of someone who'd never met anyone she didn't turn into a friend.

Burkhalter was a common enough name in Pennsylvania Dutch country. Chances were she didn't even know Zach.

"I'm Caroline Hampton."

"Oh, sure. Your grandmother is Katherine Unger. Everyone knows her youngest granddaughter came home."

"I'm not sure I care for that much celebrity."

Karen grinned. "It's a small township, and most of us have known each other since birth. You'll get used to how nosy we all are about each other's lives."

That was an uncomfortable thought. "You have a great assortment of baskets." She picked one up, admiring the stripes worked into the weaving with different colored reeds. "Is this an egg basket?"

Karen nodded. "They're popular with the tourists, not that any of them are likely to be gathering eggs."

"As long as they buy." That, after all, was the whole point. If she could make a decent amount on the show, she wouldn't feel as if she dangled on a financial precipice.

"The crafters' slogan," Karen agreed. "It's hard to tell whether people will be in a buying mood or not. Usually around here the shows start pretty small, but as we move on into spring, sales pick up."

"If there's a good turn-out—" She stopped, because a familiar figure was headed toward Karen's booth.

Zach Burkhalter. It wasn't a coincidence, then, about the name.

Karen leaned across the table to hug him. "Hey, it's about time you're showing up. I want my coffee."

In jeans and a flannel shirt instead of a uniform, Zach should have looked less intimidating. He didn't.

His gaze shifted from Karen to her, his hand still resting on the other woman's shoulder. His wife? There was absolutely no reason for that possibility to set up such a negative reaction in her.

"Caroline. I didn't realize you were jumping into the craft-show circuit."

"You two know each other, then," Karen said. "I should have known. Being the police chief gives my brother an unfair advantage in meeting newcomers."

"You're Zach's sister." And that shouldn't give her spirits a lift, either. The marital status of Zach Burkhalter was nothing to her.

"The woods are full of Burkhalters around here," Zach said easily. "Mom and Dad each had five siblings, and then they had another five kids to add to the mix."

"You're lucky you just have sisters," Karen said. "Brothers can be such a pain." She threw a light punch toward Zach's shoulder.

"Well, I'd better finish setting up." Standing there looking at Zach was not conducive to her peace of mind. It just made her remember those moments when she'd told him far too much. And had had the sense that he understood even more than she'd told.

Things had been quiet since then. With a little luck, they'd stay that way, and she could stop wondering what had become of that sketch Zach had faxed to Santa Fe.

Caro pulled the quilt from its protective covering and slid her metal chair over next to the screen to climb on.

"Let me give you a hand." Before she could say no, Zach had rounded her table. He took the end of the quilt, lifting it over the screen as she unfolded it. "Is this how you want it?"

"Yes. Thanks." *Now please go away, and let me get*

back to concentrating on the craft show. It wasn't Zach's fault that he made her tense up, sure that at any moment he'd say something about the prowler. Or the sketch.

He drew the quilt down behind the screen, and she smoothed it out with her hand. It fit perfectly, falling to table height in a cascade of rich, saturated color.

"That's lovely, too." Karen took a step back to admire the quilt. "Handmade. Are you selling Amish quilts, as well as your jewelry?"

Caro shook her head. "I just wanted it to give me a colorful background. My sister found a treasure trove of quilts stored in the attic."

She started to climb down from the chair, and Zach caught her hand, steadying her. Solid, strong, like the man himself. He wouldn't be a featherweight in a crisis, but she guessed he'd expect a lot from anyone he got close to.

"It's a lot better than looking at cement-block walls," Karen said. "Would you mind if I borrowed the idea and did something similar in my booth?"

"Not at all." She took a step away from Zach's supporting hand. She didn't need support. She did quite well on her own.

"As long as you don't try to borrow the quilt, as well," Zach said.

His sister shot him a haughty look. "I happen to have quilts of my own. Although I'm not sure I have anything as fine as that one." She fingered the stitches, so even and neat that it was hard to believe they were done by hand.

Quilts seemed to be a safe topic of conversation. "Do you know anything about restoring antique quilts? I found one that dates back to pre–Civil War, and I'd love to get it into shape to display."

Karen shook her head. "Not me. The person you should talk to is Agatha Morris. She's a local historian and something of an authority on old quilts and coverlets."

"To say nothing of being the mother of Churchville's mayor, as she'll be sure to point out to you," Zach said.

"You just don't like Keith because he tried to get the county commissioners to cut your budget. And he only did that because you gave him a speeding ticket."

Zach shot his sister a warning glance. "Don't go around saying things like that, Karrie."

She wrinkled her nose at him, in the inevitable manner of little sisters everywhere, and then nodded. "Okay. But how about my coffee? And bring one for Caroline, too. She looks thirsty."

"You don't need—" she began, and then lost track of what she was going to say under the impact of Zach's rare smile.

"Cream? Sugar?" His eyes warmed, almost as if he knew he'd had an effect on her.

"One sugar. No cream." If he kept looking at her that way, she might have to reassess her opinion of him.

Straight-arrow cop, she reminded herself as he sauntered off toward the food stand. Maybe he was one of the good guys, as her sister said, but that didn't mean he could ever understand someone like her.

Zach hadn't intended to spend so much of the day at the craft show. Usually he came by whenever Karrie was exhibiting, just to help her set up or tear down. Somehow today he didn't feel like heading for home.

Ruthie was here, somewhere, with his mother. Mom had been teaching her how to crochet, and that had sparked her interest in Aunt Karrie and the craft show. Thank goodness his daughter had Mom around to handle the girlie stuff. He could teach her how to catch a fish, but he was pretty clueless in some departments.

He rounded the corner of the row of stalls and spotted his sister, leaning across her table to show something to a customer. Beyond her, he could see Caroline, also busy with a customer. Her face was animated as she displayed a bracelet, draping it across her wrist.

His gut tightened at the thought of those bruises on her right wrist. Nobody should treat a woman that way. On the other hand, could he believe her account of how it had happened? He wasn't sure, and until he was, until he knew for sure she wasn't involved in something criminal, he'd tread carefully where Caroline was concerned.

He'd expected to hear something from that Santa Fe P.D. by now about the sketch he'd faxed them, but so far they'd been silent. His request was probably pretty far down on their priority list.

As he neared the stand, he realized that the person she was talking to was that photographer, Tenley. Interesting that the guy was still around. Something about him hadn't quite rung true from the first time Zach saw him.

Zach picked up one of Karen's baskets and turned it over in his hands, trying to separate their conversation from the buzz of talk that surrounded them.

From what he could make out, Tenley was intent on asking her out, and Caroline was equally intent on selling him something. It seemed to be a bit of a stand-off.

"Are you planning to buy a basket today?" Karen turned to him as her customer moved off, dangling a bag containing one of her smaller items.

"Why would I do that, when you keep giving them to

me? If you want your family to buy, you'll have to stop being so generous."

"Small chance of that," Karen said. "You have a birthday coming up, don't you? What kind of basket would you like?"

Caroline, seeming to overhear, turned to smile at his sister. "That's what it is to be related to a crafter. As far as I can tell, my sisters like my jewelry, but they could hardly tell me anything else, could they?"

"Of course they like it," Tenley put in quickly. "Your adaptation of Zuni designs is inspired. As a matter of fact, I'll take the bracelet for *my* sister's birthday."

"Excellent." Caroline beamed. "I'll gift wrap it for you."

"You seem to know a lot about Southwestern design." Zach leaned against the table. "You spend some time out there?"

Tenley looked startled at the direct question, but then he tapped his camera. "My work takes me all over the place. I know enough about Zuni art to appreciate it." He turned quickly back to Caroline, pulling out his wallet. "Don't bother to gift wrap it. I'll take it as it is."

In a moment he'd paid, claimed his package and moved off. Frowning, Caroline turned to Zach.

"You just scared off a customer. I might have been able to sell him something else."

He shrugged. "If someone's scared of the police, it's usually because they have something to hide."

Her reaction to that might have been invisible to anyone else, but not to him. He was looking for it, and he saw it—that faint withdrawal as muscles tightened, the slightest darkening of those clear green eyes. Caroline took that personally. That meant she had reason to do so.

And that meant he should do the thing he'd been putting off for days—run a check on her and find out just what it was about her past she wanted to hide.

"Caroline, here's just the person you should talk with about your quilt." Karen's voice had both of them jerking toward her. His reaction was mild annoyance, but he suspected Caroline's was relief.

The annoyance deepened when he found Agatha Morris and her son Keith standing behind him. He jerked a nod. "Mrs. Morris. Mayor. Enjoying the show?"

Agatha gave him an icy nod before turning to Caroline. With her iron-gray hair worn in a style reminiscent of Queen Elizabeth, her sensible shoes and the flowered dresses she wore whatever the season, Agatha was a formidable figure. "I understand you're Katherine Unger's granddaughter." The words sounded faintly accusing.

Caroline smiled, extending her hand. "I'm Caroline Hampton."

Agatha glanced toward the jewelry, seeming not to notice the gesture, but Keith slid past her to take Caroline's hand. "Welcome to Churchville, Caroline. I'm Keith Morris."

You couldn't fault Keith's manners, even if you did think him too much of a featherweight to be mayor of any town, no matter how small. Maybe the voters had been bemused by the freckles and aw-shucks smile.

"My son is the mayor of Churchville, you know." Agatha never missed an opportunity to mention that. She cast a critical eye at the quilt. "Karen says you had some question about an antique quilt. If it's that one, it's not nearly old enough or unique enough to be of interest."

Caroline seemed to stiffen at the slur. "No, I'm familiar with the history of this one. I found an older quilt in the attic at Unger House, one made by my grandfather's grandmother during the 1850s. It has an interesting design—a combination of flying geese with a star. I'd like to know more about it."

He expected Agatha to welcome the opportunity to show off her expertise. She could be counted on to launch into a lecture at a moment's notice.

But she didn't. She stood perfectly still for a moment, staring at Caroline as if she'd said something off-color. Then she shook her head. "I'm afraid that would hardly be worth pursuing. Such quilts are rather common—of no historic interest at all." She turned away. "Come, Keith."

With an apologetic glance at Caroline, Keith followed his mother down the crowded aisle between the tables.

"Well." Karen sounded as surprised as he was. "I've never known Agatha to miss an opportunity to tell someone exactly how to do almost anything."

Caroline shrugged. "Obviously she didn't think my quilt was worth her time."

Could be. But it was still odd. Odd things seemed to collect around Caroline Hampton, for some reason, and he'd like to know why. Until he did—

"Daddy!" A small hurricane swept toward him, and Ruthie launched herself as if she hadn't seen him for months, instead of hours. "Grammy said you'd be here."

He lifted her in a hug and then set her back on her feet, overwhelmed as he so often was at the way God had brought her into his life. He ruffled her dark-brown curls as his mother came up behind her.

"Ruthie, you shouldn't run off that way." Mom divided a smile among them, sounding a little out of breath.

"Mom, Ruthie, this is Caroline Hampton."

Ruthie caught the edge of the table with two probably

grimy hands and propped her chin on it, eyes wide as she looked at the jewelry. "Wow. Did you make those?" Before Caroline could answer she'd ducked down and crawled underneath the table cover, to pop up on the other side next to Caroline, beaming at her. "I love your jewelry. Someday I want to have earrings just like yours."

Smiling, Caroline bent down to let Ruthie touch the dangling spirals of silver that danced from her earlobes. His daughter touched the earring, making it shimmer.

"Ruthie, come out of there now." Instead of waiting for her to crawl under, he reached across the table and lifted her in his arms. "You know better than to go into someone's booth without permission."

But that wasn't what put the edge in his voice. It was the sight of his daughter leaning against Caroline.

Caroline took a step back, her face paling as if he'd struck her. He was sorry. He didn't want to hurt her.

But like it or not, Caroline was a question mark in his mind. He'd give the woman the benefit of the doubt in any other instance, but not where his daughter was concerned.

Chapter Six

"You really don't need to stay and help me." Caro opened the trunk of her car, peering around the lid at Rachel, who'd walked over from the house to help unload.

"It's no problem." Rachel seized a cardboard box. "Andrea wanted to stop by the show to help out, but she's swamped, with tax time approaching."

Rachel seemed to take it for granted that the family would pitch in to help. A wave of guilt moved through Caro. She hadn't done much in the way of helping Rachel or Grams since she'd been back, had she?

"You have the inn guests to worry about. I'm sure you should be prepping for tomorrow's breakfast or something." She tried to take the box from Rachel's hands, but her sister clung to it, laughing a little.

"Don't be so stubborn, Caro. How many times did I say that to you when we were kids?"

"Pretty often. But not as often as Andrea did." She had to return the smile. "That used to be her theme song when it came to me, as I recall."

"And how you resented it."

Yes, she had. She'd wanted to do things for herself,

but Andrea, always trying so hard to be the big sister, had been just as determined to help her.

Until Andrea had left, headed for college, and she hadn't come back. And then Rachel had taken off in her turn. She could hardly blame them for that, could she? Except that it had left her alone with Mom.

"I'm a big girl now. I've been doing my own loading and unloading from craft shows for a long time—" She looked up, startled, at the sound of another vehicle pulling up behind hers.

Rachel lifted a hand in greeting to Zach as he slid out of the car. "Okay," she said. "I'll let Zach do the heavy lifting, then."

"Glad to," he said, approaching. "Believe me, my sister has me well trained in the whole craft-show routine." He reached past her to begin sliding the folding screen out of the trunk.

Rachel gave her a quick hug. "Come over and we'll raid the refrigerator for supper whenever you're hungry. Grams won't want much after her tea party today." She scurried off, leaving Caro alone with Zach.

He hefted the screen. "You want to get the door?"

"Actually I want to know why you're here. Again." She unlocked the door as she spoke. After all, there was no point in refusing a hand in with the heavy things.

"There's something I need to talk to you about." He stepped inside and set the screen against the wall.

She paused on the doorstep, stiffening. Whatever it was, she didn't want to hear it.

Zach leveled that steady gaze at her. "You look like you're tensed up for bad news."

"I can't imagine that you're here to bring me good news." She shoved the door shut behind her, aware of the alien scent almost before she registered it mentally. Her head lifted, face swiveling toward the kitchen.

"Coffee smells good." Zach's tone was casual, but his eyes were watchful.

"Yes." She had to force the word out. "But I didn't make any coffee this morning."

He frowned, and then crossed the dining area and rounded the breakfast bar into the kitchen. "Somebody did. The pot's still on—the mug rinsed and left in the drainer. You sure you didn't start it and then forget about it?"

"I didn't make any." She walked to the counter. "I didn't have time."

Her mind flickered to those moments when Zach had brought her coffee at the show. When she'd actually felt as if they were becoming friends. It had been an illusion, like so much else.

"I don't see how you can be sure," he began.

"Because I know what I did and what I didn't do." She snapped the words. "Because even if I had planned to make coffee, I wouldn't have made that kind. Hazelnut. I don't care for hazelnut. I don't have any in the house." Her voice was starting to veer out of control, and she caught herself, breathing hard.

"Who does like hazelnut?" he asked quietly. As if he knew the answer already.

"Tony." It took an effort to swallow. "Tony liked hazelnut. It was all he drank."

He stood for a moment, watching, and then came to plant his hands on top of the counter. "Tony's dead. So how could he be here, making coffee in your kitchen?"

She sank onto the stool, her legs trembling. "He couldn't. He couldn't."

"You said the man who threatened you claimed he was alive." His gaze was so intent on her face that she could feel its heat.

"He was wrong. Or lying. Tony died in that accident. If he hadn't, he'd have come back."

Or would he? He'd already taken everything she had. What else was there to bring him back?

"There's more to it than that." Zach's frown deepened. "That man, the one you drew the sketch of—"

"You've identified him." Her gaze flew to his face. "You know who he is."

"I had a call from the police in Santa Fe. They're familiar with him. His name is Leonard Decker. Mean anything to you?"

She shook her head slowly. "Leonard Decker. I don't remember hearing the name. What was he to my husband?"

"Good question." Zach ran his hand absently along the edge of the granite counter. "According to the officer I talked to, Decker has a finger in a lot of pies, some of them probably illegal. They've never managed to convict him, but he's been under suspicion several times—fencing stolen goods, gambling, that sort of thing."

"Gambling." She repeated the word, her heart sinking, mind flashing back to Francine's speculations about Tony.

"You have any reason to think your husband was involved in anything like that?"

She started to shake her head, but something about that steady gaze seemed to stop her. She didn't trust Zach. But what was the point of denying something he already seemed to guess?

"There was money missing from my account." She

pushed her hair back from her face, aware of the throbbing in her temples. "That was what we fought about, that last night. He'd cleaned out my savings and checking accounts."

"Did he say why he needed the money? Give any explanation?"

"No." His only defense had been in cruel, cutting remarks. "He seemed to think I'd cheated him in some way, letting him believe I had family money when he married me." That accusation had left her numb and speechless. How did you defend against that?

Zach was silent for a moment. Maybe he knew there was nothing safe to say in response to that.

Finally he spoke. "Sounds as if Decker is nobody to fool around with, but I can't see what he'd hope to gain by following you here. Unless he thinks you're going to lead him to Tony."

"Tony is dead." But not even she was convinced by her tone.

"If he isn't, would he contact you?"

"I don't know." Everything she'd thought she knew about Tony had turned out to be a lie. How could she be sure of anything? "Francine—my friend at the gallery—thinks so, but she doesn't know everything."

"You haven't told anyone else about the money."

"No."

She thought he was going to ask why she'd told him, but he didn't. He just shook his head.

"Why not move into the house? Nobody would risk paying you any surreptitious visits there, to make coffee or anything else."

"That's why." She pressed her palms down on the counter. "Don't you see? If Tony is alive, I have to know.

If he's trying to get in touch with me, I have to be where he can reach me."

"Why wouldn't he just walk in, then? Why fool around leaving you hints that he's been here?"

"I don't know. We didn't exactly part on the best of terms. Maybe he's afraid I'm being watched. I don't understand any of it." She squeezed the back of her neck, trying to press the tension out. It didn't help. "But I can certainly understand why you didn't want your daughter anywhere near me."

"Ruthie." His gaze was startled, but she could read the truth there. To do him credit, he didn't try to deny it. "She's my child. I can't expose her to—"

"A criminal like me?"

"I was going to say to someone who might be surrounded by trouble."

"You're a wise parent." If her own parent had been a little wiser, how different might her life have been? She wouldn't have ended up spending those terrifying months in the juvenile detention facility. She wouldn't have carried that around with her for years. Or would she have ended up the same even with good parents?

"I try. Picking it up along the way, I guess. I'd like to help you, Caroline. I'm not sure what I can do."

"There's nothing anyone can do." Anyone except Tony. If he was alive, sooner or later he'd show himself. And then what? Did they try and put the pieces back together again, when there'd been nothing real to begin with?

"Get in touch with me if anything happens that worries you." He put his hand over hers where it lay on the granite, and his grip was warm and strong. Reassuring. "If there's any way I can help you find the truth, I will."

Tears stung her eyes, and she blinked them back. "Thank you. But I don't think—"

His grip tightened. "Promise me. If there's a way I can help, you'll tell me."

There wasn't a way anyone could help, so the promise was a small price to pay to be left alone.

"All right. I promise."

What would anyone have to gain by making Caroline believe that her husband was still alive? Zach drove slowly down the bumpy lane to the main road, his mind still revolving around that odd incident with Caroline.

And the coffee. Was that remotely believable? He came back to the same question. If someone had gone into the apartment while she was out today and deliberately made a pot of her husband's favorite coffee—

It was stretching his imagination to believe that much, but Caroline's reactions had seemed genuine.

So get back to the question. If someone had done that, what would his or her purpose have been? To taunt Caroline about her husband's death? To accuse her, in some veiled way, of contributing to that death? Or to make her think that her husband was still alive?

To think that. Or fear that. He didn't believe for a moment that Caroline had told him everything about that relationship. Had there been reasons why she might have feared Tony Gibson? He hadn't forgotten the bruises on her wrist, and his natural skepticism had made him question her explanation.

Still, the Santa Fe police had identified Leonard Decker, and there was a certain logic that would fit Tony Gibson into the picture with him.

On the other hand, and he had the feeling he was now

on his third or fourth hand, Caroline could have engineered the entire story herself. He didn't pretend to be a psychologist, but he'd seen enough human behavior in his years as a cop to know it was seldom entirely rational, especially when driven by strong emotion. If Caroline felt guilty in regard to her husband's death, she might find a way to punish herself through these hints that he was still alive.

He knew a bit about survivor's guilt himself—enough to accept that such a thing could happen, at least. He couldn't forget—would never forget—that Ruthie might not be an orphan if he hadn't failed to do his duty. He ripped his thoughts away from that. This was about Caroline, not him.

There was the least-palatable explanation—that Caroline had set up the situation deliberately, for reasons that had nothing to do with her feelings for Tony. Think about it. What would have happened if Zach hadn't come along just when he did?

Rachel would have helped her carry the craft show things into the apartment, and Rachel would have been the one to hear the odd story about the coffee. She wouldn't have his skepticism. She'd rush to her little sister's defense.

He couldn't dismiss the niggling fear that this could all be part of some elaborate scheme to get money out of Katherine Unger. She'd do anything if she believed her granddaughter needed her help.

Caroline could be telling the exact truth as she understood it, in which case she deserved sympathy and help, not suspicion. But he was a cop, and he couldn't stop thinking like one. In any event, the only way to help anyone, innocent or guilty, was to find the plain, unvarnished truth.

He pulled up to the curb at the police station, glancing at his watch. It was past time he went home for supper, but he had something to do first.

He unlocked the door and went inside. It was just as well that everyone was gone. He didn't want anyone listening to the conversation he was about to have, always assuming he could reach the detective in Santa Fe he'd talked with earlier.

A few minutes later he was leaning back in his chair, listening to Detective Charles Rojas of the Santa Fe P.D., who had still been in his office thanks to the time difference.

Rojas seemed to have decided to be a bit more forthcoming. "The thing is, and this is strictly in confidence, Gibson had been under investigation in the weeks before his death."

"Investigation of what?"

Silence on the line.

"Look, someone has been dropping hints to his widow that Tony Gibson is still alive. If through some bizarre chance that's true, it's in both our interests to work together on this." He waited.

A rustling of papers sounded through the phone. "You've got a point there." There was a thud, as if Rojas had propped his feet up on his desk. "Okay, here's the story. Gibson was thought to have been involved in a fairly sophisticated series of scams."

"Thought to be? If he tried to con someone, they ought to be able to identify him."

"You don't know these people." Rojas's voice betrayed

his frustration. "Upper-crust society, whatever you want to call them. They don't relish letting the world know they've been made fools of. Seemed like most of them would rather write off the con and forget about it. No one would identify Gibson directly. Maybe, eventually, we'd have pinned it to him, but he drove his car off a cliff first."

"You're sure about the identification of the body?" That was the crux of the matter, as far as he was concerned.

Silence again for a moment. "The car burned badly. Very badly. So far we haven't received complete confirmation as to the driver's identity. But Tony Gibson was seen driving the car about fifteen minutes before it went over the cliff. I think it's a pretty safe assumption that he was the one in the bottom of that ravine."

"If he's dead, who would want his widow to think he was still alive? And why?"

"Good question. And a good reason for you to keep an eye on the Hampton woman. Thing is, she had access to the kind of people Gibson liked to con, through that gallery job of hers. There's no reason to believe she was involved, but there it is. She could have been."

A few more exchanges, and he was off the phone, but he sat staring at it. Rojas had talked because he wanted to keep a line on Caroline Hampton, however tenuous.

If Tony Gibson had been involved in the kind of scam Rojas suspected, he had been a dangerous man to know. Caroline might be an innocent victim.

Or she might be involved.

He knew more now than he had fifteen minutes ago, but he couldn't say that it made him any happier.

* * *

Caroline had never intended to go to church that Sunday. However, she hadn't been prepared to combat Grams's calm assumption that of course she'd go to the worship service at the small church across the road from the inn.

If she'd thought about it, she might have come up with some reason, or rather some excuse, that wouldn't hurt Grams's feelings. As it was, she'd nodded, smiled and tried to close her eyes and ears to the service.

She had a deal with God. He left her alone, and she left Him alone. She didn't want to change that, but she also didn't want to try to explain it to Grams.

The churchyard gate creaked shut as they exited, and she took a breath of relief. It was over, with no harm done. Next Sunday she'd be ready with an excuse.

Grams linked arms with her as they started across the street, Rachel behind them, chatting with Andrea and Cal. "What did you think of the service, Caro?"

Caroline glanced back at the stone church that had stood within its encircling stone wall for the past two hundred and fifty years. The green lawn was splashed with color from spring dresses—in Churchville, people obviously still believed that worship called for their best. In their own way, they were as traditional as the Amish, meeting in someone's house or barn today.

Realizing Grams was looking at her for an answer, she managed a smile. "Nice." That didn't seem to quite cover it. "I noticed Zach Burkhalter with his little girl." She was sorry the moment the words were out. She didn't want to sound as if she were asking about him.

"Not just Zach," Rachel commented as they reached the sidewalk in front of the inn. "I think the Burkhalters have expanded to two pews, haven't they? That was his mother, sitting on the far side of Ruthie."

"I met her at the craft show. And Karen was very helpful." Did that sound stilted? Probably. She hadn't been able to forget the way Zach had snatched his little girl away from her, as if her troubles were contagious.

"They're all helping him raise that child," Grams said. "It's a lovely thing to see."

"He's not married?"

Grams shook her head. "Oh, no. Ruthie is the daughter of some friends he made when he was stationed in the Middle East with the military. The parents were killed very tragically, and Zach adopted her."

She blinked. "I didn't realize." She'd been making assumptions that were amazingly far from the truth.

"She's a dear little thing." Grams smiled. "And so appropriately named. Ruth, finding a home in an alien place."

She nodded, the story from long-ago Sunday school days coming back to her. Apparently this little Ruth had found the place where she belonged, thanks to Zach.

She'd figured him for a straight arrow, but he obviously wasn't the cold fish she'd assumed. She'd seen that when she'd seen him with his little girl.

"I have a casserole in the oven." Rachel headed back toward the kitchen the moment they got inside. "We'll be ready for brunch in a few minutes."

"I'll help you." Caroline followed her to the kitchen, catching the look of surprise that was quickly hidden by Rachel's smile.

Fair enough. She hadn't been much help to anyone since she'd come back, obsessed as she was with her own problems. It was time she changed that.

"What can I do?" She washed her hands quickly and turned back to Rachel, who was pulling a casserole from the oven, her cheeks rosy.

"There's a fruit salad in the fridge that goes on the table. I'll just stick the rolls in to heat up for a minute."

She nodded, lifting the glass bowl from the fridge and removing the plastic wrap that covered the assortment of melon, blueberries, pears and bananas. "Lovely."

Rachel shrugged. "Everything's left over from the guest breakfast. Makes Sunday easier—otherwise I'd never make it to church."

That would suit her. Maybe she could offer to stay behind and make dinner next week, but somehow she didn't think Grams would agree to that.

"Your schedule is pretty tight. I didn't realize what went into running a B & B."

"It's worth it." Rachel's expression softened. "I feel as if I came home when I came back here. Mom certainly never gave us anything that was remotely like a home."

She carried the fruit in and set it on the table. Rachel, following her, took silverware from the massive corner cupboard.

"You and Andrea had more memories from this place than I did. I was too young to have built up much." Was that jealousy she felt? Surely not.

"Doesn't mean you can't start now." Rachel set the table swiftly. "I saw Keith Morris talking with you after service. What do you think of our mayor?"

"Not bad, but his mother tried to freeze me dead with a look. Guess she doesn't fancy me for her baby boy."

Rachel grinned. "She's more likely to snub you for insulting her knowledge of local history."

"On the contrary, I asked very humbly for her advice. About the 1850s quilt we found, remember?"

"You mean she didn't take the opportunity to lecture you on the history of the township?"

"Just said it was 'of no historic interest' and walked off."

"She probably hates that someone else owned it. You ought to talk to Emma's mother-in-law about it. She knows everything there is to know about quilts."

"Who knows everything about quilts?" Grams came into the room, followed by Andrea and Cal.

"Levi Zook's mother. Caro wants to find out more about the flying geese quilt that grandfather's grandmother made."

Grams nodded. "I think there might be something about it in some family letters your grandfather collected. I'll see what I can find."

"Thanks, Grams. I'd like that. I'm not sure why it fascinates me so. I actually had a dream the other night about the geese." She'd been flying with them, soaring away from everything that held her back.

"You must have the quilt, since it seems to have touched you," Grams said gently.

Tears stung her eyes, sudden and unexpected. "You shouldn't—I mean, it might be valuable, whatever Mrs. Morris thinks."

"It's yours." Grams pressed her hands. "We'll say no more about it."

She looked from face to face, seeing…what? Love? Acceptance?

Panic swept through her for a moment. She'd told herself that what they thought of her didn't matter—told herself that she was better off relying on no one but herself.

It wasn't true. The longer she was here, the more she became enmeshed in something she'd given up a long time ago.

And the more she risked, when they would eventually let her down.

Chapter Seven

So that was what Caroline was hiding in her past. Zach had known instinctively there was something.

He leaned back in his desk chair, hearing its familiar squeak, and stared at the computer screen in front of him. It hadn't even been that hard to find—the record of the arrest of the then-sixteen-year-old Caroline Hampton, charged in the robbery of a convenience store in Chicago.

Sixteen. The criminal record of a sixteen-year-old shouldn't be so readily available, but sometimes the legal system didn't work the way it should.

He frowned, leaning forward to read through the report again, filling in the blanks from experience. Two older boys had actually done the crime, roughing up the elderly store owner in the process. Caroline had apparently been the driver, waiting outside.

His frown deepened. She was only sixteen, and she hadn't been inside the store when the crime was committed. A good attorney should have been able to get her off with probation, with her record wiped clean at the end of it. That hadn't happened. Why?

There were only two possibilities that he could see. Either she was far more involved than the bare facts would indicate, or she hadn't had decent representation. Hard to believe that the Unger family wouldn't have hired a lawyer for their granddaughter, but it was always possible they hadn't known. It was the mother who had custody, not Fredrick and Katherine Unger.

He flipped through the text, looking for the resolution of the case. And found it. Caroline Hampton had been confined in a teen correctional facility until her eighteenth birthday.

Pity stirred in him. That was pretty harsh, given her age and the fact that she didn't seem to have been in trouble before. Still, everyone's life wasn't an open book on the Internet. There might have been—must have been—other factors involved.

He drummed his fingers on the scarred edge of the desk. No one had mentioned this serious blip in Caroline's past, at least not to him. Well, they wouldn't, would they?

Still, he'd give a lot to know what the family knew about it. And what they thought about it. Was that a piece of whatever had kept the sisters apart for so long?

More to the point, could it be related to what was happening now? On the surface that seemed unlikely, but he'd learned not to discount anything.

There was a tap on his office door, followed by the creak as it opened. The face of young Eric Snyder appeared. He looked worried, but that meant nothing. Snyder always looked worried, as if he were completely convinced that whatever he decided to do, it was wrong.

As it usually was. He'd never seen anyone with less natural aptitude for police work, but the boy's uncle was a county commissioner, which meant the police force was stuck with him for the moment.

"What is it, Snyder?"

"Ms. Hampton is here to see you, Chief."

Rachel? Or Caroline? Well, he didn't want either of them to see the report in from of him. He saved the file and clicked off.

"Ask her to come in."

A moment later Caroline sidled through the door, looking around as if expecting trouble. "I wanted to see you," she said abruptly.

He stood, noting the by-now-familiar flinch away from him. Well, now he knew why. That aversion of hers to anyone in a uniform could be a sign of guilt. Or it could be the reaction of injured innocence.

"I promised I'd let you know if anything else happened."

"I'm glad you remembered." He reached out to pull his lightweight jacket from the coatrack. "No reason why we have to stay inside on such a nice day. Let's take a walk and talk about it."

Her sigh of relief was audible. "Good." She turned, moving back through the door so quickly that it was almost flight.

He followed, glancing at Snyder. "I'll be back in a few minutes. Take any calls that come in."

The boy gulped, nodding. He didn't like being left in charge of the office. Again, not a desirable quality in a cop.

Caroline was already out on the sidewalk, waiting in the sunshine, hugging her dark denim jacket around her. Under it she wore a blouse that seemed to be made of handkerchiefs sewn together, and her silver and turquoise earrings tangled in her hair.

He joined her, falling into step as she strode away from police headquarters. "Even warmer than yesterday was. Nice Sunday, wasn't it? Did you enjoy the sermon?"

He'd intended the casual comment to relax her, but it seemed to have the opposite effect. She jammed her hands into the pockets of the denim jacket, her shoulders hunching. "Yes. It made my grandmother happy to have all of us in church with her."

"That sounds as if you wouldn't go on your own."

She shot him a look that bordered on dislike. "That doesn't have anything to do with why I came to see you."

He shrugged. "Just making conversation." But he really did wonder where she was spiritually. It seemed as if Caroline could use a solid underpinning of faith right now. "Sorry. Something else has happened?"

They'd walked past the bakery before she nodded. Reluctant. Caroline was always reluctant when it came to him. He understood that a little better than he had before he'd unearthed the story of her past.

"I got something in the mail." Her hands were shoved tightly into her pockets. "I can't explain it."

He came to a halt at the bench in front of Dora's Yarn Shop, planting his hands on its back and looking at her. The pot of pansies next to the bench gave a bright spot of color to the street. "You plan to let me see it?"

She didn't want to—that much was evident in the apprehension that darkened those green eyes. So why had she come? She was perfectly capable of ignoring that promise he'd screwed out of her.

Maybe she'd run out of excuses. Probably he was the least of a number of bad choices.

She yanked an envelope from her pocket and shoved it toward him. "This came in today's mail. I didn't know what to do about it."

He took it, handling it by the edges automatically. A business-size envelope, Caroline's name and address printed in computer-generated letters. No return address. The postmark read Philadelphia.

She shifted her weight from one foot to the other impatiently. "Open it."

She obviously already had, no doubt further obscuring any fingerprints that might have survived the handling of the postal service, unlikely as that was. He teased out the enclosure—a folded fragment of copy paper with something hard inside it.

He flipped it open. The briefest of notes in block printing. A small key held fast to the paper with a strip of cellophane tape.

"It's a safe-deposit key," she said impatiently. "I'm sure of it."

He studied the key more closely. "I think you're right. It may be possible to find out what bank it's from, especially if it's in Philadelphia."

"It will be." She stared at the note as if it were a snake. "Tony had family there. Anyway, he said he did. I never met them. Never even talked to them. Tony was going to tell them about our marriage when we came east. That's what he said, anyway."

He nodded slowly, frowning at the words on the page. "Is this your husband's handwriting?"

She took a breath, the sound ragged, as if she had to yank the air in. "I think so."

Black letters. Three short words. She couldn't be positive from that small a sample, but she probably had a fairly good idea who wrote those words.

"For my wife."

What had possessed her to tell Zach, of all people? He stood there on the sidewalk looking at her, gray eyes intent and watchful, as if weighing every word and gesture. Judging her.

Still, what choice did she have? Who else would she tell?

A brisk breeze ruffled the faces of the pansies, making them shiver, and she shivered with them. The truth was that she couldn't keep this to herself any longer. She didn't know what to do or how to find out what it meant.

She certainly couldn't take this to Grams. And while Andrea's cool common sense might have been welcome, she'd have to tell her everything for the story to make any sense.

At least Zach already knew. She might not be happy about that, but it was a fact.

He nodded, murmuring a greeting to someone passing by. The woman sent a bright, curious gaze Caro's way, and she turned, pulling the collar of her jacket up, as if that might shield her from prying eyes.

Zach folded the envelope and pushed it into his jacket pocket. He took her arm.

"Let's go to the café and have some coffee. You look as if you could stand to warm up. And it won't be crowded this time in the afternoon."

He steered her down the street, turning in to the Distelfink Café. The door closed behind them, and they were enveloped in the mingled aromas of coffee, chicken soup and something baking that smelled like cinnamon.

"See? Empty." Zach led her past several round tables to a booth against the far wall. The tables were covered with brightly painted stencils of the Distelfink, the stylized, mythical bird that appeared on so much Pennsylvania Dutch folk art.

She slid into the booth. The wooden tabletop bore place mats in the same pattern, and the salt and pepper shakers were in the shape of the fanciful birds.

Zach folded himself into the booth and nodded toward the elderly woman who'd emerged from the kitchen. She was as plump and round and rosy as one of the stenciled figures herself. "Two coffees, Annie."

"Sure thing, Zach. How about some peach cobbler to go with it?"

"Sounds good."

She disappeared, and Caroline shook her head. "I don't want any cobbler. I just want to talk about this—"

"If we take Annie up on the peach cobbler, she won't be popping out of the kitchen every two seconds to offer us something else." He turned a laminated menu toward her. "Unless there's something else you want."

She shook her head. The menu, like everything else, was decorated with stenciled figures—birds, stars, Amish buggies. She flipped it over.

"I see they still offer a free ice cream to any child who memorizes the Distelfink poem."

He smiled, his big hands clasped loosely on the table in front of him. "Sure thing. It's a rite of passage in Churchville. You must have done it."

"Oh, yes." Memory teased her. "As I recall, I insisted on standing up on my chair and declaiming it to the entire café. I'm sure I embarrassed my family to no end."

"I imagine they thought it was cute. Ruthie's been

working on it every time we come in. She'll probably get the whole thing mastered by the next time we're here."

His doting smile told her that he wouldn't be embarrassed by anything his little daughter chose to do.

Annie bustled out of the kitchen with a tray, sliding thick white coffee mugs and huge bowls of peach cobbler, thick with cream and cinnamon, in front of them.

"Anything else I can get for you folks?"

"We're fine, Annie. Thanks." Something in his voice must have indicated this wasn't the time for chitchat. The woman vanished back into the kitchen, leaving them alone.

Caro took a gulp of the coffee, welcoming the warmth that flooded through her. But it wouldn't—couldn't—touch the cold at her very center; the cold that she'd felt when she saw the letter.

Zach didn't pull the envelope out again, and at some level she was grateful. "Have you showed it to your family?"

"No." She thought of all the reasons why not. "I haven't told them much about Tony. Showing them this would mean I'd have to tell them everything. They'd be upset, and I don't want that."

That wasn't all the reason. She knew it. Maybe he did, too. He watched her, the steady gaze making her nervous.

"Your choice," he said finally. "Question is, do you really think it's genuine?"

She stared down into her mug, as if she could read an answer there. "It looks like Tony's handwriting. I'm not an expert."

"If someone had a sample, it wouldn't be that hard to fake three words."

"I guess not." She pressed her fingertips against her

temples, as if that might make her thoughts clearer. "What would be the point of faking it?"

He shrugged. "What would be the point of sending it, even if it's genuine?"

"Exactly." At least they agreed on that. "It's not as if the sender is asking me to do anything. It's just a key."

"Seems like if someone sends you a key, they intend you to use it to open something," he said mildly.

"I get that." She found she was gritting her teeth together and forced herself to stop. "It's postmarked Philadelphia. As I told you, Tony said he had family in Philadelphia."

"That's a link. Still, it's odd, assuming this is from your husband—"

"I don't think we—I can assume that. It could be a fake, or it could be something Tony wrote that someone else sent me."

"Why?"

"I wish I knew." She rubbed her temples again. "Just when I get a line of logic going, it falls apart on me. Why would anyone do any of the things that have happened?"

"Good question." He was silent for a moment, but she felt his gaze on her face. "Should I assume you want to get to the bottom of this?"

"What I want is to be left alone, but it doesn't look as if that's going to happen." *You could run,* the voice whispered at the back of her mind. *You could run away again.*

But she couldn't. At some point, for a reason she didn't quite understand, she'd stopped running. She was here. She was staying. So—

"Yes," she said, surprised by how firm her voice was. "I want to get to the bottom of this whole thing. But how?"

She looked up at him when she asked the question, finding his gaze fixed on her face. For a moment she couldn't seem to catch her breath. He was too close.

Don't be ridiculous, she scolded herself. *He's clear across the table.* But he seemed much nearer.

"I might be able to identify the bank where the safe-deposit box is." He frowned a little. "And with some more information, I might also be able to trace any family he had. What did he tell you about them?"

"Not much." Almost nothing, in fact. Now that seemed suspicious, but at the time, it hadn't surprised her. After all, she didn't see much of her family, so why would she expect something else from him?

"What exactly?" He sounded remarkably patient, and he pulled a small notebook and pen from his pocket, setting it on the place mat in front of him.

She took a breath, trying to remember anything Tony had mentioned. Trying not to look at those strong, capable hands that seemed to hold her future.

"He was named for his father, I know he said that. Anthony Patrick Gibson. He mentioned a married sister once. I helped him pick out a piece of jewelry for her birthday."

Zach scribbled some unreadable notes in a minuscule hand. "Any idea where in Philadelphia? City or suburbs?"

She shook her head slowly. Incredible, that she knew so little about the man she'd married. "I suppose it would all have been in his PDA, but that was in the car with him. I had the impression they lived in the suburbs, maybe on the Main Line."

Nothing definite, she realized now. Tony had managed to convey, just by how he looked and acted, that he'd come from money. Society, the kind of people who learned which fork to use before they learned their ABCs.

Zach raised his eyebrows. "Money?"

"I guess that's what I thought." That was what Tony had thought about her, wasn't it? That Unger House, the grandfather who'd been a judge, the great-grandfather who'd served in the state senate, had automatically conveyed an aura of wealth and privilege.

"Look, we just didn't talk about our families all that much. I suppose, if I'd thought about it, that it was odd I didn't know more, but we were going to see them when we came east. I'd have found out all about them then." She blinked, realization dawning. "But there was an address—there must have been, because the police said they'd notified his family. I don't know how I could have forgotten that."

She'd been numb—that was the only explanation. She'd gotten through those days in a fog of misery, not thinking much beyond the next step she had to take.

"Well, that gives us a place to start, anyway. I'll make some calls and see what I can come up with."

She looked at him, wondering what was really going on behind that spare, taciturn expression. "I... I don't know. Maybe I should just let it drop. I mean, without anything else to go on, how much can I expect to learn?"

He put his hand over hers where it lay on the table, startling her. "Let me tell you what just happened. You've been stewing about that letter since the mail came this morning, working yourself up until you had to tell someone about it. And then you told me, and saying it out loud relieved some of the pressure. So now you're thinking that it's not so bad after all."

"Are you setting up as a psychiatrist on the side?" She

couldn't help the edge to her voice, because he'd nailed it. That was exactly how she'd felt—that pressure to tell someone, that feeling that she couldn't carry it another minute by herself. And then the release, as if by saying the words, she'd convinced herself it wasn't so bad.

"Normal human nature," he said. His fingers tightened around hers. "Don't kid yourself, Caroline. There's something going on here. Something—" he paused, as if wanting to be sure he had the right word "—something malicious about all this. I think we need to find out what's behind it. We, not you."

His gaze was steady on hers. Questioning: Will you let me help you? Will you trust me that much?

She bit her lip. She didn't trust, not easily, and certainly not a cop. But she was running out of options, and Zach Burkhalter was the best choice she had.

Something winced inside her, but she managed to nod. "All right. Will you help me find out what's going on?"

His grip eased fractionally. "Okay. Assuming I can get any answers by then, let's go to Philadelphia tomorrow."

For better or worse, they were committed.

Caroline's hand clenched on the car's armrest, but her nerves had nothing to do with the traffic Zach encountered as he took the off-ramp from the interstate toward the Philadelphia suburb where he'd determined the bank was located.

He shot a sideways glance at her. "Don't you trust my driving?"

"It's not that." She released the armrest and slid her palms down the creases of her lightweight wool slacks. Well, not hers, exactly. The art of dressing to impress a banker was Andrea's style, so she'd borrowed the tan pantsuit from her sister. Even brightened with her favorite turquoise necklace, it didn't look like her.

"There shouldn't be any difficulty accessing the safe-deposit box." Zach glanced in the rearview mirror before swinging around a double-parked car. "You brought all the paperwork, didn't you?"

"Yes." Not only had Zach found the bank, he'd determined what she'd need in order to prove her right to claim the contents of the box. "I'm not worried about that. I was just thinking about how fast you were able to get the information. And how much more of my life must be spread out there for anyone to see who has the skill and the authority."

He glanced at her, his gaze shielded behind the amber sunglasses he wore. "You don't care much for authority, do you?"

That tightened her nerves, but she managed a cool smile and what she hoped was an equally cool tone. "My sisters would tell you that I've always been the rebel."

Whether he wanted to or not, Zach exuded authority. Even today, wearing khakis and a dress shirt instead of his uniform, there was no mistaking that. It was present in the calm gray eyes, the strong planes of his face, the whipcord strength of his long muscles. He was a man who would always take control, whatever the situation.

"You were the one to test all the rules, I guess." He frowned at the GPS system on the dashboard, as if assessing its accuracy.

With their mother the rules had been whatever capricious notion had taken her fancy at the moment, but Caroline had no desire to get into that. "Pretty much. Andrea was the perfect one, of course, and Rachel was the peacemaker. The role of rebel was open, so I took it."

His hand flexed on the gearshift. "I was the oldest in my family. Does that make me perfect?"

"It probably makes you think you are."

"Touché." His glance flickered to her. "Does that rebellion of yours extend to God?"

Her stomach clenched. How had she given so much away to this man that he could even guess that?

"Let's just say I never want to get too close." She hoped he'd let it go at that, but suspected he wouldn't.

"I've felt that way at times, I guess when things were going fine and I thought I could handle everything on my own. Unfortunately in my line of work I get plenty of reminders that I can't, and I have to come running back, looking for help."

She stared out the window, not wanting him to see her face. "And do you get it?"

"Always. But not always in the shape I think it should come."

What about not at all? But she didn't want to hear his answer to that, did she?

The GPS beeped, its metallic voice announcing a right turn at the next intersection. Zach jerked a nod toward the unit.

"Be nice if God was like that, always alerting you when you were about to make a wrong turn. I guess sometimes you just have to make the mistake first before you're ready to admit it."

"So God stands back and lets you sink." She snapped the words out before she could censor them.

"Was that what you felt happened when you landed in trouble as a teenager?"

She winced as if he'd hit her. So he knew. Well, was that so surprising?

"I take it my so-called criminal record is out there for anyone to see."

"Not anyone." His voice softened, as if he knew he'd hurt her. "The records should have been sealed, given your age, but mistakes happen."

"Don't they, though." And always, it seemed, in someone else's favor. "Well, now that you know, I'm surprised you're helping me. Or maybe you're not. Maybe you're just trying to prove I've done something wrong."

He wouldn't find anything else, no matter how much he searched her past. She'd been scrupulous since the day the gates of Lakecrest closed behind her. No matter how hard he looked, he wouldn't find so much as a parking ticket—nothing to involve her with the police, ever.

Until now. Maybe Zach wasn't dressed like a cop today, but that was who he was, bone deep.

"Look, I didn't want to try and hide the fact that I'd checked into your past. That doesn't mean I'll let it influence my attitude toward you."

Her chin lifted. "As far as I can tell, your opinion of me was set from the first moment you saw me. This was just confirmation, wasn't it?"

He didn't answer for a moment, occupied with turning into a parking lot. The bank parking lot, she realized, and her stomach churned.

Zach pulled into a parking space and switched off the ignition. Then he turned to her. He pulled off the glasses, and his eyes were intent on her face, so intent that it seemed her skin warmed.

"I'm probably not going to convince you of this, but I came into the situation thinking you're innocent, not thinking you're guilty. Of anything. The fact that you got into trouble as a teenager doesn't have any bearing on anything." He paused, and a muscle twitched at the corner of his mouth. "Except, maybe, that it's made you prejudiced against anyone who wears a uniform, including me."

He didn't give her time to come up with an answer. He just turned and slid out of the car.

Chapter Eight

"Now, Mrs. Gibson, if you've brought all the proper documentation, I'll just need to have a look at it."

Caroline swallowed hard as she pulled papers from her shoulder bag and handed them to the bank officer. She couldn't stop being aware of Zach, sitting in the chair next to her. Anyone looking at the scene might think them a married couple, applying for a home loan or something else equally routine.

But there was nothing ordinary about this situation. She glanced at the man behind the desk—Dawson, that was it. His name had gone into her brain and fallen back out again as quickly, a tribute to the nerves that seemed to be doing a tango at the moment.

Thin and balding, with a fussy, precise manner, he peered so intently at each document that it seemed the bank itself, with its arched ceilings and echoing tile floors, might tumble down around them if he didn't get this right.

"Mrs. Gibson—"

Her fingers clenched. "Ms. Hampton, please. I kept my birth name."

"Yes, of course." He frowned as if that were, in itself, a suspicious action. "If you don't mind waiting a few minutes, I'll just need to make copies of these."

She nodded, leaning back in the chair with an assumption of ease. Mrs. Gibson. No one had ever called her that, other than a desk clerk at the hotel where they'd checked in for their three-day honeymoon. She'd never had a chance to get used to the name. Maybe that was just as well.

Zach seemed perfectly ready to wait as long as it took. He had a gift of stillness, and for an instant her fingers itched for a pad and pencil to capture that.

But if she did, what would it say about the man? The ease of his long body in the chair, the carefully neutral expression on his face—everything about Zach seemed designed to camouflage his emotions, assuming he had any.

Well, of course he did. She was being ridiculous. She'd seen him with his daughter, and there was certainly no lack of feeling there. The fact that he wore that shuttered look with her just confirmed that he saw her as part of his job, nothing else.

He knew about her past. She still had difficulty swallowing that. To do him justice, he hadn't let that prejudice him against her, but she suspected it had to weigh in the balance he kept in his mind, with each new fact he learned about her being dropped on the scale.

He didn't know everything. Her stomach twisted. He couldn't. The ugliest thing about that time would never appear in any official report, even though it had left an indelible stain on her life.

She straightened her back, clasping her hands loosely in her lap and trying to behave as she imagined Andrea would in such a situation—cool, confident, perfectly at ease.

"He's been gone a long time." The words came out before she could tell herself that saying them made her sound anything but cool and confident. "Maybe he found something wrong."

The faintest of frowns made a crease between Zach's level eyebrows. "What could he find wrong?"

"Nothing. Nothing at all." She'd say she was just nervous, but that was probably pretty obvious to him. "I... I don't like this."

"Why?" He leaned forward, his gaze probing.

"I just feel that way. Does there have to be a reason?"

He considered that calmly. "There usually is."

She clamped her mouth shut to keep from snapping at him. She counted to ten. "All right." Maybe she should have made it twenty. "I guess it bothers me to feel that I'm being manipulated. That I'm doing exactly what someone wants me to."

To her surprise, he nodded. "I understand. And you're probably right, but what other choice did you have?"

"None." Unfortunately, he was right, too. "That doesn't mean I have to like it."

"I'd say the best thing would be to move cautiously. No matter what is in that box, you don't have to act on it today."

"Right." She took a deep breath and tried a smile. "You're right. Whatever it is, I don't have to rush into dealing with it."

Dawson came toward them, sliding papers into a file. "Here are your originals back, Mrs.—Ms. Hampton." He handed them to her. "Naturally, I'd like to express our sympathy in your loss."

"Thank you."

"As you probably know, Pennsylvania law requires that a safe-deposit box be sealed upon the death of the owner until it can be inventoried by a representative of the Department of Revenue."

"No, I didn't know that." If she had, she wouldn't be here. What was the point of this exercise, if she couldn't access the box?

"However, since you and your husband rented the box jointly, that's not an issue. If you'll just come along, I'll get the box out for you."

Jointly. She felt as if she'd stepped onstage in a play where she didn't know the lines. She hadn't rented the box—at least not knowingly. But the bank officer clearly thought she had.

And Zach—what did he think? Did he assume she'd been lying all along about this?

Moving automatically, she followed the man, aware of Zach, close on her heels. Down one long hall, footsteps echoing on the tile, and then a flight of stairs. Dawson led them into a small room lined with storage compartments, its only furniture a table in the center of the room. Obviously the bank didn't encourage its patrons to hang around here.

Murmuring the number under his breath, Dawson retrieved the box, placing it on the table. Once it was unlocked, he stepped back with a suggestion of duty fulfilled.

"There you are. I'll wait until you're finished."

She was barely aware of the man moving to the doorway, turning his back as if to give them some semblance of privacy. All her attention was focused on the box. On the feeling it aroused.

Dread. There was no other word for it. Whatever Tony had put in that safe-deposit box, she didn't want to know. And however he'd gotten her name on the box, she didn't want to know that, either.

"Would you like me to wait outside?" Zach said.

She shook her head slowly. "No. Stay. Whatever it is, I think I'd like a witness." Besides, if she didn't let him stay, that would simply make him more suspicious.

"If that's what you want."

He was probably pleased. He saw this as one more step toward solving a puzzle, nothing more.

She couldn't be that detached. Tony's secrets hadn't died with him, and she was about to see one of them. Somehow she didn't think it could be anything good.

She reached out, her hands a little unsteady, and lifted the lid from the box. It clattered when she dropped it back onto the table. She heard a swift intake of breath from Zach.

She didn't seem to be breathing at all. She took an involuntary step back, not wanting to admit what she was seeing.

Money. The safe-deposit box was stuffed to the brim with cash.

Zach leaned against the back of the park bench, trying to look anything but as tense as he felt. Caroline was upset enough already. The last thing she needed was for him to add to that.

She sat on the other end of the concrete-and-redwood bench, staring out over the wide, placid river, as if intent on the rowing sculls that zipped along its surface like water bugs. But her hands clasped each other so tightly that the knuckles were white, and even the warmth of the spring sunshine didn't keep the occasional shiver from going through her.

"Have a little more of your coffee," he urged.

She lifted the foam cup to her lips and drank without looking at it. When they'd finally gotten out of the bank he'd wanted to find a restaurant where they could sit and talk, but she'd just kept shaking her head.

Well, he could understand why she didn't want to feel hemmed in. He'd finally gone through a fast-food drive-through and ordered her a large coffee with sugar. Something hot and sweet seemed the right remedy for shock.

Was the shock genuine? The analytical part of his cop's brain weighed her reactions. She'd certainly acted surprised when Dawson had pulled out the rental lease with her name on it. To suppose that she'd already known about the box was to imagine she'd been taking him for a ride all along, and he didn't think he was that gullible.

And she couldn't have mimicked that shock when she'd flipped the box lid back and seen the money. Whatever she'd expected to find in that safe-deposit box, it wasn't that.

"You feel like talking about it now?" He edged a little closer, even though there was no one within earshot.

The ground sloped gently from where they sat down to the river, and the few people who were in the park at this hour were on the paved path that led along the water—a couple of joggers, a couple of women pushing strollers.

Caroline lifted her hand, palm up. "I don't know what to say. I don't understand any of it."

"You didn't have any idea Tony had rented that safe-deposit box in your names?"

She shook her head, the movement setting her dangling silver earrings dancing. "No. I didn't even know he'd been in Philadelphia. Why wouldn't he tell me that? I wouldn't have found it suspicious if he'd said he had to go there on business."

Some people lied even when it would be easier to tell the truth, but it seemed pointless to say so. "The rental form had what looked like your signature on it."

She rubbed her forehead. "I guess it's faintly possible that he slipped the form in with some other papers to sign, and I didn't notice what it was."

She didn't sound convinced. Well, he wasn't, either. Caroline might be something of a free spirit, maybe a tad irresponsible, but he doubted she'd sign something without even looking at it.

"And the money? You didn't know he had that much salted away?"

Nearly two hundred thousand dollars. Caroline had refused to so much as touch the contents of the box, but finally she'd agreed to let him count it.

Afterward, he'd put the cash back into the box, and Caroline had returned it to the bank's care. What else was there to do? If it hadn't been for Caroline's name on that lease, the bank officer would have sealed the box himself, not letting them do anything but look for a will until someone was present from the Department of Revenue.

Caroline transferred her gaze from the sculls to him. "It's not my money."

She'd been saying that, in one variation or another, since they'd left the bank.

"If it belonged to your husband, then it belongs to you, unless he made a will leaving it elsewhere."

"As far as I know, Tony didn't make a will. But then, there's a lot that I don't know, obviously." Her voice held an edge.

"Barring a will, it would go to you as next of kin."

"I don't want it." The suppressed emotion in her voice startled him. "Even if it did belong to Tony, I can't imagine that he came by it honestly."

"You said he took money out of your account. You could probably legitimately claim that, even if—"

He stopped, because she was shaking her head. "I don't want it, I tell you. I just want to forget I ever saw it."

Her voice had the ring of truth. She had to be hard up for money, if Gibson really had cleaned her out, but she seemed adamant about that.

"I can understand, I guess," he said slowly, "but I don't think you're going to be able to do that. Seems to me you ought to notify the Santa Fe police."

Fear flared in those green eyes. "No! I mean, I don't want to have anything to do with it."

Anything to do with the police—that was what she meant. He hated to push her. What he wanted to do was put his arm around her shoulder, pull her close and tell her everything was going to be all right.

But he couldn't. It wouldn't be professional, for one thing. And he couldn't promise things were going to be fine. His instincts told him a law had been violated somewhere in all of this, even if he couldn't put his finger on it yet.

"Where do you think the money came from?" Maybe if he could get her thinking, the fear would leave her eyes and they could talk about notifying the police in a rational manner.

"I don't know." She rubbed the sleeves of her suit jacket. "Based on when he rented the safe-deposit box, it was several months ago. I just can't imagine, but obviously I didn't have a clue about his finances."

"What about gambling winnings?"

She winced a little, but she kept her back ramrod straight, reminding him of her grandmother. "I guess that's one possibility."

She clearly didn't want to admit that, but it seemed the obvious answer to a lot of the problems she'd been having. A compulsive gambler, losing money he couldn't repay, might resort to stealing from his wife or even driving his car off the side of a mountain.

The trouble with that scenario was that it didn't fit the facts. Tony, with a safe-deposit box stuffed with cash, didn't look like any loser he'd ever seen.

He studied Caroline's face. Those normally clear green eyes were clouded, the shadows under them looking like bruises on the fair skin. There were lines of strain around her generous mouth, and he had the sense that she was hanging on to her composure by a thread.

Sooner or later, information about the money would have to be passed on to the Santa Fe police. Since Tony's death wasn't being investigated, he didn't feel an urgency to do it today.

He could give Caroline another day, maybe. But if she hadn't decided by then to talk to the New Mexico cops, he'd have to do it.

"Do you want to head home now?" He planted his hand on the top slat of the bench, ready to get up.

She looked up, startled. "We're going to try and find Tony's family, aren't we? You said that you had a possible address."

"I do. But I thought maybe you'd had enough for one day."

She managed a smile. "Think how offended my grandmother would be at the idea that an Unger wouldn't do her duty, no matter what."

"You don't have to prove anything, Caroline." But maybe, in her mind, she did.

She rose, slinging the strap of her leather bag on her shoulder. "I'd rather get it over with. If Tony has family here in Philadelphia, I think it's time I met them."

"Are you sure this is the right address?" Caroline stared through the windshield. The row house, its brick faded and stained, sat behind its wire mesh fence with an air of cringing away from the street. Small wonder. This wasn't the worst neighborhood in Philadelphia, but it had an air of having come down in the world considerably in recent years.

Zach consulted the address in his notebook, checked the GPS monitor and nodded. "This is it, all right. Not what you expected?"

"No. I can't imagine Tony growing up here." She thought of the safe-deposit box stuffed with money, and her stomach tightened. "But I seem to have been wrong about plenty of things where Tony was concerned."

Tony, who were you? Was there anything real about our marriage?

The look Zach sent her seemed to assess her stability. "Are you sure you want to do this now?"

She took a deep breath. In a situation like this, her grandmother would rely on her faith. For a moment she felt a twinge of something that might be envy. To feel that Someone was always there—

But she couldn't. She grabbed the door handle. "Let's go."

"Wait a second." He reached across her to clasp her

hand before she could open the door. For a moment she couldn't seem to breathe. He was too close, much too close. She could smell the clean scent of his soap, feel the hard muscles in the arm that pressed against her.

"Why?" She forced out the word, her voice breathless.

He drew back, as if he'd just realized how close he was. "Maybe it would be better if I took the lead in talking to them. If they don't already know that Tony was married—"

"Yes, of course you're right." That was yet another nightmare to think about. Tony's family would have no reason to welcome, or believe in, a previously unknown wife. "Just—"

"What?"

She hesitated a moment and then shook her head. "I was going to say be tactful, but maybe there's nothing left to be tactful about."

He squeezed her hand, so lightly that she might have imagined it. "I'll do my best."

She slid out of the car and waited until he joined her on the sidewalk. The gate shrieked in protest when he pushed it open, and she followed him up the walk, stepping over the cracks where weeds flourished unchecked.

Three steps up to a concrete stoop, and then Zach rapped sharply on the door, ignoring the doorbell. Moments passed. The lace curtain on the window beside the door twitched. Someone was checking them out.

They must have looked presentable, because the woman swung the door open. "Something I can do for you?"

She was probably not more than thirty, Caro guessed. Blond hair, dark roots showing, was pulled back into a ponytail. She wore a faded navy cardigan over a waitress uniform, and the bag slung over her shoulder seemed to say that she had either just come in or was just going out.

"We're looking for Anthony Gibson. Does he live here?"

She jerked a nod and turned to look over her shoulder. "Somebody for you, Tony. Listen, I have to go. I'll see you later."

She held the door so that they could enter and then slid past them as if eager to make her departure.

"What do you folks want?" The tone held a trace of suspicion. The man thumped his way toward them with a walker. Tall, like Tony, with dark eyes.

But the world was full of tall men with dark eyes. Surely this couldn't be Tony's father. The setting was wrong, and he must be too old—he looked nearly as old as Grams, rather than being a contemporary of her mother.

"You're Tony Gibson?" Zach nudged her forward as he spoke.

"That's right." The man came to a stop at a mustard-colored recliner and sat, shoving the walker to one side.

"I'm Zachary Burkhalter, Chief of Police over in Churchville in Lancaster County. This is Caroline Hampton. We wanted to talk to you about your son."

She opened her mouth to say that this couldn't be her Tony's father, and then she closed it again, because Tony's picture sat on top of the upright piano in the corner. A much younger Tony, but that smile was unmistakable.

The lines in the man's face seemed to grow deeper. "My son died a month ago. If he owed you money, you're wasting your time coming here for it."

"No, nothing like that," Zach said easily. "We're just

trying to clear up some questions that came up after Tony's death. We weren't sure we had the right family."

The old man—Tony's father, she reminded herself—leaned back in the recliner, grabbing the handle so that the footrest flipped up. "My son, all right." He pointed to the picture on the piano. "If that's the Tony Gibson you're looking for."

"Yes." She forced herself to speak. "Yes, it is."

"Died out west. New Mexico, it was." He didn't look grieved, just resigned. "I always figured it would happen that way. Somebody'd call and tell us he was gone."

"What made you think that?" Zach's voice had gentled, as if he recognized pain behind the resignation.

He shrugged. "Always skating too near the edge of the law, Tony was. You can't keep doing that and not get into trouble at some point."

"Had you heard from him lately?" *Did he tell you about me?* That was what she wanted to ask, but something held her back.

"Not for months. He sent Mary Alice a hundred bucks back in January, I think it was. Said she should get Christmas presents with it."

Mary Alice was apparently the woman who'd opened the door to them. Tony's sister, she supposed, left here to look after their ailing father.

"Were you expecting a visit from him this spring?" She put the question abruptly, hearing Tony's voice in her mind. *We'll go back east in the spring, sweetheart. We'll surprise both our families.* He'd spun her around in a hug. *My folks will be crazy about you.*

"No. And I wouldn't have believed him if he had said so." He planted his hands on the arms of the recliner and leaned toward her. "What is all this, anyway? Why do you want to know about my son? What are you to him?"

"We just—" Zach began, but she shook her head.

"Don't, Zach." She took a breath. For good or ill, the man had a right to know she was his son's widow. "I'm sorry to blurt it out this way, Mr. Gibson. I'm actually Caroline Hampton Gibson. I was married to Tony."

He didn't speak, but a wave of red flushed alarmingly into his face. He jerked the recliner back into the upright position with a thump.

She took a step backward. "I don't want anything from you. I just thought you ought to know—"

"You're crazy, that's what you are." He grabbed the walker and took a step toward her. "Or you're trying to pull something. Some of his friends, most likely, just as crooked as he was."

"Nothing like that." Zach's tone was soothing.

The old man ignored him, glaring at Caroline. "I don't know who you are. But I know who you're not. You're not my son's wife. Mary Alice is Tony's wife, and she's the mother of his little girl."

Chapter Nine

Caroline spread the old quilt over the table in the barn, handling it as carefully as if it were a living creature. Maybe working on the quilt would distract her from the memory of yesterday's shocking revelations.

Maybe, but she doubted it.

She forced herself to concentrate on the pattern. The research she'd done had told her that the particular way the flying geese and star were combined on this quilt was unusual. She wanted to see it more clearly, but the colors were muted by an inevitable coating of dust. Going over it with the brush attachment of the vacuum cleaner on low power was the recommended process.

The soft hum of the vacuum blocked out other sounds. Unfortunately, it couldn't block out her thoughts. They kept leaping rebelliously back to that disastrous trip to Philadelphia.

Maybe *disastrous* wasn't the right word. The revelations, one after the other, had been painful, but would she be better off if she didn't know? The truth would be the truth, whether she wanted to hear it or not.

She still wasn't sure how she'd gotten out of that house

after Tony's father had dropped his bombshell. Zach had taken over, of course. That would always be his automatic response. He'd soothed the man as best he could and piloted her back to the car.

She hadn't been able to talk about it during the drive back. Maybe it would have been better to get it out, but she couldn't. She'd been numb, maybe in shock.

Zach hadn't pressed her, other than to urge her to tell her grandmother or her sisters what happened. He'd left her with the promise that he'd check the records and find out the facts.

She hadn't taken Zach's advice, good as it probably was. She'd been in limbo, unable to decide anything. She'd spent the evening with Grams and Rachel, taking comfort in their chatter, listening to Grams's stories, reviving a sense of belonging she hadn't had in a very long time.

She switched off the vacuum and stood back to look at the results. The experts appeared to be right—the area she'd gone over was discernibly brighter, the deep, saturated colors coming to life.

The sound of a step had her turning, seeing the shadow he cast in the patch of sunlight on the barn boards before she saw him. Zach stood in the doorway, his figure a dark shape against the brightness outside.

His uniform didn't induce that instinctive revulsion any longer, but her stomach still tightened at the sight of him. He might have found out. He might know the truth about her marriage.

"Hi. Your sister told me I'd find you here." He came toward her, heels sounding on the wide planks. A shaft of sunlight turned his sandy hair to gold for a moment, and then it darkened when he moved out of the light. He studied the quilt. "Are you taking up quilting now?"

"This is the quilt your sister and I were talking about. It apparently dates from the 1850s. I'm trying, very cautiously, to clean it up." She was a coward, but she'd rather talk about the quilt than what had brought him here.

"I'm surprised Agatha Morris wasn't interested. I'd expect her to be here leaning over your shoulder, telling you you're doing it all wrong."

"I may be, but eight out of ten experts on the Internet agreed that vacuuming with a soft brush was a good first step."

"What would we do without the Internet?"

He said the words casually, but she heard something beneath them that alerted her.

"You've found out, haven't you?" She let go of the vacuum hose, and it clattered to the floor.

He nodded toward a bench against the low wall that separated the hay mow from the rest of the barn floor. "Let's have a seat. I see Cal left behind some of the improvements he made when this was his workshop."

She followed him, not interested in whether her brother-in-law had made the bench or not, just intent on sitting down before her knees did something stupid.

"The Internet does make searching records easier. Tony married Mary Alice seven years ago in Philadelphia."

She ought to be shaken, shocked and appalled. Maybe she was, but at the moment she mostly seemed numb. "You're sure—" She shook her head. "Of course you're sure, or you wouldn't be telling me. What about the child?"

"Their daughter, Allison Mary, was born seven months later. A shotgun wedding, maybe."

It would be tempting to try and rationalize what Tony had done in that light, but she found she couldn't. He'd had a wife. A child. He had a duty to them, not to her.

"Did he get a divorce?" A voice she barely recognized as hers asked the question.

He hesitated for a moment, as if knowing how much this would hurt her. His very silence told her the answer before he said the word.

"No." His stretched his arm along the back of the bench and touched her shoulder. "I'm sorry, Caroline."

She nodded, trying to think this through. "So the marriage he went through with me wasn't legal. Am I—did I do anything against the law in marrying him?"

"No. He was the bigamist, not you."

She took a deep breath. "I guess mostly I don't understand. He must have known I'd find out the truth eventually. Why would he do such a thing?"

"That's a good question. Can you think of any reason—anything that might explain what was going through his mind?"

"If I could, don't you think I'd have mentioned that by now? There's nothing." She planted her hands on her knees. "Maybe if I threw something I'd feel better—preferably something at Tony's head."

"I don't think that would help." His voice was mild, as it always was. That didn't tell her whether he believed her or not. "It's natural enough to be angry at him."

"He's well beyond the reach of my anger now." That in itself was cause for wrath. Tony had escaped, and left her to deal with everything. "I'm relieved about one thing, though. Since I wasn't really his wife, I don't have to do anything about that money."

He didn't answer. Didn't move. How, then, did she know that he wanted something—something in relation to the money?

"What?" Impatience threaded her voice.

"You should talk to the Santa Fe police about it. They're the ones investigating his death, and it could have an impact upon that case."

"I don't want to." Her fingers twisted together in her lap. He put his hand over hers, stilling the restless movement.

"That's pretty obvious. Would you mind telling me why?"

Zach studied the expression on Caroline's face. What was going on with her? For that matter, what was going on with him? He ought to be looking at this situation, at her, with his usual professional detachment.

He wasn't managing to do that, not where Caroline was concerned. She got under his skin in a way he'd never experienced before.

She wasn't his type. Take that as a starting point. Sure, he was attracted to her. Any man would be. But this was about more than creamy skin and eyes so deep a green that a man could drown in them.

He was drawn by what he sensed beneath that—the creativity that sparked and sizzled in her, the gentle smile that didn't come often enough, the hint of vulnerability mixed with strength and independence.

His arguments seemed to be heading him in the wrong direction. Against that, he stacked who he was. A cop. A family man. A father who wouldn't bring a woman into his daughter's life unless he was sure she was the right woman. A Christian woman.

He must have been silent too long, because Caroline turned her head to look at him.

"Aren't you going to argue with me?"

"I guess I should." He didn't want to. He sympathized with her, maybe too much. She'd been through a tragedy that would be tough for anyone to handle, especially someone who didn't have a relationship with Christ to see her through.

He looked up at the lofty barn roof, where dust motes danced in the stripes of sunlight. Something about the quiet, open space made him feel as if he was in church.

Lord, show me how to deal with this. Caroline is hurting. I want to help her, but I have to do my duty.

"I don't see why I should do the police's work for them." Caroline's tone was defensive, and she sent him a sidelong glance that was reminiscent of Ruthie when she was in a stubborn mood. "I haven't done anything wrong, and even if Tony did, surely his liability died with him."

He studied her averted face. "Is Tony dead?"

Her gaze flashed to him. "Yes. The police said he was. I buried him."

"So the things that have happened since you came here—the letter, the coffee, the safe-deposit box—were they coincidences? Someone trying to make you think Tony is still alive?"

Her lips trembled for a moment, and she pressed them firmly together. She shook her head. "I don't know. Nothing else has happened. Maybe nothing will. Maybe—"

"Do you really think that?" He was sorry for her, but he couldn't let her convince herself that she could just walk away from this.

She shoved her hair back from her face in that characteristic gesture. "I'd like to, but I guess I can't. Still, according to you I'm not Tony's wife. So why should I be involved?"

He couldn't tell her that Tony had been under investigation by the Santa Fe police—that was their business, and he couldn't interfere unless they asked for his help. But she already suspected gambling, didn't she?

"If Tony was involved in something that skirted the law, as his father said, that money could be important. The police should know."

"Why should I be the one to tell them? It properly belongs to Mary Alice, doesn't it? Let her tell them."

"She doesn't know about it. Come on, Caroline, stop evading the issue. Why won't you go to the police?"

She swung to face him, anger flaring in her eyes. "You know the answer to that, don't you? I don't know what happens to other people who've been where I was, but I know what effect it had on me. I've spent the past eight years being so law abiding it's painful—obeying every last little rule and regulation, never jay-walking, never so much as getting a parking ticket."

"Because you learned respect for the law." He was feeling his way, not sure what lay behind that vehemence.

"No! Because I can never put myself in that helpless position again. Because I learned I couldn't trust anyone—not my family and not the police."

She swung away from him, breathing hard, as if sorry she'd revealed that much of herself to him. He couldn't let her stop, not when she was so close to letting him see what was going on inside her.

"What happened? Tell me. You got into trouble, but there's more to it than that."

She shook her head, mouth set, eyes shimmering with tears that she no doubt didn't want him to see.

"You were riding around with two guys," he said deliberately. "You stayed outside in the car as a lookout while they went into a convenience store and beat up the elderly proprietor."

"No." The word seemed torn from her. "I didn't. I didn't know what they were doing. I had no idea they were robbing that man." Her voice trembled, the pain in it almost convincing him.

"Did your lawyer bring that up at the trial?"

"My lawyer didn't believe anything I told him." A touch of bitterness. "Or maybe he didn't care."

"Your family could have gotten different representation for you." They hadn't; he knew that. Why not?

For a moment she stared, eyes wide and clouded, as if she looked into the past. "The authorities couldn't find my mother. Turned out she'd run off to Palm Springs with her latest boyfriend. You couldn't expect her to pass up a trip like that just because her kid was in trouble, could you?"

The insight into what her life had been like with her mother shook him. He'd heard bits and pieces from time to time about Lily Hampton, none of it good.

"Your grandparents, your sisters—"

She shook her head. "I guess they tried to help, when they finally heard, but by then I was in the system. There wasn't much they could do. Besides, my mother was my legal guardian." Her voice shook a little. She might deny it, but that youthful betrayal had affected the rest of her life.

He understood, only too well. Once a juvenile was in the system, everything affecting them had to grind through the legal process. "Your grandmother must have been frantic."

"I suppose." Doubt touched her eyes. "At the time, all I could see was that they'd let me down."

"You got through it." He couldn't imagine how much strength it must have taken for her to deal with that situation alone at her age.

"Not without scars."

Lord, help me to understand. "That's not all, is it?" He knew, without questioning how, that there had been more. That something worse had happened to her when she was alone and vulnerable. "Locked up in a place like that—the other kids must have—"

"Not the other kids." Her body tensed, as if she drew into herself. "I dealt with them."

"Who?" He had to force the word out, because he thought he knew the answer, and he didn't want to hear it.

She hugged herself, as if cold in spite of the warmth of the day. "I don't want—"

"Who was it?" His voice was sharp to his ears. "A cop?"

She pressed her lips together. Nodded. "When I was arrested." It came out in a whisper. "He took me into a room by myself at the police station. Left me there. I thought my mother would come, but she didn't. He came back. He—" Her breath caught, as if she choked on the word.

"He attacked you." He managed, somehow, through the red haze of fury that nearly choked him, to keep the words gentle.

The muscles in her neck worked. She nodded. "Someone came in, finally. He said I was faking, trying to get him in trouble. I didn't care what he said, as long as I didn't have to see him again."

She should have filed a complaint, but he could understand why she hadn't. She'd been alone, and she'd just had a harsh lesson in how helpless she was. Small wonder she didn't trust the system or anyone involved in it.

If he'd been the one to walk into that room, he'd have been tempted to dispense some harsh justice of his own to the man who'd abused his position and shamed his badge. Even now he wanted to put his fist through the barn wall.

But that wouldn't help Caroline. He was probably the last person who could help her, but he was the one she'd confided in, and he had to try.

"He was a criminal wearing a badge, and I'd like to see him get the justice that's due him. But he was only one person. You had the misfortune to have run up against him."

To say nothing of the poor excuse for a mother she'd had. Seemed as if Caroline had been given the raw end of the deal too many times.

"I know." She straightened, quickly blotting a tear that had escaped as if ashamed of it. "Intellectually, I know that. But that doesn't keep me from wanting to stay as far away from the police as I possibly can."

"Understandable." It was a good thing she'd pulled herself together, because he longed to put his arm around her, pull her close, tell her—

No. There was nothing he could tell her. He might understand her better now, but that understanding had only served to emphasize the barrier between them.

She pushed herself off the bench, taking a few quick steps away from him. Maybe she sensed the feelings he was trying so hard to suppress.

"Look—about the money. You could tell the Santa Fe police about it, couldn't you? Tell them it isn't mine. That I don't want anything to do with it."

"I can tell them." That wouldn't end her involvement, but he didn't have the heart to tell her that now. Push her too hard, and Caroline might just run again.

He could understand why she always seemed to perch on the edge of flight. Nothing in her life had given her the assurance that she could trust people, and running away had been her only defense.

"It'll be okay." He stood, went to her. Wanted to touch her, but he didn't quite dare, knowing what he did. "You're not a helpless kid any longer, and you have family to love and protect you."

She had him to protect her, too, even though she probably didn't believe that and wouldn't welcome it. Still, he was the one she'd told. That had to mean something.

"Since you haven't called me again, I realized the only way I'd find out how you're doing is to call you." Francine's voice was clear and crisp over the cell phone. Possibly a little annoyed, as well.

"I'm sorry." Caroline curled into the corner of the leather sofa. She'd closed the curtains against the darkness outside and told herself she was perfectly safe. Still, it was good to hear another person's voice. "It's been so hectic here, getting settled and trying to get into the craft-show circuit. That's no excuse. I should have called."

"Craft shows?" The words were dismissive. "Really, Caroline. You have a position waiting for you here. I've told you that. Why don't you come back to Santa Fe where you belong?"

"I'm not sure I do belong there." Odd, how far away

that life seemed now. "Maybe what happened with Tony changed everything."

"Nonsense. You had a good life here before you ever met Tony, didn't you? There's no reason why you can't have that again."

"I'll think about it." That was an evasion, but how could she know what she wanted? She'd been battered by one shock after another until it was impossible to do anything except tense up, waiting for the next one. "What's going on with the gallery? Are you all right?"

"Never mind me. How are you?" Francine's voice softened on the words. Caro could picture her, leaning back in her custom-made desk chair, her sleek blond hair shining under the indirect lighting she insisted upon. "I didn't mean to snap, but I've been worried about you. So many people have asked how you are, and I don't know what to tell them."

"I'm fine. Really." It was good to feel she had friends who cared about her. "It's just—things have been a little crazy." She could trust Francine, but it didn't seem fair to unload all her worries on her.

"You're not. I can hear it in your voice. What is it? Have you heard from Tony?"

The question had her sitting bolt upright. "Why would you ask that? Tony's dead."

Francine didn't speak for a moment, but her very silence communicated her doubt. "I know that's what the police said. What we all believed. But after you told me about the man who accosted you that day—"

"You've found out something." She was shaken, but at some level she wasn't surprised. Francine knew everyone who was anyone in Santa Fe, and she heard every rumor first.

"Nothing that I'd want to take to the police." Francine sounded unsure of herself, and that was unusual. "People have been talking. People liked Tony. He was good at selling upscale real estate, probably because he was so likeable. But now there are rumors of gambling debts—enough rumors that there must be some basis in fact, I'd think. You had no idea?"

"No." It was hard to look back and see how naive she'd been. "But now—" She didn't want to tell Francine about the safe-deposit box stuffed with money, but if that didn't indicate gambling, what else could it have been?

"Now it seems likely to you. Don't bother to deny it. I can hear it in your voice." Francine had become her usual brisk self. "Well, that increases the possibility that Tony is still alive. And if so, he'll get in touch with you. You're his wife, and he—"

"I'm not." She couldn't let Francine go on any longer making assumptions that weren't true about her relationship with Tony. "I found out yesterday Tony had a wife in Philadelphia. He didn't bother to divorce her before he married me."

"I can't believe it. Caroline, are you sure? He must have been divorced. He couldn't hope to get away with anything else."

"But he did, didn't he? I had no idea the woman existed, any more than she knew about me." Her throat tightened, and she had to force the words out. "He had a child with her."

"Oh, my dear. I'm so sorry."

Somehow the sympathy in Francine's voice broke through the control Caroline had imposed on her emotions. A sob burst out before she could stop it, then another. She could only hold the phone like a lifeline and let the tears spill out, vaguely registering the soothing words Francine uttered.

Finally she managed to take a deep breath, mopping her face with her palm. "Sorry." Her voice was still choked. "I didn't mean to let go that way."

"Well, it's not surprising. But look, are you positive about this? How did you find out? Did your family help you, hire a private investigator?"

"No, nothing like that. I haven't told them about it yet. The local police chief got involved. He's the one who found the record of Tony's marriage, and no record of any divorce."

"A country cop?" That was Francine at her most superior. "My dear, if you're depending on someone like that, you're really in trouble. It sounds as if what you need right now is a friend you can count on."

She pressed her palm over her burning eyes. "I know how lucky I am to have you."

"Well, I'm not much use to you when I'm way out here. Let's see—" she could hear the tapping of computer keys "—there are a few things on my calendar I can't rearrange, but I ought to be free in a couple of days. I'll let you know when my flight gets in."

Her mind grappled to keep up. "You're coming here?"

"Why not? I suppose that inn of yours can rent me a room, can't it?"

"But I can't let you do that. You have so much to do. The gallery—"

"I own the gallery, remember? I can give myself a vacation whenever I want to."

"Francine, I appreciate it." Her voice choked again. "I can't tell you how much. But I can't let you change your plans for me."

"There's no point in arguing about it. I'm sure you think you can handle things by yourself, but right now it sounds as if you can use a friend."

She'd make another attempt to dissuade her, but Francine was right. She did need a friend, and it was far better to rely on someone she'd known for over two years than someone she'd known for less than two weeks.

An image of Zach's frowning face formed in her mind. What did she know about him, really? And what had made her trust him with secrets she hadn't told another soul?

Chapter Ten

Caroline folded the tortilla over the chicken-and-pepper-jack-cheese filling. She'd come over to the house to show Grams how the quilt looked after its initial cleaning, and ended up offering to cook supper. She just hoped they'd like her chicken enchiladas. There weren't too many recipes in her repertoire. She'd had to make some substitutions, since Snyder's Grocery apparently considered that one kind of pepper was sufficient for anyone's needs.

Grams came into the kitchen, carrying a large document box—that sort that was used to store fragile paper and photographs. "Here it is. I'm sure you'll find something in this batch of papers and letters about the quilt."

Caro gestured with the tortilla she'd just warmed in the microwave. "Great. I don't dare touch them now, but I'll look through them after supper."

Grams found nothing unusual about her interest in the quilt, attributing it to a natural desire to learn about her family history. Caro didn't think it was that, exactly, but she couldn't explain, even to herself, the fascination the old quilt held for her.

"There's no hurry. You can take the box back to the apartment with you."

Grams turned to set it on the end of the counter, her earrings swinging. Caro couldn't help a smile. Grams wore the earrings she'd made for her almost every day.

"I'll be careful with it," she promised.

"I know you will, dear. And after all, family documents belong to you as much as anyone."

That calm assumption that she had a place here still took her aback, even though she'd already encountered it several times. To Grams, it was as if Caroline's time away was just a visit to another world, and now she was back where she belonged.

"Your grandfather started collecting family papers and letters after he retired, with some idea of writing a family history." Grams's smile was reminiscent. "He should have known he wouldn't be content with something that sedentary. He loved to be out and about, meeting with his friends and taking an interest in civic affairs."

"I wish I had more memories of him." She'd been too young when Mom took them away, and time had blurred whatever memories had been left.

Grams came to hug her, her cheek soft against Caro's. "He loved you, you know. You'd sit on his lap and listen to his stories until you fell asleep in his arms."

Her throat tightened. "Thank you, Grams." For the memory, and for the sense of belonging. She wiped away a tear. "And thanks again for being so welcoming about Francine coming."

"Well, of course it's fine for your friend to come. She can have the blue bedroom. We don't have any guests booked until the weekend." Grams pulled the wooden stool over so that she could watch the enchilada-making. "Goodness, Caro, wouldn't you know we'd welcome your friend?"

"I know nothing hampers your hospitality. I just thought it might be an imposition if you have other guests booked. Although I'm sure Francine will insist on paying."

"She'll do no such thing." Grams's response was prompt. "She's your friend."

Grams and Francine could battle that one out, she decided. They were both so strong-willed that she didn't have a clue which one would win.

She transferred the enchiladas to one of Rachel's ceramic baking pans, trying to concentrate on that instead of on the vague worry that had possessed her since hearing of Francine's plans.

The thing that bothered her about the proposed visit didn't have anything to do with Grams's hospitality. It was more of a reluctance to see two such different parts of her life meeting. The truth was that she felt like a different person since she'd come back to Pennsylvania. With Francine here, who would she be?

She didn't think she wanted to go back to who she'd been in Santa Fe—the woman who'd fallen in love with Tony and who'd also fallen for his lies. But she wasn't sure she was ready to move forward, either.

"Are you all right, dear?" Grams touched her arm, her fingertips light as the wings of a butterfly. "You know I've been worrying about you. And praying for you, of course."

Her throat tightened. "I know. I'm going to be all right."

"Grieving takes time," Grams said, her voice gentle. "You can't rush it."

Shame flooded her. She couldn't keep doing this—couldn't go on letting Grams imagine she was grieving for a beloved husband. She set the casserole dish in the oven, closed the door and turned to face her grandmother.

"It's not what you think. The situation with Tony—" She stopped, because Rachel walked into the kitchen, the dog at her heels.

Rachel glanced from one to the other of them, obviously knowing she'd interrupted something. "Should I make some excuse none of us will believe and go away?"

"No. Don't go. I want both of you to hear this." They deserved to hear the truth. Caro took a breath, trying to frame the words she needed to speak. "I fell in love with Tony at first sight, I guess, enough in love to agree when he wanted to elope. But I didn't know him very well." That was a massive understatement.

Rachel came to lean on the table, as if wanting to be closer to her. "You found out you made a mistake."

"That's a nice way of putting it." She tried to smile, but she couldn't manage it. "It didn't take long to find out that Tony lied constantly—about where he'd been, about his business dealings. He wiped out my savings and checking accounts. When I confronted him—" They didn't need to know about all the hurtful words Tony had thrown at her. "He was furious. He left, and that was the night he died."

"Oh, honey—"

She held out her hand, stopping Rachel's instinctive embrace. There was more to be said before she could let herself accept comfort. "I never did find out what he was doing, but I think he might have been involved in gambling. The other day, when I went to Philadelphia..." She couldn't watch their reactions. "I learned he was married before. Apparently he never got a divorce. So it looks as if our wedding wasn't even legal."

Silence for a moment. And then she felt Rachel's arms go around her, strong and comforting, the way she had been when Caroline was eight and had broken her arm falling out of a tree. "Caro, I'm so sorry."

She nodded, those weak tears spilling over again. Grams's arms went around both of them, holding them tight.

"You cry all you want, Caro. You don't have to be brave for us."

Maybe that was what she needed to hear to give her strength. "I'm all right." She pressed her cheek against Grams's, and then hugged her sister. "I've cried enough over it. I just wanted you to understand that—" She stopped, not sure what she wanted to say.

"That some odd things have been happening since you got back," Rachel finished for her.

Caroline drew back, shock running through her. "How did you know that? Did Zach tell you?"

"No, he didn't say a word, but I'm not an idiot. I can see what's right in front of me. If he's helping you...well, he's a good man."

"We want to help you," Grams said. "But we don't want you to think we're interfering." Grams brushed her hair back from her face with a gentle touch. "We're on your side, that's all. We love you. Just remember that."

She nodded, wiping tears away, and gave a watery laugh. "I'll remember. I love you, too."

She'd told them the worst of it. No one had blamed her or looked at her with that pitying expression that she dreaded. Only with love.

* * *

Caroline came down the stairs from the loft, still yawning, and squinted at the bright sunlight flooding through the living room windows. She crossed to the sofa, mindful of the papers she'd left spread across it and the coffee table.

She'd sat up far later than she'd intended, absorbed in the contents of the box Grams had given her. Those fragile papers, with their faded ink, shouldn't be left where sunlight might touch them. She didn't know much about preserving old documents, but common sense told her that.

Still, her fingers lingered as she started sorting them back into the box. Grandfather hadn't, as far as she could tell, done anything more than put together whatever he'd found relating to the 1850s and '60s. The papers weren't grouped in any way, and she'd found the Civil War enlistment papers of one Christian Unger shoved in among a sheaf of household bills and letters.

The letters were what fascinated her. Most of the ones she'd found so far dated from the 1850s. Elizabeth Chapman Unger, Grandfather's grandmother and the maker of her quilt, had come from Boston, Massachusetts. She seemed to have kept up a lively correspondence with her sister, Abigail, after she married and moved to Churchville. Judging by Abigail's replies, Elizabeth had found plenty to say about her new surroundings and her husband's family, apparently not all of it complimentary.

Caro smiled at one passage, where Abigail urged her sister to be tactful with her new mother-in-law. Human nature hadn't changed very much in the past 150 years.

She laid the papers gently back into the box and put the lid on. There'd been no mention of the quilt in what she'd found so far. Maybe the best thing would be to sort out everything she could find that related to Elizabeth and then go through it chronologically. Grams had promised to continue looking for anything else that related to her. The old house held the accumulated belongings of at least ten generations of the Unger family, and finding any one thing could be a challenge.

Grams had also suggested that Emma Zook would be a good person to give advice about repairing the quilt. She had a long tradition of quilting, as most Amish women did, and she'd know how to handle it.

But that could come later. Right now she was starving, and Rachel had insisted she come to the house for breakfast this morning to taste a new frittata recipe. Over supper last night, as if by unspoken consent, they'd kept the conversation on quilts and food, not on Caro's painful revelations.

She slid the box into the closet and headed out the door, careful to lock it behind her. Nothing had happened recently, but still, she didn't intend to take any chances.

She paused, hand still on the knob, wondering at the turn of phrase. Chances of what? Was she afraid that someone was trying to convince her that Tony was still alive? Or afraid that he was?

Tony wasn't her husband. At some point over the past two days she'd accepted that. She didn't have any obligation to him.

But she'd made the promises before God. She'd meant them, even if Tony had been lying the whole time. Her mind winced away from the memory of that ceremony. Tony, so tall and handsome in the dark suit he'd worn, seeming so solemn when he took his vows.

Had he been laughing inside, even then? She didn't

know, and the more she thought about it, the less sure she became that she could rely on anything she thought she knew about him.

Well, standing here obsessing about it wasn't going to help. She started down the path that led around the corner of the barn. She was far better off to get on with things. She'd have breakfast, see if there was anything helpful she could do at the inn this morning.

This afternoon she'd work on the quilt and try to get a few more things ready for the next craft show. Once the moving company got around to bringing the rest of her belongings, she'd have a better choice of things to sell. There was an entire box of jewelry and some weaving that she'd left for the movers.

She ought to be working on jewelry instead of the quilt. Some simple pendants that she could price at under twenty dollars would be a good balance to the more expensive pieces. Plenty of people went looking for bargains, or what they thought were bargains, anyway, at craft shows.

The path led around the pond, past the gazebo toward the house. She glanced back at the barn and stopped. One of the double doors into the barn stood ajar a couple of inches.

Had she left it that way after that disturbing talk with Zach yesterday? Surely not. She was careful to lock things up, although there wasn't much in the barn to attract a thief—just the quilt frame she'd set up and the table on which she'd laid the quilt to vacuum it. She'd packed the quilt up afterward to take to the Zook farm.

Coffee and frittata were waiting at the house. She sighed. It would worry her all through breakfast if she didn't check now, just to be sure.

She cut across the lawn toward the barn doors, the damp grass soaking her sneakers in only a few steps. Well, that was foolish. She should have backtracked along the walk instead of trying to save time.

She went up the gravel ramp to the upper level of the barn, slowing as she reached the door. Silly, to be worried about it. She'd probably left it that way herself. Certainly she'd been cut up enough emotionally after betraying herself to Zach. Hardly surprising if she'd forgotten a little something like shutting the barn door.

But at some level she knew it wasn't true. She'd closed the door and made sure it was latched, just as she always did.

She reached out, grasping the handle. Everything was perfectly still, except for the family of barn swallows who chirped under the eaves. If someone had been there, he or she wouldn't hang around to be found. She shoved the door open and took a step inside.

Sunlight poured through the opening, casting a spotlight on the interior. Nearly empty, just as she'd left it.

Except that the table she'd been working on had been tipped over, and the quilting frame she'd brought down from the loft had been smashed to pieces.

Zach sat at the kitchen table at the inn, steam rising from the coffee mug Rachel had just set in front of him. By the looks of her, Caroline was the one who needed the coffee, but instead she was holding a cup of chamomile tea that her grandmother had forced on her.

Mrs. Unger and Rachel were hovering over Caroline, so he waited, letting them do all the fussing they needed to before he started in with more questions.

Come to think of it, their concern seemed a bit out of

proportion to the cause. If so, that probably meant Caroline had finally told them about her husband. High time, too. They were capable of dealing with that trouble.

He'd sat in this kitchen before. The Hampton women seemed to be—well, not trouble in themselves, exactly. It was more as if they found trouble.

Or in Caroline's case, brought it with her. He took a sip of the coffee, nearly scalding his tongue. Everything that had happened since she arrived had its roots in her life in Santa Fe—that seemed certain.

"You ought to have some breakfast." Rachel gestured toward a casserole that sat on top of the stove, still bubbling from its time in the oven. "I'm sure we called you out before you had time to eat."

"No, thanks. I had breakfast with Ruthie before she left for school. Now, about the damage—"

"It's just a good thing Caro left the quilt in the house last night," Mrs. Unger said. "I'd hate to think what they might have done to it."

So she was assuming the unknown intruders were vandals. Most likely that was true, but he didn't want to take anything for granted.

"This quilt—was it the one I saw you working on yesterday?"

Caroline nodded. Her face was a little pale. Natural enough, having vandalism strike so close to her.

She'd been getting the dust off it with a vacuum brush when he'd come in, he remembered. "Is it valuable?"

She looked up, seeming startled. "I don't know. We hadn't really looked into the value of it."

"I gave the quilt to Caro because she loved it," Mrs. Unger said. "No one is thinking about selling it, so its value is immaterial."

"Not to someone who planned on stealing it," he pointed out.

"Surely this wasn't intended to be a theft." Rachel poured a little more coffee in his cup, even though he hadn't taken much more than a sip. "If someone wanted to steal an antique quilt, they'd hit a quilt shop. There are several between here and Lancaster."

"I suppose, but I can't ignore the possibility. The more valuable the quilt, the more likely, it seems to me."

"I suppose we could find out." Caroline threaded her fingers back through her hair, letting it ruffle down to the shoulder of the white shirt she wore with jeans. That was probably the most conservative outfit he'd seen her wear yet. "I described the quilt to Agatha Morris, though, and she seemed to disregard it."

"Agatha doesn't know everything." Mrs. Unger's voice was tart. "We could call an expert for a valuation, if you think it's important."

"That wouldn't be a bad idea." It also wouldn't be a bad idea if he could speak to Caroline alone, but that didn't seem likely, the way her grandmother and sister were protecting her.

"I'm not worried about what it's worth. There's just something about the quilt that speaks to me." Caroline gave him an assessing look. *Can you understand that?* That was what it seemed to say.

"Right." He pulled a notebook from his pocket and put it on the table next to his mug. He didn't need to write any of this down, but somehow people seemed to find the action reassuring. "Now, who might know about the quilt?"

She frowned down at the straw-colored brew. "I talked about it at the quilt show, I know. To your sister. She was the one who suggested I speak to Mrs. Morris." She shrugged. "There were a lot of people milling around. I suppose anyone might have heard us. But if someone did want to steal the quilt, why smash up the quilting frame?"

"Good point. It's most likely vandals. Something about spring seems to bring them out of the woodwork. I don't suppose any of you have seen anyone hanging around the place?"

Blank looks, heads shaken. People didn't notice, unless they were the type who saw lurkers in every innocent bystander.

"Maybe you should move into the house." Mrs. Unger's brow wrinkled as she looked at her youngest granddaughter. "If you had run into them, whoever they were—"

Caroline patted her grandmother's hand. "I didn't, and I hope I'm smart enough not to go wandering around investigating strange noises by myself."

"Did you hear any noises?" He slid the question in. She should have—that was the first thing that struck him. The damage had to have made considerable noise, and her apartment was on the other side of the barn wall.

She was already shaking her head. "No. I've been thinking about that, and I should have if they were in there at night. But I spent the evening in the house, and we wouldn't have heard anything from here."

"That explains it, then." He supposed. It got dark fairly early, so the damage could have been done any time after, say, seven in the evening. Still, whoever had done it was taking a chance on being seen.

He wasn't accusing her of lying to him, not even in his mind. But no matter how sympathetic he felt toward Caroline, he couldn't let that affect his judgment.

He put the notebook in his pocket as he stood. "Well,

I think that's it for now." He looked at Caroline. "If you'd like to walk out with me, maybe we could have a word about the locks."

She nodded, getting up quickly. "I'll be back in a minute," she said, and followed him to the door.

The patio was sun drenched and bright with spring flowers. Caroline stopped at the low wall that surrounded it and looked at him.

"This isn't about locks, is it?"

"No, I guess not, although it wouldn't hurt to put dead bolts on all the doors. More to the point, why don't you want to move into the house? Seems like that would be the sensible thing to do."

She shrugged, evading his eyes. "No one has ever described me as sensible."

"Your grandmother would probably feel better."

"You mean she'd be able to fuss over me more." She folded her arms across her chest.

"That's not a bad thing, you know." He could understand why she was prickly, given her history, but her grandmother obviously loved her.

"I like my independence." Her mouth set in a stubborn line.

He looked at her for a long moment, weighing how much to say. "I hope that's it," he said slowly. "I hope you're not just staying there because you want to make it easier for Tony to reach you."

He thought she'd flare up at hearing her words parroted back at her. She didn't. She just looked at him, her gaze defiant, and he knew that was exactly why she was so determined to stay.

Chapter Eleven

"That is just right." Emma Zook smiled at Caro over the quilt that was spread out between them. "You already know how to take the tiny stitches so they will not show."

"I've never done anything like this before." She traced the line of stitches she'd used to repair the fraying edge of a triangle. As Emma said, it was nearly invisible.

Nancy, Emma's daughter-in-law, came to look over her shoulder at the quilt. "That will fix up nice, it will. It is good to keep such a quilt in the family."

"Yes, it is."

Funny. For years she'd told herself she got by very nicely without family. Her priorities seemed to have gotten turned around in recent months.

Nancy smoothed a strand of hair back under the white prayer cap that sat on the back of her head. "Sticky buns are almost ready to come out of the oven. We'll have some with coffee when you finish work."

She'd decline on the basis that a sticky bun contained probably her entire daily allotment of calories, but that would no doubt be an offense against hospitality. Nancy fed her family in the way that Amish women had done for generations, and they seemed to thrive on it. Of course, they had no need for organized activities or gym memberships to keep fit. Dealing with the daily needs of the house and farm without electricity or other modern conveniences did the job.

Emma fingered the binding on the edges of the quilt, frowning a little. "The binding shows wear first. Could be you should just put on a new one."

"I'd hate to replace it with modern fabric. From everything I've heard, that takes away from the value. Maybe I can repair it."

Emma nodded. "It is worth a try. You have the patience to do it right. Like with the jewelry you make."

Emma didn't wear jewelry, of course, but that didn't seem to keep her from appreciating the workmanship that went into it. The difference was, she supposed, that the Amish made useful things beautiful, while she attempted to make beautiful things that were also, in their own way, useful.

"You were the one who started me on the way to being a crafter," she said, putting in a final stitch and knotting it. "You taught me to crochet before I even started school. Remember?"

Funny how that memory had come back to her—of herself and Rachel sitting at the kitchen table with Emma, the woman's work-worn hands guiding their small ones as they made an endless chain of crochet loops to be formed into pot holders.

"Ach, you remember that." Emma beamed. "You were so tiny, but you caught on fast. Like my own girls."

It went without saying that Amish girls knew such useful things, learning them from their mothers almost before they could talk. Had she and Andrea and Rachel learned anything useful from their mother? Offhand, she couldn't think of anything, unless it was how to evade bill collectors.

"I remember you always welcomed us into the kitchen, no matter how busy you were. You'd find something for us to do." Now, looking back, she knew they'd escaped to the kitchen when her mother was in one of her moods or when their parents were quarreling.

"It made no trouble." Emma had probably known why they were there, but she'd never said. "I liked having you with me for company."

Probably Emma had been lonely, working by herself in the kitchen at the mansion instead of in her own kitchen, surrounded by children, visiting with her mother-in-law while they did the routine chores of taking care of a large family.

"You told us Bible stories." Caro smiled. "Sometimes they came out half in German, I think."

"My English was not so *gut* as the children's. But the stories were the same, whatever the tongue."

"Yes." She supposed they were. "I have a feeling I was a pest, always asking questions. I wanted to know why you wore a cap, I remember."

The prayer cap now covered gray hair, instead of blond, but it was identical to the one Emma had worn then.

"The Bible says that a woman should pray with her head covered, and also that we should pray at all times."

"Do you pray at all times?" The words were out before she could think that Emma might not want to answer so private a question.

But Emma just smiled. "Often enough that I would not want to be taking a cap on and off, for sure. I know the English don't hold with that rule. The praying is the important part, *ja*. And I pray for you, little Caro."

Her throat tightened. "Thank you. I haven't…haven't prayed so much. Not in a long time. God always seems pretty far away to me."

Emma took a final stitch and bit off the thread. "If God seems far off, it is because we have moved. Not God." She stood, apparently feeling that was all she needed to say about it. "Come. We will have coffee with Nancy."

Heart still struggling with the concept, Caro followed her to the farmhouse kitchen. Nancy sat at the long wooden table, her workbasket in front of her, but she greeted them with a smile and set it aside to get the coffeepot from the stove. The room was filled with afternoon sunlight and the mouthwatering aroma of the sticky buns that sat cooling on top of the gas range.

A faceless rag doll lay atop the basket, hair in braids, awaiting its replica of Amish children's clothing. She picked it up, wanting to think about anything but her relationship with God. "This is lovely, Nancy. Is it for one of your daughters?"

"Ja." Nancy's smile was the thank-you she wouldn't say in response to a compliment. "I had a bit of time after finishing the baking to work on it."

She made sewing the doll sound as relaxing as if she'd taken a nap.

"Do you ever sell them at the local craft shows? I'd think they'd be very popular." They were unique in their lack of features, reflecting the Amish adherence to not making any images.

Nancy shook her head. "We put some out when we have our produce stand in the summer, that's all."

"Would you like to have me take some to the shows

on consignment?" She had second thoughts almost immediately. Was she breaking any Amish taboos with the suggestion?

Nancy glanced at her mother-in-law, and Emma nodded. "That would be a fine thing, I think. We would like that, Caroline."

Actually, once they committed to it, both Emma and Nancy showed a lot of enthusiasm for the idea. By the time Caroline was ready to go home, she carried not only her quilt and several Amish cloth dolls but also some carved wooden toys created by the Zook men. And the promise of the loan of a quilt frame so that she could finish her work on the quilt more easily.

She pulled the car into her parking space behind the barn and began unloading. Something else was sticking with her from that visit. Emma had played a huge role in her young life, and she hadn't even realized it until this afternoon.

The memories of that time, which came back more strongly with each day she spent here, proved that. Emma, in her quiet way, had made her feel safe. Secure. Loved. Loved by the Heavenly Father who was such a strong presence in Emma's life.

Emma's words came back to her. If she no longer felt God's presence, was it God's fault? Or hers?

Arms filled with a box containing the dolls and toys, the quilt folded on top, she followed the walk that led around the corner of the barn. It was too much. She wasn't ready to face any tough spiritual questions right now. All she could do was try to get through things as best she could. She—

She rounded the corner and nearly walked into the man who stood at her door.

* * *

The bag Caroline was clutching slipped from her grasp, but he caught it before it could hit the ground.

"I'm so sorry. I didn't mean to startle you."

Easy smile; open, boyish face; a disarming twinkle in his eyes. Churchville's mayor—she'd met him at the last craft fair. For an instant she couldn't think of his name, and then it came to her. Keith Morris.

"No problem. I just didn't expect anyone to be here. I don't get many visitors, but that doesn't mean I should overreact when someone comes to my door." She fished her key from her bag, hoping she didn't look as embarrassed as she felt.

"I'm sure it's only natural for you to be edgy under the circumstances." Keith's mobile face expressed concern.

Circumstances? For a moment she imagined he knew about Tony, but that was impossible.

"What circumstances?" She pushed the key in the lock, juggling the packages in her arms.

"Here, let me help you with those." He relieved her of her load so quickly she didn't have time to refuse. "I heard about the vandalism. That's a terrible thing. That's really why I'm here."

"You know something about it?" She could hardly object when he followed her inside since he was carrying her things. She nodded toward the dining room table, and he set everything down.

"No." He looked startled at the suggestion. "No, I don't. I just wanted to apologize on behalf of the town. As mayor, I'm afraid I feel responsible when a newcomer to our little community gets such an unpleasant welcome."

"I could hardly blame the town, could I? But thank

you for your concern. I'm sure you have plenty of more important things to do in your position."

"Important?" His right eyebrow quirked. "You do realize that the most significant part of the mayor's role in Churchville is to sign proclamations, declaring that it's Pennsylvania Apple Week, or American History Month. And did you know that this coming week is Community Festival Week?"

She had to smile at the self-deprecation in his voice when he talked about his job. "I'm sure it's more complicated than that."

"A little. I oversee town departments, of course, such as the police department. So I feel a little responsible when our police chief lets vandals run around loose."

"I hardly think it's fair to blame Chief Burkhalter for that." She snapped the words before she could think that it was odd for her to be defending Zach.

"I'm sure you're right." He backed down without, it seemed, a parting glance at what he'd just said. Was telling people what they wanted to hear part of a politician's job?

"Yes, well—" She turned away, appalled at herself for springing to Zach's defense. She didn't owe him that. "I was lucky I didn't have anything very significant in the barn. And believe me, it has a nice, sturdy lock on the doors now."

"Good, good." He rested his hand on the back of a chair. "I have to confess that wasn't the only reason I came to see you."

"No?" She raised an eyebrow, wondering if this was the prelude to a pass.

"I'm interested in the quilt you talked about with my mother. The 1850s one."

She blinked. Did he realize it was one of the things he'd carried in? "I'm pretty fond of it myself."

"I collect quilts—in a minor way, that is. I wondered if you were interested in selling it."

She could only stare at him for a moment. Was this some sort of game he and his mother played to get the price down?

"According to your mother, my quilt doesn't have much historical value." The woman's quick dismissal of her quilt was still annoying.

"I'm sorry about that." Again that boyish smile disarmed. "Mother can be a bit difficult at times. So many people see her as an expert and ask for advice that she just doesn't want to be bothered with it."

"Odd." In her experience, crafters were the nicest people on earth, always willing to help each other. She must be the exception.

"In any event, I think that quilt would be a great addition to my collection. What are you asking for it?"

The usual rule at shows was that everything was for sale if the price was right, but she didn't feel that way about the quilt. "I'm afraid it's not for sale."

"Oh, come on," he said. "Name a price."

She shook her head. "It's a piece of family history."

"One thousand dollars?"

She had to keep herself from gaping. "I'm afraid it's not for sale," she said again, infusing her words with a note of command.

He glanced toward the quilt, lying folded on the table. "Is that it?"

She nodded. Since he'd shown so much interest, she could hardly refuse to show it to him. "Would you like to see?"

"Of course."

He helped her unfold the quilt onto the table. She had to force herself not to say irritably that she'd do it herself. Really, she didn't understand why she was so possessive about the thing.

"There you are."

He took a step back to survey the quilt. "Very interesting. It's an unusual combination of patterns for that time period, from what I know."

"That's what I understand, too." She touched the edging. "Maybe that's why it interests me. I'm trying to research its history, and my grandmother has begun finding some letters and papers that relate to the time period. Hopefully I'll find some mention of the quilt."

He nodded toward one of the torn triangles. "You know, there are people who specialize in repairing and restoring old quilts. If you'd like, I could give you some names."

"No, thanks. I'd prefer to do it myself." She was sure of that, even if she didn't quite understand why.

"But it's a big job—"

"I can manage." Really, what business of his was it if she wanted to do it herself? She'd already told him it wasn't for sale.

"Now I've annoyed you." He gave her a rueful smile. "I'm sorry. I was just trying to be helpful."

"Well, thank you." She hoped she didn't sound too ungracious. "Everyone has been very helpful—I guess I'm not used to that after living in the city for so long. The Zooks are even bringing over a quilting frame to replace the one destroyed by the vandals."

"That's good. And you said you'd put a new lock on the barn door?"

"My brother-in-law took care of that, but I doubt the vandals would strike twice in the same place."

"Still, better safe than sorry." Keith's smile was a little warmer than friendly. "I'm glad the incident hasn't given you a distaste for our little town."

"Not at all. I'm happy to be here." To her surprise, she realized that was true. In spite of the problems that seemed to have followed her, she felt more at home than she had in years.

"That's good." His smile broadened. "I'm glad."

She couldn't help smiling back. Some simple, uncomplicated flirting was a welcome change from dealing with the betrayal hidden behind Tony's smooth facade.

Or with Zach's intensity. A pair of frowning gray eyes appeared in her mind, and she tried, without success, to dismiss them.

"That is such a clever idea." Karen Burkhalter leaned across from her booth at the Spring Festival to take a closer look at the children's activity Caro had set up.

"Since it's a community event, I thought it'd be good. I've done it at this kind of show before, and most kids like to string beads." She'd made a trip to the nearest craft store for supplies for the simple craft, and it had been a pleasant distraction from everything else that was going on in her life.

"You're really getting into the swing of things here." Karen's pert, freckled face lit with a smile. "I'm glad. That means you want to stay."

Karen's insight startled her. Was her attitude that obvious? "I guess I am enjoying it here." But for how long?

"They're opening the doors," Karen said. "Get ready to be swamped."

She didn't really expect that, but over the next hour it looked as if Karen's prediction would come true. People flooded through the aisles between the booths, locals and visitors alike. She should have realized that it would be difficult to supervise the children's activity and deal with adult customers at the same time.

She was trying to untangle the mess one overeager ten-year-old had made of her necklace when someone slid around the table and into the booth with her. She looked up to see Andrea.

"You can use an extra pair of hands." Andrea shoved a strand of blond hair behind her ear and took the string of beads from her. "I'll do this. You take care of the customers."

"I...thank you. I didn't expect this."

Andrea, who managed to look crisp and businesslike even in jeans and a button-down shirt, deftly untangled the beads. "Rachel would have come, but she was too busy at the inn. Hey, it'll be fun."

It would? She enjoyed it, but it hadn't occurred to her that Andrea might. There was a lot she didn't know about her sisters, it seemed. She turned to a woman who wanted to argue her down on the price of the Amish dolls.

"Well, I don't know if my grandkids would like them. Don't you have any with faces?" She picked at the fine hand stitching on the doll's dress, and Caro had to restrain herself from snatching it away from her.

"It's handmade by an Amish woman," she said firmly. "Amish dolls don't have faces because the Amish don't believe in making images of people. If you want a cheap machine-made doll with features, I'm sure you can find that somewhere else."

She held her breath. She didn't usually turn away

customers, but she wouldn't insult Nancy by selling her handmade dolls for less than they were worth.

"I guess you have a point at that." The woman looked over the display. "I'll take four of them."

She managed to keep a straight face until the woman had paid and walked away, and then she turned to Andrea, a laugh escaping. "I can't believe I just did that."

"You sounded like my husband. Cal feels the same about his handmade furniture. If you want cheap machine-made, go elsewhere." Andrea, having a moment's respite from the demands of the children, leaned against the table. "You know, you really have a feeling for Pennsylvania folk art. Maybe that's what you're meant to be doing."

The idea startled her. First Karen, now Andrea pointing out something she hadn't seen in herself.

Andrea glanced over her shoulder. "Looks as if you have another customer."

Caro turned, and her breath caught. The woman who stood on the other side of the table wasn't a customer. She was Tony's wife.

"Mrs. Gibson." Caro said the words with a sense of fatality. Of course the woman would seek her out. What else could she do? She should have seen this coming.

"I thought you were claiming that name." The woman's tone was combative, but Caroline saw past that to what lay beneath. Grief. Despite what he'd done to her, Mary Alice had loved Tony.

"What do you want?"

"To talk, that's all. You can spare me a few minutes, can't you?"

Caro glanced around. They couldn't talk here, not in

the midst of the crowd. "Andrea, can you take over for a few minutes?"

Andrea nodded, controlling the questions that no doubt seethed in her mind.

Caro slid out of the booth, struggling to find composure. She had to do this. She didn't want to.

Please. She wasn't sure whether it was a prayer or not, it had been so long. *Please show me what to say to her.*

"Let's go out back. Maybe we can find someplace quiet to talk." She touched the woman's arm. Mary Alice winced away from her, but she followed when Caro started down the aisle toward the rear of the fire hall.

They got there too fast. She hadn't come up with anything to say by the time she pushed through the metal door and went out to the gravel lot.

The area around the door was piled with boxes left there by the exhibitors, and a couple of pickups were parked nearby, but there was no one around. It was as private a place as they were likely to find in the midst of the festival.

She turned to the woman. "I guess this will have to do. I'm sure you don't want to come back later."

"No. Let's get this over with." Mary Alice's thin face tightened. She'd probably been a beauty once, with those soft curls and huge brown eyes, but years of tending a child and an ailing father-in-law had taken their toll.

For an instant Caro felt an irrational fury at Tony. What right had he to betray this woman—to betray both of them? Hadn't he had any sense of morality at all?

"How did you find me?"

The woman shrugged. "Your friend told Tony he was police chief here. I stopped at the station, asked for you. The guy on duty said you'd probably be here."

Simple, wasn't it? "All right, what can I tell you?"

"You told my father-in-law that you were Tony's wife." Mary Alice folded her arms across her chest, as if holding back pain. "What did you mean by that?"

"I wasn't trying to hurt you or him. I wanted to find out—"

"Are you after what Tony left?" Mary Alice blurted out the question. "Because if you are, you're going to be disappointed. He didn't leave a thing, and if he had, it would belong to me and his child."

The thought of that child was a fresh source of the pain she'd thought she was finished with. "No. I don't want anything. Just the truth."

"The truth is that Tony was my husband. Maybe not a very good one, but mine." Her thin cheeks flushed. "You have no right to say anything else."

"I'm sorry. I thought I was married to Tony." She tried to harden her heart. She had her own pain to deal with. "We got married in Las Vegas. But if you two were never divorced, then it was all a sham."

"I don't believe you." The woman's face was taut with pain. "Tony wouldn't do that. We were married in the church. He might do a lot of things, but not that."

Caro fumbled in her shoulder bag and pulled out the photo she still carried around. She should have gotten rid of it. Having it was like biting down on a sore lip, but she hadn't been able to bring herself to throw it away.

"Here." She held the image out to the woman. "Is that your Tony?"

Mary Alice took the photo, hand trembling. Looked at it. Shoved it back toward Caro, turning away. Her shoulders shook with sobs.

"I'm sorry." Her voice was thick, too. She grabbed the

picture, taking a brief glance at the smiling bride and groom, and shoved it back in her bag. "I didn't want to hurt you. But I was victimized by Tony, too."

Mary Alice took a deep, rasping breath. She turned back to face her, clearly still fighting for control. "Sorry. I thought—"

"I'd have thought that, too, in your place. But honestly, I don't want anything that was Tony's."

Mary Alice wiped tears away with her fingers, managing a weak smile. "Good thing. As far as I know, he didn't even leave enough to bury him. I guess you did that."

"Yes." A fresh twinge of pain hit at the thought of the tears she'd shed at the graveside. Not only wasn't she Tony's widow, but she couldn't even be sure Tony was dead.

She pushed that thought away. Someone had sent that safe-deposit key, but that didn't mean it was Tony. A thought hit her. If that money had been come by honestly, it would belong to Mary Alice and her child.

"I'm not sure if this is going to help you, but when I came to Philadelphia, it was to check out a safe-deposit box that Tony had rented. It was filled with money."

Something that might have been hope dawned in the woman's eyes. She hated to squelch that, but she couldn't let her believe that her money troubles were over.

"The police out in Santa Fe think Tony might have been involved in something illegal, so don't get your hopes up."

"Hope?" Anger flared in Mary Alice's voice. "What do you know about it? Hope doesn't feed a kid or put shoes on her feet."

"I know how you must feel, but—"

"You don't know anything about what I feel. Don't

you dare feel sorry for me. At least Tony actually married me. What does that make you?"

Before Caro could say a word, she'd whirled and raced away.

Caro stood there for a few minutes, dealing with the emotions that boiled up and threatened to explode. She didn't have the luxury of collapsing in tears or even kicking a few of the stacked boxes. She had to pin a smile on her face, go back inside and take over her stand. So that's what she'd do.

The crowds seemed to have thinned out as she moved through them to the stand. Maybe most people had gone outside to the food stands and the rides. Andrea sent her a questioning look.

"Everything okay?"

She summoned a smile. "Fine. Do you want to take a break? I can manage."

"Maybe a little later." Andrea gestured toward the children's table. "I still have a few customers."

Caro glanced at the four children grouped around the table. Three flaxen heads—common in this area with its German heritage. And one little girl with curly dark hair and an engaging smile. Ruthie, Zach's daughter.

He wouldn't like the fact that Caro was anywhere near his little girl. He'd made that clear at the last show. But what could she do about it? She could hardly chase the child away.

Even as she had the thought, the little girl lifted the necklace she was working on. "It's pretty, isn't it?"

Since Ruthie was looking right at her, she could hardly avoid answering. "It sure is. Are pink and purple your favorite colors?"

She nodded gravely. "My daddy says they're princess colors. My princess doll has a dress that color."

"Your daddy will really like your necklace, I'm sure."

"Someday I want to make pretty necklaces like yours." Ruthie leaned across the table and reached up to touch the aqua and silver cross Caro wore. "It's be-yoo-ti-ful."

Karen, overhearing, grinned at her niece. "I'll bet you could ask Daddy to get one just like that for your birthday. Maybe Ms. Caro would even make it, wouldn't you?"

"Well, yes, of course, if he wanted me to." It wasn't Karen's fault that she was in such a sticky situation. Karen didn't know that her brother's only interest in Caroline was that of a police officer.

She turned away, relieved, at the sight of a potential customer, and went to the other end of the booth, switching places with Andrea, determined to stay as far away from Zach's daughter as possible.

Once she'd persuaded the woman that she shouldn't pass up the earrings that went with the necklace she wanted, the other three children had wandered off to look at something else. To her surprise, Ruthie still bent over her necklace, totally absorbed in stringing beads on the cord.

Her sketching pad, never far away, lay on the corner of the table. A pencil in her hand was usually a sure remedy for thinking about things she'd prefer to ignore.

Her gaze was drawn back to the little girl, and the pencil started to move. She didn't have quite the angle she wanted, so she edged closer quietly, not wanting to distract the child. She didn't want to talk to Ruthie—she just wanted to capture the intent look an artist, no matter how young, had when absorbed by the work.

She didn't know how much time passed before she realized someone was watching her—had probably been watching her for some time. She looked up to find Zach leaning against his sister's booth, his gaze fixed relentlessly on her face.

Her heart seemed to skip a beat and then proceed to thud too loudly. Foolish, but she couldn't seem to ignore the effect the man had on her.

"Your daughter decided to make a necklace." He could hardly blame her. The activity was open to any child who wanted to do it.

Ruthie looked up at her words. "Daddy, Daddy!" She launched herself into his arms.

"Hi, sweetheart." He caught her, his face lighting with a love that made Caro's breath hitch. "What are you doing?"

"Making a necklace, see?" She scurried to hold it up for his inspection. "It's all finished. Isn't it pretty?"

"It's beautiful." The pink-and-purple creation dangled from his strong hand. "I'm proud of you."

"Ms. Caro showed me how." Ruthie turned to her, and her gaze touched the sketch pad. Her eyes widened. "Is that me?"

Caro nodded. And what exactly would Zach think of that?

He took the pad, his fingers brushing hers, and turned it so that he could see. It seemed to Caro that his face gentled. "Look, Ruthie. It is you."

While Ruthie exclaimed over the image and called her aunt Karen over to see, Zach's gaze met hers. For once there was nothing guarded in it.

"You've really captured her. That expression of total concentration—I've seen that so often, always when she's making something."

"You have an artist on your hands," she said lightly. She tore the sketch carefully from the pad and handed it to him. "For you."

"Thank you." His voice was low, and she couldn't seem to look away from his gaze.

After a long moment, Zach turned away. He took Ruthie's hand. "Say thank you to Ms. Caro, honey. We'll find Grammy and show her what you made."

"Thank you, Ms. Caro." Velvet brown eyes sparkled, and a pair of dimples flashed in her cheeks. "I love your necklaces."

"You're welcome, Ruthie. I'm glad you came." She would not let her confused feelings for Zach affect the way she treated the child. "I hope I'll see you again."

Zach wouldn't like that, she supposed. Well, too bad.

He gave her a slight smile, raised one hand in a sketchy salute and walked off with his daughter.

Chapter Twelve

All Ruthie could talk about for the next several hours was her new friend, Ms. Caro. Zach eventually turned her over to his mother at home, still chattering, and headed back to the festival.

They'd be closing down now, and he'd take a quick look around the grounds to be sure everything was all right. And if he saw Caroline, well, that was inevitable, wasn't it?

The bond that had started to form between his daughter and her Ms. Caro would be a nice thing to see, if only Caro were not involved in who-knew-what.

She could be perfectly innocent of any wrongdoing. But even so, he didn't want his daughter around someone who seemed such a magnet for trouble.

Caroline knew that. He'd seen it in her eyes when she looked at him.

He didn't like the thought that his attitude hurt her. She'd been hurt and betrayed enough. But that was all the more reason to be cautious of any relationship with her. Duty came first for him, and that duty could very well cause him to do something that would hurt her still more.

All very good reasons for staying away from her. So why was he headed straight for the spot where her booth had been?

His sister was already gone. One of his brothers must have stopped by to help her pack up.

Caroline seemed to be down to several boxes that looked ready to take out. He stopped behind her as she picked up one.

"Can I give you a hand with those?"

The box she balanced wobbled in her arms at the sound of his voice, and he grabbed it. "Sorry. I didn't mean to startle you."

"That's fine." She tightened her grip on the box. "I didn't hear you coming. Thanks, but I can manage these."

"No point in making two trips when one will do," he said. He picked up the rest of the boxes. "Lead the way."

Her brow furrowed, as if she were about to argue, but then she shrugged. "My car's out back."

They made their way to the back door, sidestepping folks tearing down their booths. "The festival had a good turnout." He addressed her straight back, since that was all that was visible to him. "The craft shows have become quite a draw for tourists. How did you make out with the things you brought on consignment for the Zooks?"

She looked at him over her shoulder. "How did you know about that?"

He shoved the door open, holding it with his shoulder until she maneuvered her box through. "I hear just about everything, it seems."

"I guess that's a valuable trait for a police officer. Everything sold pretty well—the dolls in particular. I think Emma and Nancy will be pleased." She crossed the gravel lot to her car and opened the hatchback. "Everything should fit in here. If I keep on with the craft shows, at some point I'll need to borrow a bigger vehicle."

He wedged the last box in on top of the things she'd already loaded and closed the hatchback. "There you go. What happened to your sister? She didn't hang around to help you tear down."

"She had a Saturday-night date with her husband, so I chased her off home. I can manage the unloading myself."

"No need. I'll follow you home and help you unload."

Her mouth tightened infinitesimally. "You don't have to do that."

"I want to." He turned toward the side lot where he'd left his car. "I'll be right along." He walked off before she could launch into an argument.

The few minutes it took to drive from the fire hall to Caro's barn were enough time to wonder what he was doing. Not, unfortunately, enough to come up with an answer.

Caroline was already unloading by the time he pulled in behind her car. He thought she was going to reiterate her insistence that she could handle this herself, but instead she gave him a thoughtful look.

"Maybe it's just as well I have a chance to talk to you. I had a visitor today. Tony's wife."

Her expression didn't tell him how she'd taken that. "I suppose that was inevitable. How did it go?"

She shrugged as she headed for the door. He picked up a stack of boxes and followed her.

"Not very happily, as you might imagine. She…well, I guess she needed to vent her anger at somebody."

"What happened wasn't your fault." He held the door while she carried her load inside and then followed her. "If she's going to be angry, Tony ought to be her target."

"Unfortunately, he's not around to hear what we think of him." She crossed to the worktable and set her stack of boxes down, so he did the same.

"What did you tell her?"

"She didn't really want to hear anything from me. I did tell her about the money, though." She swiveled to face him. "Of course, I don't know if it's still there. Did the police take it?"

"Not that I know of." At her skeptical look, he held out his hands. "I'm not in the confidence of the Santa Fe police. I told them about it, as you asked me to. They haven't kept me posted on their plans."

He could guess, but they hadn't told him. If it were his case, he'd probably leave the money where it was to see if anyone showed an interest in it.

"And if they did tell you, you couldn't pass anything along to me in any event."

"No, I guess I couldn't. So where does that leave us?"

"Destined to talk about something else, I suppose. Your daughter is adorable."

As a change of subject, it was a good one. "I think so, but I might be prejudiced."

"The proud father." Her smile seemed to relax. "I can understand that."

"You had a nice activity for the kids today. Not many of the vendors bothered to do that."

She moved into the kitchen and began putting coffee on, seeming to assume he'd stay. "Maybe they didn't think of it. I've been at other shows where vendors have had kids' activities. Or had displays of work in progress. That always seems to draw an audience."

"You enjoyed participating in the show." He didn't really need to ask. She'd been completely wrapped up in what she was doing.

"I did, yes." She leaned against the counter, waiting for the coffee to brew. "I'd gotten away from the craft-show circuit when I was working at the gallery. Francine always seemed to have so much going on that there wasn't time for anything else."

"What kind of things?" He put his elbows on the breakfast bar countertop, curious about what her life had been like in Santa Fe.

"Charity events, for the most part. Francine's late husband, Garner, was very active in the social scene in Santa Fe, and running charity auctions was something he'd started. She got involved and then carried it on after his death." The coffeepot clicked, and she lifted a couple of mugs from the shelf. "I was busy so many Saturdays that I got out of the craft-show circuit. Besides—"

"What?" He liked that she was talking to him so easily, as if they were friends.

She shrugged. "Much as I love the Southwestern art, there's just something about Pennsylvania folk art that speaks to me. It feels so familiar."

"It's part of your childhood, even if you got away from it for a while." He wrapped his hand around the mug she shoved toward him. "Sometimes I think I should be trying harder to keep Ruthie's Afghan culture alive for her, but I'm not sure how to do it. And her parents were Christian, so they were already isolated from their culture to some extent."

"I didn't realize." She leaned on the counter opposite him, so that they were close but with a barrier between them. "How old was she when you brought her back here?"

"Four. She still has some memories, mostly of her parents. I hope she doesn't remember the fighting."

"Were her parents killed?" Her voice was very gentle.

He nodded. It wasn't easy, even after all this time, to think about that. "They were both doctors, doing good work in an isolated area of Afghanistan, but there was a lot of prejudice against them because of their faith. When our team was sent there, we got to know them pretty well."

"How did they—" She stopped. "I'm sorry. I shouldn't bring up something so painful."

His fingers tightened on the mug. "It's okay. The good Lord knows my memory of that is never very far away. What happened to them was my fault."

"Zach—" Her voice was troubled.

He shook his head. "Sorry. I didn't mean to sound melodramatic, but that's how I see it. I left my post because a car overturned in front of me and I ran to help. The terrorists were waiting for that—they got into the village and attacked the clinic. David and Miriam were both killed. Thank goodness Ruthie survived."

Her hand closed over his. "I'm so sorry you lost your friends. But anyone would have done the same."

"Maybe. But if I'd stayed at my post, they'd be alive today."

"You don't know that."

He shook his head.

"Zach—" Her fingers moved comfortingly on his hand. "If something I did made you think about it, I'm sorry."

"Not your fault." He turned his hand, so that he clasped hers. "I guess it was seeing her so absorbed in making that necklace. Her mother loved to make things, too. She'd do these little crafts with Ruthie whenever she had the time. Seeing her like that reminded me of Miriam."

"They'd be proud of the way you're raising their daughter."

"I hope so."

"I know so." Her mouth curved in a smile. "Anyone can see how she adores you."

"The feeling is mutual." He smiled back at her, and somehow those smiles seemed to touch a deep well of understanding. Her green eyes darkened with awareness. But she didn't look away.

The moment drew into an eternity. And then he leaned across the counter and kissed her.

Her lips were soft under his, and she made a small sound that might have expressed surprise. Then she leaned into the kiss, reaching up to touch his cheek with her fingers.

The counter was a barrier between them. Maybe that was just as well. It forced him, eventually, to pull back.

Caro's eyes were soft, almost dazed. He touched her hair, and one of those wild curls tangled around his fingers, seeming to cling with a mind of its own.

He couldn't do this. He drew back, shocked at himself. "I'm sorry. I shouldn't have."

She turned away. "No. I mean…we shouldn't. It's not a good idea."

It wasn't. But that didn't keep him from wanting to kiss her again.

So probably he'd better go before he got himself into any more trouble.

Caroline folded the quilt carefully, wrapping a sheet around it. She'd come to the house for a family dinner and couldn't resist showing off the repair work she was doing on the antique quilt. "I've actually found references to a quilt Elizabeth was making. I'd like to believe it was this one, although there's no proof, of course."

"It's like a treasure hunt," Andrea said. She folded napkins, setting the table with the same efficiency she used to prepare a spreadsheet. Rachel's Tyler had come up from Baltimore for the weekend, and she was busy in the kitchen, having chased the others out to the breakfast room to set the table. "I wonder if there are any other primary sources. Journals, other letters, family histories— that sort of thing."

"I hadn't thought of that." Caro carried a stack of Grams's favorite Lenox plates to the table. It was far better to keep herself occupied with the mystery of the quilt rather than let her mind stray to Zach and that kiss.

He'd known immediately that it was a mistake. They both had. Why did she find it upsetting that he'd been so quick to admit that? She knew as well as he did that there couldn't be anything between them.

"Caro?"

She blinked, jerking her mind back to the present to find Andrea looking at her questioningly.

"Sorry. My mind was wandering. What did you say?"

"I asked if you wanted me to do an Internet search to see if I could locate any other information."

"That would be great. As it is, it's like listening to only one side of the conversation. If only I had Elizabeth's letters to her sister, instead of just her sister's to her."

"That would be pure gold if I could find that," Andrea said. "And about as rare. But let me take a look and see what I find."

"Are you talking about the quilt?" Grams carried a pitcher of daffodils to the table.

"If it is the same quilt, and that's a big *if,* Elizabeth's sister mentions getting the pattern for her from a Reverend Albright. You wouldn't expect a minister to be passing on quilt patterns."

"Maybe it was from his wife." Grams tweaked the blossoms. "I think everything is ready in here. Do we dare interrupt Rachel to see if she's ready?"

"Not I," Caro said quickly. Rachel was the mildest of creatures, but she could turn violent if interrupted in the midst of culinary creation.

"Nor I," Andrea said quickly.

Caro grinned. "Up to you, Grams."

Grams gave a ladylike snort. "I'll get her."

But the kitchen door popped open, and Rachel burst through carrying a laden tray. "Where are the men? The food is ready now."

"We're here." Cal's voice sounded from the hallway. He never strayed far away from Andrea, she noticed. Tyler loomed behind him, and Rachel's gaze caught his.

Something clutched Caro's heart. Surely she wasn't jealous, was she? Her sisters deserved to find happiness with good men who loved them.

It was just that she felt…bereft, she supposed. Not at the loss of Tony, but at the realization that what she'd imagined they'd meant to each other was an illusion.

There was no one for her, and she was left standing on the outside, watching her sisters' happiness but unable to share it.

Rachel carried platters to the table, and for a few moments all was confusion as she and Andrea brought the rest of the food, filled water glasses and finally took their places around the long table.

Grams reached out, and they all linked hands around the table. She'd forgotten, in all those years away, that family custom. Rachel held her hand on one side and Andrea on the other. She could almost imagine she felt love flowing through the link as Grams asked the blessing on the meal and on the family.

They loosed hands at the Amen, and platters began to fly around the table—fried chicken, baked corn, fluffy mashed potatoes, the relishes that were characteristic of a Pennsylvania Dutch dinner.

"Rachel, you've outdone yourself." Cal took a biscuit and passed the basket to Grams. "This is wonderful."

"Well, she had an incentive," Andrea teased, with a sidelong glance at Tyler. "Tyler was coming."

Tyler grinned. "Then you should thank me, right?"

"I guess so." Andrea took a forkful of mashed potatoes and looked at Grams. "Can we tell Caro yet?"

"Tell me what?" She couldn't help a spasm of apprehension. Most of the surprises in her life had not been happy ones.

"I suppose we'd better, since you've given it away," Grams said.

"What?" Surely they wouldn't all be smiling at her if it were bad news.

"We've seen how much you love dealing with the local arts and crafts," Grams said. "So we thought a good addition to the bed-and-breakfast would be a crafts shop in the barn. Which you would run, of course."

She could only stare. "But…that would be very expensive, renovating the barn, getting the stock. I don't have any cash to put into a project like that."

Thanks to Tony. If he hadn't wiped her out, this might be a possibility. But if he hadn't, she might never have come home and realized that what she wanted was right here.

"Your contribution would be your expertise," Andrea said. "Grams will front the start-up costs with the settlement she received from the embezzlement of Grandfather's business. And I'm sure I can get you a small-business loan for whatever else we need."

Her mind whirled with possibilities, and for a moment she let herself hope. "But the renovations—"

"You have a carpenter and an architect right in the family," Tyler said. "I've already drawn up some preliminary plans, but Cal and I need your input. We thought you might want some space for craft classes and groups to meet."

She tried to combat the tears that welled in her eyes. "I can't let you do all this for me. It's too risky. There are other craft and gift shops…."

"You have access to Amish-made crafts that many others don't." Grams smiled, her eyes soft with tears. "Emma loves you as if you were one of her own children."

"She mentioned the idea to begin with," Andrea said. "Rachel and I just took it and ran with it."

"So, Caroline." Grams smiled through her tears. "What do you say? Will you do it?"

She couldn't speak. Couldn't say anything in the face of this overwhelming love. She could only nod and put up her hands to try and stem the tears that overflowed, washing away the barriers that remained between them.

Zach had stayed away from Caro for several days, trying to forget that kiss. It hadn't worked. Still, he'd managed to rationalize it to a certain extent.

They were attracted to each other, and they'd had a moment of closeness that took them both a little too far. More serious for him than for her. There was no actual investigation going on, so he hadn't violated any regulations, but he knew in his heart that was a cop-out.

Attraction or not, he had a responsibility to check on her. The Santa Fe P.D. might not want to involve him in their investigation of Tony Gibson, but he wouldn't ignore the odd things that kept happening in Caroline's vicinity.

At least, that was what he told himself when he pulled up to the side door of the inn. He wanted to touch base with Rachel. If she could talk her stubborn sister into moving into the house, he'd feel a lot better about Caroline's safety.

But when he tapped at the door nearest the kitchen, it was Emma who answered. "Morning, Emma. Is Rachel around?"

"She has gone to New Holland for groceries. Is there some way I can help you, Zachary?"

Emma had moved to a first-name basis with him when her son had been injured last year.

"It's nothing important. I'll catch her later. What about Caroline?"

"Ach, she is not here, either. She has gone to the airport to pick up her friend who comes for a visit."

That was the first he'd heard of a friend coming. Someone from her life in New Mexico? Maybe someone who knew Tony? "Was that her friend from Santa Fe?"

"*Ja*, the lady she worked for out there. I have the blue bedroom all ready for her."

"Guess it wasn't my day to find anyone home. Stay well, Emma."

She nodded, shutting the door.

That was a pointless trip. Still, it was interesting to learn that her employer was coming. Francine Carrington—the woman who'd reported her missing.

He went down the steps, glancing toward Caroline's apartment, and came to a stop. Caroline might not be there, but someone was. He caught sight of a flicker of blue, maybe a shirt, disappearing around the corner of the barn.

Could be nothing. Could be the person who'd been in the apartment a couple of times, back for another try.

He glanced toward the patrol car, but it would be faster on foot. He jumped lightly off the patio and ran across the grass.

Better this way, in any event. The prowler, if that's what he was, would hear a car coming. This way, he'd catch him unawares.

It worked out just about that way. He rounded the end of the barn, moving quietly on the grass instead of the path, and there the man was, looking in the window.

"Police. Stop right there and turn around."

Somehow he wasn't entirely surprised when the man turned around. Jason Tenley, supposed photojournalist. He hadn't bought that from the moment he'd met the man.

"Just looking for Ms. Hampton, Chief. That's all." Tenley held his hands up, palms toward him, as if to show he wasn't holding a weapon.

Not that he expected a weapon. If the prowler had intended harm to Caro, he wouldn't do it by making coffee.

"Looking in her window?" He shook his head. "You'll have to do better than that, Mr. Tenley. Suppose we go back to my office and talk about it."

Tenley looked chagrined. "You're not really going to

arrest me, are you? I suppose technically I'm trespass-ing, but…"

"*Prowling* was the word I had in mind," Zach said. Something was off-key here. The man wasn't reacting the way he should be, having been caught by the police.

"Guess maybe it's time to come clean." Tenley tried a disarming smile.

"It wouldn't hurt." He wasn't disarmed.

"I'm not a peeping Tom. I'm an insurance investigator. Let me reach into my pocket, and I'll show you my ID."

Zach gave a curt nod. Insurance investigator. The words sounded more reasonable than the photojournal-ist bit.

Tenley handed over an ID folder. Zach studied it and then slid it into his pocket.

"You won't mind my hanging on to this until I check it out."

"Wouldn't do any good arguing, would it? Especially since I'd like your cooperation."

"It's a bit late for that."

"I guess it looks that way from your viewpoint."

"From any cop's viewpoint." The guy might be legit, but that didn't mean he was letting him off easily. "If you come into my jurisdiction on an investigation, you ought to know enough to check in with me. Now, why are you here?"

And what did it have to do with Caroline?

"You're right. I shouldn't have tried to take a short cut. The truth is, my company is on the hook for a substantial sum over a charity auction in Santa Fe, and they're not eager to advertise the fact that they've been had. A very expensive piece of Native American jewelry that was do-nated for the auction has turned out to be a skillful fake."

He didn't need the man to connect the dots for him. "Caroline Hampton was, I assume, the jewelry expert on the gallery's staff."

Tenley nodded. "She's the only one, so far as we've been able to determine, who had the skill to make such a convincing switch."

"I take it you don't have any actual evidence, or this would be coming from the police."

"That's about the size of it." Tenley ran a hand over his graying hair, then massaged the back of his neck. "It's been a real headache. Both the owner and the insurance company want to keep this a private matter as long as there's a chance of regaining the object."

"And what progress have you made?" He wouldn't let himself focus on the Caroline he'd grown to know. He couldn't.

"Precious little." Tenley spread his hands. "Ms. Hampton hasn't made a suspicious move since she's been here. Only thing that might have caught my attention was that trip to Philadelphia, but since she went with you, I assume she wasn't contacting any fences."

"No." He was tempted to hold the man until he'd checked out his story, but that would be more a product of his own irritation than good police work. "Where are you staying, Mr. Tenley?"

"White Rose Inn, out on the highway."

"All right." He gave a curt nod. "Stop by my office tomorrow afternoon. I'll have checked this out by then. In the meantime, stay off this property. We clear?"

"Right." If Tenley was relieved, he didn't show it. "I'll be on my way."

He went quickly, rounding the end of the barn at a lope. A moment later his car bounced out the lane toward the road. Zach watched, automatically noting make and model, license number.

Now what? Go back to the office, check out the story Tenley told.

It would check out. Tenley wouldn't make up something so easy to disprove. And then—well, then he was going to have to tread very carefully.

He'd begun to have feelings for Caro. But those feelings could explode and hurt both of them if she wasn't the woman he thought her to be.

On the other hand, if she was innocent in all this, she'd feel betrayed when she learned he'd been investigating her. And she'd been betrayed too many times in her life to forgive that again. There was no possible happy ending in all of this that he could see.

Chapter Thirteen

"Now we're getting into typical Pennsylvania Dutch country." Caroline nodded toward the dairy farms spread across the rolling landscape. Once she'd picked up Francine at the airport in Philadelphia, she'd been eager to get off the interstate and out into the country again.

"Very pretty." Francine barely turned her expensively coiffed ash-blond head to glance out the window.

"You didn't look," Caro accused, half laughing.

It was good to see Francine again, but rather odd, too. They'd had a good relationship, a friendship even, but she'd always been aware of their employer/employee relationship.

Francine gave an elaborate sigh. "Really, Caroline. You should be aware that I'm not a scenery person."

"True. I've never known anyone who was more urban than you." Even in Santa Fe, where most people gloried in the magnificent outdoors, Francine had looked slightly too sophisticated to fit in.

She'd been surprised that Francine hadn't gone back to her native San Francisco after her husband's death, but she'd been devoted to running the gallery and continuing Garner's charities. There had been rumors of a suit launched by Garner's children from his first marriage, contesting his will, but Francine had never mentioned it.

Francine touched her hand. "Now you know how much I care about you, to be willing to spend time in this rural wilderness. I suppose there's not even a decent coffee bar in this small town of yours."

"Well, no." She tried to imagine one of the stolid Pennsylvania Dutch farmers picking up the latest mocha cappuccino before heading out to do the milking. "But my sister makes a fine cup of coffee."

How long would Francine last here? Probably not for more than a few days, but she was touched that Francine would make the effort at all.

"I'll defer judgment on your sister's coffee until I've tasted it, if you don't mind. Now tell me. Has anything more happened with regard to Tony?"

She'd been keeping Francine up to date at her insistence, so there wasn't much new to tell. "Not since I talked with you after we found out about that safe-deposit box and Tony's wife. Believe me, that was enough of a shock to last quite a while."

Francine frowned for an instant and then smoothed the frown away, always careful to preserve her flawless complexion. "I'm not sure it was a good idea to take the local cop along on that expedition. Why tell the police something they don't already know?"

"He's all right." She pushed the memory of that kiss away. "Anyway, I could hardly hide the existence of all that money. If Tony was involved in something illegal, I don't want it in my possession."

"I suppose not. But as for that first wife—well, darling, he should have told you about her, but I refuse to believe there wasn't a divorce. Tony was hardly the type of man to commit bigamy."

She had to smile, even though the situation wasn't humorous. "Is there a type of man likely to do that?"

"You know what I mean." Francine dismissed that with a wave of her hand. "I'm relieved nothing else has happened. Perhaps whoever was playing games has tired of it."

"Maybe." She wasn't convinced she was at the end of this trouble, but maybe she was just being pessimistic.

"So, are you about ready to give up your rural solitude and come back to Santa Fe where you belong?"

"I don't think so." She couldn't imagine how Francine was going to take her news. "As a matter of fact, my family wants me to create and run a crafts center and shop in conjunction with the inn."

Francine's head swiveled to give Caro the full effect of a disbelieving stare. "You're not going to tell me you're settling in here for good."

"Well, maybe not forever. But for the foreseeable future, anyway."

To her surprise, Francine didn't jump into telling her what she should do, as was her usual practice. Instead she turned back, to stare absently at the winding road ahead for a long moment.

"Much as I hate to say this, maybe that's the best thing for now."

An odd note in her voice set Caro's nerves on alert. "What do you mean?"

"That's really the reason I came." Francine didn't seem to want to look at her. "I hate to be the bearer of bad tidings, but I feel as if I have to warn you."

"Warn me about what?" Her hands tightened on the steering wheel.

"Something happened at that last charity auction we ran." Francine's voice was slow. Reluctant. "There was an elaborate turquoise and silver pin—an original design by a noted Zuni artist. Do you remember it?"

"Yes, of course I remember it. I set up the display and did the photographs." She'd held the beautiful thing in her hands, marveling at the artistry and craftsmanship, knowing that however good she was, she'd never make anything that perfect.

"The new owner had it valued. It's a fake."

Her head spun. "How could that be? I worked on it. I know it was genuine. It was checked out by the insurance expert before it went on display. Surely they don't think that the gallery had anything to do with the fraud."

"Not the gallery," Francine said. "You."

Caroline narrowed her eyes, trying to make out the sign that was nearly hidden by a rampant growth of wild roses. It would be hard enough to see in the daylight; in the dusk it was nearly impossible. She had to come to a stop to read the sign, and even then it wasn't reassuring. She wasn't supposed to be on Twin Forks Road, was she?

She'd followed Emma's directions to reach the Stoltzfus farm and arrived there without incident. Even now, several carefully wrapped quilts rested on the back-seat, ready to be shown in the craft center once it opened. Now getting back home was the problem.

Maybe she was jumping the gun, collecting materials for the shop while it was still in the planning stages, but she wanted to be sure she had enough inventory to give her new project a chance of success.

Besides, it had been a distraction from the bad news Francine had brought with her when she arrived three days earlier. Since then they'd gone over the counterfeit backward and forward, exploring every possibility, without coming to any conclusion.

Francine had reiterated her support a number of times, but Francine was also concerned for her gallery's good name. She wouldn't sacrifice that for the sake of friendship, and Caro didn't want her to. But where did that leave her?

She hadn't been able to bring herself to tell her grandmother and sisters about this new complication. How long could she expect even their support to last?

Grams would say that there was Someone who was always there to support her. Emma had said that if God seemed distant, it was because she had moved away, not God. Maybe that was true, but if it was, how did she bridge that gap?

Lights flashed in her rearview mirror and she looked up, startled. Apparently she wasn't the only one on this lonely road. Good. It felt a little less isolated. It must lead somewhere, hopefully to a road whose name she'd recognize before it was completely dark.

The driver behind her came up fast—too fast on this narrow road. His lights reflected in her eyes, and she flipped the rearview mirror to diminish the glare. Irritation edged her nerves. If he was in that much of a hurry, why didn't he just pass her?

She eased ever so carefully closer to the side. There could be a ditch or a drop-off, hidden by the lush undergrowth. She raised her hand to motion him around—

The car rammed her, snapping her neck back and taking her breath away. Shock ricocheted through her, and she stepped on the gas in an automatic reflex.

The car surged forward, but he was right on her tail, bumping her again and sending the car fishtailing before she regained control. Crazy—he had to be crazy.

She clutched the wheel, hunched forward as if to ward off a blow, pressing down on the gas. *Please, please. Help me.*

No hills to deal with, thank goodness, but she went shrieking around the bends blindly, terrified that she'd meet someone coming, but at least then she wouldn't be alone out here with a maniac on her tail—

He came up fast, lights glaring, and rammed her again. She fought the wheel, but it did no good, she couldn't regain control, she was losing it—

The car spun dizzyingly and plunged off the road. Her body was thrown backward, then forward as the car lurched to a stop in a mass of rhododendron bushes. The airbag deployed, muffling her. For a moment she couldn't move, couldn't even assess whether she was hurt.

But she had to move. She could hear the other car, coming back toward her, engine roaring. She had to get out, now, before he reached her.

She fumbled with the seat belt, freeing herself, shoving at the folds of the airbag, and slid across to the passenger door, shoving it open, clambering out.

Taking a quick glance toward the road, she saw the car stop, a dark figure get out. No time to see more; she just ran. Into the dark, anywhere away from him.

She stumbled through the undergrowth, brambles tearing at her clothes, and then burst into the woods where dry leaves rustled with every step.

She couldn't worry about being quiet—he was too

close behind her. She rushed through the woods blindly, panic harsh in her throat, breath dragging painfully.

She'd gained a little on him, hadn't she? She could hear him crashing through the underbrush. Stop. Think. Once he got in the clear he'd overtake her easily.

She looked around, eyes adjusting to the dimness. There—that clump of trees surrounded by bushes. If she could get in there before he came any closer, she could hide.

Please, please. She ran to the bushes, threw herself on her stomach and squirmed her way beneath, reaching back to ruffle the dry leaves so that she'd leave no telltale traces.

Just in time. She could hear him now, closer, so close she could hear the ragged gasps of his breath.

She curled into a ball, hiding her face against her knees. *Please, Lord. Please. If You're there. If You hear me, protect me.*

The footsteps came closer, crunching the leaves. A low chuckle chilled her bones. Did he see her?

A whisper, so soft it might have been a flutter of birds' wings. It came again, a little louder.

"Caro." A whisper, just on the edge of hearing. "Caro, come out. Come out."

She pressed her face tight against her knees, clenching her teeth. He knew where she was, she would feel a hand grabbing her, dragging her out—

He turned. His feet rustled through the leaves, going back toward the road.

She let out the breath she'd been holding. *Wait, wait, don't move yet, not until he's farther away.*

Finally she couldn't hear him any longer. She crawled out. Don't go toward the road, he could be waiting. The other way—that was the only safe thing. She moved slowly, cautiously, one step at a time.

Nothing. If he heard her, if he was coming, she'd know it. She hurried blindly through the woods, away from the road, falling, getting up, running, falling again, until finally she was in a field, the stubble of grass under her feet, and ahead of her the lights of a farmhouse.

The brightness of electric light, not Amish, then. They'd have a phone. She started toward the house at a staggering run. She was safe.

Thank You. Thank You.

Zach sent a cautious glance toward Caroline as he drove down the lane from the Miller farm to the main road. "Are you sure you don't want to stop by the E.R., just to be on the safe side?"

Caro shook her head, reaching up to lift a strand of hair away from the bandage that adorned her forehead. "You heard Mrs. Miller. Nothing but bumps, bruises and abrasions."

"Margo Miller is used to patching up three accident-prone sons, but that doesn't make her a doctor."

She turned her head slightly to smile at him. "I'm all right, really. I just want to go home."

"If you're sure." His stomach had been tied up in knots since he got the call from John Miller that Caro had turned up at his door. It began to ease, just a little, at the smile. "Have you thought of anything else about the car?"

She moved restlessly. "We've already gone over all that."

They had, but he suspected she needed to talk it out before she reached the inn. "Sometimes something else comes back once the initial shock has passed."

"I didn't really get a good look—just lights in my rear-view mirror." Her voice tightened on the words, as if she didn't want to relive those moments.

"What about when you got out of your car? Did you try to see where the other vehicle was?"

She glanced toward him, her breath catching. "You're right. I did. It was just a dark shape, but I'm sure it was a sedan. I guess that doesn't help much."

"It eliminates all the pickups in the county," he said lightly. "We might find something when we go over your car. When he rammed you, he might have left a paint chip that would tell us the color."

"I didn't think of that." She shook her head. "I haven't been thinking of much of anything, to tell the truth. Just...scared."

"That's not surprising." It took an effort to keep his voice level when he thought of her in danger out on that lonely road. "You're entitled after what you went through. Any chance you got a look at the driver?"

"It was dark. I couldn't see anything about him." Her voice tightened, alerting him. There was more, he was sure of it.

"Notice how he walked? Did he give the impression of a young man?"

"I didn't see him, I told you."

"Hear him, then. Did he speak?"

Her hands twisted together in her lap. This was it. She'd heard him.

"Not to say 'speak.' He...whispered."

He wanted to reach out, to cover those agitated fingers with his, but he couldn't. "What did he whisper?"

"My name." Her voice was the whisper now.

"You're sure?"

At her nod, his jaw clenched. It wasn't a random thing, then. He hadn't really thought it was, but there was always a chance. He glanced at her.

"There's something else, isn't there?"

She held out against the question for a moment, and then she nodded. "He didn't say Caroline. He said Caro." Her fingers twisted again. "Tony called me that. He... I didn't believe he could be alive. But who else would know?"

She sounded at the end of her rope, and for a moment he couldn't think of her as a suspect, only as someone he cared about, someone who was hurting.

"I don't think you can assume that." He tried to keep his feelings from sounding in his voice. It wouldn't do either of them any good to let her know he cared. "Your sisters call you Caro. I've heard them. Probably a lot of people around here have."

"I suppose." She didn't sound convinced.

He could hardly blame her. The bottom line was that the attack on her wasn't a random thing, so whether the attacker was Tony or someone else, this situation had taken a turn to the dangerous.

They were almost at the inn, and once her grandmother and sisters saw her, to say nothing of her friend, he wouldn't have a chance to say anything in private.

"Look, I want you to promise me something."

She looked at him. "What?"

"Promise me that you'll stay at the inn tonight, okay?"

She nodded. Her eyes were wide and frightened in the intermittent illumination of the streetlamps. "That's not a permanent solution. Why is this happening, Zach?" Her voice choked on a sob. "I have to know."

He did reach out then, clasping her hand briefly in his. "I wish I could answer that. But I won't stop looking until we know the truth. I promise."

Chapter Fourteen

Caroline turned away from the stove and nearly tripped over Barney. When she'd made it clear she was returning to the apartment the next night, Grams had insisted that if she wouldn't listen to reason, she'd at least take the dog along for protection.

"You'll take care of me, won't you, sweetie?" She ruffled Barney's silky fur, and he gave her a foolish grin and a soft woof.

She was afraid Grams didn't understand her insistence on coming back to her own place. It wasn't about asserting her independence, not anymore. She loved and trusted them.

Just as important, she'd taken her first step toward trusting God again last night. Funny. She'd wrestled with how that would happen, and then when it came, it had been as natural as breathing.

She walked into the living room, carrying her mug of coffee, and Barney padded at her heels. Much as she'd learned to love this place, it did seem lonely with darkness pressing against the windows. But she hadn't really had a choice. Danger was coming closer, and she wasn't going to let it get anywhere near her family. She'd face it here.

Barney put his head on her knee, as if he sensed that her thoughts were getting too grim. She petted his head. "Sorry. I guess I'm not very good company, am I? Maybe if I talk to you, I can keep from thinking about what happened last night."

But she couldn't. She kept hearing that voice whispering her name. She'd heard it last night, too, but at least she'd had the comfort of Rachel's soft breathing in the other twin bed to help block it out.

Caro. No one in Santa Fe had called her that but Tony. Still, Zach was right. Plenty of people here had heard the nickname. Even Zach had used it once or twice. Wasn't it more rational to assume that the dark figure was someone, anyone, other than Tony?

She was thinking too much again. She took a sip of the coffee and made a face. Why on earth had she made coffee? It would keep her up all night. Not that she expected to do much sleeping, in any event.

Barney's ears pricked, and he raised his head, giving a soft woof. A knock at the door followed a moment later.

The dog didn't act as if it were a stranger. She went to the window nearest the door and drew the curtain back. Her sisters stood on the doorstep.

She'd thought this was settled. She opened the door, trying to look perfectly calm and confident.

Before she could say a word, Andrea had elbowed her way in, arms laden, with Rachel right behind her.

"Since you won't come to us, we've come to you," Andrea announced. She tossed a couple of sleeping bags on the rug in front of the fireplace. "We're going to have a pajama party."

"Andrea, Rachel—" She choked up before she could say anything else.

"Don't argue." Rachel carried her bundles to the kitchen. "We have the makings of a first-class pajama party—brie, crackers, fruit, my special panini sandwiches, hot chocolate and marshmallows, the works."

Andrea grinned. "Doesn't sound remotely like any pajama party food I can remember."

"Well, I trust our palates are a little more sophisticated now." Rachel moved from stove to countertop to refrigerator as if she were perfectly at home. Maybe, for Rachel, any kitchen was home.

"I hope Tyler knows what a treasure he's getting." She crossed to the breakfast bar.

Andrea followed her. "She reminds him with every meal. I'm sure when Cal faces one of my meals, fresh from the deli, he thinks he's married the wrong sister."

"I had first shot at Cal, you'll remember, and he never got past looking at me as a little sister." Rachel turned the heat on under the hot chocolate pot and slapped a fry pan onto the front burner. "He took one look at Andrea and he was a goner."

Andrea's smile was tender and reminiscent. "He didn't act that way. Spent most of his time yelling at me for one thing or another, as I recall."

"He adores you, and you know it." Caro looked from Andrea to Rachel. "You're lucky, you know. Both of you, to find such good men."

Andrea gave her a quick hug. "Baby, it's going to happen for you, too. Just because Tony turned out to be a jerk—"

Rachel made a soft murmur of dissent, but Andrea shrugged that off.

"Don't give me that look, Rach. We all know the man was a con artist if not something worse, and Caroline deserves way better than that." She glanced at Caro's face. "Okay? Or would you like to slug me?"

That surprised a laugh out of her. "Tact isn't your strong suit, is it? But you're right. It's just taken me a while to accept."

Rachel turned a sandwich. "I can understand that. It's one thing to accept something intellectually, but another to really get it in the heart."

Caro could almost feel the tension drain out of her. "How did I get two such wise older sisters?"

"It took us a while." Andrea's expression grew serious. "We let you down. We know that now. We were both so eager to get away from Mom that we didn't think about what it was going to be like for you, left alone with her."

Tears welled in Caro's eyes. It was far more than she'd ever expected to hear from Andrea, who was always so sure of herself. "It's okay." She forced the words past the lump in her throat. "Really."

"Okay, enough serious stuff." Rachel slid plates in front of them, then turned back to get the platter of brie, grapes and crackers. "Wrap yourself around that, and I guarantee you'll feel better. Prosciutto, goat cheese, roasted red peppers, sautéed mushrooms—"

"And your secret sauce?" Andrea teased.

Caro took a bite, the flavors exploding in her mouth. "Wow, Rachel. This is prize-winning food. You're right. This would bring a dying man back from the brink for one more bite."

"Oops, almost forgot." Andrea turned to scrabble through her bag. "I brought something that's going to cheer you up almost as much as Rachel's food." She put a sheaf of fax papers onto the countertop. "My Internet research paid off faster than even I expected. I found a family historian in Boston who is writing a history of Elizabeth's family. And—wait for it—he actually had some of Elizabeth's letters written to her sister from Pennsylvania."

Caro put down her sandwich. "You're kidding! How on earth did you find him that fast?"

"Genealogy sites." Andrea smiled, a little smugly. "You'd be amazed at what's out there, and most of the serious researchers are eager to share. He faxed these when I promised to send him photos of the quilt and any additional information we find."

"Hurry, look at them," Rachel urged. "Andrea wouldn't let me get even a peek. She said you had to be first."

Caro bent over the faxed sheets, deciphering the faint, faded script. It had become easier since she'd been reading the letters from Elizabeth's sister, and she was able to go through them fairly quickly, reading out pertinent bits to her sisters.

"Listen to this." She frowned at the page. "She says, 'I have completed the quilt according to the pastor's instructions, and I eagerly await the first opportunity to put it out.' That's a little odd, isn't it?"

"Maybe she just means to use it," Rachel said, scooping up melted brie with a cracker.

"Could be." But something was niggling at the back of Caro's mind—something she'd read or heard, that had to do with quilts.

"Listen to this one." Andrea had picked up another of the sheets. "This really is odd. She says, 'Thank you, my dear sister, for your concern. I am upheld by your prayers. As you say, this venture can be dangerous, but when I think of the perils of those we help, our dangers are nothing. If only I could be sure who to trust. A Friend was taken into custody two nights ago, and all are praying for him and questioning who could have betrayed him.'"

"Wow," Rachel said again. "I always pictured women of those days living a pretty quiet life. Sounds like Elizabeth had something more serious on her plate. I wonder what it was."

"Well, my new genealogy friend promised me more letters in a few days, so maybe the answer will be there." Andrea looked toward the stove. "Are you going to give us some of that hot chocolate, or just let it steam away over there?"

"Goodness, I forgot." Rachel scrambled to get the hot chocolate served up, along with a shoofly pie that she said was Emma's contribution to the party.

Between the food and the lively chatter her sisters put up, Caroline realized to her surprise that she actually wasn't worrying any longer. She had a new life, and plenty of new things to occupy her mind. With so much support, she'd get through this dark time.

They cleaned up together, chattering in a way she couldn't remember since they'd been children. Her sisters had grown into women to be proud of. Andrea, so smart and efficient, but with a new softness about her since she'd come back home and met Cal. And gentle Rachel—there was strength behind that gentleness that surprised her.

What did they think of how she'd turned out? She wasn't sure she wanted to know. She'd certainly made more than her share of mistakes.

They finally settled in front of the fireplace with refills of hot chocolate. "I guess we should have asked your friend to join us," Rachel said. "But she went out to dinner, and I didn't like to interfere with her plans."

"You mean you thought she'd put a damper on the party," Andrea said, smiling.

"It's just as well," Caro interceded. "I don't think Francine is the pajama-party type." And Francine certainly didn't have to tell Caroline where she was going for the evening, although she was a little surprised that she hadn't.

"It was nice of her to come here to support you," Rachel said.

"It was. She's bravely doing without her gourmet coffee for the sake of being here for me."

"I did manage to fix some hazelnut this morning that she said wasn't half-bad." Rachel's grin said that she wasn't offended.

Andrea stretched. "Look at the time. I'd better get some sleep. I'm supposed to meet with a new client in the morning."

Caro was about to say that they could go and sleep in their own beds when the noise came. Rachel froze, half into her sleeping bag, and stared at the back wall—the one the connected to the barn. "Did you hear that?"

"How could you help but hear it?" Andrea demanded. "Somebody knocked something over. Sounds like your vandals are back, Caro." She was already dialing her cell phone. "Cal, there's someone in the barn. Yes, all right. We will, just hurry."

She snapped the phone shut. "Cal says to stay inside and keep the door locked. He's on his way, and he's calling Zach."

When Caro would have moved, Rachel grabbed her.

"It's all right. They'll be right here. Cal was staying in the house tonight. It'll only take a couple of minutes."

"I don't have a couple of minutes." Caroline pulled free and headed for the door, seized by a compulsion she didn't really understand. "I can't wait. Don't you see? The quilt is in there. Vandals—" Words failed her, but the pictures filled her mind—some ignorant kids slashing at the quilt, stretched on its frame, throwing paint at it—

She reached the door and grabbed the flashlight that hung next to it. Barney, excited, jumped at her heels, barking. "I'll be all right. I'll take Barney—"

"We'll all go." Andrea coolly pulled a poker from the fireplace rack. "It's our history, too."

"Right." Rachel rushed to the kitchen and returned brandishing the fry pan. "Let me at them."

Caro's fear was swept away by the desire to laugh. "All right. Let's go."

She opened the door. Barney ran ahead of them, barking wildly. How they must look, running after the dog in the dark. The fear she'd felt the night before in the woods was a distant memory. She could take on anything with her sisters behind her.

They rounded the corner of the barn. Barney gave a fierce bark, followed by snarling and snapping, and a man's frightened cry. She swung the torch's beam wildly, trying to focus on the melee.

The dark figure—was it the man from last night?— tore free of the dog and started to run.

But there was no place to run. The police car surged down the lane, siren wailing, just as Cal, breathing hard, burst out of the path from the house.

The man froze, caught in the converging beams of the

headlights and the torch. Zach got out of the police car and came toward him.

"Out kind of late, aren't you, Mayor?"

The man turned, full into Caro's light. Keith Morris stood there, and in his arms was the antique quilt.

Zach led Keith to a straight-backed chair in the barn apartment and planted him in it, none too gently. In his opinion, Keith should be sitting in the police station right now, but he'd given in, partly because of Keith's frantic appeals to be allowed to explain, but mostly because Caroline said she wanted to hear him. After what she'd been through, she deserved to hear.

At the moment Caroline and Rachel had spread the quilt on the table and were going over it, stitch by stitch, to be sure it hadn't come to any harm. Andrea had given up her poker, a little reluctantly, and now sat in the corner on the sofa, her husband's arm around her.

"Okay, Keith." He frowned down at Churchville's mayor. "Let's have an explanation. Breaking and entering, theft—those are plenty serious charges."

"No, no, you can't arrest me." Sweat broke out on Keith's forehead, and his gaze swiveled from side to side and settled on Caroline. "You have to believe me. I just wanted a look at the quilt, that's all. I wanted to know what you had before I made an offer. But then I heard the dog barking, and I ran without thinking."

"You expect us to buy that? You could have come to Caroline anytime and asked to see the quilt if you were interested in buying."

"He already saw it," Caroline said. "He offered to buy it."

"I... I hardly got more than a glimpse then." Keith

looked at him and quickly away. "I mean, I thought the price would go up if I showed too much interest—she'd already turned me down once."

"If all you wanted was to look at it, why did you take it out of the frame?" Andrea leaned forward, apparently unable to stay out of it any longer. "You were trying to steal it."

Keith shied away from the words. "I couldn't help it. I mean, it was my mother." He looked up at Zach again. "You know what she's like. She's so proud of being the final authority on things historical in the area, proud of her ancestors being First Proprietors, going back to William Penn and all that. She couldn't take the idea that someone might have something of more historical significance than she does." He sat up straighter, apparently gaining confidence from this line of argument, which just might be closer to the truth.

"So you decided to steal the quilt for her?" He let skepticism weigh his voice.

"Not steal, no. I thought if I showed it to her, maybe she'd decide it wasn't that great and lose interest. Or if not, I'd return it, come to Caroline, make her a fair offer. I thought I'd have it back before anyone even knew it was missing. You don't want to arrest me for that. Think of the ugly publicity."

That was the wrong argument to use on him. In his book, no one was above the law. Maybe it would be tough to go up against the Morris family, but—

"That's not why your mother wants the quilt." Caroline walked toward Keith, her gaze fixed on him.

Zach took a sidestep that put his body between them, shocked by the wave of protectiveness that surged through him. "What do you mean?"

She didn't veer from her focus on Keith, and she spoke to him as if there were no one else there. "You don't know what we found out. We already had Elizabeth's letter from her sister. Now we have copies of the ones she wrote."

Zach shot a glance toward Andrea, who seemed like the one most likely to give him a sensible explanation.

"The Elizabeth Unger who made the quilt," she said. She turned her attention back on her sister. "Go on, Caro. What did you figure out?"

"Elizabeth talked about making the quilt according to the directions she'd been sent. About putting it out for its first use. About a Friend being betrayed and arrested, and how their courage was nothing to that of the people they were trying to help." She turned toward the others then, her eyes alight with excitement. "Don't you see? I remember reading about it—some scholars believe that quilts were used as signals on the Underground Railroad, guiding escaping slaves to safe houses."

"This area was one of the major routes." Everyone knew that. There was even a historical tour of Underground Railroad sites.

"Elizabeth was a perfect person to get involved—deeply religious, coming from Boston, which was a center for the abolitionist movement." Caroline went on as if he hadn't spoken. "The Friend she talked about…the word was capitalized because she literally meant Friend, one of the local Quakers who were part of the network. She said someone in the area betrayed him to the slave-catchers." She swung back on Keith. "That's what your mother didn't want me to find out."

He'd become so involved in her story that he'd almost

forgotten about Keith. Now he saw that the man's face had blanched.

"What about it, Keith? Time to stop dancing around the truth."

"One of your mother's prized ancestors was the traitor. That's it, isn't it?" Andrea was on her feet now, shaking off her husband's restraining arm. "You're trying to save your family reputation."

Keith shook his head helplessly, sagging in the chair. "Mother knew the family stories about it. When she heard about the quilt, heard that Caroline was going to display it, was looking into the history—she thought it was all going to come out. She wouldn't let me alone about it. She said I had to destroy the quilt, make it look like vandals had broken in, anything. I didn't want to, but I couldn't help it."

Zach planted his hands on his hips. "And what about the rest of it? Breaking into this apartment, forcing Caroline's car off the road last night."

Cal cleared his throat, the sound breaking through Zach's fury. "Much as I hate to sound like the attorney I used to be, Chief, don't you think you ought to caution him before he answers that question?"

The words restored his common sense. He was appalled at himself. He was letting his feelings for Caro get in the way of his duty.

He reached for Keith's arm. "Come on. Let's continue this down at headquarters."

"No, no, don't." Keith shrank away from him. "I don't need an attorney. I didn't do anything else, I swear it. I heard about her troubles, but it wasn't me. And I couldn't have done anything last night—you should know that. I was at the town council meeting. It went on until nearly eleven. The council members will tell you. I was there the whole time."

"I won't press charges."

The quiet statement had him swiveling toward Caro. "What are you talking about? He's admitted it."

"But he didn't do the other things. I never thought he did."

No, she wouldn't have believed it could be that easy. Besides, she believed Tony was still alive. "We caught him red-handed running away with that quilt in his arms."

"We got it back. There's no harm done." For a moment she looked ready to burst into tears. "I don't want the trouble it would cause."

"That's not an excuse for not doing your duty." Now it was as if they were the only two people in the room. She knew how he felt about duty. And why.

"Your duty. Not mine." She looked immeasurably tired. "If I don't press charges, you can't arrest him, can you?"

"No. He can't." Keith straightened. "I'm very grateful, Caroline. I hope you won't—"

"That's not all." Now it was Rachel. He'd always thought her the gentle one of the sisters, but at the moment she had fire in her eyes. "There's a condition to not pressing charges."

Zach's gaze crossed with Cal's. Cal gave a rueful shrug. "I suggest both of us contract temporary deafness. Whatever she's going to propose, we shouldn't hear."

That was probably good advice, but he couldn't pretend none of this ever happened.

"You resign." Rachel said, the tone of her voice allowing no wiggle room. "It's in the paper tomorrow, or we press charges. And you and your mother walk on egg-shells around us from now on. No more tricks, no gossip, nothing."

"I agree. Anything. Everything." Keith was practically babbling in his efforts to get this over with. "I'll do it."

Rachel glanced at her sisters. She must have seen agreement in their faces. "That's it, then."

He watched, fuming, as Keith gave them all a vague, meaningless smile and bolted from the apartment. He couldn't arrest him if they wouldn't press charges. He resented having the decision taken out of his control. His duty—

"Relax, Chief." Cal nudged him. The sisters were hugging, half laughing, half crying. "It wasn't done according to the book, but at least my wife isn't going to jail for braining the mayor with a poker, Caroline knows the story of her quilt, Rachel got her licks in and Keith is losing the thing that's most important to him. Besides, you're getting rid of the worst thorn under your skin who ever took office in the township. It might not be according to Hoyle, but seems to me it worked out pretty well."

"Not according to the law."

Cal shrugged. "The law has its limitations. I'd rather see justice."

It wasn't his interpretation of doing his duty, but clearly he could do nothing about it. He went to Caro. "I'll be leaving, then."

This wasn't over, not by a long shot. Keith might be removed from the running, but Caro was still in trouble, whether she knew it or not.

"Thank you." Her green eyes glistened with tears when she looked at him.

"You're welcome. I hope the three of you know what you're doing."

He thought about the possible charges hanging over her in regard to the museum theft. She'd been generous to Keith. He suspected the insurance investigator wouldn't be generous toward her.

Zach sat in his office the next afternoon, scowling at the day's issue of the *Churchville Gazette*. True to his word, the announcement of Keith's resignation appeared prominently on the front page. Keith must have run straight home and called the paper to make the deadline.

He tossed the paper aside. Maybe Cal had a point, but he still wasn't satisfied. He had a duty that Cal didn't, and he didn't like being finagled out of doing it for the sake of convenience.

He ignored the phone ringing in the outer office, shoving his chair back. He knew what was really sticking in his craw. He'd let himself start to care about Caro Hampton against his common sense, against his professional duty, against everything he knew was right and sensible. He'd told her more about himself than he'd told anyone other than family, and look where it had gotten him— compromising his duty for a woman who obviously didn't return his feelings.

Eric Snyder opened the door without knocking and poked his head in. "You'd better take this call, Chief. It's the Santa Fe police."

Zach glared at him. "I've got it. Shut the door. And hang up."

He picked up the phone, waiting until he heard the

click that told him the line was private. "Chief Burkhalter here."

"Chief. This is Charles Rojas. We spoke a while back about Tony Gibson and his widow."

"I remember, Detective." The neutral tone of his voice must have alerted the man that he wasn't feeling particularly cooperative. They'd pretty much told him to buzz off, hadn't they?

"Yes, right," Rojas said quickly. "And you were real helpful, sending along that sketch of Leonard Decker the way you did."

He grunted. That hadn't seemed to lead anywhere, as far as he could see.

"Ms. Hampton still there, is she?"

"Yes." He sat up straight. Something was going on. The Santa Fe P.D. hadn't called him just to chat. "What about it?"

"We just found his body."

He clutched the receiver, mind working feverishly. If Leonard Decker was dead in Santa Fe, it was highly unlikely he'd been running around this part of Pennsylvania trying to make Caro believe her husband was still alive. "When?"

"That's the thing." The tone of the detective's voice told him there was bad news coming. "He's been in the river, but the ME pegs the time of death as somewhere around the same time Ms. Hampton left Santa Fe. We consider that an interesting coincidence."

"If you're suggesting that Ms. Hampton killed him—" He stopped. He wouldn't do Caroline any favors by alienating the investigator. Not that he could do her favors in any event. His duty was all he could do. "Do you know anything about the forgery of some jewelry at the gallery where she worked?"

He could almost sense the interest on the other end. "How do you know about that, I wonder? Have you been holding out on us, Chief?"

"I might ask you the same thing, Detective." This was his jurisdiction, after all.

Rojas paused. "Okay," he said finally. "We've been hearing rumors, but no one is talking—not the gallery people, not the victim, certainly not the insurance investigators."

"One of the insurance investigators is here. Keeping an eye on Ms. Hampton. He claims she had the expertise to make the switch, but no proof."

Rojas whistled softly. "Told you more than they have us, then."

"He had to. I was about to arrest him for trespassing."

"That'll do it, all right." Rojas chuckled. "Look, Chief, seems to me it's time for us to put our cards on the table. Maybe we can help each other."

And who will help Caroline? The voice at the back of his mind was insistent, but he managed to silence it. If she was innocent, Caroline would only be helped by finding out the truth. And if she was guilty—

If she was guilty, his feelings had nothing to do with it. He'd do his duty.

"I'm listening," he said.

Chapter Fifteen

Caroline stood by the barn doors, watching as the movers carried the remnants of her life in Santa Fe into the barn. With a new lock once again installed by Cal and with Keith frightened off for good, her things should be safe until she had the heart to go through them.

She fidgeted restlessly as box after box was carried inside. Who would have thought she had so much stuff? If she'd packed it herself, she'd have gotten rid of things, including most of Tony's belongings. As it was, she'd simply taken what would fit in her car and left the rest to the movers. They'd have packed everything down to the Sunday paper and the cans of tuna fish in the cabinet.

Tony's things rightfully belonged to Mary Alice now. Would she want them? That was yet another hurdle, one she didn't want to face.

Speaking of facing things, maybe she ought to admit what was really bothering her. Not the task of sorting through her old life. It was the fact that she hadn't seen Zach since the night before last, when they'd exposed Keith's activities.

She should have realized she was treading on his devotion to duty when she took matters in her own hands and settled with Keith. But didn't he see that she and her sisters had done him a favor? If it had come down to the chief of police arresting the mayor, it would have been a three-ring circus. No one could predict how something like that would turn out. Zach might have been the one to suffer most, not that he'd let that stop him.

She sensed movement behind her and turned to see Francine picking her way along the path gingerly as if it were lined with snakes. She wore capri pants and a snug top with a pair of high-heeled sandals that were inappropriate anywhere outdoors.

She teetered to a stop next to Caro. "I see your belongings have finally arrived. It might have been faster to have sent them by mule train."

Caro shrugged. "I suppose. I wasn't in any hurry to get them. It just means I have to sort everything out."

"No need to rush into doing it." Francine touched her lightly, sympathetically, on the arm, surprising her. Francine wasn't a touching person, generally. Caro had never seen her hug anyone other than her late husband or a potential big donor to one of her charities.

Hearing Francine voice what she'd just been thinking made her reconsider. "Thanks, but I'd better face it. After all, Tony's things don't really belong to me."

"If you believe that hick sheriff knows what he's doing." Francine's tone made it clear that she doubted it.

"Police chief, not sheriff," she corrected, a little pang reminding her that she was unlikely to be talking with Zach on that subject, or any other, anytime soon.

"At least that business with the quilt has been cleared up." Francine seemed to be looking for something to distract her from that rather sad parade of belongings. "The things these small-town folks don't get up to. Imagine committing robbery to cover up something that happened 150 years ago."

"If someone threatened to expose something harmful about Garner's family, you'd jump into action quickly enough."

Francine stiffened a little at the mention of her late husband, but then she smiled and shrugged. "Believe me, I'd find a better way of dealing with it. A little blackmail goes a long way in some circles."

"Maybe so. Keith isn't as sophisticated as you."

"You're convinced he wasn't the man who forced you off the road? Maybe your police chief was too quick to accept that alibi."

"Not my police chief. And no, it couldn't have been Keith, unless he has an identical twin no one knows about. He was in full view at a town council meeting all evening."

"Well, I suppose it'll sort itself out." Faint lines appeared between Francine's brows. "If there is any chance it was Tony, that's another reason not to do anything about his belongings, you know."

"I suppose so. But I hate having this unfinished business hanging over me. And, frankly, I'm not sure I owe Tony any kind of loyalty at this point."

"But, Caroline—" She stopped, because a familiar police car was pulling up behind the moving van.

Zach got out, very stiff and correct, dark glasses hiding his eyes. Something in her tensed as he approached. If only he'd let her explain why she'd intervened with Keith, maybe she could clear that air between them.

"Zach." She forced a cheerful note into her voice. "You remember my friend Francine Carrington."

He gave Francine a curt nod and turned back to her.

"I'm afraid I'll have to ask you to come down to the police station with me."

She blinked. "Look, if this is about Keith again—"

"It has nothing to with that."

"What, then?" She couldn't keep her voice from rising. "What's going on? You're scaring me."

A tiny muscle twitched at his jaw, the only acknowledgment of her words. "You need to come with me now. Two detectives from Santa Fe will be arriving shortly to question you."

She heard Francine's sharp, indrawn breath. She didn't seem to be breathing at all. "Question me about what? Tony?"

"About Leonard Decker. The man you said threatened and harassed you."

"I've already told you everything about that." Why are you doing this? That was what she wanted to say. Why are you looking at me as if I'm a criminal?

"He's been found. Dead. He was murdered about the time you ran away from Santa Fe."

She was vaguely aware of Francine murmuring that she'd get her sisters and hurrying off toward the house, teetering a little on her heels. Silly, to notice that at a time like this.

And then all she could feel was the iron grip of Zach's hand on her arm as he led her to the police car.

They filled up Zach's tiny office at the police station—she, Zach and the two officers from Santa Fe— one short and burly, the other tall, young, almost elegant in his Western dress. She felt as if they were using up all the air in the room, leaving none for her.

"Now, Mrs. Gibson, you must see that it's in your best interest to be honest with us." The younger one was smooth and persuasive.

"Hampton." That was all she could think of to say. "We—I found out that Tony had a wife in Philadelphia he hadn't bothered to divorce before he married me."

That probably only increased their suspicion of her, but she was too tired to think what was the best thing to say. If Zach, who knew her, could believe her capable of murder, what chance did she have of convincing anyone else?

Zach. The pain cut deeper than any she'd ever known, even deeper than the knowledge of Tony's betrayal. Maybe that was because she'd always suspected, at some level, that Tony wasn't honest. Zach was a man of integrity. If he believed this, maybe she really wasn't worth being loved.

Zach moved slightly in his chair. "Ms. Hampton has not been apprised of her right to have an attorney present."

The detective shot him a look of dislike. "I'm sure Ms. Hampton would rather have a friendly talk with us than a formal interrogation with an attorney present."

What Zach would have said to that she didn't know, because the door opened and Cal burst in. Zach shot to his feet. "Burke, you're not licensed to practice law in Pennsylvania. Get out."

"I'm not, but I've brought someone who is." He ushered in a graying, distinguished-looking man who reminded her in some way of Grandfather. "Caro, this is Robert Hanson. He's an old friend of your grandparents' and he's your attorney. Don't answer any questions unless he tells you to." Cal bent to press his cheek against hers before anyone could object. "It's going to be all right," he whispered. "We're all waiting outside and praying for you."

"Out." The older of the detectives grabbed Cal and shoved him out of the office. He grinned and gave her a thumbs-up as he went.

The ice that encased her began to thaw. They were here. They were taking care of her. Even Zach, in his way, hadn't let them bully her into talking without an attorney. Maybe somehow she was going to get through this.

There were moments when she doubted that, over the next two hours, when the wrangling between Hanson and the detectives turned into a blur of noise that made her dizzy. When that happened, she clung to the thought of them—her family, waiting for her.

Someone else was here with her. *Draw near to God, and He will draw near to you.* She'd looked for a reference to what Emma had said in the Bible she'd found on her bedside table. Those were the words that expressed Emma's thoughts perfectly. *Draw near to God, and He will draw near to you.*

She listened to the attorney and answered only the questions he allowed, convinced that those questions made no sense. She'd never spoken to Decker before that day in the plaza, never heard Tony mention his name. She didn't know what Tony had been involved in. He'd lied to her from the first time she met him.

Maybe her voice had trembled on that, because the attorney's hand had closed warmly over hers, as if it were Grandfather there next to her.

"I think that'll be all Ms. Hampton will answer today," he said.

The detective lost his urbane charm, leaning toward

her with a quick, threatening movement. She didn't think she reacted, but Zach was between them in an instant.

"You heard the attorney. Now either you're going to charge Ms. Hampton or let her go."

"Stay out of this, Burkhalter. This is our case."

"This is my jurisdiction." Zach's voice carried no expression at all, but it was like a door clanging shut. "Charge her or let her go."

"Of course Chief Burkhalter knew perfectly well they didn't have enough evidence to charge her." Robert Hanson leaned back in the leather chair that had once been her grandfather's, accepting a mug of coffee from the tray Emma held. They'd all come back to the library at the inn for a council of war once she'd finally been released. "He's a good man to have on your side, my dear."

She could only stare at the man from her place on the couch between her sisters. "I don't think he is."

"Listen to Mr. Hanson," Cal advised. He took a tray of sandwiches Emma had put on the table and began forcing them on people. "That could have been a lot worse if Zach hadn't been looking out for your rights."

Her rights. Yes, she supposed Zach would do that for anyone. It was part of doing his duty. She suddenly felt an overwhelming urge to cry.

She got to her feet, drawing startled glances. "I… I know we have to talk this over, but I can't seem to think. I need to take a hot shower, change my clothes, and then maybe I'll be able to eat something."

Cal glanced toward the attorney. "Maybe we'd better get this over now, Caro. Mr. Hanson has a busy schedule."

But Hanson waved with a thickly piled ham sandwich. "Not at all. I'll just sit here and catch up with Katherine. Take your time, my dear. I know the atmosphere of suspicion can seem to contaminate you when you're not used to it."

Andrea and Rachel stood up, one on either side of her. "We'll go with you," Andrea said firmly, and took her arm.

All she wanted was to be left alone to let the tears out, but she knew she'd never get rid of them that easily. She let them walk with her back to the apartment, trying to nod and smile at their attempts to distract her.

Once Rachel had run a hot tub, more relaxing than a shower, she insisted, and Andrea had laid out a change of clothes, she shooed them toward the door.

"I can handle the rest of it," she said firmly. "I know how to take a bath by myself. I'll come back as soon as I feel a little more together. You go now and keep those two lawyers from scaring Grams with their stories, all right?"

Her sisters exchanged glances. "She has a point," Andrea admitted.

"Maybe we are hovering a little," Rachel said. "All right. But if you're not back in an hour, we're coming for you."

"I will be. Go." She shoved them out the door and locked it behind them.

The confident manner only lasted until the door closed. She had to drag herself back up to the loft. She peeled off her clothes, tossing them to the back of the closet. Maybe she'd throw them away.

Only when she lay back in the tub did the tears come. Whatever they might say about Zach defending her, she knew things were over between them. She'd known all along it couldn't possibly work, but she hadn't been able to quash that tiny flicker of hope. Well, now it was gone for good.

She sat up, sloshing water over the tub. How ridiculous was this, hiding away to cry while people who loved her made plans for her defense. She wasn't a child who needed protection, much as she appreciated what they were trying to do.

The familiar urge to run had disappeared completely, she realized with surprise. She'd grieve, and go on grieving for the loss of whatever she might have had with Zach, but she wouldn't run. She'd stay and face this.

She got out, dried herself, made up her face and brushed her hair free of tangles. Then she put on the clothes her sister had laid out and went down the stairs.

They'd be surprised to see her back so soon. Well, she was surprised, too. But it was time she started acting like one of the grown-ups.

She opened the door, stepped outside and turned to shut it. She sensed movement behind her, felt a fierce pain in her head and then slid into blackness.

Chapter Sixteen

Zach leaned back in his chair, leveling a gaze at Rojas, the senior of the detectives. The past hour had been an exercise in futility since Caroline left, surrounded and supported by friends and family.

Not by him. He'd done what he could for her, but it hadn't been enough.

Doubt had been growing in him throughout the endless afternoon. If you followed the rules, you got the right result. That was what he'd always believed, but it didn't seem to be working out that way this time.

Where is the truth in this, Lord? Help me to find it, whatever the cost.

"Let's stop the posturing, Rojas. It's pretty obvious you don't have anywhere near enough evidence to charge Ms. Hampton in Decker's death. What's this really about?"

Williams, the younger man, opened his mouth for what would probably be another jab at hick cops, but Rojas waved him to silence.

"Go out there and get the dispatcher to give you a cup of coffee."

Williams gave him a mutinous look, but he went. When the office door closed behind him, Rojas spread his hands wide.

"Okay. Here's the truth, or as much of it as I can tell you. Tony Gibson was involved in a scam worked through a series of charity auctions at the gallery where Ms. Hampton was employed. Someone at the gallery had to be involved, and she seemed the obvious suspect."

"*Obvious* isn't always good enough."

A slow anger simmered inside him. If Rojas was content with the obvious, the truth would never come out.

"True," the man admitted. "We don't know how long this was going on. The people involved aren't ones to run to the cops if they think they've been defrauded. More likely to write it off or hit up their insurance company." He shrugged. "You figure they're smart enough to handle fortunes, but seems like they check their business sense at the door when it comes to these fancy society affairs. The Carrington name means something in those circles."

"That'd be Francine Carrington's late husband?"

Rojas nodded. "Carrington had a heart condition. That seems to be common knowledge. He died, and the widow kept up the charities he'd started. Everybody found that admirable. Just lately, though, Carrington's kids from his first marriage have been making noises about the merry widow."

"You knew she came to see Ms. Hampton," he said slowly. "That's why you're here." If the detective was suspicious of a woman in Mrs. Carrington's position, he wouldn't want to raise the wrath of his superiors by leaning on her. "You figured it was safer to lean on Ms. Hampton than on her."

Rojas looked affronted. "Hey, don't tell me it doesn't

work the same in your little corner of the world. Some people you just can't jump in and accuse, not if you want to come out with your job intact."

He thought of Keith Morris. "It's better to risk that than to harass an innocent person."

"Well, now, we don't know that Ms. Hampton is innocent, do we? She could be involved, could be the one who faked the pieces. Or maybe she knows something. There has to be a reason why those two women are here together."

The anger was coming to a boil now. It wasn't his case, the sensible side of his mind insisted. It was his jurisdiction, though. His obligation to find the truth.

"You decided Ms. Hampton was the weak link. You figured if you leaned hard enough, she might break."

"It works, more often than not," Rojas said.

"Not when you're leaning on an innocent woman." A woman who deserved better than she'd ever gotten from the law he and Rojas both claimed to represent.

Rojas's brows lifted. "Sounds to me as if you've gotten involved with the woman."

Zach shoved his chair back. "I'm going to get some air. Feel free to use my office." He slammed out before he could say something he'd regret.

The day had slid away while they were arguing. Dusk was drawing in. Unease trickled down his spine.

Caro was safe. Of course she was. Her family would protect her. So why did he have the urge to drive over there, just to be sure?

He shouldn't approach her now, not when she was part of an ongoing investigation conducted by another department. Doing so could cost him. He had to follow the rules on this one.

But maybe following the rules wasn't good enough. His job was a small sacrifice in exchange for the truth. Or for Caroline's safety.

Driven by a need stronger than anything he could explain, he slid into the cruiser and pulled out.

Voices penetrated the darkness, forcing Caroline's eyelids to flutter. She didn't want to wake up. She couldn't. Her head hurt. She wanted to lie here quietly....

But she wasn't in her bed. Hard wooden boards beneath her, not a soft mattress. And the voices—

"You shouldn't have hit her that hard." Francine, but a Francine who sounded different. "We'll never find it without her help."

There was the sound of something heavy sliding along the floor. Her mind began to function. The apartment. She'd been leaving, going back to the house. Now...she opened her eyes a cautious slit.

Now she lay on the barn floor, amid the boxes the movers had brought in this morning. Francine had one of the boxes open, hauling things out and holding them up to examine in the dim light.

"...don't see why I had to hit her at all." It was a voice she struggled to recognize. "You should have offered to help her unpack and sort things out, like any good friend would."

He stepped into the light. Jason Tenley. The photographer. Except that he obviously wasn't. Why was he here with Francine?

"And what if she found it first?" Francine's tone was waspish. "You should have made sure you had it before you killed Tony."

The words penetrated, and Caro gasped. A tiny sound,

but they heard. They were on her in an instant, the man hauling her to a sitting position. The movement sent pain shooting through her head. She struggled and realized her hands were tied behind her back.

"Now we're getting somewhere." Francine leaned over her. "Think, Caroline. Where would Tony have hidden something of value? Something quite small. It has to be here. We've looked everywhere else."

"I don't know what you mean." Which was the truth, and better than any lie she could imagine. "What are you doing, Francine? Who is he?"

Francine didn't bother to answer the questions. She surveyed Caroline for a moment. Then, before Caro could guess her intent, she slapped her.

"Think," she demanded. "Where did he hide it? Help us, or my brother might have to do to you what he did to Tony."

She could only gape at the woman. Her friend. The person she thought she knew. She hadn't known Francine, any more than she'd known Tony.

"Shut up, Francine." The man, Tenley, if that was really his name, smiled pleasantly. "You talk too much."

"It doesn't matter what she hears now." Francine turned on her. "Help us, if you want to go on living. We're not leaving here without it."

They didn't intend to let her live in any event. She knew that as surely as she'd ever known anything. That was what Tenley meant. Francine wouldn't talk so freely in front of her if she was going to let her live.

Tenley intercepted her gaze. "Yes, she really is my sister. Half sister, at least."

"You're not a photographer." Think, keep them talking. Don't sit here and wait for them to kill her.

"Just an honest insurance investigator. Until I ran into my dear sister, and she suggested that there was far more money to be made by skirting the law a little."

Francine gave a low sound that might have been a laugh. "You were never honest, whatever else you were. Stop chatting. We have to find it. If she won't help us—"

The menace in her voice sent a surge of energy through Caro. She wouldn't be a helpless victim. "I'll help you. I know what should be in the boxes. But you have to tell me what I'm looking for."

Francine frowned at her for a moment. Then she came to Caro, bent over and fumbled with the bonds at her wrists. "All right. You're looking for a pill vial. Find it, and you might get to go on living."

"And do be careful, my dear." Jason Tenley waggled the thing that was in his hand. A gun, small and deadly. "I'd hate to have to use this."

No, he wouldn't want to use a gun. They'd want it to look like an accident, like Tony's death. Or even suicide. Widow, depressed over her husband's death, under suspicion herself, decides to end it all. That made sense.

She stumbled to her feet, rubbing her hands together and then grabbing the nearest box. She had to think. *Please, Lord, help me think. Show me what to do. Someone could come looking for me at any moment. Walk in the door and face a man with a gun. Please, help me.*

She felt her control slipping as she pulled things from the box and took a deep breath. *Draw near to God, and He will draw near to you.* The words seemed to steady her.

Please, Lord. Let me feel Your presence. Show me what to do.

If Zach came—she didn't doubt Zach's ability to handle Tenley. But Zach wouldn't come. Zach thought she was guilty.

Be with me, she prayed again. She opened another box, this one containing clothing, and began feeling carefully in the linings and pockets. Her hands felt stiff and cold.

"Something so small could be anywhere," she said, needing to hear the sound of a voice. "Why do you need it?"

"You don't want to know the answer," Tenley said, leaning against a stack of boxes, the gun drooping.

"What does it matter?" Francine tossed aside a file folder that was probably from Tony's desk. "She's the reason all of this fell apart." She turned on Caro, face twisting with anger. "You never even realized, stupid little idiot. You didn't know what you were saying when you told Garner the one thing that showed I was playing his wealthy friends for suckers."

"I did?" She could only stare at Francine. "I hardly knew Garner. He died the night of that first charity event, right after I came to work…" Her voice trailed off.

Her first event. She hadn't been working at the gallery for more than a few weeks, and she'd been so eager to do well. Garner Carrington, tall, courtly, distinguished, coming into the gallery unexpectedly looking for his wife. He talked to her, probably seeing how nervous she was, and she'd babbled about whatever it was Francine had her working on. He'd already been suspicious, or something she'd said had tipped him off. Francine must already have been substituting fakes for the real donated objects.

"Yes, you." Francine stalked toward her, fury filling her face. "I never planned to harm Garner. I just wanted to make sure I came out of that farce of a marriage set up for life. You're the one who forced the issue."

Horrified, Caro could only stare at her. Garner's heart attack, that very night. Francine, the grieving widow, mourning that if only she'd gone to his bedroom sooner, she'd have found him in time to help.

But she could only be this frantic to find a pill vial if it were somehow evidence that she'd killed him. And the only way it could have come into Tony's possession—

"Tony knew." The words came out before she could suppress them. Tony had known and done nothing.

"Tony knew." Francine shrugged. "We were having a little fling, Tony and I. Nothing serious, but he was coming to the house that night. He was out on the balcony, and he saw me with the pill bottle. He took it. Blackmailed me. If he hadn't gotten so greedy—"

"This is futile." Tenley walked between them. Before Caro could guess his intent, he knocked her to the floor. Pain shot through her. Half-conscious, she felt him pull a rope tight around her wrists and ankles.

"What are you doing?" Francine clawed at his arm. "We have to find it."

"We can't." He shook her off. "We've played around with this stupid plan of yours for too long. The only solution is to burn the place down. The vial will be destroyed, and your little friend with it."

"The police—" Francine began.

"The police don't know a thing," he said shortly. "I'm going to get the gas cans. Here." He handed her the gun. "Make sure she behaves." He stalked toward the door, switching on a penlight as he did. His figure was a dark silhouette in the doorway for an instant, and then he disappeared.

Nearly dark. How long had she been here? They'd come looking for her—Andrea and Rachel would come—

No, Lord. Don't let my sisters walk into this. Keep them safe. Protect them. Protect me. She reached out in longing, in certainty, and felt His presence.

She couldn't be sure how much time passed. She didn't attempt to talk to Francine. She just waited, wrapped in God's love.

Footsteps finally, coming back. A dark figure appeared in the doorway, carrying a flashlight. Awareness shot through her. A bigger, heavier torch than the tiny penlight Tenley had carried, surely.

"About time," Francine said, apparently not noticing anything wrong.

But she would, she'd see— Shoving with her elbows, she pushed herself toward Francine as the fierce beam of the flashlight shot into the woman's eyes. Francine lifted the gun, arm flying up to shield her eyes. Caro raised her bound feet and aimed a frantic kick at Francine's legs.

Deafening shots, flashes of light, loud voices. She didn't know where Francine was. Zach—was that Zach's voice?

The overhead lights went on, blinding her for an instant. Then her vision cleared and she saw Zach, holding Francine in a hard grip. Other men rushing in—the detectives, local patrolmen. And a moment later Zach was holding her, releasing her bonds, drawing her gently into the safety of his arms.

"Now, you sit quietly here on the bench, and you can watch them work on your new business for a while." Rachel, at her most maternal, guided Caro to a seat on a garden bench that had a view of the barn. "You know what the doctor said."

"He said I should take it easy for a couple of days," Caro pointed out. "Not that you and Grams and Andrea should coddle me for the rest of my life."

Still, she had to admit that it had been healing to spend the past two days doing nothing, floating in a soft cocoon of family concern. She hadn't seen Zach. No detectives had come with questions.

All of the belongings she'd had stored in the barn had been taken away for a police search. Maybe that was just as well. She was ready to concentrate on the future, not the past.

Right now that future was taking shape before her eyes. Rachel had stopped to talk to Tyler, looking very professional with his hard hat and blueprints. Inside the open doors of the barn, she spotted Cal with a crew of Amish carpenters, beginning the work that would transform the barn into the Three Sisters Arts and Crafts Center. It was an ambitious title they'd decided upon. She just hoped she could live up to it.

The quilt would have a place of honor, hung in a glass case inside the entrance, with as much as they knew of its history posted beside it.

That history wouldn't include any mention of treachery, she'd decided. That could be left for others to argue. She simply wanted to celebrate how the work of a woman's hands had helped lead courageous souls to freedom.

She leaned against the bench, half dreaming in the warm sunshine, and watched as a familiar police cruiser pulled up. Zach. She'd known he'd come at some point. What she didn't know was what they would say to each other.

He came toward her slowly and stood looking down at her. "Any chance you feel up to talking? If so, I'll risk your sister's wrath and sit down."

She gestured to the bench beside her. "Please. I think it's time I stopped floating and found out what's happening."

He sat down next to her, studying her face with that intent gaze. "Is that what you've been doing? Floating?"

"Pretty much," she admitted. "You can tell me. You don't need to hedge around the subject. Did you find the vial?"

He nodded. "Stuffed inside a ski boot, as a matter of fact."

"They were right to be worried. That's one of the first things I'd probably have gotten rid of, since I don't ski."

"That was what motivated all of this, apparently." Zach linked his hands on his knee. "Francine had to find the vial before you did and got curious about why Garner Carrington's medicine was with your husband's things."

"She thought if I believed Tony was still alive, I wouldn't get rid of them." Her brain was starting to work again. Apparently she'd figured some things out while she'd been drifting. Everything Francine had engineered—the love letter, Tony's favorite coffee, the sense someone had been watching her, even sending the safe-deposit key, had one aim—to keep her thinking Tony was alive, so she wouldn't do anything with his belongings until they'd found the evidence.

"That's what her brother claims." Zach wore an expression of distaste. "They're tripping over themselves to blame each other for everything that happened. I guess that'll be for the Santa Fe courts to sort out. They're out of my jurisdiction, anyway."

"They're gone? Don't the detectives want to talk to me?"

"Not at the moment. Rojas seems satisfied that your role was that of an innocent bystander."

"A stupid bystander, you mean." She shook her head. "I can't believe I didn't see anything. I worked on those charity events with Francine and never suspected a thing."

"Francine was one careful lady. Sorting out the truth from the accusations, I'd say she started the scam with help from her brother. Carrington must have already been suspicious the day he spoke with you, though."

She nodded slowly. "I've been thinking about that. At the time, I thought he was just being nice to a new employee, but in light of what happened, he must have been trying to see what I knew. Whatever I told him confirmed his suspicions."

"He let her see that he was on to her. A deadly thing to do with a woman like that. She acted immediately."

"And Tony saw her." The words tasted bitter, but she got them out. "She told me that. She and Tony were having an affair, and he saw what she did. He took the pill bottle and blackmailed her."

Some of the tension in Zach's face eased, as if he was relieved he didn't have to convince her of what Tony had been. "According to the brother, Tony got greedy, and Francine decided he had to go. They thought they'd have plenty of time to search for the vial."

She nodded. "I had a feeling that someone had been in my apartment several times during the couple of weeks after Tony died. I thought it was Decker, the man who threatened me, but it must have been Francine."

"Decker messed up their plans. He scared you into

running, and suddenly your belongings were out of reach. Tenley followed you here to keep tabs on you while Francine, playing the devoted friend, found out that most of your things were in a moving truck, making their way slowly east."

"So they had to wait until everything got here to find it," she said. "But I don't understand what happened to Decker. Was he one of the people they scammed?"

"Rojas thinks so. He figures when Decker couldn't get the money out of you, he went to Francine, and she killed him. But neither of them are talking about that, and we may never know."

Maybe it didn't matter whether she knew. Let the law take care of Francine and her brother. But there was one thing she had to come to terms with before she could move forward.

"About Tony." She looked down, realizing she didn't want to see Zach's face when she asked this. "Why? Why did he get involved with me? Why marry me?"

His hands clenched. "Tenley claims Francine told Tony to make sure you weren't suspicious about her husband's death. As to the marriage—well, we know it wasn't the real thing. He may have thought it gave him more leverage over Francine, having you and anything you might remember about Carrington in his pocket, so to speak. Or maybe he just couldn't resist." His voice softened. "People have been known to fall in love. Even the bad guys."

She took a breath, feeling the last of whatever shackled her to Tony falling away. "You're trying to spare my feelings, but you don't need to. I know now it wasn't love with Tony."

"I…" He hesitated, as if not sure what to say. "Is that a good thing?"

She nodded, managing a smile. "I think so. I'd rather know what love isn't, so I can recognize what it is."

Zach touched her hand, very gently, and her breath hitched. Her heart seemed to be fluttering somewhere up in her throat.

"I'm sorry," he said softly. "For the times when I doubted you—"

"Don't." She closed her hand over his. "There were times when I doubted my own sanity. Anyway, you wouldn't be you if you hadn't questioned. You're a man of integrity, and you did what you thought was right."

His fingers moved caressingly on hers. "If there's anything I've learned, it's that when there's a choice between duty and right, God expects me to do what's right." His voice roughened, as if with emotion he was trying hard to control. "Look, I know you're going to need time to come to terms with everything that happened to you. I just hope you'll do it here. I'll be waiting."

She turned to look at him and saw the love shining in his eyes. Her heart melted, and she reached up to touch his cheek, feeling the strong line of bone and the warmth and aliveness of his skin.

"Not so much time," she said softly. "I've stopped running now."

God had brought her back to the place where she belonged—the place He'd been preparing for her all along. And the man He'd intended for her from the beginning.

Zach's arms went around her, and she was home.

* * * * *